THE CHINA MAZE

This is a work of fiction, in which the events are entirely imaginary.
Any coincidence between living persons and named characters
in the novel is purely fortuitous.

This edition published by Gibson Square for the first time

UK   Tel: +44 (0)20 7096 1100
US   Tel: +1 646 216 9813

info@gibsonsquare.com
www.gibsonsquare.com

ISBN   978-1-78334-136-8

Papers used by Gibson Square are natural, recyclable products made from wood grown in sustainable forests; inks used are vegetable based. Manufacturing conforms to ISO 14001, and is accredited to FSC and PEFC chain of custody schemes. Colour-printing is through a certified CarbonNeutral® company that offsets its CO2 emissions.

THE CHINA MAZE

by

Joseph Clyde

GIBSON SQUARE

Praise for

A State of Fear
A Tony Underwood thriller by Joseph Clyde

'Compelling... deserves to be a bestseller.'
Daily Mail

'Remarkabl[e].'
Sunday Express

'Exciting, horrific, and poignant.'
Literary Review

'Echoes of the best of Len Deighton or John Le Carré with darkly
humorous touches.'
Times Literary Supplement

'Thrilling.'
Spectator

'A gripping read and a good way to scare anyone.'
Plymouth Herald

'Dystopian... Hard to put down.'
Adrian Tahourdin, *TLS*

'Dark fast and pitch perfect....'
Michael Burleigh

'A talented novelist ... enjoyable, for all its grim realism.'
Edward Luttwak

'A page-turner.'
entertainment-focus.co.uk

'Amazing attention to emotional realism.'
Sosogay.org

Praise for:

The Oligarch
A Tony Underwood thriller by Joseph Clyde

'Layers of violence, deception and moral confusion: the oligarchs,
the mafia, the ruthless vulgarity of today's have-it-all Russians...
sardonic, sharply paced... a page-turner... in the tradition of
Frederick Forsyth and John le Carré... manipulative sex, the
inventively coarse language and brisk changes of scene...'
The Times

'Echoes of Frederick Forsyth and Gerald Seymour,
you're... reminded of French or Russian literary fiction,
... cleverly resolved.'
Sunday Times

'Sit back in wonderment and enjoy this romp around a parallel
universe that exists – I assure you, it does. [Joseph Clyde] serves up
a treat of acute observation and dead-pan humour that testifies to
a highly-informed eye.'
Independent

'Subdued tension throughout... a well-paced thriller with a
refreshing sense of realism.'
Evening Standard

'Gripping and enthralling tale of intrigue and double-crossing...
racy... dialogue, everyone is even more devious than they already
appear... for once "unputdownable" as the cover claims.'
John Ure, *Country Life*

'Neatly sidesteps many of the traps by being set not in a spy
agency but among Russian emigrés.'
Standpoint

'Very believable.'
Mail on Sunday

'Swift, tight, skillful. A horribly plausible thriller which is also a forensic dissection of the many-layered Russian criminal diaspora of a London increasingly fit only for kleptocrats and their dependent flunkies.'
Jonathan Meades

An Amazon Top 5 Spy Story

1

'So where you gonna hold him?' Zach Boorstin asked Captain Tang. 'In the cells?'

'No more cells. We are full up.' The Captain cocked his head towards a window of his office in the Public Security Bureau. 'You can hear why.'

It was seven in the evening and for the fifth night Urumqi was exploding. The difference today was that the low growl of the riots was closer and spiced with gunshots.

'Never mind, gentlemen', Tang went on, 'we have found somewhere for him. We give him special place. We keep it for distinguished guests. Perhaps you would like to see?'

'We'd be privileged', said Alyosha Benediktov, his American English perfect except for his Russian accent. 'Sounds like a special guy all right.'

'Sure we would.' Zach, the real American, sprang from his chair. 'So let's go!'

Tony Underwood, English and the oldest in the three-man posse of visiting security men, brought up the rear as they followed Tang out of the office, across the corridor to the stairs. The Captain led them to the lift to the ground floor then down winding steps, deep into the basement of the twenty-five storey concrete pile. A slim, short-haired fifty-year-old in a clean-cut western suit, he walked sedately, a hand on the rail, as though this were a ceremonial event, and in a sense it was. There were no precedents for operatives from the FBI, M15 and the Russian FSB visiting a Category One prisoner in a jail in Xinjiang province, any more than there was a precedent for the captive.

The lower they descended the stronger the smell of the

day's food cycle – boiled mutton, rancid dough, shit – everything overlaid by the stench of stale tobacco. Guards with T65 assault rifles, unwieldy-looking in the tight space, stood on every landing. Seeing the visitors approach one of them stubbed out his cigarette and, snatching up his gun, looked listlessly alert. After Tony had passed another spat noisily into a spittoon. At the hawk and the splat Tony started round. Puzzled at the foreigner's interest in his expectoration the man stared back, summoned more mucus and, an eye still on him, spat again.

Hearing the Englishman's steps falter Alyosha, the Russian, turned, saw what had happened, and laughed.

'Take it easy, Tony. No offence meant. This is China!'

Four levels down, leaving behind galleries of cells packed with captive rioters, they came to the lowest floor. Passing through a heavy steel door – when it closed it was suddenly quiet – they continued along a corridor into a room big enough, just, for the four of them. After closing the door Tang drew back a curtain the length of one wall. Behind were bars protecting a sheet of one-way glass.

'Here is prisoner', the Chinese said with a welcoming sweep of his hand, his formality out of place in the cramped, chilled space. 'Please look.'

The three of them did, intently and in silence. The minutes passed. Someone had to go first. It wouldn't be Tony, never a big talker, and for all the respect due to his age in some undefined way the junior of the group. The Russian seemed too engrossed by the tableau in the cell to say anything, so the first to speak was garrulous Zach.

'So there he is, the rare specimen in his cage!' The American drew a slim camera from his hip pocket. 'Mind if we take pictures?'

Tang seemed to blanch.

'I do not think it will work. The glass may not allow it. We have camera inside. We can give you pictures. Everyone.'

'Well, thanks.'

Zach had the camera ready cocked, an eye to the viewfinder, and put it away reluctantly, as if re-holstering a weapon.

'Funny thing', he mused, still staring. 'He's young, but sitting there scribbling he looks like some kinda scholar. An old-time scholar in his pyjama suit.' He stared on. 'See the way he holds up his pen, looking for – what's it the French call it?'

'*Le mot juste*', the multilingual Russian supplied. 'The right word.'

'You got it. Fastidious guy. Always the way, isn't it? Fucking mass murderer and fastidious with it.'

'We don't actually know whether he's killed anyone', Tony murmured.

'Now it's you being fastidious!' Zach gave Tony's grey-suited back a light slap. 'Maybe we can't prove it, but there's a point where you gotta stop drawing a line between action and intent. You're in on the jihad game, you *are* a mass murderer, whether you get to do it or not.'

His eyes went back, greedily, to the cell.

'Hey, look at that! Way he smoothes his parting with his middle finger – he just did it. Not that you left him too much to smooth, Captain. Great barber's job. Preens what's left like a cat.'

The cell they were inspecting was a low-ceilinged room eight feet by twelve. A table and chair, a rattan mattress on a fixed wooden bed, a toilet and a sink filled the space. Luxuries for the Captain's special guests included a green desk lamp and – incongruous among the Spartan furniture – the pink fluffy cover the lavatory seat had somehow acquired.

'Love his facilities', Zach grinned at Tang.

'Facilities?'

'Toilet.'

'It was left by an English man', the Captain explained, unsmiling. 'A smuggler of antiquities. It took many months to get expert opinions and arrange trial, so we accommodated him here. His mother sent the cover.' He looked round at their faces. 'Now you have seen our prisoner it would be interesting to know what race you think he is. You, Mr Underwood, I believe you know already. But Mr Boorstin and Colonel Benediktov, where do you think he is from?'

The man at the table was in his mid-to-late twenties. Dark hair close-cropped, reading spectacles low on his nose, he was dressed in loose grey pyjamas and canvas shoes. Other than his age it was hard to tell anything about him. Ethnically he seemed indeterminate.

If he hadn't known, Tony thought, he would never have guessed. Passing him in a London or New York street this man would melt into the background, his skin neither dark nor white, his features regular in the sense of nothing excessive, his eyes maybe Eurasian, maybe not. Their view of him was sideways on and at that angle he appeared to be of Chinese build, though Northern Chinese, tall and lithe. The lamplight was poor, casting shadows, so that certain movements of his head gave his skin a brownish tinge: a Turk perhaps, of light complexion.

The kind of man who doesn't like to be wrong, for once Zach was taking his time before opining. He's European he thought, when the prisoner turned further into the light: a dark-haired European, Spanish or Italian. Or maybe southern Russian. A Chechen perhaps, yes Chechen, that would fit. Not that he had met too many Chechens, it was just that you were surprised to see jihadis looking not too different from yourself. Next moment something about the not quite level eyes made him Chinese again. Or a half-caste.

'Tell you one thing', he said in a puzzled voice. 'He's an immigration officer's nightmare. Whaddya say, Alyosha?'

The Russian thought, then said slowly: 'He's a sort of no-man. A no-man and everyman.'

OK', Zach said. 'We give up, we surrender. So what is he?'

'Ultimately he is a Tungan', said Tang. 'Tungan with a bit of Ukrainian.'

'A *what*? Zach's brows shot up. 'Tungans don't figure on my mental map. Or my terrorist map. Who in hell are Tungans? They from the tundra or something?'

'They are Chinese Muslims. Not too far from the Uighurs, culturally.'

'So he's Uighur.'

'He claims he is.'

'So a Uighur by adoption', Zach persisted, 'taken on the ethnicity of his customers, along with their religion.'

'That is right, he has become a mongrel', Tang said coldly, 'like a dog.'

'Careful, Captain!' Zach grinned. 'I'm another one. A mongrel Jew. Lucky I don't bark. So what's his name again?'

'His name is Osman. Khalil Osman. His father was a Tungan, his mother was Ukrainian.'

'A lot of Tungans lived in the old USSR', the Russian threw in. 'Central Asia. Kirghizstan, Kazakhstan, Uzbekistan.'

'So why'd they leave China?'

As if inviting him to answer Alyosha turned to Tang. The Captain said nothing, declining to explain that it was the revolt and bloody repression of the Tungans in the 1870s that had driven them north, across the Russian frontier. The American filled the silence.

'So are these Tungan guys Chinese or Uighur?'

'Those who live in China are citizens of China. In the same way black people in New Orleans are American.'

'Thing is our black folk are black-coloured. This feller doesn't look like anything to me. It's like the joke about the guy on the subway. Somebody asks him whether he's Jewish and he says no I ain't, but the guy keeps asking, so in the end he says well if it's so goddamned important to you OK, so maybe I'm a Jew. Now can I go on reading my paper? So the first guy says, 'funny, you don't *look* Jewish.'

Tang was trying hard, his eyes attentive, his mouth tensed, ready to smile, but it was useless. At the end of the joke his lips were in the same configuration as at the beginning: a small, strained arc of anticipation. Tony and the Russian grinned widely, though out of courtesy to the Chinese neither laughed.

'So the man was Jewish after all', Tang said, and laughed, too hard.

'Forget it, Captain.' One of Zach's freely dispensed pats on the shoulder made the Chinese stiffen. 'I'll have the same problem when you start telling me Chinese jokes. Which I hope you will over a drink once we've nailed our multi-ethnic prisoner, our man for all seasons.'

'A man for each season?' Tang raised a brow. 'Who was that man?'

'Jesus, there I go again! That's a tough one. I can't even remember.'

'Sir Thomas More', said Tony. 'The philosopher beheaded by Henry the Eighth. It was a play.'

'Wow! You knew that?'

'Sometimes I go to plays. Or rather my wife takes me.'

Tang glanced from Tony to the Russian with a puzzled look. Zach was back at the window.

'There he goes, he's getting up.'

In his excitement he placed his hands on the bars, so for a moment it was as if it was the American inside a cell, gazing out.

Searching still for *le mot juste,* the prisoner pushed back his chair, got up and began walking. It wasn't pacing – there was no suggestion of anxiety and three strides would have covered the cell. He just walked, placidly, round and round, eyes down, as if to stimulate his thoughts. The three faces stared harder, as though to divine them.

'When he's on his feet he moves like a cat', Zach pronounced. 'A stalking cat. Kinda cat who might go for your throat.'

'No, that's not a feline motion', the Russian quibbled. 'Cats are slinky, insinuating. That's not him at all. Look at that rigid back. The guy's stiff with pride.'

Or pain, it occurred to Tony. Examining his movements more closely he decided to stay quiet about two things that struck him: the way the prisoner placed his right foot on the ground, tentatively, to take the weight off it, and the reason for the rigid back. As if to confirm his suspicions Osman stopped in his tracks and put a hand to his spine, grimacing.

Zach was onto it too.

'Something wrong with his back? *And* that foot – the right one.' He took his eyes off the prisoner long enough to smirk at Tang. '*And* something on his cheek. The right cheek – see it? Looks nasty. A burn, is it?' He shook his head in mock condolence. 'Hate to see a murdering man in pain.'

'He is fine. The prisoner is fine', Tang said.

Zach wasn't giving up.

'Looks a little whacked, don't he? Late night, was it?' He gave Tang the closest thing to a wink. 'Hope you got something out of it. If you did do me a favour, Captain, could you?' The American plugged his ears and closed his eyes, grinning. 'For Christ's sake don't tell me! Otherwise I'll be up before some congressional committee on a charge of rendition, complicity in torture and generally infringing a cutthroat's inalienable human rights.'

Tony and the Russian watched Tang's face for his reaction. There was nothing to see.

'I have not seen him since two days ago, when he was well.'

'Oh come on, Captain, I didn't mean you personally.' Zach touched Tang's arm, confidentially. In return the Chinese gave the American a set, silent look, though to Tony there seemed a lot in it. OK, he seemed to be saying, we have different styles of interrogation, I'm not going to deny it. Or argue about whether our methods are worse or better than your hypocrisy.

The silence became awkward.

'What I meant', Zach said, rowing back splashily, 'was that the main thing is we've got him. Catching him was an intelligence coup that'll bring us all a whole lot of information on this corner of the world, and I'd like to convey my congratulations to the Chinese authorities formally, from the FBI. And to you personally, Captain Tang.'

'I second that, from MI5', Tony said.

'And the Federal Security Bureau,' Alyosha came in.

The courtesies accomplished, everyone turned back to the cell, where Osman had sat down again.

'What's that he's writing?', Alyosha asked.

'I don't know. Something for his lawyer, perhaps.'

'He has his own lawyer?' Zach grinned, back to his sardonic self.

'Yes, his own lawyer. That is to say, ours. He didn't want one but we gave him one. A prisoner has to have lawyer. It is our system.'

'But if he's yours, and he didn't want one, why does he bother writing to him?'

'He asked for paper and we gave it to him. He writes about many things, literary things sometimes. He writes down poetry, from memory. He has been well educated. In England.'

Tony spread his hands in a 'What can you do?' gesture.

The prisoner, he was thinking, must have known someone might be there – why else would there be all that glass? – and it showed in his behaviour. It seemed unnatural, the way he sat and walked about the room without a glance, determined perhaps to avoid dignifying whoever might be watching with a glance in their direction. At the same time there seemed a certain self-consciousness in his manner, and next moment he showed it.

'Whoa', Zach said. 'Maybe we should turn our backs, gentlemen!'

Osman was standing over the toilet, lifting the fluffy lid. A hand on his fly, with the other he reached back to the lamp suddenly, trying to turn it off at its base. It stayed on. In frustration the hand thumped the desk.

The lavatory was to the viewers' right. To undo his fly he turned his back on them, putting himself at an awkward angle to the bowl. In a practised movement he swivelled his hips just enough to project his stream while guarding his privacy. Then stood with his back to them, tore off a piece of toilet paper and wiped.

Zach was loving it.

'There you go, what did I tell you! The fastidiousness! Keen as hell to turn innocent folk into body parts but he wipes his prick after a piss! Doesn't shake it, wipes it!'

'Zach.' Tony spoke in a small, dogged voice, 'I told you, as yet we have no proof.'

'And there's no proof it was his prick he just wiped, is there? 'Cos we didn't see it!'

It was the moment Tony decided not to pull the American back every time fact and speculation became intertwined, because with Zach he would never stop.

He glanced at Tang in a way that suggested maybe they'd

seen enough, but the others seemed content to stay on, easing the Englishman aside. His sight obscured, Tony contemplated the back view of his colleagues.

Two good heads of hair, Zach's dark spread just beginning to go at the crown, Alyosha's dirty blond mane fuller. Twenty years between him and them, Tony reckoned, minimum. He hadn't spent too much of his career with foreign colleagues – wasn't senior enough – but he'd resolved to get on with these two. The way things were going they could be spending a lot of time together.

Zach would be a problem. In his years in counter-terrorism Tony had seen enough of the FBI to expect one of two types: the old-style, bruising loud-mouth or the more recent genera- tion of smart, techie graduates. An evening in Zach's company – they were staying at the same hotel and had had dinner together the night before – led him to the conclusion that the American was a mixture of the two: a clever-dick motor-mouth capable of behaving like a dick in the alternative sense.

His appearance sharpened the impression. A smallish man, everything about Zach seemed concentrated in his beak-like face. If there were such a thing as a know-it-all nose Zach had one, a perky, upturned affair, a nose that looked as if it had sniffed the way the wind was blowing before anyone else and was mightily pleased about it. The satisfaction of the nose was reflected in his perpetually smiling mouth. He must irritate a lot of people, Tony thought. Maybe that's why they'd sent him to Urumqi, in the back of beyond.

The Russian he had not encountered before today. Physically he was a less than pleasing specimen. A large, meaty body was topped off by a baby face, round and soft, as if in apology for the brutishness of his frame. But it was a baby with a precocious intelligence. Behind the amused indifference, the small, voracious eyes seemed to be drinking in other folk's every word and gesture. As someone posted in Xinjiang province the Russian knew Captain Tang already. Maybe why he hadn't troubled to dress in a suit for their meeting. Although he held the rank of FSB colonel, his open shirt and jeans seemed studiously slobbish.

Seeing the Englishman excluded, courteous as ever the Captain invited him to step closer to the window. Tony shook his head. It wasn't the first time he'd done it, but there came a point where observing a prisoner surreptitiously was beyond the call of duty.

Zach had an endless patter of questions and Tang went on answering patiently, in his over-precise English. He did it with a touch of satisfaction, even smugness. The prisoner was his catch, and in his undemonstrative way he was enjoying his moment. 'We are all professionals together', a read-out of his expression would have said, 'and we meet at a moment when the world is learning that there are times when we Chinese can be more professional than others.'

2

When Captain Tang took it into his head to be present at the interception of a suspect truck on the outskirts of the city the night after the riots began, his colleagues in the police department knew that something unusual was afoot. Previously a military man – it was why everyone called him captain – and now a model bureaucrat at the *Guoanbu*, the Ministry for State Security, he was known for sticking to his intelligence brief, resisting the temptation to meddle in operational matters, even as an onlooker. This time something about the source of the tip-off on the truck – he wouldn't say what – had excited his interest, and he was anxious nothing should go wrong.

It was at his insistence that a fair-sized detachment was deployed: twenty-five PAPs, the paramilitary police, were stationed in a narrow lane leading off a main road into a Uighur district in the south of the city. Secreted in one of a row of abandoned houses, their olive green uniforms blending into the shadows of the unlit street, they waited. Their leader, Commander Pei, stood behind the half-open door of the building, wondering why such a force was necessary to intercept a single truck, and aching for a cigarette.

It was a long wait, and several times he'd been on the point of putting two requests to the senior intelligence officer at his side: the first to ask him to observe the no-smoking rule on such occasions, the second to enquire whether he would be kind enough to explain what in hell's name this crazily over-manned operation was about? He didn't dare, and it was two hours and several of Tang's cigarettes later before he learned the answer.

The street was on an incline, the truck heavily laden, and its gears ground noisily as it laboured up the hill towards them. It had rained a little while they waited, and when it hit the bed of nails strewn in its path, with a kind of startled sigh the cumbrous vehicle braked, before skidding to a halt. The PAPs poured from the house silently – orders were to avoid a commotion in a volatile area – and ringed the truck. Thinking the intelligence officer was expecting a truckload of insurgents (it was the only explanation that made sense) the Commander had instructed them to surround the vehicle in double ranks. So there they were, in the semi-darkness, the truck with its two flat front tires marooned in a silent circle, its engine off.

In the cab sat two men: the driver and his baseball-capped companion. Their arrest proceeded with a decorum unusual for the notoriously muscular PAP. The driver – a Kirghiz to judge by his skullcap and curses at his blown-out tires – stepped down quietly into the ring of paramilitaries wielding automatics. Once on the ground he flattened himself against his cab, a hand to his face, the other to his privates, in anticipation of a rifle butt to the head or a boot to the groin. The fact that neither came had a lot to do with Tang's presence: the Captain, it was rumoured among the PAP and the police, was apt to be a little legalistic in his views on the treatment of prisoners.

The figure in the baseball cap sat on in the truck's cab, as if all this were no concern of his. Opening his door the Commander signalled up at him to get out. *You wenti ma?* the man said in Mandarin, looked down nonchalantly, and didn't budge. 'What's the problem?' Feeling he'd done sufficient to satisfy the Captain's scruples, the Commander ordered the nearest PAP, in vigorous tones, to fetch him down. Reaching them at that instant Tang stepped between the cab and the brute-faced PAP who was about to oblige. Gesturing up courteously, he invited the driver's companion to descend.

Shrugging, the man clambered from the cab and stood head down in the street, in such a way that his cap continued to hide his face. A wasted effort: the Captain reached up and removed it. After staring at him for almost a minute he said in English:

'Yes, there is a problem Mr Osman. A problem with your cargo.'

'A problem with nuts and raisins?'

'Please give me the key. And your passport.'

Commander Pei did not understand English. He looked on with interest as with a kind of calculated languor the man pulled them from his jerkin pocket. Leaving Osman amidst a semi-circle of raised weapons Captain and Commander went to the rear of the truck and ordered it opened. Inside were no insurgents, in fact no one at all, only stack after stack of wooden cases. One and a half metres long by half a metre wide, each was labelled in fancy Chinese characters: Nuts and Raisins, *Sunshine* brand.

The Commander searched the Captain's face for signs of disappointment, but nothing showed: the expression of quiet resolution had not changed. A curt signal invited a PAP to bring one of the boxes to him and tear it open. The man climbed up, humped one down and, wielding his bayonet, prised off the lid. Nuts and raisins, packed in plastic bags. 'Probe underneath', Tang instructed. With a stabbing, raking motion that tore open some of the bags, the PAP did. Nuts and raisins.

'Bring down another case, from the bottom this time.'

Another was carried down, opened, probed, and after an impatient gesture from Tang, emptied onto the street. The same. More cases were brought and opened, the contents spilling into the road till the fellows doing the work were ankle deep in nuts and raisins.

Unhappier now with every case, Tang wouldn't let up. The

Commander had respect for the Captain, and to avoid being a witness to his humiliation found a compelling reason to go to the front of the truck, check that Osman was secure. It was when he returned that he saw the Captain standing among the scattered boxes, a freshly opened case at his feet, a lightweight sub-machine gun in his hands, and a smile on his face as he chewed contentedly on a nut.

*

Riots in the town of Yining close to the old Soviet frontier, incendiary bombs lobbed at police stations, an attempt to bring down planes before the 2008 Olympics, the 2009 uprising in Urumqi, another attempted high-jacking of a plane in 2012 by a terrorist on crutches, an attack with knives at a train station in Kunming and a car bomb in Tiananmen Square – Uighur attacks were growing in frequency and viciousness. The Commander had been involved in many, but it was in the 2009 riots that he had seen things he would not forget.

Hundreds died, but to this day he was unsure what had started the slaughter. A website claimed that migrant Uighurs working in Guangdong province had been set upon for raping Han girls, and true or false that had been enough. A spark can start a prairie fire, Chairman Mao used to say, hatreds in the province were tinder dry, and next thing his men were confronting thousands of young Muslims on the streets. 'Social garbage' was their official designation, though Pei didn't like that kind of talk: to him they looked like students, though these were fine distinctions. The Commander was a patriot and seeing his Han brothers set upon with iron bars, bricks or knives, he waded willingly into the 'garbage.'

And so did his Han brothers. Bands of them armed with clubs and machetes swarmed the streets looking for Uighurs, as what had begun as a rowdy demonstration degenerated into a contest of barbarity: bludgeoned faces, throats slashed, castrations. Things got so bad there'd been rumours of decapitations, even if no heads separated from bodies had been located, but the Commander had seen something worse. The image he had trouble putting out of his mind was of a Han boy, a car mechanic, sprawled on his back in a garage, his entrails arranged on the ground beside him in a rough approximation of the Chinese character for *Uighur*.

Composing himself enough to order that on no account should the body be photographed (if it leaked the retribution of the Hans would be appalling) he left the garage quickly. Now he'd seen everything, the Commander thought, but he'd been wrong. Till today knives, bricks, and iron bars had been the Uighurs' favoured weapons. A truckload of pistols and sub-machine guns destined for the insurgents promised an even higher pile of corpses.

*

Captain Tang, on the other hand, appeared pleased with his find. 'Thirty-six cases', he announced, consulting his tally, 'plus ammunition.'

'And they're ours', the Commander said in a flat, contemplative voice, picking up a sub-machine gun. 'Chinese-made. Type 79. They are good weapons.'

'Which is why we export them. They even reach the Taliban, via Iran. And that's how they came back here, I would imagine.'

He walked back along the side of the truck to the cab. Reaching Osman he stood before him.

'It's as I said. Your cargo raises questions.'

As he spoke he took out a cigarette and, the packet still in his hand, flipped on a lighter. The flame went out. While he re-ignited it Osman said, 'may I?', stretched a hand to the packet and helped himself to a cigarette. Then, as Tang stood frozen, to a light. While he drew in smoke and exhaled the Captain watched, silently. The cigarette was half-way to his lips for a second drag when, after a nod in his direction, a paramilitary reached out a black-gloved hand, crushed it against his cheek and held it there, extinguishing the cigarette in the process.

Taking a slow draught on his own the Captain walked off, leaving Osman with a hand clamped to the burn on his cheek and surprise in his eyes.

3

The reason for Tony's diffidence towards to his Russian and American colleagues was not that he felt standoffish, just that diffidence was his style. That and a feeling he was something of an interloper among these representatives of three big powers. A hundred and fifty years ago, he'd learned from his hurried reading before coming, it would have been a different matter.

He'd never been too clear what the Great Game had been about, but now he knew. The British and Russian empires had faced each other across a waste of deserts and mountain ranges, with India as the prize. The British had it, Moscow wanted it, and for years the Russians had played the game with stealthy moves: 'the Tournament of Shadows' was their name for it. In the event neither side was to win: after World War II India ended up with independence and Xinjiang with Red China. Today the Great Game was jihadism and everyone was a player, though in the Central Asia of today Zach's and Alyosha's countries were bigger players than his.

Not that he deferred to them in other ways; he hadn't spent a lifetime in the security services for nothing. The IRA, Soviet espionage, Islamist terrorism – all of these and more he had worked on for as long as he could remember. At a modest level, it was true, but it added up to almost forty years of solid, boots-on-the ground experience. Real boots when he'd started.

Two years ago, after decades of dutiful service, it had looked as though his career was about to end in the obscurity in which it began, and it was the Islamists who'd saved him. In the security fraternity the role he'd played in a major counter-

terrorist operation had given the 58-year-old veteran something of a name. The first thing the American said when they
shook hands in the hotel lobby the night before had given the
unassuming Englishman a jolt of pleasure:

'Tony Underwood! Great to see you! You're the Safia guy,
right?'

And he was: the lowly M15 operative who by a one in a
million chance was the key player in the investigation of one
of the biggest terrorist plots mounted in Britain. Safia was a
Muslim girl who'd gone on trial for aiding and abetting her
brothers in an Al Qaeda dirty bombing, and it was Tony who'd
brought her in. The Americans and Europeans were clamour-
ing for details of the case, which meant that the M15 under-
ling found himself briefing the FBI, the DST in Paris, the BfV
in Berlin, and the anti-terrorist department of the Russian
FSB.

'That was some case you cracked', Zach had told him over
dinner.

'Bit of luck, really.'

And so it had been, for Tony and the country.

'Heard somewhere that you'd retired. Gone out in a blaze
of glory.'

'Don't you believe it. All I got was a lengthened sentence.'

'Meaning?'

'They kept me on.'

'So what you been doing since?'

'Oh, you know, this and that, here and there.'

This was not quite the truth. The service had kept him on
because, with his horror of retirement, Tony had asked them
to, and because his performance in the Safia case made it hard
for his bosses to refuse. So Tony got his wish and stayed. The
question was, what to do with him? It was the Chinese, of all
people, who'd solved the problem.

*

When another bout of rioting broke out in Urumqi someone in the *Guoanbu* had a brainwave. Instead of closing the place to foreigners for the duration the Chinese decided to open it up, and not just to the press: the FBI and M15 were formally invited to send their people (the FSB had Colonel Benediktov in Urumqi already). The idea was for their Western counterparts to see for themselves the scale of the insurgency – and to be fed the Chinese line about what was behind it.

Grinding the Uighurs' faces into the sand over many a decade was the explanation favored by Western intelligence agencies, but the *Guoanbu* view was different: to their eyes the uprising was evidence of a brazen new jihadi thrust into the Central Asian heartland. For them the Islamist assault on Xinjiang was part of a war against the East as well as the West, first by Al Qaeda then by ISIS, and the West should be made to care.

Not knowing where Urumqi or Xinjiang province might be, let alone anything about Uighurs, Tony was hardly the obvious man for the job. But then M15 was up to its ears in domestic matters – the fall-out from the Syrian, Libyan, Afghan, Pakistani and Somali emergencies – and specialists on Central Asia were thin on the ground. So it was that Beijing was informed that M15 were grateful for the invitation to see the situation in the province for themselves, and were pleased to inform the Chinese People's Republic that Mr Anthony Underwood, a senior figure in the service (which wasn't true) who as a long-serving officer had distinguished himself in a major Islamist counter-terrorist incident (which was), would be their representative.

Tony had been consulted, but needed no time to think it

over. Happy to escape the routine, pre-retirement tasks he had been assigned, not to speak of family problems (he had a wife and daughter and there were troubles with both), he saw no objection to decamping to the other side of the world at short notice, or to the prospect of a few weeks' swanning in a warm climate. He'd never set foot further East than Moscow and a visit to a remote and exotic corner of China would fit the bill nicely.

Only when M15's personal envoy to Xinjiang province was squeezing himself into his economy seat for the seventeen hour flight to Urumqi via Beijing (he'd tried to upgrade to business class, with no joy – his modest rank again), wondering how the tight, anti-thrombosis stockings his wife had insisted he wear for the trip could do anything except make a blocked vein more likely, did the agency learn that the mission had changed, and that it had sent the wrong man.

*

In the arrival hall of Beijing International Airport a loudspeaker paged *Mi-s-teh An-teh-ni An-de-woo*, travelling to Urumqi, several times in English and Mandarin, so advertising to the Chinese nation the arrival of the M15 man in what seemed to Tony menacingly precise tones. *Go at once to information desk for message*, the announcer instructed, in a voice suggesting he'd be in trouble if he didn't show up, pronto. So much for the anonymity the *Guoanbu* had guaranteed.

The girl at the information desk gave him a number to call. It turned out to be Edward Collinson, a First Secretary at the British Embassy and the security liaison man accredited to the Chinese government. Collinson sounded harassed. Something had arisen that Tony needed to know before he continued his journey, something he'd prefer not to discuss on the phone.

When was his onward flight to Urumqi, tonight or tomorrow? In three hours ten minutes, Tony replied. In that case Collinson would come out to the airport to talk, there being no time for Tony to get through the Beijing traffic to the Embassy and back. He'd be there in an hour, and they agreed to meet in the departure lounge, by the bookstall.

For Tony it was a handy rendezvous point. Books, never an important feature in his life, were prominent in his mind at that moment. Before the decision to send him out here his knowledge of modern China was confined to Jung Chang's *Wild Swans*, something his wife had insisted he read. Now he was better informed about the place where he was going. In the last few weeks he'd worked his way through a small library of works on Xinjiang and its history: the Silk Road and Marco Polo, the Great Game, Muslim insurrections and blood-drenched massacres.

Then the communist victory in 1949, the flood of Chinese settlers, the Chinese atmospheric nuclear tests at their base in the wilds of Lop Nor, the frantic exploitation of the province's mining resources, and today the resurrection of the Silk Road to the West, where Urumqi would once again be a major staging post. Oil, gas, coal, uranium, gold – Xinjiang, the size of Western Europe and the place he'd scarcely heard of, had it all.

Waiting for Collinson he scanned the shelves hungrily, but there was nothing; almost everything was in Chinese, and so far as he could see confined to economics and business methods. Familiar figures stared from the covers of translated works: Donald Trump's gilded mane, the jovial mien of Richard Branson and the golden grin of Warren Buffet – tycoons, self-improvement men, gurus of every sort.

Alongside the bookshelves a DVD was playing of a bow-tied American management type giving a lecture. It had attracted quite a crowd, and for a while Tony watched. The keynote, it seemed, was the importance of self-belief. No lack of that in China, he'd concluded after an hour on the ground of Asia's busiest and most imposing airport. Go lecture the British.

From briefings by his colleagues at Thames House about Chinese counter-intelligence methods – they seemed to amount to a kind of systematized paranoia – he assumed they would monitor his meeting with Collinson, declared to the *Guoanbu* or not. To spot his shadow he inspected the throng of men watching the DVD, but soon gave up: in their anonymous suits and ties the whole lot looked like shadows, an entire surveillance team immersed in a course of self-improvement.

Collinson arrived late, still sounding harassed.

'Sorry to keep you. There's been a lot happening.'

For some reason Tony had assumed that our Beijing security man would be a portly old China hand his own age, but, not for the first time, he was behind the game. Collinson was in his mid-to-late thirties, thin and academic-looking, from his abstracted manner to his untidy carroty hair and almost wilfully ill-fitting clothes. He ought to have guessed. More and more of his newer colleagues in the service looked to him like adolescent nerds: keen-eyed, tech-friendly young men with degrees in God knew what, or alarmingly self-possessed young women whose paper qualifications tended to be even better.

This one was a Chinese speaker, he noted when Collinson ordered Tony's beer in the language, appointed no doubt for his linguistic skills. It couldn't have been for his hair. And not a man who'd spent too much time on the beat as a humble watcher, by the look of him; a three-week course in the latest electronic surveillance techniques, probably, then onwards and upwards to higher things. Not for him Tony's interminable hours drinking in Irish pubs, loitering around mosques or standing in the rain on some godforsaken industrial estate while a KGB officer with Soviet Trade Delegation cover picked up his consignment of embargoed goods.

Not that he felt resentment at Collinson and his kind; it wasn't in him, and after his Safia coup he had no need. It was just that in his last years in the job he couldn't help but reflect on the way the counter-espionage world was going. Wherever you looked human intelligence was giving way to human machines, and the change was not for the better.

His beer ordered (Collinson asked for coffee) the embassy man glanced at his watch:

'You've got a plane to catch, so I'll be quick. There's been a change of mission.'

'Don't tell me I'm on the next plane home. I don't think my legs could take it.'

'Absolutely not.'

Tony scoured the younger man's face for clues: relieved at the 'not' he distrusted the 'absolutely.'

'It's just that it's developed into something more than a PR function, and there's a chance it may last longer. Would you be all right with that?'

'Absolutely.'

In a version tailored for Tony's consumption Collinson relayed the story. While Tony had been standing in line at security at Heathrow, one hand supporting his beltless trousers, the other removing his shoes (showing his M15 credentials would have been more trouble than it was worth), a Counselor from the Chinese Embassy had requested a meeting with the Deputy Director at Thames House, and delivered an important-looking package.

The contents included pictures of a box-load of sub-machine guns, a photo of a pyjama-clad man sitting at a desk in a cell, his features indistinct but a toilet with a fluffy cover weirdly prominent in the background, and for the DNA people a generous clump of hair (it was dark and curly). Finally there was a photocopy of his passport, made out in London to one Khalil Osman, a 29 year old male with dual British and Kirghiz citizenship.

Handing over his package with a sense of occasion and a satisfied smile, the Counselor explained that Osman had been involved in gun-running in his country, and that his government would be more than happy for the M15 man, currently en route to Xinjiang, to interrogate the newly captured man. At which the Deputy Director smiled in turn: getting access to anyone detained in China could be a gruelling process, especially if there were security considerations, yet here was the *Guoanbu* offering an invitation. A first, in his experience.

Most grateful, the Deputy Director replied warmly, adding something about the increasingly close cooperation between our two nations in the security field yielding increasingly beneficial results. At which more smiles were exchanged. Reflecting when the diplomat had left on the implications of a British terrorist rotting in a Chinese jail, and its media potential, the Deputy Director's face swiftly regained its familiar, lugubrious expression.

Presented with the Chinese bag of goodies the technicians did their stuff. The counter-terrorism folk were enthusiastic: Osman they knew of, Osman had form, Osman they would be happy to see interrogated at the earliest opportunity, preferably by one of their senior men experienced in the international field. Who did not include Tony Underwood.

With a lot of shouting into phones and scurrying along corridors it took little more than half an hour to get clearance to pull Tony off the job, in favour of a top man specialising in the Afghan-Pakistani-Central Asia area. And a further three minutes to discover that flight BA352 to Beijing was already taxiing down the runway with Underwood aboard, his contentment marred only by his long and horribly tight black stockings.

*

Tony listened to Collinson's account, his lower lip protruding glumly. Yet another book on the history of the Silk Road, swallowed whole on his sleepless flight, had whetted his curiosity about the place further, and with plenty of time on his hands (he'd supposed) he'd already been planning forays into the Gobi and Taklamakan deserts. Now it was starting to sound as if there'd be work to do. Interrogation reports, interpreters, liaison with his Russian and American colleagues, secure communication problems – there'd be no end to it.

Collinson pointed to his briefcase.

'I've got a copy of the stuff the Chinese gave us.'

'Good.'

The embassy man set the case aside.

'You're going to let me have it?'

Collinson inclined his head to one side with an apologetic smile. Like this the carrot hair looked even whackier.

'It's tricky, security-wise.'

'But if the Chinese gave them to us, what's the risk?'

Over-secure security men, more grey matter than common sense. Another problem with the younger folk.

'Bit convenient for them, isn't it?' he grumped.

'Meaning?'

'The timing. Just as we and the FBI come to town they lay their hands on an Al Qaeda suspect.'

'What we thought', Collinson nodded. 'On the other hand we've done a bit of preliminary work on Osman, and it's looking persuasive.'

'The passport's forged I assume?'

'Can't be sure from a copy. We're asking them for the original but I imagine it'll take time. Chinese bureaucracy.'

'So he could be a genuine Brit?'

'Everything suggests he is.'

'Christ.'

Tony studied his beer, his spirits not down exactly, but deflating. He could see it all coming: consular issues, human rights to everything under the sun, and the sensationalist reporting in the British press...

'Have they announced his capture?'

'No, and they don't intend to. In China they don't have to. They're holding him under emergency legislation, insofar as it matters.'

'Will it get out? To the media I mean?'

'Who can say?'

I can, Tony thought. Everything always did. A British subject couldn't just disappear into Central Asia, and no questions asked: he'd have family, friends, sympathisers. If there was a leak – and there always was – he could see the headline: *M15 man interrogates British terrorist in Chinese jail.* The thought of it gave him no joy. He wasn't the kind to relish public attention, or any attention, come to that.

'It'll depend on what they – and we – discover', Collinson went on. 'The Chinese will want to show the world they were right. That Al Qaeda is active in Xinjiang, and ISIS is on its way, and their Uighur problems are nothing to do with rioting for human rights.'

'And who exactly is the bastard?'

'A Central Asian Muslim educated at a British boarding school and London University.'

'Age?'

'Twenty-nine, but his importance belies his youth.'

A maxim of modern life, Tony sighed to himself. Prime

Ministers, billionaires, now even terrorist bosses seemed the merest striplings. Not to speak of his M15 colleagues.

'And how and when did they catch him?'

'Very recently. *In medias res*, apparently.'

'Sorry?'

'Red-handed, with his guns.'

'How many?'

'Thirty-six cases.'

'Doesn't seem much.'

Play it down, his instincts were telling him, play it down.

'The Chinese think there's more of them there already, smuggled in before the riots. And they're taking it seriously. Trainloads of extra troops are being sent in from Gansu province next door.'

'They're worried about a mass revolt?'

'It's not so much the numbers – three quarters of Urumqi is Han Chinese after all – it's that they've got their hands on weapons. Hard to do in China, though in Xinjiang, with all those frontiers – Afghanistan included – a matter of time. Anyway that's how they got Osman.'

'Just the smuggling?'

'More, they think. A lot more possibly, the *Guoanbu* are hinting.'

'Of what?'

'Terrorist plots. And there could be a British angle.'

'And they're giving us access, promptly. Bit of a turn-up, isn't it?'

Tony's tone was rueful, as if he'd rather they didn't.

'Can't recall a precedent. Maybe they think we can reach parts they can't. Or perhaps it's political – political and economic. A big chunk of their raw materials comes from Xinjiang, plus it's the gateway to the New Silk Road the Chinese keep talking about. The biggest and longest trade route the world has seen, from Beijing and Shanghai all the way to Greece or Calais, via Kazakhstan, Pakistan, Afghanistan and so on, complete with integrated rail services. The containers will take two weeks from here to there, but it'll be a frequent service.

'And Xinjiang will be key to the whole project. The idea of developing their own Central Asian Texas gives the Chinese an extra incentive to join the war on terror, as we're no longer allowed to call it. They're not going to stand by and watch the province turn into a religious battlefield, even if it means cooperating with the West to stop it.'

'Is that why they've got the Americans and the Russians in?'

'Partly, though there's an element of reciprocity I suspect. The Americans let them have a crack at the Uighurs they were holding in Guantanamo a few years back, after 9/11, and the Russians are in there because of the Shanghai Cooperation agreement.'

'Remind me...'

'Sort of Central Asian NATO, writ small. Cooperation on terrorism and drugs, a few military manoeuvres and suchlike. Russia and China are the chief members.'

'You say Osman has connections in Kirghizstan. Sorry, my geography's a bit hazy, but is that –'

'– one of those ex-Soviet republics no one can remember. North West of Xinjiang, they share a frontier. Lots of mountains, part of the Tian Shan and Pamir systems. Sunni Muslim, Turkic-speaking. Some rioting a few years back between impoverished Kirghiz and minority Uzbeks. And there's evidence that Al Qaeda's in there, fishing.'

'So how did Osman wind up in London?'

'Molybdenum.'

Tony confined himself to raising a brow. There was a limit to the number of times he could say 'sorry?'

'A metal. Used in steel alloys, withstands intense heat. Aircraft parts, electrical contacts, industrial motors.'

'Got you. And the Osman connection?'

'His father started out as a mining engineer. Made a killing in molybdenum when the Soviet Union fell apart. The Russians pulled out in 1991 and they privatised the mines. Which is when the mafia came for him. It got so hot Osman senior sold up and took his family and his cash to London.'

'So our terrorist's dad's an oligarch.'

'Mini-garch. Worth a couple of hundred million or thereabouts, but he plays the same game. He hasn't bought a football team yet but he's done the rest. Got himself a piece of Hampstead, put his kids through boarding schools and swapped his wife for a Czech model half his age. And dumped his religion along the way. A classic.'

'And Osman junior?'

'Classic reaction. Comes to the UK when he's eight years old, a smart kid who speaks Chinese and Russian, and soon he's speaking English better than the natives. Brilliant at school, studies economics because his father wants him to go into business. Gets a first, collects a fancy pad in Chelsea and a million or two by way of reward, so he's at liberty to live it up. Which he does for a couple of years in the usual way. Then it all goes bad. His dad pushes him to get involved in family investments, instead of which he gets the Islamist bug. Gives up the drink and the girls and goes back to University to study comparative religion.

'His dad tries to claw back the flat and the money but it's too late, legally he can't. So he drops the case and disinherits his boy, who by now is deep into his religious studies. Next thing he's probing his Muslim roots and getting involved in Islamic politics of the friskier kind. That's how we got a line on him.'

'Good source?'

'Student friend who turned against him. Said that the playboy he used to go clubbing with had turned into a nihilistic, narcissistic, God-struck bastard – those were his words – who was getting in deep.'

'Nihilism doesn't usually go along with Islamism.'

'We don't know enough about his beliefs to get into points of doctrine. Sounds like the kind of fellow who would want his personal brand. He's had a troubled background, remember. His dad made him drop his religion when he dropped his, just after he went to prep school. Which was about the time he got rid of his mother. Must have been a difficult time for him.'

'The heart bleeds.'

'He's turned against everything Western, apparently, but he's clever with it.' He paused before adding, '"An intellectual hatred is the worst", as they say.'

'Who says?'

'W.B. Yeats. The poet.'

'Ah.'

An intellectual hatred is the worst. Smart folk, in other words, did most damage. Tony liked that, stored it away in his mind. It would join the collection of quotes he'd built up over the years, his substitute for a university degree. Blessed with a good memory, he had a knack of getting things by heart, and while he'd never had time for on-the-job study he was curious about the doctrines that drove his adversaries. During his stint tracking Soviet agents he'd invested in a few lines from Marx and Lenin, and after mugging up on the Muslim faith for his anti-terrorist assignments he could reel off a passage or two from the Koran.

'And after University?'

'Did a bit of scribbling. Journalism, reviewing, preparing a book on Central Asia. His great works are still awaited.'

'And he's travelled.'

'Got around under the umbrella of his comparative religious studies. Though the only religions he seemed keen to compare were Islam and Christianity, to the detriment of the latter. Never made it to Syria so far as we know. Seems more interested in his home territory. Spent eighteen months in Central Asia, maybe not all of it doing research.'

'So the Chinese may be onto something serious. Not just arms smuggling.'

'I'm sorry to say they may.'

'Sorry?'

'Because they've cried wolf on Al Qaeda in Xinjiang so often and we've scoffed so loudly that it would be one in the eye for us. Particularly as Osman's British. All we need. We've got British Muslims fighting in Syria, Afghanistan, Iraq, Somalia and Pakistan, British Sri Lankans plotting away there, and now British Central Asians getting at China. Talk about the empire strikes back.'

Collinson's sigh was unconvincing. The look in his eye suggested something else – that he was privately not unhappy to see the frontline in the terror war shifting eastwards. For a Sinologue, Tony reflected, it would be more scope for bureaucratic empire building.

'But if it turns out to be no more than a bit of schoolboy exuberance, shipping in a few weapons to rioters, and it's a one–off, I don't see that HMG should worry.'

'Agreed. Except the Chinese are telling us they think our schoolboy's been trained in the Fergana Valley.'

'That part of the tribal areas in Pakistan?'

'No, it's new ground, further up. Between Kirghizstan, Uzbekistan and Tajikistan. A hideout for jihadis from all three countries. Couldn't ask for a handier place to do their business. It's getting on for the size of England, hideously remote, and somewhere the Yanks are not at liberty to use their drones. I'm in touch with the *Guoanbu* about it – we think there are people up there from Afghanistan too.'

'So what exactly do the Chinese think?'

'They think Osman could be involved in setting up a sort of Central Asian Taliban, and that he could be the brains behind an operation in Xinjiang.'

'And the riots?'

'Just the beginning. A prelude to something bigger.'

'Well they'll find out from him soon enough, won't they? I mean to judge by what I've heard about their interrogation techniques.'

'They'll do their best, and he won't enjoy it. Not something he'll be prepared for, even after his public school. But there's a limit to how much they can rough him up. I mean him being British.'

'Sounds like I'm in for a messy time. At least the locale will be interesting.'

'Oh yes, no question. I've been there on holiday and it's an evocative part of the world. The deserts, the ruins, the history – though that's pretty much it. I can't say that Urumqi itself is much to rhapsodize about. The Chinese settlers are an unattractive bunch. A lot of them were criminals sent there under Mao, as forced labour. Now they've been given someone to look down on and it doesn't bring out the best in people.

'Not that the Uighurs are that inspiring, though they're not at the fanatical end of the Muslim spectrum. Historically they had a reputation for jollity, music, dancing girls and the rest, but nowadays they seem a sour bunch. Oppressed and oppressive. And they're not the only minority. White Russians, Kazaks, Kirghiz, Tadjiks, Uzbeks, Mongols, Tartars – the place is not so much a melting pot, more a cauldron. And one way and another it's always on the boil.'

'And they're throwing me into it.'

'Don't worry, you may not be on your own for long. Way things are going Thames House say there may have to be a follow-up visit. Depends how far you get.'

In other words, Tony thought, seeing Collinson lower his eyes, the situation might escalate beyond his rank.

'By the way, there's a guy at the table behind you', Tony said quietly, 'taking a close interest in our conversation.'

Over his shoulder he indicated a young Chinese a couple of tables away. Without turning Collinson shrugged and smiled.

'I'm sure he is. Their security people work like clockwork soldiers. Don't know when to switch it off, and unlike us there's no shortage of personnel. The intelligence guy handling your visit, by the way, will be Captain Tang.'

'You know him?'

'By reputation.' Collinson leant closer, whispering. 'One of their bright young things, the young being fifty in China. Liberal side of the fence. Too much so, perhaps, in Beijing's eyes. We think they've given him a demanding assignment to toughen him up. I'll be interested in your impressions. If he does a good job up there he could go far.'

An announcement came over the Tannoy.

'That's your plane.'

'Before I go, I couldn't trouble you for a sight of my instructions, could I? I think there's time.'

'God I'm sorry. And there's a brief they telegraphed, for your interrogation.'

Collinson retrieved his briefcase and opened it. Tony held out a hand for the papers. There weren't any. Instead Collinson took out his computer, and began fiddling.

Ah, the laptop generation. Years ago the tech boys at Thames House had run a computer exam for people of Tony's generation. The assessment in his case had been to the effect that, technologically speaking, whilst not a child exactly he was an adolescent who showed few signs of maturing. And there things had rested. A series of emergencies, notably the Safia affair, had spared him all manner of improvement courses. When they'd warned him the Internet had been cut off in Xinjiang, content at the thought of being out of touch, he'd left his own machine behind.

Collinson was still fiddling.

'Paper's so much easier, don't you find?' Tony sighed, 'plus more secure. You lose it, you've lost one item. Leave that thing in a car and you've lost the whole show.'

Collinson's smile was tolerant, as if directed at an infant. Clearing a space between them on the table he turned his laptop to face Tony.

There were half a dozen pages: four on what the Chinese had told them about their catch, the rest angles on the interrogation they wanted him to cover. Tony read quickly, scribbling one-word notes to himself. When he'd finished Collinson said:

'Communications with Urumqi are intermittent. There seems no logic to when they're on or off. It's driving the correspondents and the business people crazy, and you'll have the same problem. Anything sensitive and we'll send a courier, or I'll come out myself.' More laptop fiddling, then he added. 'Oh, and you should see these. Background on your American and Russian colleagues.'

He brought up two more pages. Personality reports marked *Confidential*, the first was on Zachary Boorstin:

A Special Agent in Charge with fifteen years experience in counter-terrorism, mainly in Washington. Has worked on a few Islamist cases with M15, competently in the main. Has a yen for the Far East following a year's internship at the FBI station in Singapore. Character assessment: sharp-witted, garrulous, impulsive, amiable in small doses.

Next was Aleksei Konstantinovich Benediktov. The Russian was a few years older, with a fuller CV.

Colonel in the FSB, Department for the Protection of the Constitutional System and the Fight against Terrorism. Son of Major-General Benediktov, formerly the senior KGB China specialist. Speaks excellent English and Mandarin following his father's posting in Beijing in the 1960s, and subsequently to the Washington Embassy. The son served in Chechnya and more recently at the Russian Embassy in Bishkek, Kirghizstan. A Russian source has reported that he was withdrawn after an incident in which —'

'Flight 2967 to Urumqi is closing at gate 23. All passengers...'

Scanning the rest hurriedly Tony pushed the laptop back to Collinson and reached for his briefcase.

'Better be off.'

Collinson paid and they prepared to leave. He'd been right about their clockwork shadow: the moment they stood up the Chinese two tables behind folded his paper, briskly. As they said their farewells, he got up. When they walked off in separate directions he stayed where he was, the mechanism jammed. A few paces away Tony glanced over his shoulder to see the poor fellow transfixed, his head inclined anxiously, gabbling away like crazy into some concealed mobile.

He smiled to himself. There he was, a *Guoanbu* man listening in to foreigners discussing things sourced from his own outfit, stuff they knew already, then reporting them back to themselves, classified secret no doubt. Not that he was surprised. Infinite regurgitation was the way of the intelligence world, and he could think of occasions when he'd done much the same.

4

Back from their visit to Osman's cell the three security men stood around in the corridor outside Tang's office, where the Captain was talking earnestly into the phone. After their underground seclusion the sound of rioting seemed louder, closer. The Bureau was evidently on some sort of alert. What sounded like instructions were being shouted from loudspeakers while police and paramilitaries stomped urgently by, with a double-take at the foreigners lingering in their path. Some were stowing ammunition and checking their weapons as they passed.

Leaving the American and the Russian trading impressions of Osman he walked to a window at the front of the building – Tang's office was at the back – and peered through the grill. Three hours before, a *Guoanbu* driver had collected him and Zach from the hotel and delivered them to the front entrance, no problem. Now the road outside the broad courtyard was empty. Beyond the high railings a ring of barricades was being hurriedly erected, with sandbag emplacements for heavier weapons. On the far side of the road shopkeepers were frantically hauling down shutters, while police from the Bureau scuttled across the courtyard and out of the gates to reinforce the thin line of PAP.

The rioting was supposed to have been a safe distance away. The situation must have deteriorated, sharply. To judge by the improvised barricade they couldn't have expected the rioters to get this close, let alone armed insurgents. If they got any nearer that rough and ready line protecting the Bureau had better hold. The rate things were going, troops and helicopters were what they were going to need, and there was no sign of either.

When he came back Benediktov turned to him.

'OK, so who gets first crack at him? The bastard's British so maybe it should be you. Whaddya say, Zach?'

'Fine by me', the American shrugged.

Though not with Tony. He hadn't been involved in too many interrogations – the preserve of more senior, lawyerly types – and to judge from the briefing Thames House had sent they were worried about how he'd get on. The fact that the instructions read like a child's guide – *probe him hard, but not to the point of alienation* – had done little to boost his confidence. One way and another he'd prefer to see what the others got out of him before taking his turn.

'Fair's fair', he said, 'we'll toss for it.'

Before they could object he'd fished a pound coin from his pocket, called heads, tossed it with Zach, won, tossed again with Alyosha, won again.

Not what he'd hoped.

'I really don't mind if one of you –'

'– you won, you go first,' said Alyosha, pointing imperiously to the basement.

'No one better than a Brit to soften him up,' Zach added. 'Just don't get all gentlemanly with him. I don't care for the fucker's face.'

With Tang still on the phone it was a subordinate who took him back underground. The guards on the landings had smartened up, he noted, their weapons at the ready now. Some were calling out to one another from floor to floor, anxiously it seemed. The one outside Osman's cell, a great bruiser with a servile manner, nodded at his approach, and reached for his keys.

By prior agreement with the Captain each of them was to see the prisoner alone. Pointing with a grin at the grill on the cell door, then at the pistol on his belt, to assure him of support in case of trouble, the man let him in, closed the door and left him with Osman.

*

He was at his desk, head down, facing away from him, writing. Hearing the door shut and Tony's steps behind him the prisoner neither turned nor looked up.

'I'm Tony Underwood', he said after a while. 'I'm a British official and I've come to talk to you.'

Moments passed. He felt stupid standing there, like a supplicant respectfully requesting an audience.

'I said I've come to talk.'

'You say you're British', Osman replied at last, without turning. 'If so I would have expected the courtesy of some notice of your intention to call.'

'This is a Chinese prison. I don't control things. And on the subject of courtesy it would be polite to face the person you're talking to.'

Slowly Osman raised his head and turned.

'Good evening, Mr Underwood. It's about time you came. I've been asking to see you for days. I want you to intervene with the Chinese on my behalf. Habeas corpus and so on.'

'I think there's a misunderstanding. I'm not from the Embassy. I work for the British security services.'

'But you said you were the Consul.'

'I said nothing. You supposed.'

'Well why aren't you?' A note of petulance. 'I asked to see someone from the embassy and by that I obviously meant a consular official. So where is he? What's the use of a British passport if they can lock you up and no-one gives a fuck? I have a right —'

'— you're in China, Mr Osman.'

'So that wipes out my rights? And my passport? And what right have M15 to interrogate me on Chinese soil? Some sort of dirty deal with the *Guoanbu,* is it?'

'I'm not a politician. We need to talk to you for our own purposes, for reasons you will be aware of. The Chinese agreed.' After a gap he added: 'I did ask about consular access.'

He had, in a manner of speaking, in the course of his talk with Collinson: what he'd asked was, had there been any?

'And?'

'The Chinese have to verify your identity.'

'Bullshit. They've got my passport.'

'It could be forged. The world's afloat with British passports – your world especially. From their point of view you could be anyone.'

Tony was still standing, at the front of the desk now, with Osman still in his chair. In that position it was as if the prisoner was interrogating *him.*

'Mind if I sit?'

Why was he asking? He took a seat on the bed.

A silence.

'Can I ask what you're writing?'

'Ask the Chinese. They'll give you a copy.'

'It's quicker to ask you.'

'It wouldn't interest you. It's about literature.'

Don't let him rile you, the child's guide had said. Though being made to feel inferior by a gunrunner and probable terrorist was doing nothing to keep him sweet.

'You never know', he said. 'Which writer?'

'Montaigne. Not your reading I imagine, so here's a line for your edification.' He read from the page before him. *'There is no hostility that exceeds Christian hostility.'* He gave a scarcely perceptible smirk. 'Not bad from a Catholic, don't you think? Though his mother was Jewish. A great man, though I hate to think what he might have become today. A raging Islamophobe, I suppose.'

Montaigne? Tony's mind was an anxious blank – anxious because the name wasn't entirely unfamiliar. French, to judge from the way Osman pronounced it, maybe a few centuries old. In which case he wouldn't know. His secondary modern school in south London had taught him little about anything old or foreign. One day he'd do some catching up, he'd been telling himself, buckle down to some serious reading. Something to fill his old age.

Feeling Osman's pleasure at his discomfort and the stares of Zach and Alyosha from beyond the glass, he was about to hurry on when – a miracle – something kicked in.

'*It is putting a very high price on one's conjectures*', he found himself saying, '*to have someone roasted alive on their account.*'

Where the hell had that come from? Ah yes: one of the new breed of eggheads in the service had put the Montaigne quote at the head of a note on the origins of religious extremism circulated to the counter-terrorism staff. Tony was one of the few who'd read it, and the sentiment had imprinted itself on his mind. A mind like blotting paper that soaked up things easily but indiscriminately, leaving a smudgy impression.

'I don't know the French', he went on, 'but to me it sounds pretty good in English. Big ideas are not worth incinerating anyone for, is what he's saying. Rather a relevant quote in the 9/11 context, wouldn't you say?'

'Well well, Montaigne and M15. Congratulations, you have excellent sources.' Osman made a supercilious face. Tony could have kicked it. 'But quotations are one thing, understanding them another, and you've got it all wrong. It doesn't prove what you think it does. He was talking about Christian persecution.'

'About all kinds of fanaticism I should have thought. Twenty-first century terrorist bombings as well as' – he hesitated, then made a stab – 'seventeenth century burnings alive.'

'Sixteenth. Montaigne died in 1592.'

'Interesting, but we'd better get on.'

Taking the miniature recording machine that Collinson had provided from his pocket, he laid it on the desk.

'Better make sure it's working.'

Osman pointed. Tony checked: it wasn't. The red light had come on, briefly, then gone out.

'Want me to fix it?' Osman smirked.

'Never mind, let's get on.' The recording wasn't essential: the Chinese would make their own tape, Tang had assured them. 'Tell me, when did you become – or rather re-become – a Muslim?'

'Ah, the interrogation is beginning.'

'So when was it?'

'What business is it of yours?'

'None at all. Just part of a process that has to be gone through to determine how long you're likely to stay in this country, and the conditions you're likely to be held under.'

'Ah. Threats already. And if I don't cooperate?'

'Then you don't. No skin, as they say. There'll be other opportunities, other interrogations. Maybe a little more informal than mine. Meanwhile let me tell you what we know already.'

Briefly, he went over what Collinson had given him: the family origins in Kirghizstan, the molybdenum fortune, the move to London, the dumped wife, the Hampstead mansion. Then the private school, university, Muslim politics, the travels to Central Asia.

'It's only a sketch, from memory', he concluded. 'We have more. And I'm open to correction.'

Listening, Osman's mask of indifference had slipped a little.

'You've been tracking me.'

'Not without reason, it turns out. Maybe you can help fill out the picture? You're a Tungan, right?'

'I was born one. Now I'm Uighur.'

'By adoption, I assume.'

'They are brothers, Muslim brothers. You've learned something about Uighurs I imagine, but Tungans, Mr Underwood, you know about Tungans?'

'Can't say I do.'

'I'll tell you. The name is Chinese, it comes from Eastern Gansu, the province next door to this: Tung means East and -gan is for Gansu. Tungans were Huis – a Hui is a Chinese Muslim – and in the 1860s the Huis revolted against the Manchus because they wanted their own country. Ninety percent of them were wiped out, the rest fled to Russia. Or in my family's case, Kirghizstan. But not all of us got away, and for those like my great grandfather who stayed the punishments were barbaric.'

'Such as?'

'Things like slicing.'

'You mean death by a thousand cuts?'

'Exotic rubbish. No one could survive half a dozen – though my great grandfather came close. He was a scholar, a brave and religious man, but then faith and courage was all the Muslims had. The Chinese had German canon supplied by the Krupps of the day. Anyway they caught him and they executed him. Shall I tell you how?'

'If you wish.'

'The slicing was done in pubic, so as to terrify the population – and entertain them. For them it was like a snuff movie, filmed before their eyes. The way the flesh was cut, the morsels selected and the sequence were not laid down in law, so the executioners could use their imaginations, like whimsical butchers. They could start with a few slices off the arms, or maybe the fleshier parts of the chest. Then cut by cut they'd proceed to the amputation of a limb or two, and finally to decapitation, or a stab to the heart. On the way they could go for the genitals if the mood took them. One of the prime cuts.

'If the crime wasn't too serious and the executioner was feeling benign, after a good lunch perhaps, the first cut would be the throat, the later ones purely to dismember the corpse. And this being China the *coup de grace* could always be brought forward, so long as you could afford a bribe.

'But my great grandfather was accused of treason, he wasn't going to demean himself by paying a bribe, so he got the whole show. Slowly. We know because the Chinese are punctilious about keeping records. You want the details?'

'Another time.'

'You find it difficult? A man in your profession? Never mind, I'll tell you all the same. Opium was sometimes administered as an act of mercy, is what historians say, but that's not quite right. They gave my great grandfather opium, though he didn't ask for it. They forced it into his mouth, and it wasn't an act of mercy.'

'So why should they – ?'

'– to prevent him fainting away after they'd taken the first slice or two. Seeing pieces of your flesh tossed to the ground can have a bad effect on the nerves. And it's no fun for the crowd if the victim wasn't in agony. That's why they administered the opium in measured doses: enough to keep him conscious, but not enough to smother the pain.'

'You seem to know a lot about it. Because of your great grandfather?'

'And because it tells you a lot about China.'

A silence.

'You like the Chinese, Mr Underwood?'

'It's my first visit.'

'Never mind, in time you will discover. With the Chinese there is always something extra. Some little touch you would never have dreamt up, like one of the most fanciful dishes of their cuisine. Like the opium.'

'We're talking about a long time ago.'

'Wrong again, Mr Underwood, it wasn't so long. They only stopped doing it in the last century – 1905 to be exact. For my ancestor, forty years too late.'

'You can use history to justify anything. People don't mull over the past any more, plotting revenge. Except jihadis, with their Caliphate and their harking back to the Crusades. If everyone were to take the slights their ancestors suffered personally there'd be no end to it. Is that your message? Terrorism without end?'

'A squaring of accounts with the past, I'd prefer to call it,' Osman came back, with a half-smile.

Silence again. Balls, Tony was thinking, absolute balls. Philosophical smart-arsing, student talk.

'You seem to see terrorism as an intellectual game, where anyone is free to use their version of the past to whip up hatred. A lot of people could die that way.' He paused for a moment before adding: 'An intellectual hatred is the worst.'

'Bravo! Yeats, in *A Prayer for My Daughter*. But I'm afraid you're off the mark again. He was talking about the Irish question, remember. Another account to be squared.'

'And your re-adoption of Islam? Is that part of the game? Or was it after your father became an apostate?'

'If I tell you it was after I went to university, what absurd construction will you put on that I wonder?'

'They don't seem to have taught you manners at university.'

'Manners? And you, Mr Underwood, how about your own? I didn't ask to see you. You're here at China's request, I imagine. I know they're buying up half the City but does that mean M15 are at the beck and call of the *Guoanbu* now? Anything to keep them sweet and pull in orders. Quite a come-down from the old days, isn't it, when the Brits did what they wanted and to hell with anyone else. Notices saying *No Dogs and Chinese Allowed* in a Shanghai park, and so on.'

'That was a myth.'

His reading was proving handy.

'We're working on your case with Russia and the FBI as well as China. And we're making progress.' It was bullshit, but so what? It would be so long before this man saw a Western newspaper again he'd never know. 'The fact that we're working together does rather reduce your chances of getting out of here in a hurry. So I would advise you to be frank about what you've been up to. In the UK as well as here.'

'If you think I'm plotting against Britain, why not extradite me?'

'Oh we'll be trying, we'll try all right. Grounds for suspicion as long as your arm, connected with the activities of one or two of your former university mates.'

Another stab in the dark – Collinson had said nothing about anyone else – but it seemed to work. Osman's eyelids batted.

'So what are the chances?'

'Of what?'

'Extradition.'

'Non-existent, I should say. To begin with we'd need something specific to extradite you for, which means you'd have to tell us what you've been up to in Britain. Names and addresses, foreign contacts, the lot. In the second place we don't have an extradition treaty with China, given their fondness for capital punishment. Though they don't shoot quite so many people in the back of the neck nowadays for minor crimes, I'm told.' He watched Osman closely as he added. 'They're going over to lethal injection instead. Part of modernizing their image.'

Osman was careful not to react, but Tony caught the brightness in his eye.

'But that's all theory. Even assuming you give us a reason to get you back, the Chinese have a prior claim. It was they who caught you and they have a right to try you according to their laws, not ours.'

He left a space for Osman to reflect, before adding:

'None of which rules out informal arrangements, you understand. Unlike ours the legal system here is...sort of flexible I gather. I suppose it's possible to conceive of them extraditing you to the UK as a one-off, or letting you serve your time at home. Assuming we can get them to commute a death sentence. But they'd need something in return, wouldn't they? Such as details of anything else you might be planning here, in addition to the guns. Targets, timing, who's in with you – the usual things.'

'So what are you driving at exactly?'

Tony wasn't sure. Irritated by the man's cockiness he'd been carried away, free-wheeling.

'I'm suggesting that in your shoes I'd be thinking in terms of a deal,' he said off the hoof, 'because the alternative might not be pleasant.'

Without speaking Osman bent forward and took off his left shoe. Tony glanced down. The foot, badly swollen, had been roughly bandaged.

'Toenails?', Tony asked.

'Nothing so crude, or so visible. They wrenched it. And they'll tell you I tripped.'

'Only did the one?'

'The guard told me they were keeping the other for future sessions.'

'The big fellow?'

'He's a sadistic lout.'

Now Osman rucked up the top half of his pyjamas, and turning away. Bruises the size of plums pitted his lower back.

Tony's sigh was part-genuine.

'Local excess I suppose, though you'll know more about what goes on here than me.'

'So why did they send you?'

'Oh, I happened to be available. And I've dealt with terrorist cases in Britain.'

With an involuntary wince, Osman was putting his shoe back on.

'Mr Underwood', he said when he'd finished. 'It's your duty to report what you've seen. If the government takes up my case and there's a lot of publicity maybe they'll deport me?'

'I wouldn't bet on it.'

Osman thought for a moment.

'You say I should make a deal. Imagine for the sake of argument that I have some influence on the insurgency. The methods it uses, whether terrorism is included or not. Just imagine. And imagine something is... pending.'

'Meaning you're involved in something beyond arms smuggling.'

'I said imagine. And if I were, and the Chinese' – he affected a shrug – 'did what they do to my category of prisoner, I wouldn't be able to use my restraining influence, would I?'

'I don't think you're in any position –'

'– what I'm saying is that injustice against Muslims is unlikely to go un-avenged. And that includes me. If nothing happens to me, perhaps nothing will happen outside.'

'You seem very concerned with your own skin. Where's the martyrdom element in all this?'

'Who said I was anxious to become a martyr?'

'Because you're afraid of death?'

'Absolutely not.' His expression did not change as he added: 'It's just that I could live without it.'

There was a silence, then in a quiet voice Tony said:

'I don't believe you have anything or anyone out there, besides your few hundred weapons. I think you're a fantasist. A nihilist and a fantasist.'

'Excellent! Then tell it to the Chinese. Tell them you know from your records that I'm a playboy terrorist, an amateur who got caught up in a bit of gun-smuggling and that relations between our two great countries will suffer if they make a big deal of it.'

At that moment the spyhole behind where Osman was sitting shot up and down, though there was time for Tony to catch sight of the guard's eye. It looked malevolent, a reminder of what Osman could be in for after he'd gone. M15 wasn't supposed to shrug at torture. Maybe a little more commiseration was required, if only for the record. He nodded towards the foot.

'I'm sorry about your foot – though I've seen worse, and you're still walking. They shouldn't have done that. I'll have a word about it.'

'How do you know I can walk? You watched me? From that glass?' He pointed to the mirror. 'I had a piss not long ago, did you watch that too? Is it in order for the security services to watch prisoners pissing? Isn't there something in the law about preserving dignity? Something else I need to speak to the Consul about.'

So much for his commiseration.

'You should have chosen another place to be caught', Tony said sharply, and made to get up.

'You're going?'

'I think that's enough for today.'

'Don't you want to ask me any more questions?'

'Not for the moment. Unless there's something you're burning to get off your chest. But then it's only our first encounter and you don't seem in a forthcoming mood. Maybe you'd prefer to let your hair down with the Russians or Americans. Or the Chinese.'

'This is tantamount to rendition! I demand to see the Consul.' Osman stood up, then turned away. 'That's all I wish to say. Now you can go. And you can tell your American and Russian friends I'm otherwise engaged this evening.'

Tony took a breath before saying.

'I think you may be misjudging the situation. Interrogations will be held at their convenience, not yours. And you're in no position to decide who comes to your cell and when they go.'

'It's my time for prayer', Osman said abruptly, checking his watch. 'So would you please leave.'

'Ah yes. Sundown, the mahgrib. As you wish. I'll pass your request about the Consul to the Chinese. As for rendition, we haven't rendered you to anyone. You rendered yourself. So you're theirs for the duration, I'm afraid.'

He tapped on the door. Grinning and bowing his colossal length the guard let him out, re-locked the cell and accompanied him up the stairs, exchanging remarks with the gun-toting guards on the way. They were almost at the top when Tony remembered that Zach and Alyosha would still be in the viewing room. Signaling to the guard to follow, he turned and went back down.

The viewing room door was shut. He opened it: the room was empty. About to leave, he turned and glanced through the glass. Osman was on his knees, head to the floor, facing in what Tony assumed was the correct direction. He'd seen a lot of mosques in his time, watched a lot of Muslims praying, and something wasn't right. Maybe it was the rough treatment he'd received, but Osman's posture seemed artificial: stiff, head not quite touching the floor, his bows insufficiently abject. And he'd kept a canvas shoe on the damaged foot.

As he turned to go Osman got to his feet, abruptly, and went to his desk.

Short prayer, Tony thought.

5

Upstairs he found Zach and Alyosha sprawled in chairs in the Captain's office, drinking tea. Tang wasn't there.

'Called away', Zach explained, 'shot off like a rocket. Not surprising, the racket out there. Listen to it.'

Tony listened.

'Seems closer', he concluded. 'A lot.'

'You bet', said Zach. 'And more of Osman's guns popping. So how'd it go?'

'You didn't watch?'

'Nope.'

'I told Tang you'd be welcome.'

'Delicacy of the profession. Figured you wouldn't want the Yanks and the Russkis snooping on your chat with your compatriot. The thought of us there might poop your party, throw you off your pitch. The Captain'll share his transcript with us presumably, in advance of our own little chats.'

'Get anything from him?' Alyosha threw in.

'It was a preliminary chat. He thought I was the Consul.'

'Your bedside manner', Zach grinned.

'He's not like any terrorist I've ever seen. He's an intellectual all right, never lets you forget it. Not much in the way of Islamic submission in him. He's a cocky young bastard. I hope I kept my temper.'

'You have one, Tony?' Zach again. 'The cool-hand Brit, with a temper?'

Tang came back at that moment, looking troubled and out of breath.

'I apologise, gentlemen. It is a busy time.'

'So we can hear', said Alyosha. 'How are things going out there?'

'The situation is fully under control –'

'– but not entirely hopeless.' Alyosha's baby face creased in a grin. 'Sorry, Captain. Old Soviet joke.'

Tang smiled bleakly. This one, it appeared, he had got.

'I'm going to presume on your hospitality', Zach said gravely. 'Your green tea is excellent for my health, but I'm hearing guns. Maybe it's my nerves but it's after eight in the evening and could I use a beer.'

'Use?'

'Drink.'

'Certainly, of course. Excuse me. I am busy, I forgot.'

He phoned and made the order, then hovered distractedly at his desk.

'This is a temporary office, for the riots. I have a State Security office with things for foreign guests, but not here.'

Tony was less interested in beer than whether the insurgents had made it through the back streets to the main road, and what would happen if they did. Might the Bureau be overrun? On the point of asking, he checked himself. This was China and direct questions, they'd told him, were thought impolite.

'Maybe this isn't the best time to talk', he said. 'I mean if our presence is obstructing operations –'

'– not at all.'

A waiter appeared with beers, opened them and handed them round. Zach sipped the Qing Tao appreciatively.

'Very nice.'

'We learned from the Germans in the colonial period', Tang explained, absently.

'You learned well. Lucky for you it wasn't the British, you'd be swigging that bitter stuff.'

'I have tasted it. It is not too bitter, but warm.'

And so on it went, for several minutes. A long way to come to talk about brands of beer, Tony thought, while a terrorist downstairs was refusing to say what his plans were for the future and all hell was let loose in the city.

'So what are you using out there?' He gestured towards the explosions. 'Live rounds now I suppose?'

'I am not responsible for operations. Only for intelligence matters. And for liaison. So please to enjoy your drink.'

The Captain coughed, picked up the phone, spoke a few phrases, sharply, then put it down, smiling.

'Gentlemen, the food will be arriving soon. Szechuan food. It is very good.'

'Very kind, Mr Tang. *I said VERY KIND.*' Zach raised his voice to be heard over the rising hubbub in the outside corridor. 'But if you don't mind I think I should be getting along back to the hotel, and I don't know about the transport arrangements.'

'You must not worry, I have checked. There is a jeep.'

'Good', said Zach.

'Armoured. With guard.'

'Better', said Zach, getting up, 'so maybe we should be on our way.'

'You cannot go to the hotel', the Captain said.

The three of them looked at him. For once Zach wasn't smiling.

'And why is that?'

'It is not safe.'

'So we stay while the shooting gets closer?'

'It is the procedure. Later we drive you home. When rioters have finished.'

The realisation that they were trapped brought silence. So much for my early night to sleep off the jet-lag, Tony sighed to himself.

'When they finish?' he said. 'And that will be?'

'It will be around eleven', Tang answered. 'I have ordered

whisky too. Jameson's whisky. We can talk about the situation regarding Mr Osman.'

'Your assessment of the situation on the streets would be of more immediate interest, Captain', Alyosha said with lazy sarcasm.

'The evening is becoming more disorderly than expected. We have information that there are Al Qaeda elements active on this occasion, using Osman's weapons. Normally people do not have guns in China. This is not America.'

'Or Russia', Alyosha, cheerier at the thought of whisky, threw in.

'I've seen a riot or two', Zach reflected, 'and when it's different ethnicities beating up on each other it's tougher than when it's just an anti-government thing. The Hans and the Muslims really don't like each other, do they? Hatreds as strong as that must be centuries in the making. How many's it been, Captain?'

'It is complicated', said Tang, and left it at that.

Tony gave Zach a look that said, back off. And for once Zach did.

The firing flared again. Someone had to say something to cover it, and it was Tang.

'The prisoner's passport said he passed through Moscow recently. En route to Kirghizstan we think.'

'May I have a look?' Tony asked.

Tang fished in his desk and gave it him. Tony turned to the photo. Osman had selected a good picture. About twenty when it was taken, during his playboy period it seemed, with his longish curly hair and a bulky scarf tied in a fashionable French loop. Something cosmopolitan about him, even then, like a frenchified version of the youngest of the Boston Marathon bombers. The girls must have gone for him in a big way, done their bit to inflate his ego.

'I am sure he has been to many places. In Pakistan, and perhaps the Fergana Valley.' Tang threw a hand towards the front of the building. 'You can hear what they are doing with all this foreign money and guns and training. Here we see what they are aiming for.'

He pressed a button and a scroll-like fixture on the wall unrolled behind his desk. It was a map of the world. A vast swathe of territory, from Algeria to the borders of Mongolia, via Egypt, Iraq, Syria, Somalia, Iran, Pakistan, Afghanistan and Kazakhstan was coloured green. A chunk of China – Xinjiang – was included. Without its north-western province his country seemed pitifully diminished.

'This is the Caliphate al Qaeda and ISIS are determined to establish', Tang instructed in school-masterly fashion, pointing to the map. 'In it there will be Sharia law and training for jihad in the rest of the globe. And with Pakistan and Iran they will have nuclear weapons. Think of it, gentlemen! Xinjiang as part of an Islamist power on the borders with China with nuclear warheads!'

Alyosha had his head down, looking bored. Tony stared up at the map, giving a dutiful nod from time to time. Sad to see Tang relapsing into spokesman mode, he was thinking.

Zach had gone silent. A manic reformed smoker, he was wafting away the plumes from the cigarette Tang had left burning on his desk like a man besieged. When the Russian lit up too, and the brute pong of his black tobacco was eclipsing the Captain's Marlboros, he looked despairing. Noting his discomfort, Tony resisted the urge to smoke a cigarillo, his little vice, though with all that was going on around them he could have done with one.

To drown the thump of boots outside the office and on the floor above Tang was talking ever louder. When the door opened for the Jameson's to be delivered the sound of people screaming into phones in the offices opposite flooded the room.

'Well that's very generous', Zach said when the door was closed and the Jameson's poured. 'Let's drink to our four-power cooperation – to our counter-terrorist Internationale! With a capital 'I', Alyosha.'

'I got you first time', the Russian grunted.

They drank. Embarrassed to feel himself reddening after just half a glass, Tang frowned. For a case-hardened intelligence officer, Tony thought, watching the flush deepen, he seemed a bit of a thin-skinned fellow. Not what he'd expected.

Till that moment the turbulence had been coming from the front of the building. Suddenly it was from the back. Megaphones, revving lorries, piercing cries.

'Lot of trucks out there by the sound of it', Alyosha said.

'That will be our troops arriving. Reinforcements we have asked for, from Gansu province. They are experienced men. We have exercised with the forces of other countries in riot control, from Russia and Pakistan. Part of the Shanghai Cooperation agreement.'

'I read about it', Zach said flatly.

Tony stood up.

'You have a toilet?'

'Over there, Mr Underwood. I am sorry, it is not very luxurious.'

He went in and closed the door. The washroom faced the rear of the building. Above the sink was a small window. He wrenched it open and looked out.

It was still light, but the view of the rear courtyard was intermittently obscured by a pall of smoke from a chimney. A steel gate, guarded by armed police, led from the compound into the road. He saw no army trucks, nor any sign of troops. Instead vans and lorries were lined up at the rear of the building, engines running. Between the trucks and the door civilian staff had formed a human chain, passing sacks and boxes. Burning papers and transferring files, Tony surmised. Preparing to evacuate.

He flushed the toilet and went back into the office, avoiding Tang's eye but conscious of his mortified look. In the room the drinking was speeding up, the bottle almost gone, and inhibitions with it. Quiet till now, Alyosha had become talkative, sluicing down beer and whisky in indiscriminate Russian fashion.

'Hope our prisoner's safe', he barked at Zach. 'My turn next for a chat. Maybe we should swap roles? You tell him you're Moscow's man and I'll say I'm the American. Like Kissinger, an American with an accent.'

'No dice. You go at him like a real Russian. Knock some of the crap out of him, tell him he's gonna be batted back and forth between China and the Lubyanka till he comes clean. Long as he doesn't end up back in Britain. You got laws against disrespecting a prisoner by farting in his presence, right Tony? Oh yes, he'd love it back in Blighty. A cell all to himself with a plasma TV so he can keep up with ISIS propaganda on the BBC, and the legal right to the forcible conversion of fellow inmates, dumbo Caribbeans for choice. No chance of him getting the soft option in Russia, right Alyosha?'

'No, because we're not an exhausted civilisation aching for annihilation, like the West.'

'Wow! Hear that, Tony? That's our Russian friends for you! The drink brings it out!'

Tang went quiet. The barroom atmosphere, Tony could see, was beginning to displease him. Zach and Alyosha had got to know each other before Tony had arrived, and conversed in a kind of vicious joshing.

More shooting, with longer bursts this time. Zach turned to Tang, nervous again.

'How're your army doing, Captain? Just how far is Gansu province? Getting here, are they?'

'There are troops here already but maybe not sufficient. In Xinjiang they have too many things to guard.'

'Like Lop Nor? The nuclear place?'

'We must protect our installations.'

'Go ahead and protect them', Zach grinned. 'Don't want that stuff blowing up and drifting across the Pacific.'

The door opened and waiters came in, set up a trestle table then wheeled in a trolley and set down several dishes.

'Looks good.' Zach's eye pored over the duck eggs, winter melon, Szechuan shredded beef smothered in chilies. 'Nice and hot too I should say. You do yourself well here, Captain! A lot better than Pennsylvania Avenue, I can tell you.'

Indicating they should begin, Tang excused himself and left the room. As he went, Tannoy announcements blasted through the open door. To Tony the voice seemed hysterical, but then to him everything in Chinese sounded manic.

Zach turned to Alyosha. 'What they saying?'

'Something about implementing procedures.'

'The procedure for getting distinguished foreign guests the hell out of here is what I want to know.'

As if in response Tang came back. Before he could speak Tony asked:

'When are we going, Captain?'

'The jeep is here. It is the soldiers we are waiting for, to guard you.'

'Hope they can get in here. Hope we're not surrounded.'

'No, not surrounded. Not all the way. We could dine downstairs for better safety, if you prefer, it is less noisy but maybe not so comfortable.'

'Know something?' Zach put down the chopsticks he'd been eager to deploy. 'I just lost my appetite. I've got beyond the point of worrying about losing face. I'd like to be on my way, Captain. Pronto if you don't mind. Guard or no guard.' With a last, tragic look at the food, he stood up. 'So where's the jeep?'

'Perhaps you are right.' Tang answered instantly, as if he'd been waiting for the moment his guests would take responsibility for their departure. 'Later there is curfew, so better go now. Yes, better we all evacuate. Then the army can protect the building.'

'You mean have a free fire zone?' Alyosha said.

'I think that is what I mean.'

A burst of shots from the front, followed by the sound of breaking glass made clear the understated nature of Tang's advice.

'This way, gentlemen.'

Outside the office a short corridor led to the rear of the building. Police, civilian staff, secretaries with squealing voices, paramilitaries humping gear – the pressure to get out and away was growing into a stampede. Some were trundling boxes or plastic bags of papers, encumbering the corridor further, others had dumped them where they stood and begun forcing a way through. Another few minutes, it seemed, and there'd be panic.

The three long-noses attracted less attention now, in fact none at all. Shouting that he had a delegation of foreign guests with him Tang pressed forward, but few gave way. And when they finally thrust a path through to the rear door Tony felt an urge to get back in: the melee outside made it feel the place was being invaded.

He scanned the courtyard for army uniforms and saw none. Only the chimney spewing its smoke, the line of vans and lorries loading, and people pouring from the building, staring round and yelling what sounded like the same thing (*where the hell's the army?* Tony surmised) before surging across the court-yard, through the gates and out into the road.

Tang stood at his side in the doorway, peering through the crowds and the smoke as he shouted into his mobile. Finally a jeep appeared, its klaxon blasting a path towards them, forcing a band of police to scatter, and drew up. In it were two men in fatigues, one the driver, the other brandishing an AK47. The Russian dashed towards it. Zach and Tony made to follow but Tang signalled them to wait.

'That is not our jeep. It is our Russian friend's. He has office in Urumqi, with official car', Tang explained.

'Lucky Russian', Zach said. 'Didn't say goodbye, or ask if we were going his way, but then he's a full colonel. Maybe we're too junior to matter. Dispensable, eh Tony?'

'I am sure that is not the case. Colonel Benediktov must have thought you would be safer with our soldiers.'

Tang had stopped talking on his mobile, his troubled eyes still searching for their jeep. Shots and screams and the noise of shattering glass were reaching them from the front of the building, louder every second.

'There is ours!'

It wasn't an army jeep, Tony noticed, and the driver wasn't in uniform. Never mind, it was four wheels, a driver, and some-body with a weapon.

The jeep drew up and Tang saw them in.

'Don't worry about us, get yourself somewhere safe', Zach had time to yell before, revving and honking to clear a path through the courtyard and onto the street, they set out for the hotel.

Tang didn't move. Absurdly amidst the mayhem he stood where he was till they disappeared from sight, waving goodbye.

6

Through frowns and urgent gestures the guard in the front of the jeep signalled that Zach and Tony would be wise to keep their heads down. The lurch as it bolted from the compound, headlights off, and the jolt when it braked to avoid a blood-drenched body sprawled in the road (were there snipers at the back of the building?) encouraged them to comply.

The hotel was a few miles off, in an area untouched by the riots. For a while they careered through small streets, worming their way onto the main route eastwards to the hotel. And there they stopped: traffic blocked the road. As they inched to a halt in a slowing tide of cars Zach raised his head, looked around and shouted in Tony's ear:

'The curfew, it's the fucking curfew. Everyone's piling out of town.'

The Chinese driver and guard conferred excitedly. They wore no uniforms, just jeans and black T-shirts. Security service operatives, Tony assumed, though their fresh, alert faces seemed extraordinarily young.

The guard spun round.

'We OK, we go round.'

Round? They couldn't turn. The road was a dual carriageway, with no break in the central reservation as far as the eye could see. Which didn't worry the driver. On the other side, fifty metres ahead, a street led off to the right. Waiting for a gap in the traffic the driver bounced the jeep over a low wall and over a bed of shrubs and flowers and accelerated towards an oncoming wall of riot trucks and fire engines. Mounting the pavement at the last moment to avoid collision with a hooting and flashing truck, he swerved the jeep crazily into the street.

The youngsters in front were laughing.

'Stupid motherfuckers!' Zach struggled up from the floor where the lurching and pitching vehicle had thrown him. 'Couldn't we just have *waited?*' He tapped the driver's shoulder. 'Hey, you! Take it easy for Chrissake!'

The Chinese turned and grinned, enjoying the appalled faces, and drove on.

'Security service drivers', Tony smiled to disguise his alarm, 'showing us what they can do. The same the world over.'

'OK, so the guy's a Chinese Evel Knievel, but where they taking us?'

Tony sat up and stared ahead. The headlights' raking glow illuminated a dark and narrow street. To judge by the driver's urgently craning head as he searched, fruitlessly, for a turn to the left, they were lost. Plunging ever deeper into the blackness, he braked suddenly: oil drums and an iron bedstead blocked the road.

'What's this?' Zach peered out. 'Fucking rubbish dump?'

'A barricade', Tony said tersely.

The driver had a hand on his door, preparing to get down, when he froze. Two skullcapped figures, scarves obscuring their faces, had emerged from behind the bed and drums. Shielding their eyes from the headlights they walked towards them. One carried a gun, jauntily, on a shoulder.

The driver closed and locked his door.

'Aiya!' the guard said softly. '*Wei-u-er!*'

Uighurs. His machine pistol was on the floor in front of him. Stealthily, without ducking, he reached down for it. Wary now, one each side of the jeep, the figures approached. At the guard's door a face looked in, a hand signaling at him to wind the window down. Fingers round the stock of his gun, the guard nodded and began lowering the window, slowly, the glass squeaking in the silence of the street. The figure outside was agitated.

'*Kwai!* – quick!'

His weapon level with his knees, out of the man's sightline, the guard wound faster. As the glass came down he raised the gun, surreptitiously, to window height. Then two things happened: the glass of the driver's door shattered and the back of the guard's head disintegrated into a crimson pulp. A second shot, to the chest this time, and the driver himself fell forward, soundlessly, over the wheel.

Heads down, their shoulders bloodied, Tony and Zach crouched motionless in the back. When a rear door opened Tony didn't move – if the next bullet was for him why look up? – yet something made him. At the same time, he spread his hands – look, empty! Muttering in a lost voice *what the fuck!* Zach did the same.

Angry eyes stared in at them along the top of a gun. It was the Uighur who had shot the Chinese. For a moment he surveyed the foreigners cowering on the jeep floor in their suits and ties.

'*Ni gan shemma jer-li?*'

Tony gave Zach a despairing look. To his surprise, Zach shot back something in Chinese:

'*Zhi zhe! Waiguo zhi zhe!*' We're journalists, we're foreign journalists!

'*Tamen shi zhi zhe!*' the gunman called out to the second Uighur, with a rancid laugh. 'Journalists!'

The second man ran towards him, shouting urgently. The first screamed something back. Understanding nothing, his mind in limbo, Tony watched as the mime unfolded. The Uighur challenging his gun-toting friend was the one who had approached the guard's window. Though younger than the first he seemed the senior of the two. When the older one jabbed the gun towards the jeep the other held out a staying hand, then grabbed the barrel, screaming *zhi zhe!* in his face.

The older man tugged it back, nodding to the dead Chinese. The second, exasperated, shook his head. A hand was reaching to the back of his belt when with a warning shout the first stepped back and began swinging his gun at all three of them, back and forth, as if preparing to mow them down. Then let out a manic laugh and, stopping to retrieve the gun of the Chinese guard, stamped off to the barricade.

Drawing a pistol from his belt the younger man stood by the open door and looked in. His eyes were nervous, uncertain.

'Tell him we're covering the riots', Tony whispered.

The Uighur must have heard.

'You are English?'

'English, yes!' Zach nodded, 'English journalists, covering the riots.'

His American accent had gone. The new one was caricature English, circa 1920.

The pistol came down 30 degrees.

'I am teacher. I speak English a little.'

Something in Tony unfroze. As his feeling returned he sensed a wetness on his face, his hair. He touched his forehead, glanced at his fingers: sweat. The fingers went to his hair and he looked again: thick, warm blood.

When he reached for his pocket the pistol rose.

'Handkerchief', said Tony, making mopping movements on his head.

Taking it out he began wiping his forehead, his blood-matted hair. For the first time he looked at Zach. Head askew, the American was inspecting a shoulder of his fawn-coloured suit, rubbing ineffectually at the scarlet stains. His expression hadn't changed, the corners of his mouth upturned as always. Had he been through stuff like this before? Well, Tony hadn't, so when he felt something hard and sharp between his fingers and saw a sliver of skull on the blood-drenched cloth of his handkerchief, he didn't feel good.

'You come out.'

The pistol was waving them from the jeep. They edged out and stood by the open door. Avoiding the bloodied parts of their clothes, the Uighur patted them down.

'Where you work?'

The pistol was back in his belt.

'The BBC', Zach got in quickly. 'Both of us.'

A cry came from the barricade: the older Uighur was shouting something in their direction, in an angry tone. The younger man shouted back, then turned to them, smiling.

'He say he saved me from Chinese in jeep, he do what he want. But I tell him he want to shoot journalists! Shoot BBC! I say no!'

'We saw', Tony said gravely. 'We are very grateful.'

'So what you say on BBC? About Xinjiang, what you say?'

'The truth.' Closing his eyes and raising his hand as if swearing an oath, the American added: 'Nothing but.'

'And which truth you say? Chinese truth, or Uighur?'

Tony glanced at Zach, expectantly. Zach would have an answer, Zach was a talking man.

'The truth we see is that Uighurs do not live as well as Chinese.'

Their interrogator gave a bitter laugh.

'A joke! That is joke! We don't live at all!'

'Also', the American went on, 'we report that Chinese are taking over a land Uighurs believe is theirs.'

'Believe?' The man frowned. 'No, no believe. We *know* it ours. They kill everything. Our culture, our religion, our economy too they kill. Now they kill us. They say we are Al Qaeda, always, Al Qaeda! Now they say ISIS too!'

In the space of a second the eyes above the scarf had gone from angry to earnest. Now, in an urgent movement, he stripped it off. The face beneath was clean-shaven and young – mid-twenties, Tony guessed. Young and intelligent-looking.

'I look like Al Qaeda?'

'You? Al Qaeda?' Zach shook his head, as if disgusted. 'Not in a million years. It's just that, well these guns you have. People are gonna' – he caught himself and reverted to BBC English – 'people will ask themselves where they came from?'

Tony shot the American a frown that said, for fuck's sake don't get into an argument.

'To defend ourselves we have them. Otherwise – no defend.'

'I understand', Tony nodded. 'We both understand. Everyone has a right to self-defence.'

'They take everything from us. In our homeland we have no home. Our young people not allowed to study their Muslim religion, to learn that it is religion of peace. And in my school I must teach Chinese. Not Uighur language, Chinese only.'

Zach's head was to one side, as if considering the point before replying. A shot from the barricade filled the silence. The older Uighur was trying out the guard's gun, brandishing it above his head, laughing.

'That's not right.' Tony nodded, vigorously. 'People should be able to learn their language.'

'So you will say the truth?'

'We will continue to tell the truth about what we see', Tony affirmed.

'You see Public Security Bureau?' A hand pointed behind him, towards the town centre, where smoke was rising. The young face, mischievous now, smiled boyishly. 'The Public Security, it will be ours tonight. It is great victory. Innocent people, many hundreds, and they torture. Now they free. You will see, you will write that?'

'Free', Zach echoed. 'All your brothers, free. That's why

we're here. We were going to have a look, we took a short cut, we got lost.' He shrugged. 'Tomorrow we'll go and report. Today' – with a theatrical flourish of his wrist he looked at his watch – 'today it's too late. There's a curfew. We have to get to the hotel.'

'Where is hotel?'

Relieved at the turn of the conversation, Tony came in hurriedly: 'Over there. Eastwards.'

The Uighur looked at the Chinese in the jeep. Tony's eyes followed. The guard's head, a shapeless mass, lolled from the open window.

'We will take them out', the Uighur said. 'Then you drive there.'

Summoning his companion, together they went to work. Untangling the guard from his seat belt with yelps and curses, the older man dragged the corpse to the roadside, its oozing head smearing the tarmac darkly. The teacher went to the driver. His body was slumped over the wheel, as if sleeping. With tremulous hands he sat him upright, unclipped his belt, hesitated, then edged him from his seat.

Half-way out, the dead man fell into his arms, as though clinging. Startled, the teacher let go and the body fell to the ground, face upwards, blood surging from its mouth. The teacher stepped back, staring down at his clothes. Snorting and laughing, his companion strode over and dragged the driver across the road to join the guard.

'You can go', the teacher said.

Zach and Tony looked at the driving seat, then each other. The American shrugged.

'I would, except I don't have my driving glasses.'

He made for the passenger door, opened it, looked in: the seat was soaked with blood, a pool forming in the indented middle.

'Jeez! Not what I signed up for.'

Shutting the door quickly, he climbed into the back.

Tony inspected the driver's seat: except for broken glass, it was clean. The Uighurs moved aside the bedstead and one of the barrels. The teacher came back to the jeep to give directions through the shattered window: to get back to the main road they should continue two hundred metres, turn left, sharp right, left again. Tony thanked him, and for a second they looked at one another. What do you say, he was thinking, to a pleasant-faced young teacher whose ethnic fervour had involved him in the killing of two Chinese the same age as himself, for no possible purpose so far as he could see? Not even the right to teach his language.

He switched on the headlights. His eyes went to the bodies picked out in the jeep's harsh glare. The Uighur followed his gaze.

'Chinese blood', the man said, defiantly. 'We lose much blood too. You say on BBC.'

Tony shook his head.

'This is not the way', he said with a despairing wave, started the engine and drove off.

A few metres down the road Zach turned in his seat.

'Oh boy, look at that.'

Tony glanced in the mirror. Crouched at the roadside, his figure silhouetted in red in the tail-lights of the jeep, the older Uighur was stripping the Chinese bodies swiftly, passing the clothes to his companion. At that instant the teacher was holding up a pair of jeans, gingerly, away from himself, as he went through the pockets.

'Identification is what they're after, and they'll find it. Step on it Tony, for Chrissake.'

And Tony did.

*

Blessed with a sense of direction – Zach was supposed to be navigating but could see little from the back – Tony made his way through the crooked streets back onto the hotel road. It was past eleven and the traffic escaping the centre of town had cleared. In the other direction fire engines were still roaring by, sirens screaming, together with convoys of trucks filled with blank-faced PAP.

Leaving the jeep in the car park they stripped off their blood-spattered jackets and walked past two armed police into the hotel. As they marched through the lobby to the lift a concierge hurried from behind his counter.

'You gentlemen all right? Maybe I help?'

'We're fine', Zach shrugged. 'A small accident. We just need to wash up.'

A shower and a vigorous shampoo helped lift Tony's spirits – till he saw the pinkish froth on the water beneath his feet. Images of the cheerful Chinese boys taking them from the Bureau came back, then of the corpses by the roadside.

He needed a drink, but first, Tang. On arrival the Captain had given him his personal mobile number. 'Anything you need', he'd said, with his automated smile, 'I am here.' Still in his underwear he rang the number. No reply. Should he try Collinson? No point, he wouldn't get through, and if he did he would only alarm him, set a hare running in favour of pulling him out.

Changing into slacks and a jumper he went to the door, came back, switched on the TV, zapped between channels. Pointless. No SKY, no CNN, no BBC, nothing in English at all. On a Chinese channel something came up that looked like news: an official-looking piece about some visiting delegation or other, Iranian he guessed.

Then pictures of Urumqi. The presenter's rigid demeanor and denunciatory style suggested he might not be giving the full picture. There were no shots of the Public Security Bureau, or of shooting, only clips of vicious-looking rioters and hero-ically cudgelling police. It lasted less than a minute, and was fol-lowed by a piece about the launch of a ship.

About to switch off, he stumbled on a Chinese English-lan-guage channel, featuring at that moment a girl in native dress talking to camera in front of a herd of camels, snow-capped mountains in the background. Awed by the desert landscape, for a minute he listened.

'So here we are in the lost city of Loulan, in the Taklamakan desert. This is where they found her, the Loulan Beauty. 3,000 years old, maybe more…'

A shot of a mummy came up: a woman, not Chinese he guessed, with her more pronounced nose and remnants of long, brown hair.

'The mummies in Xinjiang were not embalmed. Exceptional conditions in the desert are the reason she is so well preserved. It is 340 square kilometres in size and either very cold or very hot. In the Uighur language Taklamakan means 'go in and you won't come out.'

Hope the same won't be true in Urumqi, Tony thought, and switched off the TV.

Waiting for the lift he was joined by two young girls with lurid make-up and insolent faces. Stripped of their high heels and piled-up hair they would have looked no more than sixteen, an impression enhanced when one of them looked him up and down while blowing bubble gum. Mixed-race, pret-tyish things, on their way from God knows what assignation he guessed. At night the hotel was swarming with them, Zach had assured him, the Chinese turned a blind eye and mere riots wouldn't stop it.

He rode down to the lobby. With the town centre out of bounds the place was more animated: people checking in from downtown hotels milled about, the bar was packed, a jazz band rendering a be-bop number at top volume, like some celebration. Everything extravagantly smart and gilded, the smiles of waitresses and reception girls included, while half an hour away their city was under siege and men lay dead on the streets.

A cleaned-up Zach was in the bar already. Changed into shirt and jeans he was settling at a table.

'I rang Tang', Tony said, joining him. 'His personal number. Engaged signal, couldn't get through. I'll try later. Somebody ought to pick up those bodies.'

'Didn't give me no number', Zach grumbled. 'But there you go, the colonialists get privileged treatment.' He looked round the busy bar. 'How do you get a drink in this place?'

'Be good to know what's going on downtown, but there's nothing on TV.' Tony looked around. 'Not that anyone here seems to care. You pick anything up?'

'Sure I did. Here's the situation', Zach half-shouted over the noise of the band, an eye still out for the bar girl. 'The PAP protecting the Bureau were caught with their pants down. Attack from the back streets, suicide-style. Uighurs lost twenty or so people getting through. Gansu troop reinforcements got held up by sabotage on the Lanzhou-Urumqi connection. Small explosion, big dent in the line. Which is why we'd still be waiting for our army jeeps.

'Uighur spokesmen are threatening an extension of the insurgency and Al Qaeda's issued a statement of support, the Chinese are saying. Bit too good to be true, that part. Statements of support are not their style. Not that I'm suggesting Tang and his boys might be up to anything, propaganda-wise, just that I'd like our linguists to go over the text of that, look out for Chinese-style locutions. – Hey, beautiful! We're thirsty. Straight from the front line!'

The bar girl approached.

'Tony, what you having?'

'Whisky.'

'One double whisky and one Old Fashioned. Plenty of ice and orange, no sugar.'

The waitress nodded, wrote it down, then said in excellent English.

'What is Old Fashioned?'

Turning his full attention to the girl Zach looked her up and down with candid appreciation. Slim figure, tall hair, a short jacket and skirt and a white blouse opened at the top a fraction more than necessary. Beguiled at the length of the legs standing inches away from him, he took a moment to reply.

'Well it's Bourbon and orange, basically, but with – nah, never mind. Whisky, two doubles.'

'Lucy Liu of a looker', he nodded after the bar-girl, 'but less frightening.'

'You were saying. About the situation.'

'OK.' Zach dragged his eyes away from the retreating girl. 'Executive summary: the rioters have turned into insurgents and they're getting smarter. As of half an hour ago clashes still going on downtown, armed. Unusual activity at the airport suggests troops planning to get through by plane.'

'And the Public Security Bureau?'

'I was saving the best for last. Minutes after we got out the back they got through the front and torched it.'

'Is Tang OK?'

'After what we just saw, I hope so.' Remembering the Chinese boys they looked at one another in silence.

'And they got the prisoners out?'

'Yep, they got 'em out.' Zach's mouth was framed for

sarcasm, and it came: 'Just that it looks like it was the Uighurs who did it, like our schoolteacher said.'

'And Osman?'

'No idea. Maybe he fried alive down there in his five-star suite. Or he's snug and warm under collapsed masonry. Or Tang may have spirited him away. Or his Muslim pals rescued him.'

'Be useful to know which. Rather affects the point of our being here, doesn't it?'

'C'mon Tony! I didn't enjoy our little adventure a whole lot either, but don't tell me you're wimping out! You're living the life here', he threw a hand round the bar, 'and it doesn't come trouble-free!'

Their drinks came at that moment. Zach raised his glass, sombre suddenly.

'To those nice Chinese kids, God rest their souls. And may their killer rot in hell.'

'Amen.'

They drank.

'Now one to you', Tony said, raising his glass again. 'That was some trick you pulled, about the BBC. I didn't realise you spoke the language.'

'I don't. Few lessons I took back home is all. Plus a bit of pillow talk from my Singapore days. Can't waste all that time before you can decently get up and out. Don't suppose I got the tones right, never could get the hang of that. But it worked.'

They drank. Setting his glass down Zach looked even more pleased with himself than usual, but for once Tony didn't mind. He felt shaken, but the idea of getting out hadn't occurred to him, and if Osman was still available for interview he wanted to see that side of things through. A prize shit, but the man intrigued him.

'Of course I'm staying,' he said. 'It's just that I don't know that we're going to be able to do anything much from here, apart from watch. Assuming they still want us.'

'There are worse places to be holed up. Think of us as observers,' Zach grinned, 'UN observers with no mandate and fuck-all to do. And of Urumqi as the new Casablanca – and we're playing Bogart!' He nodded at the Russian-looking pianist dragging out a melancholy number; the jazz band had packed up at midnight. 'At least no one's gonna come bombing us here.'

'The hotel doesn't seem so sure', Tony said, pointing at what looked like net curtains over the plate-glass ground-floor windows facing the street.

'What about them?'

'They're not cotton, they're kevlar. Blast-proof.'

'Good. I feel even safer.'

'By the way, where'd you get the information? A reporter?' He indicated a group of Europeans at the bar, correspondents by the look of them.

'I got a friend there', he indicated a tall man dressed in rather smart fatigues and talking to a woman at the bar, 'but he got in before us to beat the curfew. So I rang home, for the hell of it, and believe it or not I got through. Hadn't had time to cut the line.'

Home, it turned out, was the FBI, who'd put him onto the CIA, who'd given him a factual rundown on what was going on a few miles from where they were sitting. The information came from émigré sources, apparently, with their own websites. One reason the Chinese kept cutting the lines.

Their drinks were low. Zach summoned the bar girl.

'What's your name?'

'My name is Ling-Ling.'

'Exquisite. My friend here will have –'

Tony said another whisky, double. Zach said he was switching to brandy.

'We have many. Which one would you like?'

The American scanned the rows of bottles high above the back of the bar.

'That one.'

He pointed to a Hennessy XO on the topmost shelf. Following his gaze, the girl checked the height. Back behind the bar, with a gazelle-like leap she hopped onto the rear counter, steadied herself, raised a hand and fetched the bottle down. While she stretched for it and her skirt rose Zach flashed Tony a grin that said, how about the view? Tony snatched a look, and smiled. *Cool off,* he had an urge to say, *we've had a tough evening, but this isn't Vietnam.*

His mind went back to the Chinese by the roadside.

'Maybe I'll try Tang again.'

He took out his mobile and dialled. To his surprise the number rang; a dedicated circuit, probably. For a while there was no reply, then a voice, faint against a fuzzy barrage of noise.

'Tang.'

'Underwood. Tony Underwood.'

'Mr Underwood, you are safe in your hotel?'

'Very safe now. And you?'

'Comparatively safe.'

Comparatively was what the background racket suggested.

'We did have a problem', Tony said, 'on the way here.'

He described the blocked road, the barricade, the two Uighurs, the shooting of the Chinese, their escape.

'Ah. That is bad. I knew them, they were good young people. And you are our guests, this is most unfortunate. You are not injured?'

'We're fine. It's the bodies of the driver and the guard I'm worried about.'

'Of course we will find them. And the ones who murdered them. From your description I think we know the group in that area. A new one. There is a teacher there, a young teacher –'

'– it wasn't him,' Tony said quickly. 'He was there, though if it's the same man it was him who saved our lives.'

'Our young boys' lives he did not save, it seems.' The Captain's tone was harsh suddenly. 'Do not trouble yourself, Mr Underwood, we will deal with him.'

The earnest young voice complaining he wasn't allowed to teach his language… The way he'd held the dead men's clothes, at arms length, squeamishly… Maybe he should have been less precise in his description, Tony thought.

'And Osman?'

'Osman, he is safe.'

A silence. The crackle – or shots? – intensified. When it diminished he asked:

'Safe in the sense he got out?'

'Yes, in that sense.'

'But not in the sense he's still your prisoner?'

A gap, then:

'In that sense he is not safe, no.'

'Let me get this straight, Captain. Your prisoner – our prisoner – has escaped.'

'I cannot discuss. It is not convenient. We will talk tomorrow. Today – I am a little busy, as you can hear.'

The rattle of an automatic sounded close. He must have held the phone up.

'Those are not fireworks', Tony said.

'No, not fireworks. We will talk again. Tomorrow.'

'Tomorrow is fine. One more thing. I assume you recorded my interrogation. Is the transcript safe? Or has it gone up in flames?'

Tony's interest was personal: there'd be nothing on his recorder and he didn't look forward to reconstituting the interrogation from memory, or to explaining the gaffe to his superiors. If there was no word-for-word record, for them there'd been no interrogation.

'No, please do not worry, it is safe. As soon as you'd finished I sent it out of the building to be transcribed and translated. I told them to work quickly, overnight. It will be at the hotel in the morning.'

'That's very efficient. I'm more grateful than you know.'

'My regards to Mr Boorstin', Tang signed off, through what sounded like a burst of gunfire.

Tony pocketed his mobile.

'The Captain sends his regards.'

'Most grateful.' Zach broke off from his dreamy survey of the bar girl. 'And our prisoner? Our terrorist for all seasons?'

'Alive', Tony said, 'but sounds like he got away.'

7

Four floors underground, Osman sat listening. It was from shouted exchanges between his guard and another on the landing two floors up that he'd tracked the progress of the riots. Around midday he'd heard him open the steel door at the end of the corridor and yell up:

'Getting any more up there?'

'Nah', came the reply, 'they stopped sending them. No room, less we pack them in lengthways. They're sending the bastards down to Turfan. Or they were, when the trucks could get through.'

That evening, after Underwood had left, there'd been more. The noise of the steel door opening, a rush of sound, then:

'What the fuck's going on up there? Can't hear nothing with this door closed, it's like the grave down here.'

'Still at it, the bastards. And they've got guns. And fuck-all sign of the army.'

Since then, nothing. The drip from the toilet cistern in his cell was all he could hear. He'd done his best to fix it with a wedge of paper, so instead of a ping now it made a splat. Ping or splat it was playing on his nerves. When he'd complained the guard looked down at him with his wolf's grin.

'Category One prisoner complaining about a dripping toilet? What do you think this is, a hotel? How about I do the other foot for you, take your mind off it?'

And so it had continued, the silence and the splat. Was it deliberate, to wear him down, the way a drip eats away at stone? He gave up limping about for exercise – it was hurting the foot – and went back to his desk. To keep his mind off his predicament he was writing out poetry, also as a source of malign pleasure. Here and there in the text of a Shakespeare sonnet or an ode by Keats he would insert a name or number:

The weariness, the fever and the fret
Here, Nawaz and Abdullah, where men sit and hear
Each other groan...

Or:

Like as the waves make towards the pebbled shore,
so do our minutes hasten 44° 46' 60 N, 85° 32' 60 E to their end...

It amused him to think of Tang and his minions scouring his texts, spotting the invented names, checking out the meaningless coordinates. A piffling revenge, but he felt better for it.

Ekrem, the driver of the truck with the weapons and a Kirghiz brother, told him how he'd once done something similar. He'd been hiding out with a friend in the country, but they were onto him. The house was close to a river, every morning he went for a walk along the bank and every morning he was followed.

Caught short one day he took a dump in a primitive shithouse along the path. There was no flush, nothing but a hole, scraps of paper and a basket. When he came out his shadow was hovering behind a tree. Walking on he looked back and saw him go into the shithouse and emerge several minutes later, wiping his hands on a handkerchief and throwing it away disgustedly. A dead letter drop, the fellow must have thought.

Afterwards Ekrem made a point of stopping every morning, for the pleasure of thinking of the security man sorting through the used paper.

'It seems a lot of trouble', he'd laughed when Ekrem told him, 'having a shit just to annoy a spook.'

'It was a small thing, a stupid thing', the Kirghiz said thoughtfully, 'but worth it. Worth it because it was the first time I'd been followed and I was afraid. Afraid and ashamed of it, so it was a way of getting my own back for my fear.'

It was the same with him. He wasn't afraid, he'd told himself when he'd volunteered to bring in the guns, never would be, not even if they caught him. And yet his fearlessness was something abstract, unproven. Now there was the reality of his cell, the interrogations and beatings that were just beginning, the prospect of execution by lethal injection Underwood had tried to frighten him with... He didn't need the M15 man to scare him, knew deep down how it felt for your fearlessness to be unproven.

The remains of his dinner were on his desk. A rice bowl, empty, a fishbone meticulously picked, a plate scraped clean of its chicken and tofu. The food had got better suddenly, for the benefit of the foreigners he assumed. The same reason they'd given him paper and pencils two days earlier, and why the interrogation had been abandoned abruptly, in mid-session, the night before that. And the reason it could start up again the moment they'd gone...

The interlude with Underwood had been a respite of sorts, staving off the next session with the state security people. The Russian and American would keep them out of the way for a while too, and the American at least was something to look forward to: whoever he was he'd be even dumber than Underwood, he could be sure of that.

It was nearly a week since they'd got him. There'd been dark moments but the fear hadn't shown – though how long could he hold out if they started on him for real? Pray to Allah, a Yemeni instructor at the camp in the Fergana valley had told him. Take your mind off what they are doing. Compared to the majesty of God, you must think, the pain is without significance, like life itself, an ephemeral thing. Wise advice, except that now he faced two uncertainties instead of one: whether he could take the pain, and whether his faith was strong enough to convince himself that it was nothing.

It was getting towards eleven, his memory clouding, his foot hurting, and it was hard to get Underwood out of his head. A lower-middle class autodidact by the sound of him, flaunting his piddling quotations, who'd needed putting in his place. Insulting of them not to have sent someone senior, though he shouldn't have let himself be drawn into provoking the man; better to have confined himself to refusing to say a word till they'd brought the Consul. Still, the fellow had got nothing from him, was obviously out of his depth. A fantasist he'd called him – but Kul and the operation planned around him was no fantasy, as they would soon discover.

Though how had they got onto him? The interception of the truck couldn't have been accidental, some random check, not with Tang there, and with that number of PAP. Nobody knew their route into the city except Ekrem, and him he trusted absolutely.

He thought back to their first meeting. It was the day he'd shown up at the camp deep in the walnut forests of the Fergana Valley. Ekrem was bodyguard to Salih the Uzbek, the strategist of the group who'd been deputed to check out the unexpected volunteer, and at first it hadn't gone well. The Uzbek, a bearded giant, sat him at a table under a tree, fanning himself in the moist heat, his lips sceptical beneath the beard, saying nothing and making him do the talking.

All the time Ekrem stood a few metres off, a gangling young figure with a hard gaze and a restless-looking trigger-finger. The instant he'd reached for his backpack the gun levelled on him. And when he took out his spray and began squirting away at the mosquitoes feasting on his arms and ankles the barrel was lowered, replaced by a contemptuous smile.

Driving over mountain roads into Xinjiang months later with their truckload of nuts, raisins and light machine guns, they would laugh at Ekrem's first impressions. The fellow in the skullcap and combat fatigues who'd come to them unannounced was a Chinese agent, he'd been sure of it. A traitor in the making whose offer to join the jihadist group should be rewarded with a good beating before he was dumped in the middle of the forest, or disposed of on the spot.

To begin with Salih had shared his bodyguard's suspicions, and looking back it was easy to see why. The public school accent, the too new fatigues, his pallid-looking features – who was this? If it wasn't a plant, maybe a journalist under cover? Or an amateur jihadi who would crumble after the first week's training, then sneak off and sell his story? It had taken many weeks and endless conversations, but in the end they'd taken him in. The $300,000 in cash he'd produced from the backpack had helped.

After that the new recruit and his interrogator had got on fine. Before long they were sharing a tent, where nights were spent dreaming up a Central Asian Caliphate stretching from Iran to Xinjiang. Yet for all his extravagant talk and guru-like appearance, Salih was a man of action. His theology, such as it was, was home-made (he had left school at 12) and his view of the world simple.

Their sacred mission was in Central Asia, the Uzbek would intone, not the West. For him the Great Satan was not so much America as the Han Chinese: the Yellow Satan, he called them. And after all, he would add with his sudden smile, say what you like the Yankee Satan had respect for religion, whereas the Chinese were heathen folk. It was they, not the Americans, who would dominate the region with their numbers and their money, then crush Islam and instil their atheist ways.

At the training camp there were Taliban and Arab brothers, but the majority were Uzbeks, Kirghiz and Uighurs, and in devising his attacks it was the Hans that Salih kept in his sights.

Cagy about his operations, all he'd told him was that he had his eye on something in Xinjiang. Not some piddling demonstration or attack on a police station, knifing people at railway stations or blowing up cars (where was their enterprise, their jihadi spirit?) No, this time it would be something to make the Yellow Satan tremble.

Next morning the Uzbek had disappeared. Over a month later he came back to the camp looking weak and ill, but on a cloud of euphoria. He'd been in Xinjiang, he explained excitedly, weeks of travelling through godforsaken deserts in freezing weather, but worth every instant!

A chill had developed into a fever, and it was while he lay shivering in his camp bed that, unable to contain himself, when they were alone together it came out bit by bit. The attack he was planning was to be mounted from Kirghizia, though contacts in Xinjiang would be needed. So off he'd gone in search of Uighur recruits, insinuating himself across the frontier to nose around Muslim communities in the south of the province, near the site of the operation. Which was how he'd come across Kul.

They'd met at his local prayer circle. There'd been the usual mixture – Uighurs, a Kazakh, a Mongol convert, a fellow Uzbek who was a cousin (it was how he'd gained entry to the circle), but among the medley of ethnicities one stood out: a man of sixty or so wearing Western clothes and with a touch of the Indo-European in his beardless features. No one in the room seemed to think the worse of him for it, in fact they treated him with particular deference.

Salih had an easy manner, and after getting himself introduced he'd begun joking about the man's clean-shaven face, asking if he was a recent convert, hadn't had time to grow his beard. Not at all, Kul came back, sharply. He was a born Muslim, of Tungan descent. Not a drop of Han blood he assured the Uzbek fervently, several times. As for his beardless face it wasn't his decision: he had a living to make and if he grew one he wouldn't hold on to his job for long. So where is it you work, Salih had asked, interested now, some government job is it? And Kul had told him, and for Salih that was enough.

Their meeting was providential, he swore, his fevered eyes alight, no mere stroke of luck but the work of Allah! Nor was the appearance at the camp of his new recruit a few months earlier coincidence, but more evidence of divine favour, for who better to make a follow-up contact with Kul than himself, a fellow Tungan?

And the Tungan had leapt at the chance. Bored of his training (though he'd stuck at it: by now he was fit and could shoot, not too precisely but well enough) he'd been keen to prove himself in the field. While Salih was on his journey he'd been working up a project of his own. What their Uighur brothers lacked, he told the Uzbek when he was back, was not so much the will to take on their Han oppressors, it was the means. The arms at their disposal were pitiful – a few pistols and home-made bombs, but no serious supply of weapons.

Why not use some of his $300,000 to buy them, together with a truck that he and Ekrem could use to get them to Urumqi, disguised as local produce? That would fit with Salih's wish for him to check out Kul. Once the arms had been delivered he could make his way south, see if he was suitable material for whatever the Uzbek had in mind?

At first Salih was non-committal: he'd need to think it over, he said, didn't want anything to cut across his own plans. Having thought a day or two, he was enthusiastic. If the weapons got through and fuelled an uprising in the northern capital it would be the perfect diversion for his operation in the south. Though for that three trips would be needed, he calculated, for a thousand weapons, and getting them through would not be easy. There were frontiers, checkpoints, patrols – after the 2009 riots the Hans were nervous.

'And what if they get you? You know what they do to Uighur fighters they capture? You think being British will save you? That they will give you biscuits and cups of tea and enquire after the health of the Queen?'

Making contact with Kul wouldn't be simple either. Was he prepared for the risks of travelling on his own, Salih had gone on, staring him in the eye? Absolutely, he'd assured him, though if he was to sound out his fellow Tungan for an operation he'd need to know more about it. At which point the Uzbek dropped his giant head to his chest, and clammed up. When he raised it, he was smiling.

'You are a clever man,' he said, 'a brave man. Your nuts and raisins plan is very good, and we have people to receive your weapons. But on Kul your question is that of a novice. What you should be asking me is *not* to be told about the operation we want him for. If they catch you, you will have less to give away.

'Later, you will know more. Everything in its turn. First, you must get the guns through. Next, Kul. We have a contact in Urumqi, somebody I have worked with, an experienced man, a strategic ally…' Salih smiled at his own cunning. 'The Turkman is his code name. I have thought how it might be done. After your third delivery you will be taken to a safe house where he will brief you about the arrangements for your trip south. Then he will tell you more. For the moment, that is all you need to know.'

The Uzbek, it was clear to him now, had been testing out his novice with the weapons, and the novice had done him proud. Two loads he and Ekrem had got through – almost 700 guns – but on his final trip Tang was waiting…

Where was Ekrem now? Here, in the Bureau, upstairs with

the others? Or somewhere worse? Wherever it was his friend would need all his courage, Allah help him. He didn't have a British passport – no passport at all – so for him there'd be no limits, though whatever they did to him they'd be wasting their time. He may have suspected something – he knew he'd be travelling back alone to the camp after the third trip, leaving his brother behind for another operation – but about Kul he knew nothing. And if he had they'd have got nothing from him.

*

With an effort of will he cut his train of thought: why agonize about events he was in no position to influence? The thing was to keep control: be self-sufficient, pray regularly, don't feel lonely – though it was the stillness more than the loneliness that was getting to him.

It was around this time that the guards upstairs locked up their prisoners and came down for a drink, yet tonight there were no boots on stairs, no clatter of rifles being parked against the corridor wall, no sound of glasses and laughter from his guard's room. Only rumbling noises, at times a distant shout and – perhaps more wish than reality – the crackle of one of his Type 79s.

He glanced at the mirror. Were Tang and his foreign friends watching him, for their after-dinner entertainment? His guard had given the game away the first day, jeered at him about his praying, something he couldn't otherwise have known; he'd been careful to pray only when the spy-hole was closed. It had been a point of honour never to acknowledge there might be someone there, but suddenly the idea exasperated him: turning from his desk he made a V sign at the glass.

A strange custom, that. He remembered it puzzling him when he'd learned it at school in Britain: you just turned the two victory fingers round and you had the fuck-off sign. So he did that too. If there were Chinese watching, that would screw their minds.

'Infidel bastards!' he shouted at the glass in English, then in Russian, then Chinese. It didn't say much for his self-control, but again he felt better for it.

Thoughts of Underwood returned. Prospects for extradition didn't sound good, though what he'd said about giving the British a reason to ask for him back would be something to ponder. Though any hint that he'd been involved in something at home could foul his chances of getting a campaign for his release going in the UK press... Which would be hard enough. They were hot on human rights in Tibet, oh yes Tibet got them going, every starlet had an opinion. But Uighurs? Muslims? Jihadis?

No use sitting here, he wouldn't write anything now, and no use going to bed, he wouldn't sleep. Though better there than here, where the stiff-backed chair was hard against his bruises.

It was from the bed that he heard the steel door open, then footsteps, from there that he watched the cover on the spyhole sliding up. At the sound of it he shut his eyes. Then opened them from curiosity – it was late for the guard to be looking – and saw his face. He wasn't wholly Chinese, sometimes he spoke a dialect, not that it mattered: the heavy brows, the close-spaced eyes, the man was a brute in all cultures. Yet tonight there was something different. Instead of leering in at him, the eyes seemed frightened.

A second later the lock ground, the door opened and the guard stood there. Stood with raised arms, his keys dangling from his right hand, his fat gut thrust comically forward. It was when he took a step into the cell that Osman saw why: behind was a short man holding a gun at his back, and behind him, more.

Uighurs.

He half-rose in his bed. The stocky man stepped into the cell.

'*Aosiman xiansheng?* Mister Osman?'

Hearing his name in Chinese, then Uighur-accented English, was startling.

'*Shi wo.* That's me.'

He got up and faced the man in jeans and a torn combat jacket with a sub-machine gun in his hands and smoke-reddened eyes. He pointed, half-smiling, at the Type 79.

'*Nimen zhexie wuqi doushi wo guo jing daijinlai de!*'

These guns of yours, I brought them in across the border myself!

'I know.' The man waved his weapon at the door. 'We control the building. Part of it's on fire. Better get out. Quickly.'

8

The courtyard behind the Public Security Bureau was strewn with dumped sacks of files, the vans and lorries commandeered by staff keener to save themselves than their papers. Abandoned by their guards, the last of the prisoners, some in underwear, had made off into the night. In the courtyard one lone figure was left: a dead woman, killed by a stray bullet, lay within metres of the street.

In the doorway where Tang had waved goodbye to his foreign guests less than an hour before, Osman and his rescuer appeared through the smoke, heads down, hands to their mouths, then bolted across the courtyard to the gates. There the Uighur stopped, coughed for a full minute, took out his mobile and dialled.

As he spoke he turned to watch the burning Bureau. Osman's eyes were drawn to the dead woman, her blue silk blouse luridly aglow in the light of the flames eating through the building. She lay on her front, head to one side, mouth ajar, as if wanting to tell him something, but instead of words there was blood. It was only the second dead body he had seen in his life: the first had been the guard to his cell, minutes before.

A car drew up. Motioning him to lie flat in the back the Uighur sat next to the driver, gun alert. As they drove off Osman stayed silent; there seemed nothing to say. Asking how they'd known where he was and where they were going was superfluous: the Turkman, Salih's contact in Urumqi, must have heard he'd been caught and arranged for his rescue when the Bureau had been attacked. And now they must be on their way to the safe house whose address Salih had given him.

As the car skidded across the debris in the street all he could sense was heat, noise and smoke. Instead of getting away from the flames they seemed to be coming closer, circumventing the building, he surmised, to get back to the street the Uighurs held. Minutes later the heat was gone and the noise had retreated, fading to a distant roar.

The Uighur lit a cigarette. Osman smoked rarely, but he wanted one now.

'*Keyi-ma?*' May I?

The Uighur passed the packet and lighter over his shoulder, silently. For another half hour they drove on, avoiding main roads, cornering abruptly, through a dizzying complex of streets. From the squalid, run-down, single storey buildings flashing past the window he guessed it was a Uighur area.

In an unlit street, they stopped. On one side, a row of buildings awaiting demolition; the other was gone already. The Uighur pointed to the door of what seemed an abandoned shop, its frontage stacked with rubbish, its rusted shutters drawn. Osman got out, turned to the window to say goodbye. Too late: before he could thank him for saving his life, or his cigarette, with a wave and a smile the Uighur was gone.

8 Karim Street was the address Salih had given. Before approaching the door he glanced around. No street name was visible, and the figure on the door was 23: they must have changed the location after his arrest, afraid he would talk. Not much of a compliment, but professional... He rapped on the door. A key ground in the lock.

A man in a black shirt and trousers stood before him. Late fifties, medium height, curly hair graying, to his eye he didn't look Uighur: a Kirghiz or Uzbek, perhaps. Beckoning him in silently the man shut the door quickly. Osman stood inside, adjusting his eyes to the penumbra. A single oil lamp struggled to light what seemed to have been a greengrocer's store. The counter was still there, the shelves behind stacked with remnants of withered vegetables. Otherwise there was a table, two chairs and a makeshift bed: a rattan mattress, a pillow, a light blanket. Apart from the man in black, there seemed no one there.

The man pointed to a chair. Before sitting down Osman shrugged off the white mac he was wearing. He'd found it on their way out, in Tang's office, and thrown it over his pyjamas in case the flames caught up with them in the final dash for the exit. It was when he tossed it over a chair that he saw the great livid stain on the lower back. For a few moments he tried to make sense of the splashy explosion of crimson, as if puzzling over a Rorshach test. Then folded the coat quickly, to cover it.

He sat down and turned to the man in black.

'Where –'

The man cut him off with a gesture, his finger indicating a storeroom beyond the counter. A beaded curtain, drawn, separated it from the shop. When Osman stood up and took a step towards it a hand on his shoulder held him back.

'Mr Osman, *Aosman xiansheng,* it is good to meet you.'

The voice came from beyond the curtain. Now he could trace the faint outline of a figure in a chair. Stepping back, he sat again at the table.

'I apologise,' the voice went on, 'for the amateur dramatics. Absurd, I know, but that's how it has to be. You'd like a shot of something? A celebratory glass? Though maybe you don't drink?'

The figure spoke Chinese, with an accent he couldn't place.

'On special occasions,' Osman murmured. 'A whisky would be good.' He looked around, sceptical, before adding, 'if you have it.'

'Naturally we have it. Hamid – that's not his name, but it will do – Hamid, give our friend a whisky. Hamid is my translator. Not for languages – I can manage those – he translates my wishes into action.'

Fetching a bottle and glass from behind the counter, Hamid almost smiled.

'No ice, I'm afraid, or soda,' the voice went on. 'The quality must compensate for the presentation.'

Hamid poured him a tot of the Chivas Regal.

'And me, and yourself. We must celebrate together.'

Hamid poured more glasses, handed one through the curtain.

'So, here's to your liberation.'

The three of them drank.

'And to whom do I owe –' Osman began.

'– your rescue? Us. Hamid found out where you were, thanks to his Uighur friends. I won't say they mounted the attack on the Bureau with your salvation specifically in mind, but let's say the coincidence was to your advantage.'

Osman raised his glass to the man in black, who nodded.

'I was given an address, and a name,' he said. 'The Turkman.'

'Well, this is the address – the new one, we changed it of course when they got you. As to the Turkman,' the voice laughed briefly, 'I am he. So, to business. The Uzbek and I have been in touch about your little accident. We agree that nothing has changed. As before, the plan is for you to go south. Our friend there is expecting you. He was eager to meet his young professor – that's what you'll be, a professor of comparative religion researching a book – but he's nervous about seeing you in Xinjiang at the moment. So your rendezvous will be at Dunhuang, Gansu province. Any problem with the law and you're an Anglo-Chinese visiting the fatherland, seeing the Thousand Buddha caves.

'Everything else is fine. The PAP have been shifting people south to north, diverting forces to Urumqi, and after tonight they'll be doing it quicker. The only problem is communications. On one minute, off the next, God knows what they're playing at. Never mind, we have a line out from our man to the Uzbek.'

'And to the Uzbek from here?'

'Don't trouble yourself, for that we have other arrangements. So it's all set up, you can go tomorrow.'

Tomorrow? Osman took a slug of whisky. Before setting out on his travels he could have done with a day or two to recover. He didn't feel good. His foot was throbbing, the running and leaping during his escape had made the swelling worse. On the other hand, for a man on the run getting out of Urumqi and Xinjiang province for a while had advantages.

'Fine, he said. I'm ready to go. Just one thing. Our Uzbek friend said you'd tell me something about the operation. To make a judgment about our man I'll need some idea of what it is we want him to do.'

'Of course. Hamid – another whisky, if you would. Then maybe you'd like to take a ten minute walk. It's a nice night. The air's a little smoky, but there you go.'

Without a word Hamid unlocked the door and left.

'The lock, if you don't mind.'

Osman turned the key.

'Here we work in units,' the voice explained when he had gone. 'Units of one. Everyone knows what they need to and nothing more. Hamid is aware there is an operation, but he knows no names or details. Later he may need to know more, but for the moment he's in charge of modalities, and that's all.

'For the same reason, with you I'm going to be parsimonious with the facts. If I go further, and you judge Kul to be unsuitable, then you will be left with useless knowledge in your head. Dangerous knowledge, for you and for us.'

'I understand.'

'Of course you do. You are an intelligent man, Mr Osman, our Uzbek friend assures me. Intelligent and courageous. Getting the first two consignments of those guns through was something. So, about your fellow Tungan...'

In brief, staccato sentences the figure briefed him about Kul: where he worked, details of the Dunhuang rendezvous, their recognition signal. Then an outline of the operation. Listening, Osman's default expression – a kind of superior scepticism – lifted. He'd had his theories about what the plan might turn out to be, but this... As the Turkman spoke he felt a succession of sensations: awe, pride to have been selected for the task, then deep in his heart, a needle of fear. Now he understood Salih's secretiveness, and the business with the curtain.

'It's a privilege,' he got out, 'to be trusted.'

'You will earn it, I assure you.' A laugh like a shot came from behind the curtain.

A rap on the door.

'That'll be Hamid. Open up.'

He did and Hamid came in.

'You won't be seeing a lot more of me,' the voice went on. 'I made it here tonight because their attention is elsewhere. Meanwhile do what Hamid tells you, and be careful. After the attack on the Bureau it'll be like martial law out there. We don't want to lose you again, like last time.'

'I did wonder about last time.'

'Meaning?'

'How they knew.'

'They knew nothing.' The voice was sharp now. 'It was a random stop and search. It must have been.'

'The PAPS seemed to be expecting me. There were twenty of them, thirty. And Tang, why would he be at a road block? I mean he's senior, isn't he?'

'Maybe he just fancied some on-the-ground experience.'

'He knew who I was. Spoke to me in English, told them to treat me properly. I didn't even get a bruise.' He fingered his cheek. 'A light burn was all.'

'Now you're complaining they didn't beat you up.'

'They did,' Osman came back, sharply. 'Later.' The whisky was making him nervy, and the hint of mockery in the Turkman's tone riled him. 'When they interrogated me. My guard beat me up and wrenched my foot.'

'But you told them nothing.'

'Of course not.'

'OK OK. Tell me about the foot. Can you walk?'

'I'll be fine. The guard was a vicious bastard. We made him help get us out – show us the fire exit from the basement. And salvage this.'

Taking his passport from the pocket of his pyjamas, he held it up.

'How the hell did you get hold of that?'

'It was Tang who relieved me of it, personally. We made the guard take us by his office on the way out – it was in a wing that hadn't gone up yet. Found it in his desk drawer. You should have seen the guard's face, grinning away, so pleased to be of assistance. Part-Uighur he swore he was. And that's why you're going to get it, we told him.'

'So you did him?'

For reply Osman took Tang's mac from its chair and displayed the splashes of blood .

'OK, I can see.' The barked laughter again. 'I'm sure you kill a man a day. Not sure what use the passport is though. They'll have put a stop on it. Give it to us, we'll fix it. Better make you an Anglo-Chinese. Let me see… how would Christopher Lang suit you?'

'Fine.'

Hamid, without a word, took the passport.

'And Hamid will fix you up with some clothes. Good luck with your travels. Meanwhile, Mr Lang, I suggest you get some sleep. Now, if you'll excuse us…'

Suddenly Osman was in the dark. Hamid, standing behind him, had turned out the lamp. The rattle of the bead curtain parting, the sound of feet traversing the shop and of the door unlocking, and the two of them were gone.

*

Early next evening, a rap on the shutters. Opening the door a crack he did a double-take before letting Hamid in: the clerkly, middle-aged figure of the previous night had turned into a hunched old man in skullcap and raggedy trousers carrying a shopping bag.

Inside he straightened up and emptied the bag onto the table. Osman's new outfit was a pair of stone-washed jeans, a black T-shirt with a silver Chinese logo on the front (*Eternal Brand*), a light denim jacket, scrupulously distressed, and a base-ball cap, also with its logo, to disguise his half-shaven head.

Putting them on he examined himself in the lavatory mirror. Pretty good. If anything the disguise seemed overdone, all that glitter, but then men in their twenties dressed like that, and the ensemble did its job. Somehow the Chinese script alone was enough to incline his features, just visible beneath the cap, in a Han direction. At a casual glance now there seemed no doubting where he came from. It was as if he could change race at will.

Pleased with the transformation, he lingered in front of the glass before saying:

'Seems fine. What do you think?'

Hamid nodded, and that was all.

He inspected the white and gold trainers.

'They're enormous.'

For reply Hamid produced his passport from his bag (for a Mr Christopher Lang now), held it up, then placed it in a trainer. With a little bending, it fitted. Osman took it out, put on the trainers, stood up and shrugged.

'Feel OK. So I'll be getting a train, right?'

From his bag Hamid produced an envelope with a small wad of renminbi and a railway ticket. Then a revolver. Nonchalantly, Osman picked it up. Before going to the camp he'd never carried a weapon, and it was a Chinese army 5.8m – not the one he'd trained on. Checking the magazine – it was full – he stuffed it into the back of his belt beneath his coat.

Last, from a pocket, Hamid brought out a tube of ointment, indicating his foot.

Osman strained a smile.

'Very thoughtful.'

'We meet again here,' Hamid said. '11 p.m., in three days' time. If there is a mark on the door of number seventy-three – the last house in the row – it is safe.' Taking a chalk from a pocket he made a two-inch cross on the table. Osman nodded, Hakim unlocked the door, and he stepped into the street.

There were a lot of things he'd been tempted to ask him, he thought as he walked off, not least about the Turkman, but it would have been pointless to try – the man had a gift for non-communication – though it was hard to get the hidden figure out of his head. The voice, the mixed accents – who and what was he? A Western-educated jihadi? An Americanised Uighur? An English-speaking Turk, as his pseudonym suggested, with Uighur associations? Or – the idea chilled him for a moment – a Turk in the pay of the CIA.

In this part of the world there could be strange alliances. He remembered Salih's words about the Americans having respect for religion, whereas the Yellow Satan had none. What if Washington was using the Uighur movement as cover to foment trouble in China? Just how upset would the Americans be to see the Chinese facing a serious terrorist movement, like the US itself. The nature of the target would be compatible with that.

A few more steps and he gave up guessing. He must concentrate on the task in hand: dirty his too-new trainers with dust, try not to limp, watch for a tail, take a roundabout route to the station, make his way to Dunhuang. Worrying his head about who the Turkman was or wasn't would be unprofessional. And after what he had learned about the operation he was glad he didn't know.

9

The hotel, recently completed, was aimed at the international mining clientele that had begun pouring into the province, and keen to make a show. Along with its fancy Chinese and Western cuisine (Uighur dishes didn't feature) a prize attraction was breakfast – one of those serve-yourself morning banquets that could blend into lunch. Along with the usual array of cereals, juices, cheeses, meats, eggs any style and the rest, there were Chinese dumplings, Japanese soups, marinated crab pieces, wine and beer, champagne if the mood took you. Not to mention a horde of sleek young waitresses insinuating themselves into your good graces (though again, no Uighurs).

For all his compact figure Zach was something of a gourmet, and when he woke up the thought of the East-West spread put him in an expansive mood. It was the morning after their escape at the roadblock, and by way of celebration he left messages inviting his British and Russian colleagues to brunch. It took a while for them to show. Tony was the first to appear: drugged by drink and jet lag he'd slept till almost eleven. After waiting a token moment for Alyosha the two of them started in. Their aborted dinner the night before and the Russian's delayed arrival served as a pretext for a second tour of the fare.

When Alyosha finally came – he'd got the message late, he explained – and they told him of their adventure the Russian's response was a snort of laughter: that's what you get, he said, from trusting yourself to Chinese hands. They'd have done better to hitch a lift in his official jeep, with his Russian guard (a crack shot, he assured them) and a driver who knew where he was going.

'Well thanks for the invitation', Zach came back, 'even if it's retrospective.'

The dishes succeeded one other, and when it got to midday it was natural that drinks should follow. Brunches were not Tony's style, but what the hell: his body clock was still on GMT, their plans in chaos, a wrecked and smouldering town centre did not beckon, so eating his way through the day seemed the best option. Eating, drinking, and talking about Osman.

'Don't give much for their chances of getting him back', Zach mused, 'he'll be up there in the Tian Shan range by now, working his way back to his friends in the Fergana Valley or wherever. Only consolation is the foot. Gives me a warm glow, thinking of him limping and stumbling through frozen snow.'

'So he escaped', Alyosha threw in, his knife and fork in the air. 'Big deal. Maybe he was a nobody to begin with? If their counter-intelligence is on a level with their military competence maybe all they lost is a spoilt boy who's looking for an identity and found one playing ethnic games.'

'A gap-year gunrunner,' Tony added 'Though I doubt it. Your people involved in finding him, Alyosha, under your Shanghai agreement thing?'

'Not directly', the Russian shrugged, 'it's a Chinese problem.'

'So what *do* you do here?'

'I cooperate. Sit in my office and cooperate.'

'With who exactly?'

'The *Guoanbu*, Public Security, customs, the frontier people. You name it, we cooperate. Tell each other stuff, copy one another's information. Assuming we know what the hell's going on, and on Osman we have no idea.'

'Total farce yesterday', Zach grumbled. 'We could have burned alive in there. Where were the choppers for Chrissake? Three of 'em on the scene and there'd have been no trouble.

One to knock out the rioters, one to evacuate our prisoner – and one to stand by while we finished dinner.'

'Helicopters', Alyosha murmured. 'For the Yanks they are mechanized gods. The American *deus ex machina*. They hover over you 24/7 and down comes the solution to every problem.'

'Pretty much', said Zach, snatching expertly at a dumpling. 'Hope they've got one standing by to lift us out of the hotel. Long as it's not Russian-made. Afghanistan's littered with the wrecks of those things. No one shot them down, they just flopped out of the sky.'

Alyosha ordered beer, ignoring him. So Zach pushed it further:

'Let's face it, Tony, only reason to be sorry Osman's gone is that the Chinks and the Ivans won't be able to give him the treatment while we keep our hands clean, and collect. 'Cos you and I ain't going to get a hell of a lot out of him, are we? Sit there stroking him with our kid fucking gloves is all we're allowed.

'Saw the transcript of your interrogation. No offence Tony, but come on! Reads like a fucking seminar. Montaigne, for Chrissake! Where d'ya get that stuff? Didn't realise you were a literary man, any more than I knew the guy was half-Jewish. Half of one of us, so there must be something to him. Maybe it's time I read him?' The know-it-all nose turned at him across the table under the ravenously chewing mouth. 'Tell me Tony, what you going to get out of him by chatting about a sixteenth century frog?'

Tony said nothing. The American was in overbearing mood and he was tired of being overborne.

'I enjoyed it', Alyosha said. 'Your approach is very subtle. You knew you were going to get nowhere with direct questions, so you went round him. You've done a lot of interrogations, Tony?'

'A few', Tony said, making an overstatement sound like its opposite.

'He's well-read alright', Alyosha mused, 'and like the Captain said, he's into poetry.'

'There you go', Zach stabbed a finger. 'Those people, it's a giveaway. Bin Laden wrote poetry. So did Chairman Mao, another poet-terrorist.'

Looking down at his plate Alyosha intoned:

I have just drunk the waters of Changsha
And come to eat the fish of Wuchang.
Now I am swimming across the great Yangtze,
Looking afar to the open sky of Chu.

Zach stared.

'That poetry? That Mao?'

'You want it in Chinese?'

'Jesus.' Zach had stopped eating. 'Montaigne one side of me, Chinese poetry on the other.'

'My dad made me learn it, when he was posted to Beijing,' Alyosha drawled. 'Seven goddamn years of Mao. Not that he had any time for the murdering bastard.'

The American turned back to Tony.

'Least you got to talk to our man. Now he's away with the terrorist fucking fairies. They get him back, he'll take some cracking, unless the Chinks cripple him a bit more. Then we can go in, spread our hands, commiserate, and tell him his best chance is to come clean with us.'

Tony shrugged: 'That's what I thought I was doing.'

'My impression', said Alyosha, 'is that he's a cocky little shit, but not a killer. I don't see him as part of anything big.'

Zach agitated a finger, looking deep.

'There's more to him than that. Way I read him he could be a new type. Terrorists of the mind who cross over into action. Anarchists hitching a ride to doom on Al Qaeda's wagon. Osama used to go on about the Crusades, with Osman it's ancient China. Death by a thousand cuts and the rest of it. Weird or what? And all because his great granddad was a Tungan. Revenge merchants is what they are, nationalists of defunct nations. *Time to square accounts with the past.* Something else that's gonna keep the three of us in business.

'They're not gonna take any of that crap here. To understand the Chinese, you gotta think of the Russians. Why are the Ivans such touchy bastards? 'Cos they got an inferiority complex – and I'm not saying they're wrong. Look at the fuck-up they made of their country. And why are the Chinese so goddamn prickly too? 'Cos they got a superiority complex. Think they're the bees' fuckin' knees, civilisation-wise. Everything that's gone wrong for them is 'cos the West was out to get 'em.' He wiped his grease-flecked mouth. 'So there you go. The Chinks and the Ivans, different cultures, both of 'em paranoid, so it comes to the same thing.'

He stopped and looked at Alyosha, as if remembering he was there.

'No offence', he said, holding his beer across to clink glasses.

'None taken', Alyosha said, clinking. 'I don't understand a word you said, so how can I take offence?'

Bewildered, Tony looked from one to the other.

'As a paranoid Russian', Alyosha smiled, 'am I allowed a question?'

'Feel free.'

'The relevance of all this?'

'Chinese paranoia explains why the three of us are here. They think one of us sent Osman. Wanted to watch us interrogate him so as to see who it was. Why would we send in jihadis to Xinjiang? For the Chinks it's a no-brainer: to stymie the unstoppable advance to world domination of the glorious Chinese people. Fuck up their country same as the terrorists are fucking up ours. And why Xinjiang? To foul up the New Silk Road before it gets underway.'

'Ah', said Tony, nodding, as if that resolved it. Americans, he'd learned from such experience as he'd had with the FBI, went in for theories. 'And after seeing my interrogation would they think the British had sent him?'

'After seeing your interrogation they wouldn't know what the hell to think.'

Alyosha was looking bored.

'The time to worry about the Chinese', he yawned, 'is when they learn to piss.'

Zach tilted his head and raised a brow.

'I had a leak before coming in,' the Russian went on. 'Know what it said above the stalls in the toilet?'

'We don't read Chinese. Tell us.'

'It says "One small step forward is a big step for civility".'

Relieved at the chance to lighten up, Tony guffawed.

It was nearly one. Zach ordered more beer, Alyosha a slug of vodka. When it came he drank it down, sighed contentedly, and wagged a finger at Zach.

'I see where you're coming from. You talk about turning terrorists on China like mad dogs, but everyone can play that game. Who knows? Maybe you'll gang up with them, like Nixon did with Mao, and turn them on us?'

'See what I mean, Tony? Fucking paranoid! Still, I kinda like the idea. Economical, too. Throwing suicide bombers at you would be cheaper than ICBMS.' Suddenly he pointed behind their backs, grinning. 'Hey, look! Our rescue team just showed up.'

Tony and Alyosha turned towards the door behind them. A group of Chinese officers, peak-capped and corpulent, had come in and sat down at the far end of the restaurant, at a reserved table, cordoned off.

'So they finally made it! Now they're here maybe they'll apologise for almost letting the elite of Russian and Western counter-
intelligence be liquidated en masse? But they're Chinese, aren't
they, so first they gotta have their chow. Who's gonna go up and
ask what happened? How 'bout you, Alyosha? You're big
buddies with them, aren't you?'

And so on it went, till after two. Alyosha goading Zach about
the US wanting the Ukraine in NATO ('You wanna watch what
you're buying into. Khrushchev was a Ukrainian and it was him
who did the Cuban missiles, remember?'), and Zach's jibes about
Putin's fears of being surrounded ('One day he'll be begging us
to surround him – to save him from the Chinese.')

The difficulty with Zach's perma-smile, Tony began thinking,
was that you could never be sure when he was talking balls and
when he was serious. With Alyosha, it was the contrary problem:
keeping his rare smiles from slipping into a leer. It could be hard
to work out where their teasing stopped and reality began, and
there were times when he suspected they weren't teasing at all.

Now he was stuck here with nothing to do, the prospect of
seeing so much of them was not enticing. Zach could be
amusing, though something about Alyosha gave him the creeps.
Together, they were too much. For an hour or so their banter
had entertained him, but already he'd begun tiring of their
company, the way grown-ups tire of children. Their goading of
one another seemed childlike too, a replay of the Cold War in
pseudo-ironic tones.

Now the Cold War was over they seemed to need new
reasons to despise and distrust each other; it wasn't ideological
any more, it was personal. Strange how they couldn't let it go.
Like the Chinese and the Uighurs the hostility seemed organic,
in the blood, and nothing would flush it out.

10

From Urumqi to Dunhuang was a fourteen-hour journey overnight. At the station Osman thought of upgrading his ticket to soft class, but decided against: the sleepers seemed fully booked – tourists were getting out of the province to more tranquil places – and in economy class, amongst the Chinese, he'd be less conspicuous.

At eight in the evening the train set off. He'd resolved to stay awake all night, but he couldn't do it. At the safe house he'd scarcely slept – the foul air, the distant shooting, anxiety about his trip. By midnight the rhythm of the train lulled him, and he began dozing off.

An hour later a cry awoke him. A few rows ahead two policemen were dragging a young Uighur from his window seat. Blood flowed from his temple, his legs were threshing, his *doppa* crazily askew. He was screaming for help yet no one in the carriage, Chinese mostly, wanted to know. Like them he turned away, taking a sudden interest in the darkened desert beyond the windows.

When they got the man onto the platform of the next carriage, the door slid shut and they started on him for real, the noise of the train muffling the blows and yells. Everyone was careful not to look that way, yet Osman leant into the aisle, instinctively, and watched the soundless mime through the glass. The man had collapsed face down on the floor and they were trying to lift him, yanking at his belt till he was on all fours, like some limp animal. In frustration one of the PAP kicked him in the stomach, then glanced back into the carriage.

His eye caught Osman's. Moving back in his seat swiftly, out of his line of sight, he began reading. His head was deep in his

Chinese paper when a shadow fell across it.

'You were looking, eh?'

'Not deliberately, officer. I just happened –'

'– you saw something?'

The man's face was closer, his voice lower. There was spittle in the corner of his mouth.

'Nothing. I only saw him… struggling. Resisting.'

'You saw correctly.'

The seat next to him was empty. In the seconds it took the policeman to go back to his colleague, who was holding up the half-insensible Uighur against the side of the train, Osman had his British passport out of his trainer and into his jacket pocket. When they'd taken the man away the officer came back into the carriage to resume his checks. Reaching Osman he stopped and leant towards him.

'Resisting arrest, right?' the man said, leering. When Osman nodded energetically, he moved on.

*

The rendezvous in Dunhuang was a pavement teahouse in a dusty backstreet. Ambling past, he checked out the clientele. Any of them could have been Kul: the place was crowded with old-timers, men mostly, but only one was sitting alone. Coming back he made for his table – then hesitated. The recognition sign, Hamid had explained, was two packs of Marlboros. In front of the sixty-year-old at the table was a single pack – of Kents.

Was it him? Or a plain clothes man in his place… Skirting the table he left the teahouse, walked round the area for twenty minutes, came back, checked again. The man with the Kents was still there. The mobile shot Salih had shown him had been blurred, and the man's features left a mixed impression. Like himself, a Tungan with a Caucasian touch. Otherwise the figure at the table looked like any Chinese office worker: short hair, sleeveless shirt and tie, the jacket on the chair next to him neatly folded. A dispatch clerk, the Turkman had told him, so that would fit.

There were three seats at his table.

'Keyi-ma?' *May I?*

'Keyi.'

The man smiled and gestured towards the empty seat. Osman sat down, ordered a juice. When the waiter had gone he leant over, pointed to the pack and asked in Chinese:

'You like Kents?'

'I don't smoke. And you? You'd like one?'

The man reached for the pack.

'That's kind, but I don't want you to –'

'– *mei guanxi!* No problem!'

Opening the pack he held it out. Osman slid one from the packet.

'You have a lighter?'

'No lighter! I only keep them for friends'

Borrowing a light from the next table, he took a distracted puff.

'They like Kents, your friends?'

'They prefer Marlboros, but here I couldn't find any. And Kents – only one pack!'

Osman exhaled smoke like a sigh of thankfulness. It was Kul, but the man seemed a moron.

'A shame', he said. 'Marlboros – two packs – would have been better!' He indicated Kul's coat on the chair between them. 'You were keeping a place?'

'For you, yes, for you I was keeping it.'

*

The din of the teahouse was welcome, even if to hear one another they had to lean close. Kul wasn't a moron: the non-smoker had assumed he could buy his cigarettes at the teahouse, they only had one pack of Kents, and he'd been afraid of missing him if he'd gone in search of his Marlboros elsewhere.

'It's a great pleasure to meet you, Mr Kul', Osman mouthed in his ear, when this was explained.

'I too am pleased to meet. The courier said you were a professor of comparative religion. I am hoping I may be able to help with your researches.'

'Courier?'

'Yes, the Uzbek, Salih's cousin, in our prayer circle.' He giggled. 'It is a long way, but he knows the road, and he is swift.'

'Of course, his cousin.'

So Salih would be getting feedback from Kul about their meeting. And via Salih, the Turkman. Something to bear in mind.

For several minutes they chatted. For something to say, he asked whether Kul would be visiting the Thousand Buddhist caves during his stay. A mistake.

Kul shook his head, vigorously.

'Why would I visit their statues?' he muttered in a low, derisory voice. 'Karma is rubbish, superstition.'

Staring away, he went silent. Then:

'Excuse me, professor, they told me that you too are of Tungan descent, and you are interested in Islam. But from your face I see that your background is a little mixed. So are you Christian or Muslim?'

'A Muslim, on both sides a Muslim. My mother was Ukrainian, but we lived in Kirghizstan, and she converted.'

'A wise woman!'

'And you?'

'A Muslim, of course!'

'And a Tungan, I gather.'

'My race? Ah, professor, only history knows!'

'How's that?'

Kul gave a quiet smile. 'They said you were researching the religions of the province. If you are interested I will tell you the tale of who I am, because I too have made researches. You have time to listen?'

'I've come a long way to meet you.'

Kul settled in his seat and leant forward. Involuntarily, Osman edged back a little: it wasn't that he smelled bad, and yet there was something – some primal atmosphere the man carried with him – you didn't want to be too close to.

'It began like an opera, something you could not believe, but it happened. It was Urumqi, 1928, a banquet given by the Governor of Xinjiang. For a Chinese he was a good man because he didn't oppress Muslims, but his rivals hated them. At the banquet they waited till his guards had left their weapons outside and come in to eat. Then assassins rushed in and shot him, six times, there, at the table.

'Now the Muslims were afraid. The new Governor brought in Chinese from outside the province to seize their lands – like now, you see, professor, like today! Then a Chinese official seduced a Muslim girl, so there was a revolt. A banquet, an assassination, a seduction – and 200,000 people died! You see how it is always the same, professor?'

'I do.'

Osman affected a patience he did not feel. Where was this going?

'Except that at that time the Muslims had a leader, Ma Zhongying. You know of him?'

'Of course. As a Tungan of course I know.'

'He called himself Ma – horse in Chinese – but for him Ma

was short for Mohammed. He was a born soldier. At seventeen a colonel, in his twenties a General. General Big Horse they named him! They say he was a warlord, a brigand, but that is not true. He was a great leader, a Muslim Napoleon! And his plan was for an Empire, a Central Asian Caliphate from Gansu to Samarkand!

'The Chinese he hated because they had murdered his father. He laid siege to Urumqi, a walled city in those days, like medieval times. And the fighting, it was medieval too. People starved to death, thousands slaughtered, everyone crazed by blood – even the dogs went mad! They had eaten the corpses in the street, and it made them mad!

'I've read about Ma Zhongying', Osman said, gently, 'many times.'

'But Ma Zhongying and my family!' Kul raised an alerting finger. 'About that you have not read.'

'Tell me.'

'My grandmother was a White Russian, and in the siege of Urumqi she was raped.'

'By a Han?'

'No, a Muslim. She was a beautiful woman, with her blond hair and fine white skin. Too beautiful for common soldiers, so she was handed upwards, as a prize of battle. I say that it was rape, but to judge from what she said no force was used that night. And the man who took her? An officer and a Tungan – Ma Zhongying himself!

'She was old when she told me, in her seventies. My first thought was that she was inventing things, to cover her shame. She talked of his youth and gentleness, as if her violator were some kind of prince, a handsome prince! Then it was his air of power and command, and the devotion of his servants.

'Nine months after that night my father was born. The child of Ma Zhongying, she assured me. It didn't trouble her that her son had Muslim blood. For her all that mattered was that his father should be a distinguished man. There are woman like that, professor, especially White Russians, with their aristocratic ways...'

'So you're a descendant of Ma Zhongying. Incredible!'

'At first it seemed unlikely, but when I compared old photographs of General Big Horse with pictures of my father, I became convinced it was true.'

His eyes were filled with intensity now, staring at him in exultation. From his jacket he took a slim, scuffed leather case, and handed it to him. Inside, in a silver frame, was an old photo. The picture was a half-length, the General in uniform. Against the straps and holster and stripes and epaulettes the oval face seemed almost soft, though Ma had been a soldier of remorseless violence – General Thunderbolt had been another nickname – especially against the Chinese. It was why Osman had admired him.

He looked up at Kul, then back at the photo.

'The resemblance is there, I can see it, no question.'

It wasn't flattery. Alongside the man's Russian genes – the larger nose, the wider face – there was something of Ma Zhongying. Especially the eerie placidity of their features.

Kul slipped the picture back into his jacket.

'My father never knew, because his mother never told him. He was a simple man, a farmer of grapes and melons. He was not religious, but he married a Uighur girl, who died in a cholera epidemic soon after I was born. Two years later, it was my father. The communists wanted to take his farm, he resisted, so they killed him.

'My grandmother and I survived. She didn't want to bring me up, so she gave me to an orphanage, a Christian one run by the British China Inland Mission. So you see, professor, I am a bigger mixture than you! In me there were three religions for you to compare – four if you count atheism! An Orthodox Russian grandmother, a Muslim mother and grandfather, a father who had no religion – and finally a Protestant education!

'Those English matrons – they were strict, I remember their soap and their punishments – but they taught me well. Though who was I, with my fairish skin and light brown eyes – see how light, professor – my mixed religions, and my atheist father? Later I understood two things: that the blood of a Muslim hero was in me, and that every calamity in my life was brought about by the Hans.'

'And your grandmother, is she still alive?'

'Oh yes, in her nineties.'

'So you live alone together.'

'I have never married.'

That I understand, Osman thought.

'A cleaner takes care of her. She is no trouble. She can no longer walk and' – he smiled as he said it, broadly, as if delighted to impart the news – 'no longer right in the head.'

'She hasn't converted?'

'She is Orthodox, but she doesn't practise. In my house I won't allow it. And how can she worship', his smile was malevolent now, 'if she is gone in the head? Maybe it was her religion that made her mad!

'At first I was a casual believer, a Friday Muslim, though I could never go to the mosque. To practice openly could be dangerous – I might fall under suspicion and lose my job. I know it is humble work, logging goods and supplies in and out at my depot, but it was steady work. And it gave me time for thinking.

'And always my thoughts were of Allah. To guide my faith I had the Internet. A young man in my circle – we have a Muslim circle, professor, they told you I imagine? – taught me where to look, and how to wipe away the trace of what I had read. Because where I work you have to watch what you do.'

Osman returned his opaque smile.

The way Salih had described him Kul sounded more than a little strange. Promising, the Uzbek had said, but strange —one reason he'd been sent to look him over – and Osman saw no reason to revise that impression. Against his tranquil features the eyes could seem over-bright – maybe a little crazed. And yet the judgment he would pass back, he decided as they sat smiling at one another in the tea-shop, was that Kul had what it took.

His hatred of the Han was visceral, his faith profound, his view of himself as the descendent of a Muslim hero rooted in his psyche. Then there was his place of work. The receiving and dispatching he'd done for over thirty years, the Turkman had told him, was at Malan, a remote spot in the south west of the province. It didn't feature on the map, but that was natural, because Malan was the centre of the Lop Nor nuclear research and storage site.

*

The plan had been to report to the Turkman before any approach was made, but Kul forced his hand. They were saying goodbye outside the teahouse, Osman thanking him for his story and promising to be in touch, when he said:

'So I will be in your book, professor, *Inshallah*? You will write your book, won't you, and tell the truth about Ma Zhongying and the Chinese infidels? Soon I will retire and have time to help.'

'You're retiring?'

Osman did his best to disguise his shock.

'Oh yes, it is time, they have told me. Already they are interviewing replacements.'

'So how long will you go on?'

'Who knows? A month or so perhaps?'

A bad moment. Even if Kul agreed, by the time the preparation was complete he could be gone from his job, and there'd be no access.

They were still in the street, Kul smiling and nodding in a senile way, in anticipation of his retirement, Osman casting round for an excuse to get him to sit back down, when chance resolved the problem. At that moment two policemen turned the corner into the narrow street. Instinctively the pair sat back down at their table, their backs towards them.

They ordered more tea, Osman lit another cigarette – the tension was getting to him – and for some minutes chattered about this and that, before choosing his moment.

'I'm sorry to hear you'll be leaving. After thirty years you'll miss the routine. Where is it you work, with your dispatching?'

'It is secret', he smiled, 'but I have told Salih so I can tell his friend. At Malan I work. You know it? The base at Lop Nor, Base Twenty-One. Everyone where I live works there. It is the desert, professor, there is nothing else. You know about Lop Nor?'

'The nuclear place? I've heard of it. I read there were protests there, over nuclear testing, in the 1990s. You must have been there at the time.'

'Oh yes, I was there. It was 1993, I saw it all. From the inside I saw it, from my office, near the security fence. They came from everywhere, miles away, because all of them had suffered. A thousand people – more! I watched them attacking the fence – it was electric – with anything they could get their hands on. Hacksaws with plastic handles, pliers they held with rubber gloves to cut the wires.

'Some of them got in and found explosives, and set fire to tanks and aircraft! The Chinese ordered us to retreat to a safe place inside the base. From there I saw them burning my office, but I wasn't indignant. I looked at those people and I thought, I am Muslim, I should be out there with them!

'Then the soldiers arrived and I saw them shooting, carrying away bodies…Then the arrests, the beatings, the executions and disappearances. A friend of mine went missing, a pious man and a Uighur. Later his wife was presented with his corpse. They had tortured him, she said, his body, so beaten. For our circle it was alarming. Maybe they had forced him to inform about us? We waited, we were afraid, but nothing happened. So my friend hadn't given us away. Such courage. Thinking of him I felt ashamed. The moment had come to test my faith, and instead of joining them I had cowered inside that building, with the Hans…'

'But they stopped over-ground nuclear tests, didn't they?'

'Oh yes, three years later they stopped. After forty-two tests – too late. The nearest big cities were 200 kilometres away but the desert winds, they are strong, they can blow radioactive particles everywhere, and there was a cancer epidemic. And around Malan the tests were terrible. The sky was dark, there was no sun and no moon, sand and dust rained down everywhere. Some of us knew, we took shelter, but simple folk, they didn't realise. It is as if they were bombarding the Uighur people with radiation to destroy them, to destroy their Muslim faith…

'It was in 1996 they stopped, but those things, they work slowly. The deaths from cancer haven't stopped, they are still mounting. Only now, decades later, do people see the effects. Today they know more about it. The Internet, it is all there, why their people died.'

Osman was silent, then said in a musing voice:

'And today we have more riots. The way things are going it wouldn't surprise me to see a bigger attack one of these days.'

'If there's more trouble they will deserve it', Kul said quickly. 'And next time, next time I will be on the right side.'

He spoke vehemently, drumming his empty cup on the table, his eyes alight, his tranquility gone. To calm him Osman put a hand on his arm.

Make contact and size him up – no more, were his instructions. Now he would have to take things further – but how? Several lines of approach came to him, yet none seemed right. Then Kul, tranquil again, filled the gap. Leaning towards him as he poured more tea, in a voice so low it was hardly audible above the noise of the street, he whispered:

'You must meet many Muslims in different countries, professor, in your researches. Maybe you know of people?'

'People?'

'You know, preparing something.'

Osman took a breath before saying in a neutral tone and with the smallest shrug:

'I have heard there are people.'

'Well tell them what I have said. Tell them I am not alone, that we have our circle. People of faith, who might help.'

'Help in what?'

'Whatever it is they are preparing.'

Osman stared him in the eye:

'And assuming there is something, you, Mr Kul, you personally, might you help? Are you ready for sacrifice?'

Kul turned to see what had become of the policemen patrolling the street: they had disappeared, but he said nothing. He'd moved too fast, Osman began fearing, when in a voice filled with a kind of acid sweetness, Kul replied:

'When I retire my employers at the base will give me a gift. It is their custom. They are generous to us, the Chinese, they have given gifts to the whole population. Their biggest gift, as they never tire of reminding us, is of the Han civilisation, and this gift is everywhere to be seen. The Chinese language they forced on us. The mosques they build for the tourists. And the secular teaching they force on us to exterminate our religion, that is another of their gifts. The drinking, the indecent clothes and behaviour to corrupt our youth. All this they give us freely.

'Then there is their gift of scientific progress. Such as the radiation poisoning that has led to leukemia, children with cancers, cleft palates, tumours, twisted limbs, birth defects – all these are gifts to us Muslims from the Hans!

'Such generosity! The question is, how should we respond? We cannot stand by and let them shower us with gifts without responding. They deserve something in return. It is only right.' The eyes were burning again. 'And if the gift we give them is that of our lives, I am ready.'

11

General Li Hesan, head of Bureau Six, the counter-intelligence branch of the *Guoanbu,* had been in the security business for six decades. Anyone else his age would have been replaced long ago, but family connections had helped him stay in his job well beyond his retirement date. As no one was allowed to forget, the General was not just another old-time cadre, but a distant relative of Mao Zedong and a teenage courier in the Chairman's first intelligence organisation.

Though a powerful man, the General was not a commanding figure. His face was pigmented with age, from the liver spots darkening his brow to his dramatically stained teeth, so black that in certain lights he seemed toothless. Reputed for his fiery temperament (*explosive farter* was his whispered nickname), his expression was either angry or grimacing, as if in referred pain from his entire body, in which the eyes alone moved quickly, kept alive by a simmering rage. Today, as he shuffled along the street close to his Beijing office on a grey and drizzly morning, his mood was more than usually vile.

He was returning from a meeting he'd been summoned to urgently that morning, together with the Minister for State Security. Much of his life was spent dozing round tables, yet this had been no somnolent affair, but a crisis meeting at Zhongnanhai on Tiananmen Square, China's seat of government, devoted to events in Xinjiang and presided over by the President himself. It had been an uncomfortable two and a half hours. Sensing the President's cold rage over what had happened – between barking out questions he frowned down at the officials ranged around him like an irate statue – the General had done his best to lie low, but it was no good: his

Minister had clearly brought him along to absorb some of the presidential anger, and kept deflecting his enquiries over to his counter-intelligence chief.

The worst moment came when, indignant at the humiliation the country had suffered at the sight of terrorists setting the centre of one of its key provincial capitals aflame, he turned in the General's direction and said with a frozen smile:

'I gather that Western security officials were on hand to enjoy the spectacle, like some kind of comic opera. Explain to me, General, how it was that foreigners had been invited to our country to witness the destruction of the Public Security Bureau and the escape of a Category One prisoner. A prisoner involved in gun-running, who seems to have been a Westerner himself.'

Explaining their presence in Urumqi at the time the General concluded:

'The coincidence with the prisoner's escape was certainly unfortunate –'

'– unfortunate?' the President interrupted. 'A mild word in the circumstances, wouldn't you say? How soon can he be recaptured? Meanwhile can we at least keep his escape out of the media?'

'Certainly, that can be done.'

On and on the meeting ground, the President pummelling them with questions about why the *Guoanbu*'s intelligence had failed, why reinforcements had been delayed, and how quickly the frontiers could be sealed against arms smuggling. A warning that he would be taking personal charge of the investigation into this 'shameful and unprecedented incident' followed them to the door.

By the time he got out the General felt a craving for air, and on his way back to his office insisted on getting out of his car and covering the last five hundred metres on foot, something he did from time to time, partly to stimulate his fading appetite. His plain-clothes protection officers did their best to dissuade him – security had been stepped up in Beijing too – to no avail. It was one of those days the goons could do nothing right. When he slipped on the wet pavement and the nearest man grabbed an arm the General shook him off, and when he tripped again, this time nearly falling, for a full minute he stood cursing the fellow for not catching him.

If he shuffled along rather faster than usual today – one reason he kept tripping – it wasn't so as to be on time for his next appointment (he kept visitors waiting on principle), but because he was eager to give a larger than usual piece of his mind to the intelligence boss from Urumqi he was due to see. Something else that would boost his appetite. His irritation increased when, arriving at his office on time, he asked for Captain Tang to be shown in, and was told that he had not yet arrived.

*

His taxi marooned in traffic, the Captain had no illusions about the interview he was about to undergo. His problem wasn't just the attack on the Public Security Bureau and the escape of the foreign prisoner whose capture he'd written up as a break-through in the anti-terrorist struggle, but the situation regarding the presence of foreign security men. The idea of inviting them when the rioting had broken out had been his, and it was only by exploiting a contact in the minister's office, a distant cousin, that he had he finally got the General's approval. The problem now was to convince him that there was some purpose in the foreigners continuing their stay.

Assuming, that is, that he wasn't on his way out himself. If so he'd be more than happy to go: working in Xinjiang was a bloody business, after four years of it he'd done his stint, and the last thing he wanted was to get stuck in that poisoned backwater. If the real purpose of summoning him to Beijing was to relieve him of his command, so be it.

Another reason he was not looking forward to the interview was that it would no doubt involve the usual hour's wait in the General's outer office. Time he could have used for something else he planned to do during his brief stay in the capital: to lobby another family contact, in the education ministry this time, about a scholarship that would allow his daughter Ling-Ling to attend a university in the West.

*

When Tang put his head through the door of the outer office the secretary turned to him with more astonishment than annoyance.

'You're late. He's been asking for you, he's waiting. You have kept the General waiting.'

Murmuring something about the traffic, Tang hurried in. The General was sitting upright at his desk, his arms folded, staring at the door.

'I've been waiting for you, Captain Tang', he said the moment he entered. 'General Li Hesan has been waiting for a captain!'

Tang stopped two steps inside the doorway. This would be just the start. Having no real excuse he offered none, simply composed himself for the assault.

'Perhaps this is a new way of behaving towards superiors. A democratic informality, where generals must hold themselves ready to receive their juniors during their lunchtime and captains are at liberty to keep their seniors waiting. Something else we've learned from the CIA and the FBI, is it? Maybe they behave like that in Public Security, I know they like Western methods over there, but I'm not having it in counter-intelligence.'

Anything he said would make things worse, the Captain decided, but then silence could be construed as insolence.

'General, I apologise.'

'Ha! As if an apology solves anything! I suspect I'm going to hear a lot more apologies in the next ten minutes, because that's all the time you've got to explain.' He looked at him over his glasses. 'Come in and sit down, why are you standing there like a block of stone?'

Tang took a seat.

'Do you know where I've been all morning? With the President, in Zhongnanhai, at a crisis meeting! Yes, the President! And let me tell you, he's an angry man. An unprecedented national humiliation, in his words. And you, Captain Tang, are you proud of your accomplishments? Your loss of your prisoner, your flaunting of our problems in front of your Englishman and your American. Your foreign liaison scheme looks a bit silly now, doesn't it? Like a comic opera. You know who said that? The President! Was this a plot to humiliate China, mounted by our enemies to demonstrate the blundering incompetence of our services? How can such a thing happen, tell me that?'

'Before the attack on the Bureau', Tang said quietly, 'things were going normally. The capture of Osman –'

'– fart talk! Don't you see? You capture a British agent delivering arms to the rebels, then you invite a British intelligence officer to Urumqi to interview him. After which he escapes!'

'General –'

'– I know what you're going to say! More fart talk, so why say it?'

'General, we must remember why the attack on the Public

Security Bureau succeeded. It was –'

'– because they had weapons! Because British intelligence gave them weapons! The British and the Americans!'

'In my opinion it happened because of the failure of the People's Liberation Army to get through in time to destroy them.'

'Are you telling me we have to rely on the PLA for safeguarding prisoners? That's a job for Public Security, who've blundered again. They ought to have sufficient trained men and weapons –'

The General stopped. This was what his opposite number at Public Security had argued – an argument dismissed by the General as an attempt to increase Public Security's manpower and budget at the expense of his own. The tide of indignation flowing over Tang retreated enough for the Captain to deploy the defence he'd thought up on the plane. The opportunity came when the General began grumbling about how long they were committed to paying the foreigners' expenses.

'It was to be a few days, that was all, so they could see the jihadi threat for themselves. But circumstances have changed.'

'They certainly have!'

'But the exercise has been far from wasted. You will recall the original purpose: to demolish all that foreign rubbish about the lack of human rights in the Uighur Autonomous Region.'

'Rubbish is the wrong word, Captain! Shit is the word, the military word!'

'All that foreign shit about human rights, by showing them that the terrorists were infiltrating operatives into China.'

'Exactly', said the General. 'They've no excuse now for pretending it isn't happening, have they? No excuse for their anti-China attitude.' He leant forward. 'Tell me Captain, how are they reacting?'

Expecting the question, Tang stood up to slide a folder of

intelligence reports about his foreign visitors across the desk. A blotched, quivering hand reached for them, greedily. The General had a bottomless appetite for eavesdropping transcripts, especially of conversations between foreigners, though the ones he was offered were not quite what they appeared. What Tang had brought were edited excerpts. Had the General seen the full transcripts of the way their guests talked privately about China his indignation would have increased.

*

The Captain had ordered his men not to bother with close surveillance of the foreigners during what was meant to have been a brief stay. As fellow security men they might have noticed, making a disagreeable impression, and anyway the emergency had left him short of watchers. Routine eavesdropping on people he was learning to call his colleagues, on the other hand, gave him few qualms: it was part of his job, the foreigners would expect it – and would do the same to Chinese visitors in their countries.

The truth was that the Captain himself liked leafing through the product. For someone who had never visited the West reading their private conversations was an education. The first thing that surprised him was how unguarded they were. Chatting away freely the way they did seemed lazy, unprofessional – unless of course they were so contemptuous of China's eavesdropping capabilities they thought they could talk privately in private places. If so, they were mistaken: the intercept devices at his disposal were top of the range. Based on American models supplied only three years ago by a patriotic Chinese research student in electronics at MIT, and rapidly reproduced by the *Guoanbu's* technical services, they were identical to the most advanced equipment used by the FBI itself.

Maybe the foreigners didn't care what their hosts thought of them? Or were they trying to convey things to them by their blatant indiscretions. Though what? The things the American said in his presence were barefaced enough, though nothing compared with his comments in the transcripts. The Russian could be worse, the Englishman less brazen. It wasn't just what they said about his country – there were elements of truth in their criticisms, you couldn't deny – it was the way they talked about each other.

Favourably impressed by Underwood – the wisest of the three, he'd decided – he was surprised to read his colleagues' dismissive opinions of the Englishman. 'An amateur if ever I saw one', was the Russian's comment on his interrogation techniques. 'It's like his government picked up a tourist from the street to do the job.' For his part the American had once described Tony as 'a middle-ranking watcher who got lucky on a single case, and was sent out here to grass.'

Not that the Russian and American thought much of one another. When they were drunk, which seemed a lot of the time, each of them shared his views about the other with the Englishman. 'A more than averagely fucked-up Russki who'll be dead in five years, the way he drinks and smokes,' was the American's description of Benediktov. While for the Russian, Boorstin was a 'typical Yankee bull-shitter and cultural prole, the only Yid I've met who could use another ten years education.'

On the American's lack of delicacy, Tang sympathised. His sexual appetites were evident from his file, but the man was shameless, unrelenting, seemed to think every Chinese woman could be bought. Ling-Ling had told him that he'd offered her $500 dollars to come up to his room and teach him to write Chinese characters.

That kind of report – there'd been others – shocked him

not because of what the foreigners were up to, but for his daughter herself. He'd never planned for her to work at the new hotel, with its loose-living international businessmen and call-girl service. She'd chosen it herself, and he wasn't happy, but then that was Ling-Ling: a good girl, but one who enjoyed a cosmopolitan style of life. It was why he'd added her to his list of informants and paid her a little above the standard rate: with her English skills she deserved it, and the money would go towards her studies abroad.

The problem was that her dream was a career in fashion, rather than getting herself a serious education. He'd been through it with her often enough to know that she was set on getting out of Xinjiang and travelling abroad, but unless it was for a course of study he approved he'd refused to pay.

*

The General was leafing through the first intelligence report – excerpts from a discussion between Zach and Tony over their first dinner at the hotel after Tony had arrived. Coming to China, the Englishman said, had given him the surprise of his life. He'd admired the modernity of Beijing airport and the Urumqi hotel, and praised the efficiency of the Chinese in general. (Tang had thought it best to omit Zach's response: 'Well if you sat on their heads their whole fucking lives and crapped all over them at the slightest mistake, even the Brits could be efficient.')

'At least we've got something out of it', the General said with a look of satisfaction when he'd finished, setting the remainder of the intercepts aside for future reading. 'And presumably they'll report to their governments that Al Qaeda is a threat to China, and ISIS is on the rise. That's what they're saying in their reports home, isn't it?'

The honest reply was that if he hadn't been obliged to shut down email and telephone traffic on the General's orders, maybe they would. As it was, Tang had restored them from time to time without seeking authorisation. Rather than switch off communications entirely he preferred to find out what the insurgents were telling their foreign contacts as they rushed to take advantage of the periods when the lines were open:

'Certainly that is the tenor of their comments. They've got the message alright, exactly as we intended. And of course if we recapture Osman while they're still here –'

'– that would be good, Captain. Very good. The President mentioned him at the meeting. We've got to show the foreigners that we're not beginners. We didn't ask them here to take lessons. Remember what Chairman Mao said about counter-revolutionary foreigners? What was it now…'

'*Despise them strategically, but take them seriously tactically.*'

'That's it, that's what he wrote! Not bad, eh? He had a phrase for everything. Yes, re-capturing Osman would show them. How's the investigation going?'

'Well it's early days, but it's underway.'

'But do you have any leads?'

'In the Uighur community, we have sources.'

'Mind they don't lie to you for money. They're a scummy lot, bad as the Tibetans. You've learnt that much in Xinjiang, haven't you?'

'Absolutely', said Tang.

'You need more officers?'

'I could do with another dozen, for surveillance.'

'You shall have them. Meanwhile I don't want anything said about Osman's escape.'

'But if we can't warn the public that he's out there on the run, how are we –'

'– nothing, you understand? Nothing!' The General

thumped his desk. 'The President insisted. You want to coun-
termand the President? But I want him back in jail. I want to
see those foreigners' faces when you've got him and screw
something out of him, show them who his jihadi backers are.
Then maybe we can get the Americans to target their bases in
the Fergana Valley, with their drones. Sometimes you have to
cooperate with the adversary when it's to our advantage, and
we get something back. And they let us talk to those Uighurs
they caught in Afghanistan, didn't they, in – what's it called?'

'Guantanamo Bay, General. In Cuba.'

'Cuba, yes. But they didn't extradite them when we asked,
did they? More shit about human rights!'

'Absolute shit, General.'

'I know we have to let the foreigners see Osman, ask their
questions, see how they go about it, watch for any sign of col-
lusion', the General went on, looking sly. 'But they can't touch
him, can they, so they'll get nothing from him. Only farts.
Though if we let them stay on, having them hanging around
won't make it harder for us to get things out of him, will it?
Stuff those foreigners will be glad enough to have in exchange
for their own feeble interrogations?'

'We had already begun interrogating Osman –'

'– I know, I know, but you didn't get anything, did you?
Because you were interrupted, by your foreigners.'

'And we will interrogate him again.'

'With Chinese methods.'

'Naturally it will be by Chinese', Tang said. Though not me,
he could have added, or anyone I control. He hadn't enjoyed
being teased by the American about Osman's foot, as if they
were some kind of primitives, and had ordered that the guard
who'd done it should be disciplined. Not that it mattered, now
the man's head had been blown apart.

'So remember,' the General said as he dismissed him. 'The

President wants results! So no soft methods! I looked at him this morning and I thought, there is a man of iron, who will take the struggle to the terrorists, a worthy successor to Mao! And remember what the Chairman said about struggle? It wasn't a dinner party, he said, or painting a picture, or doing embroidery. So it can't be...'

The General's quote tailed away.

'*It cannot be so refined, so leisurely and gentle, so temperate, kind, courteous, restrained and magnanimous,*' the Captain finished for him.

When he came out of the General's office the private secretary gave him a look that said, *Don't worry, it happens the whole time, people get other jobs.* If that was what his expression was meant to convey he was wide of the mark. The reason Captain Tang was looking a little dejected was because the General had confirmed that he'd be returning to his post in Xinjiang, and wanted him back there the next day.

12

After passing on his impressions of the Dunhuang meeting Osman was once again on his travels, en route to a second meeting with Kul. His report had been to Hamid, not his boss. 'He cannot come this time, so you tell me what happened – but please, no names.'

His message to the Turkman had been simple: psychologically speaking he was convinced they'd got the right man, who saw himself as a martyr in the making. Everything suggested he would respond to an approach – in fact he'd come close to volunteering. The only problem was that he'd been forced to tell him more than they'd agreed. There'd been no choice: he was due to retire before long, so they'd have to work quickly.

The Turkman's response had come late the following day. (The time it took for him to consult Salih, Osman supposed, though with the lines down most of the time, how the hell did they do it?) He'd done an excellent job, the Turkman said, and it was agreed that he should see his friend again, urgently, and make an open approach. At which point Hamid had pulled an envelope from his pocket, wordlessly. In it were more train tickets, the destination this time a station in Qinghai province, east of Xinjiang.

Another overnight trip. He'd done his best to disguise his dismay. It wasn't the length of the journey, it was the perils of travel: the police and paramilitaries at railway stations, the plain clothes men he was convinced he'd spotted on the Dunhuang journey. A second trip would be pushing his luck…

'You will meet at Qinghai lake,' Hamid had told him. 'It is like Dunhuang, there are many tourists, to see the birds. There is a restaurant, the Yellow Gull, where you will have lunch. And this time, the Turkman says, you may tell him more.'

*

The lake was the biggest in China, its five islands had been made into bird sanctuaries, and May was the migratory season. From their restaurant table above the crystal green water Kul and Osman watched flocks of cormorants, gulls and geese soaring, hovering, or swooping for fish.

'Every year I come here for the migration,' Kul said. 'A miracle of the deity, the Chinese call it, and for once they are right.'

Birds, it turned out, were his passion, and somehow the hobby fitted: you could picture him at it, alone, watching, brooding, obsessing. For some time he instructed Osman, a novice, in the ornithological riches of the lake. He spoke like a mentor, patiently, but his student was in no mood to learn: Kul's simplicity of mind had begun to annoy him. As he rhapsodized about the scene before them Osman searched for ways to remind him that birds and fish were not the purpose of the meeting. He hadn't travelled hundreds of miles to hear about the mating habits of the bar-headed goose.

He was ill at ease in the restaurant: his youth and clothes made him feel conspicuous. In the street outside, China Travel buses were unloading another cargo of elderly, overweight Westerners every fifteen minutes, their loud voices demanding tables at the edge of the terrace closest to the lake. Americans, French, Germans, British – how he hated the petulant, imperious bastards! He wasn't alone: beneath their glassily accommodating manner the Chinese staff were enjoying themselves at their expense. 'Better give this old bird-nose a good table, he wants to see himself in the water, can't think why,' a waitress murmured to a colleague as she passed, ushering an ancient

American and his wife smilingly to their seats.

When their order was delivered Kul interrupted his lesson to smile down at his naked carp, one of the delicacies of the lake. Osman was on the point of turning their talk to the matter at hand when, spotting something in the distance, Kul set down his chopsticks, pulled a pair of binoculars from his jacket, and was lost to conversation.

'You see?' he said after a minute, pointing excitedly. Peeling away from the flock in a predatory dive, a cormorant had emerged with its prey, its scales flashing silver as the bird gobbled it down. 'The water is so clear the fish do not stand a chance. They come from so far, these birds, from India, Burma, the whole of South East Asia. They eat their fill then they breed on the islands. It is like the Chinese and the Muslims. We are the fish and they are the greedy, migrating birds. The Hans feed on us and breed in our lands. The more they breed the more birds will migrate with them, and the more fish they will eat.'

'Maybe you should do something to dissuade them?'

Kul put down his binoculars.

'And what do you recommend?'

'To get rid of predatory birds? Well, you frighten them off, don't you? Though not just with a scarecrow or firecrackers.' Osman half-smiled. 'Something louder.'

Kul said nothing. It was a fine day and as he stared at the lake's placid surface, mesmerised, he seemed about to slip into one of his silences. After his nineteen hour journey Osman himself was tired and hot and in bad need of a drink. Everyone around them was swilling beer, but out of deference to his guest, he resisted, and gulped water.

It was a relief when finally, without lifting his eyes from the lake, Kul murmured:

'You are right. To frighten ravenous birds we must be bold.

When we met in Dunhuang you said there were people planning. But the plan must be serious, not just another demonstration with hacksaws.'

It was the opening he needed, and Osman was ready.

'There was great joy among our brothers', he said softly, 'when I told them you might join their enterprise. And great admiration, because what they have in mind will be serious all right. And risky.'

'Risky?' Kul said it like a question, though in his face there was no alarm. 'In what way? You mean something that risks not working?'

'No, not that. I meant personally. Risky for you.'

'I do not want that risk either. I do not want to be caught and spend the rest of my life in prison. Or be executed, like my friends in 1993, for nothing. No, risks like that I do not want. I want certainty. Certainty that our brothers will be avenged and that, Inshallah, Paradise will be my reward.'

For the first time he stared Osman in the eye. A strange look, hard yet soulful, a kind of misty determination. Determination to die, was Osman's reading.

'So what is it I must do?'

Now was the time. Osman looked around, and leant closer.

'Your responsibilities will be minimal. Just two things. First, you must recruit two martyrs from your circle. Second, you must use your position to prepare documents and passes for entry to your base.'

'That is all?'

'The best operations', Osman said, 'are the simplest.'

'But what will they do, inside? And how can I find brothers to give their lives if I do not know what it is for? I cannot ask them just to go in and burn something and be shot, like before.'

It was a fair question, and this time he had more discretion: let him know as much as necessary, the Turkman had instructed.

'I understand. I'll tell you some details, to help you recruit the right people, but you must keep them to yourself.'

'Of course.'

To the left of the main restaurant was a small observation platform. At that moment there was no one there. Nodding towards it, Osman got up, and together they walked towards it.

Slowly, repeating certain phrases to make sure they were understood, he described how the plan would work.

The base would be Kirghizstan. A truckload of timber would arrive at a minor crossing point into Xinjiang. A Kirghiz brother would drive it as far as the border. Sometimes – though not always – the Chinese customs post would inspect the loads for drugs. To lessen the chances of a search the brother would hand over the truck to the martyrs Kul would enlist. To reduce it further they would be armed with delivery documents for the timber, courtesy of Kul, marked *special consignment, Lop Nor construction.*

Kul gave a contented nod.

He would also provide passes for the driver and his mate, Osman continued. Finally he would leave his office when the truck arrived, to be on hand to take care of any difficulties.

'To get into the base, that is a good plan. But what will there be in the truck, beneath the logs? People?'

'No, not people.' He hesitated, then said: 'PETN.'

'And what is that?'

'Pentaerythritol tetranitrate.'

Kul shook his head.

'I am a clerk, not a technical man.'

'An explosive, the best available. The size of the truck will give us room for a huge charge. It is easy to get hold of but hard to detect, even if they scan the truck.'

'And how is that?'

'It has low vapour pressure, which means very little gets into the air, so they can't sniff it out.'

Kul's eyes simultaneously glazed and smiled.

'So Allah willing, a big explosion!'

'Colossal.'

'And the ugly birds will scatter, and never return!' He thought for a moment before adding. 'Yes, it will be wonderful, but there is a problem. The Lop Nor region is salt lakes and sand marshes, between two deserts. The Taklamakan and Kuruktag deserts. Over time it has shrunk but is still big, very big. Hundreds of kilometres, many installations.'

'And so?'

'It is no use exploding your truck just anywhere. They will want to get into the inner perimeter, won't they, where secret things are stored.' He leant forward. 'So tell me, what are they to aim for? What is the target exactly?'

Osman rocked his head, looking wise. The truth was that he had asked the same question and the Turkman had declined to answer. The driver would brief the martyrs at the frontier, he explained, the only people who needed to know. The truck would be able to go wherever it was needed. A Russian-made *Ural* logging truck, it would be massive, its fenders strengthened to bulldozer levels by strips of steel. Together with the impetus of a heavily laden truck, it could break through any barrier. The martyr at the wheel would get experience of driving it by trying out a smaller model with a similar cab at an import depot the *Ural* firm ran in Urumqi.

Insofar as his expression ever changed, Kul seemed happy.

'History', he murmured when Osman had finished, 'it is history we are making. Our Muslim history this time, Allah be praised!'

On the plan Kul had a single query.

'It is a serious plan, a concrete plan, I do not wish to change it in any way but I have a personal question. If it is our martyrs who will make the truck explode, they will be sacrificed, as servants of Allah. But what of me? How can I be sure to die?'

It was a question Osman had not foreseen. For that reason, together with Kul's pleading expression, it annoyed him. Trying not to sound sardonic, he said gravely:

'Where there is a will there is a way.'

'The will is there', Kul came back, 'but the way – a sure way to die – I do not see.'

His eyes clouded with something like anguish.

He's right, Osman thought. How could they not have thought of that? They must have assumed he'd be killed in the explosion, like the others, but it couldn't be left to chance. It was vital that Kul should die. Not just for himself but for them all.

'It will be fine', he said, a hand on his arm. 'I told you, you should come out of your office and be on hand. You will find a way of boarding the truck at the last moment, before it drives further in.'

The anguish returned.

'What you say, it sounds…risky. And I told you: no risks!'

'OK. There'll be no risk, I promise.'

'How can you know?'

'Because next time', Osman said quietly, 'I will bring you a revolver.'

The doglike gratitude on Kul's face made Osman avert his eyes.

13

After sleeping off another three-hour brunch Tony spent the late afternoon shopping. The centre was sealed off but there were stores in the hotel and more a short walk away. It was late May and warmer than he'd expected, a bright, clear 25 degrees, and if they were going to wait around for Osman's recapture he'd need a lighter outfit. Zach and Alyosha seemed to compete with each other in casualness, making him feel over-dressed in his business suits.

A light, cream jacket, linen trousers and a straw hat blended better with the other hotel guests, and with his mood. He never spent much on clothes, or luxuries of any kind – everything went on Penny, his troubled daughter – and strolling back in his new gear he felt less than his fifty-nine years; younger still after the girl who trimmed his hair in the fancy coiffeur off the lobby asked whether he worked in television, she was sure she'd seen his face. The sun, the pretty women, the comforts of the hotel – riots or no riots, so long as the Uighurs weren't gunning for you personally, life here had its attractions.

On his way from the barber shop to the lift he called at reception for messages. There was one, from Collinson (God knew how he'd got it through, hotel channels he supposed). Providing Diwopu airport reopened the following day as promised (it had been closed to civilian transport) he'd be flying in next morning. Something of a downer, but what could you do? He'd be coming to see what was happening, he assumed, after all the dramas, and for a copy of the transcript of Osman's interrogation they'd be waiting for in London.

The airport didn't reopen and it was another day before Collinson turned up. The delay was handy: it gave time to tidy up the transcript, something it badly needed, on the laptop he'd been obliged to buy. Surprised to see his less consequential exchanges with Osman solemnly recorded, not to speak of the crazy English, in which Montaigne had come out as Mutton, he cut the Frenchman out. And since it was from Collinson that he'd picked up the Yeats quotation ('Yites' in the transcript), about an intellectual hatred being the worst, the Irishman came out too.

*

'It doesn't sound', the Embassy man said after scanning it, 'as if you pressed him very hard. The guidance they gave contained specific questions, I seem to recall. Contacts, dates, addresses.'

At Collinson's suggestion they were doing their business while walking in a small park minutes from the hotel. Tony stopped to face his moist-browed, wild-haired colleague.

'It also said I was to concentrate on forming a relationship. Not something you can do if you're firing questions he has no intention of answering. Plus the Chinese had started in on some rough treatment and I wanted to keep a line out.'

'Rough treatment?' Collinson frowned. 'Did he complain?' He held up the record. 'There's nothing about rough treatment here.'

'Because the Chinese took it out. I saw what they did to his foot and back and he wasn't happy about it. Deniable stuff, but they did it.'

'Did you protest to Tang?'

'The point was made to him', Tony said, remembering Zach's sardonic comments about not wanting to know how the Chinese got things from Osman, 'that stuff they got out of him by heavy methods would give us problems. He sort of implied he wasn't involved.'

'Osman's a British citizen, so for God's sake watch out.'

'I know. If anyone tells me anything I shouldn't know on account of the way it was extracted I'll take good care to un-know it.'

'It's just that –'

'– admissibility of evidence in court.' The younger man was beginning to rile him. 'I don't just read the papers, I've been working on this kind of thing for some time.'

'Tony, I'm not trying to teach my grand –'

'– I know, and I'm not your grandmother.'

Collinson was thumbing the transcript again, earnestly puzzled.

'There's some weird stuff in here, isn't there? That business about his great grandfather's execution, and this being pay-back time.'

'I know what you mean. On the other hand if it's the idea of historical revenge that motivates him it makes more sense than taking the world back to a seventh century Caliphate. But you're right, he's a strange customer. A new type. I prefer my terrorists more conventional. At least you know where you stand.'

Walking back to the hotel for dinner Collinson gave him a sight of a telegram from Thames House. Consultations with the CIA and FBI, it said, confirmed suspicions about Osman's training in Central Asia. It was consistent with his activities in Xinjiang, but could equally have included preparations for operations in Afghanistan or the UK. Assuming he was recaptured, and depending on what he had got out of him first time round, Tony was to follow up his first interview with more. Meantime he was to stick close to the Chinese, report any progress in the search and, provided his hosts didn't object, stay on as long as it took.

Fine by me, Tony thought.

'Will the American –'

'– Zach –'

'– will he be staying on too? If so and they get Osman back we'll get more stuff from the Russian and from him I assume. How do you find them by the way?'

'Zach's a smartarse. Sharp but none too subtle. Alyosha's what you would expect, only more so. Lugubrious, drinks like a whale, looks like one too. Between the two of them they'll give our man a good going over if they get the chance. I figured I'd be the good cop, in the hope of ending up with the most. Anything the others get will be a bonus.'

'If you need me to help out –'

'– I'll be fine.'

A certain eagerness in Collinson's manner suggested that he wouldn't mind getting in on the case. Over dinner in the hotel Tony was careful to mark out his turf. He may have been sent out here by accident but they were stuck with him now.

Almost as an afterthought he told him about the confrontation with the Uighurs, and the dead Chinese.

'Good God Tony! You might have been killed. Why didn't you tell us?'

''Because I wasn't, because it's not easy getting through to you, and because it won't happen again.'

'Just one thing', Collinson said at the end of the meal, looking embarrassed. 'There's a new squeeze on expenses. The Chinese invitation was for a week. They've extended it, but given that you'll stop being their guest at some point, you may have to think about –'

'– a cheaper hotel?'

'Perhaps.'

'Absolutely not! I'd rather stump up the difference. Old men like their comforts. It's not as if it's a fortune. Five-star, and less than £100 a suite. In Britain it'd be £400. And in between trying not to get shot or burned to death I think I've worked my passage. Keeping an eye, getting some feedback from Zach and Alyosha, striking up a relationship with Tang. He's stiff but unwinding a little. We get on well.'

Collinson closed his eyes, suggesting acquiescence.

It wasn't that top-class hotels were a novelty. He'd spent plenty of time in grander places than this – the Ritz, the Berkeley, the Connaught – though usually in the bar, watching. Staying in one as a guest was all the more agreeable after the kind of places the M15 money-men used to insist he squat in when he was on the road in the UK.

It didn't take long to get used to seeing your laundry disappear and return shop-new a few hours later, to be pampered by invisible staff, or to have taxis whistled up the moment you pointed your steps towards the doors. All this with no need to register anyone's comings and goings, or devise means with nervous hotel managers to tap into their clients' conversations.

Nor did he object to being surrounded at his restaurant table (by now he had his own) the moment he sat down by a trio of girls, one to advise on the menu, another to take his order, a third whose sole purpose seemed to be to butterfly around looking pretty. It was strange to find yourself staying in a high-class joint that was virtually incommunicado with the outside world, though that too had advantages. To be shut off from news from home – mostly about his daughter, and mostly bad – was no penance. Extraordinary how pleasant life could be when you blanked out your domestic obligations and lived in luxurious surroundings in exotic places at someone else's expense.

On the joys of being incommunicado, Collinson was to prove him wrong.

'Oh sorry, I nearly forgot.' The Embassy man reached into

a pocket. 'There's this. Arrived just as I was leaving.'

Tony took the letter. It was from his wife.

Darling, I know you've not been gone long, but they said the phones weren't working and there was a diplomatic bag I could put a letter in. I hope you're alright, it's terrible the things they've been showing on television. I must say the Chinese seem to be behaving pretty brutishly, it's six of one and half a dozen of the other so far as I can see. I still don't know why they sent you, it's not as if it's your part of the world. I don't suppose the accommodation is up to much out there either, and the food must be trying.

The only news from here is about Penny I'm afraid. The rehab people say she's progressing but if she's to make a go of it this time she'll need another few months. I'm a bit behind with the payments, and they've started making noises. And I'm afraid there could be a big bill for the boiler. I know you said just to patch it up, but they said it's an old model.

The way things are mounting up I think we're going to have to cash in that endowment. Is there somebody I can speak to at the bank, to get things moving? It's so difficult, you not being around, and not knowing when you're getting back. The way things are going I don't know whether I should go ahead and book our holiday in Cyprus. I was looking forward to it, a bit of sun will do my back good the doctor says.

Looking after little Suzy while Penny's away is a business. Of course it's lovely having her, she's a bright young thing, but such a chatterer! And the business of getting her to school, all that way to Camberwell. I know you said I should squat in Penny's flat, so as to be nearer, but I can't face it, I feel claustrophobic in basements. And the thought of living in that street full of…well you know what. You feel you're taking your life in your hands every time you go there. And the way they look at you, as if you've no right to be there, in your own country.

I'm sorry there's no more cheerful news to report. The weather's been good, so that's something, though we'll pay for it in August. You take care of yourself, and get back as soon as you can. And don't forget the stockings, and take some vitamin C. God knows what there is going round where you are, and the last thing we need at present is for you to go down with something.

Let me know if the phone comes back on so we can be in touch.

Lots of love,

Jean.

He slipped the letter in a pocket, feeling suddenly sour. Nothing like news from home to get your spirits down.

'Not alarming I hope?'

'My wife.'

'Any reply?'

'Not for now.'

'You want us to get someone in Thames House to phone her?'

'Good idea. Tell them to say I got the letter and I'm fine, and to leave everything till I get back. Make sure they don't tell her about my little adventure with the Uighurs, and tell her not to worry about whatever she hears on the news. And that I survived the flight without thrombosis.'

'I'll do that.'

A bit of chat about the latest economic disasters at home, of a kind that made the prospect of another few weeks in an obscure and tumultuous Central Asian town attractive, and they were done.

Collinson left next morning. From the hotel forecourt Tony watched as he climbed into his taxi, with his dishevelled suit and triple-locking briefcase containing a laptop full of stuff the Chinese already knew, or would be unsurprised to learn. A strange new type: the overgrown student as security man. The policemen really were getting younger.

14

Osman got back from Qinghai late in the evening to find the Turkman as well as Hamid waiting in the safe house. Slumping into a chair – the tensions of the trip had left him nervously exhausted – he faced the curtain.

'Glad you could make it this time,' he said tetchily when Hamid indicated his boss was there.

'I had a tail,' the Turkman explained, 'but I appear to have lost it. Maybe they're too busy hunting for you? You're sure you weren't followed? You checked the street before knocking?'

'Of course,' Osman rapped back, sensitive as always to intimations about his youth and experience.

'It's good you made it,' the voice soothed. 'You've been doing fine work. I think a tête-à-tête is called for. Give us an hour, Hamid, if you wouldn't mind?'

'A drink before you go,' Osman growled.

After setting up the whisky Hamid let himself out into the night.

'So tell me,' the Turkman resumed, 'how is our martyr in the making shaping up?'

Pushing back his whisky, Osman described his trip, at the same time filling out what he'd told Hamid about the Dunhuang meeting.

'How much did you have to tell him? Not too much I hope.'

'As much as necessary,' Osman shot back, 'like you said. If he's to recruit his martyrs there are things he has to know. For example, if we're using a truck he'll need a truck driver, won't he?'

'You sound tired, my friend, but don't worry. Just one more tourist trip.'

Osman suppressed a sigh:

'And where is it this time? Tibet?'

'No, the south, via Turfan. To his house.'

'Jesus.'

'It troubles you?'

'Absolutely not,' he said, too quickly. 'It's just that he lives near Lop Nor. A restricted zone, isn't it?'

'His house is just outside, in the middle of nowhere. One of the last places they'll be looking for you. They won't expect you to be travelling into the desert.'

'And the reason I'm going?'

'A few things need checking out on the spot.'

'And when do I go?'

'As soon as we can fix it with Kul. This retirement thing worries me. You say there's no terminal date, but what if they find a replacement in a week or two, and he's off the job?'

Then we're fucked. And don't think I can go down there looking for someone else, Osman forbore to say. The Uzbek would have to do that himself.

'No idea.'

They went through the arrangements for the trip: code-names, the emergency drill, new instructions for Kul.

'Amazing they need to be told all this stuff', Osman grumbled when they'd finished.

'The way it is. Folks like them, you have to hold their hand all the way to paradise.'

'Which reminds me. He asked about the target, but I dodged the question. Not difficult since I don't know myself. How about telling me, so I can make more sense? The base is huge, he said. What exactly are we intending to hit?'

'How about we keep things professional?' the voice said tersely. 'The place you know, the means you know – and for you that's enough. You're a courier, a contact man. The rest you leave to us.'

A wave of anger hit him. *Courier? Contact man?* He'd done what they'd asked, fought back his fears, risked his life, showed what he was made of, while this patronizing bastard sat there behind his curtain, sniping. With an effort he resisted a compulsion to rip it aside.

'Another thing,' the Turkman went on. 'I don't like depending on Kul for his choice of martyrs. How do we know he won't come up with a couple of crazies, the kind who are so high on religion they can't keep a code name in their heads or point their truck in the right direction when they get inside? You'll need to check them out.'

'You're sure a mere courier is up to that?'

A gust of laughter.

'OK, I take that back.'

Osman stared on silently, sourly, at the shape behind the curtain.

'Speaking of crazies,' the Turkman continued, 'I'm not happy about this half-dead Russian you told me about either. I'm not happy about *any* Russians. She lives in his house, you said, like it was normal, but I don't like the idea of some mad old granny snooping around. Maybe she's not crazy? Maybe she listens, takes things in, remembers, talks to people?'

'I told you, she's bedridden. In her nineties, comatose half the time. It's what Kul told me and we have to take his word. Why would he tell her anything? She's not Muslim, she's a Christian, Russian Orthodox. The guilty side of the family. It's one of the reasons Kul's doing it, I would guess, because he feels tainted. You have to understand the psychology. For him she's a living reproach.'

'Forget the amateur psychology. If he's serious he'd have got rid of her, pumped in more drugs or whatever. If they're living alone no one would ever know.'

'It's the Chinese he's got it in for, not Russians.'

'Not the point. You said that for a Muslim she's guilty blood. And mad old bats can do crazy things. And how can we be sure she's mad?'

'I told you, because Kul said so.'

'Hardly a model of sanity himself from the sound of it. Make sure you check her out. Tell Kul you need to see her.'

'OK. No need to get paranoid about someone's granny.'

He poured himself more whisky.

'That's quite a habit you've got,' the Turkman laughed. 'What's the calculation, if you don't mind me asking? That if you render Him a big enough service Allah will overlook the booze? I'll never get my head round that.' More laughter. 'Another thing, something I meant to ask. When they beat you up, was Tang there while they did it?'

'No. He asked his questions, got no answers, and cleared off before they started. I get the impression he's of a delicate disposition.'

'A squeamish intellectual.'

'Squeamish, yes.'

'Well he won't last long here. Talking of squeamishness, you didn't shoot him, did you?'

'Who?'

'Your guard. You told me you did, but I heard on the best authority you didn't. They handed you the gun and you didn't do it. They did.'

'I never said –'

'– easy now! I must have misunderstood. You seem a touchy fellow, Mr Osman, but as an older man may I give you a piece of advice? If you didn't kill him, you should have done. In this business you should never miss an opportunity to toughen up. You see what I'm saying?'

Their hour was up. Hamid returned at that moment, and Osman let him in.

'Just in time. The money, Hamid my friend.'

Fishing in his back pocket Hamid drew out an envelope. Opening it Osman took out a stack of pink-red bills. He flipped through them: 20,000 in yuan, some $3,000.

'A sweetener for our martyrs,' the voice explained. 'A down payment for their ticket to heaven.'

'And me? How about a little help for me?'

'You're not going.'

'Staying alive costs money. I'm running a bit short, all this travelling. I need topping up, just in case.'

'What case?'

'I don't know. If something goes wrong I may have to go somewhere in a hurry.'

'Be our guest. Hamid – another 10,000.'

Reaching into his pocket Hamid counted out the cash. Separating it into manageable wads Osman stuffed it into pockets.

'Well, good luck. Now, Hamid, if you'd be so kind…'

Two swift movements, the light went out, the key turned, and the Turkman was out of the door and into the street.

15

Days had passed and still no news from Tang. MI5 and the FBI had gone quiet too. Now things were off the boil Thames House and Pennsylvania Avenue appeared to have forgotten Urumqi's existence, together with that of their men in the field.

From time to time Zach and Tony wandered around the centre of the city, checking out the atmosphere, keeping an eye. Troops – in over-supply now – had cleared up the debris of looted and gutted stores, burned-out cars and shattered barricades. In Er Dao Qiao, the main commercial street, boarded-up shops had reopened and the fruit barrows and kebab stalls were back in business.

Yet nothing was as before. A pall of acrimony hung over the city, and there could be no easy return to what had previously passed for normality, as Hans and Uighurs passed each other with alert yet averted eyes. The street-vendors' cries seemed muted, as if to avoid the attentions of knots of police on corners, or files of armed men muscling a path through the streets in light black body armour, while auxiliaries in green camouflage outfits and red armbands hung around checkpoints. As in 2009, justice had been swift and in Uighur areas posters had gone up announcing executions. If hundreds hadn't escaped when the Public Security building was torched there would have been many more.

When the Grand Bazaar reopened they'd looked round a couple of times and been disappointed. Instead of the ancient, bustling souk of Tony's imagination it turned out to be a modern pastiche, no more than a decade old. A cavernous new building in Islamic style, it was packed with niche-like cubicles selling everything he didn't want or need: carpets, over-carved furniture, rolls of silk, phony-looking antiques, women's tights, fancy knives and ornamental daggers. Lots of knives and daggers.

Outside the Bazaar was a square, a fountain, a smart new mosque – and a Kentucky Fried Chicken. Another of those sanitised areas that were proliferating everywhere, deadening the oriental appearance of the city. Nearby a sign in Chinese, Uighur and English read: *Folk Tourism Spot*. The effect was of a Muslim stage-set erected by the authorities to keep the natives sweet.

Tiring of these excursions and marooned in their enforced leisure, Tony and Zach began looking for ways of escape. While they sat around waiting for Osman to be recaptured the fine weather was going to waste and a spot of tourism beckoned. Hanging about the hotel in the hope of something happening had been fine for a few days but was beginning to feel like hard work, and they deserved a break.

The closest of the old Silk Road towns to Urumqi was Turfan. When they told him they were planning a trip Alyosha offered to put his number two in charge and act as guide. Proud of the Landrover he'd recently acquired from a mining company, in addition to his official jeep, he insisted on driving them there himself and dispensing with his guard. 'I can look after myself, 'specially when no-one's gunning for me.'

Grapes, wine, melons and ancient ruins – Turfan sounded promising enough to justify the two-hour drive through what Alyosha assured them was a spectacularly unappealing landscape. He was right about that, Tony decided, contemplating the stony, moonlike flatness, a letdown from the dune-filled desert sands he had expected. What Alyosha had omitted to tell them was that modern-day Turfan itself had limited attractions.

Time and a frantically modernizing regime had obliterated

almost everything of interest, with virtually nothing to remind them of its history as an ancient watering hole and trading centre. The lush oasis Tony had pictured could have been one of the less appealing suburbs of Urumqi: a featureless place of 200,000 souls whose centre consisted of the usual glass and concrete structures strung out along extravagantly broad avenues. 'Gotta be able to get two tanks abreast each way', Alyosha explained.

An hour of touring mournful esplanades, markets with more stalls than customers for the packs of henna, dried grapes and crystal sugar, and a near-empty museum was enough: they fled the town to a more promising attraction beyond. Jiaohe was an entire city abandoned to the sands over a thousand years ago. Approaching it through fields and vine-yards clothed in midday sun Tony's spirits revived; climbing the winding steps to the plateau on which the dead city was built over two thousand years ago, they soared. For the first time since his arrival in the province he felt the breath of antiquity.

The city lay on an island at the confluence of two rivers, and its remains were an arresting sight. It was not like ruins in Europe: here the devastation was absolute. Remnants of build-ings at ground level remained, but the rest was gone. The impression that was left – of a headless city, veiled in sand – was sombre.

Their guide, a bearded Uighur in a black scullcap, so antique-looking he seemed to have stepped from the ruins, added to the sense of melancholy. Taking them through the town's history he relished enumerating the deaths, the murders and the battles, the conflicts rather than the interludes of peace, the decay rather than the reasons it had flourished. At the final site they inspected – a newly excavated pit that seemed no more than a vast hole in the sand – the lugubrious old fellow was in his element:

'The administration of the time was highly organised. They even had a home for orphans, and the wars and killings meant there were plenty of them. This pit was dug up only a few years ago. In it we discovered the bones of more than two hundred children, many of them babies. Murdered, all of them, one by one. We know it from the size and disposition of the skeletons, and the battered heads. And they were not just killed, but eviscerated. Such was the fury of those times. So when the entire city was razed by Genghis Khan in the thirteenth century, it was a kind of deliverance.'

'Amen', Zach muttered, looking up from the pit to stare across the levelled bleakness of the city. 'When ISIS gets its nukes this is pretty much what New York or London will look like too. And they won't have to finish our kids off one by one.'

'Genghis Khan a liberator', Alyosha took up, 'I love it. Reminds me of the old Cold War joke. Guy says "these are dangerous times, comrade, will there be a war?" No way, his friend replies, there won't be no war but there'll be such a fight for peace there won't be a stone left standing.'

They paid off the guide – he took his money with a bow, as if accepting alms – and started back along the circuitous path leading from the plateau to the entrance. It was hot, they were thirsty, the flattened city had left its mark on their mood, and for a while no one spoke. But nothing silenced Zach for long.

'Fucking house of horrors, the history of this place. Wherever you go it's massacres, torture, disembowelling, assassinations. And it isn't all ancient times. Listen to this.'

He flourished the guide book he'd been reading:

'"*Hami, the melon town. Exotic fruit etcetera.*" Gotta go there you think – then you read on. Chinese guy called Chang gets himself appointed to gather taxes. Screws the Muslims, goes easy on the Hans. Bit of a paedophile, takes up with an underage Muslim beauty – and away they go. A mass revolt, bride and bridegroom murdered in unspeakable fashion, decapitated bodies everywhere, so many there's no time for religious burials. Muslims, Tungans, Buddhists and Mongols tossed into a pit together.'

'Something to be said for headless people', Alyosha grunted. 'When they got no heads they got no religion.'

'And that wasn't a thousand years ago', Zach went on, a finger stabbing at his book, 'it was 1930. While guys round here were shovelling headless trunks into mass graves Herbert Hoover was president and we were dancing to Guy Lombardo. And look at this place now. All those billions the Chinese spent making it crappily modern, and fuck-all changes. Now they're gunning for each other again. In 2009 the Uighurs were stabbing Hans in the street with syringes infected with Aids, and the Chinese were putting pork in the drinking water. And now they're getting guns the body count will soar. Awesome!'

'Talking of horror stories', Tony came in, remembering his own reading, 'how about this? A German comes to Urumqi in 1916 and the first thing he sees is someone being executed in the street – slowly. He's tied into a sort of cage, with his head sticking out of a steel collar and his feet on a board.'

'So how did he die?' Alyosha asked, interested.

'They came back and lowered the board by an inch or two every day till finally his neck breaks.'

'How long it take?'

'Eight days. The thing is, nobody thought anything of it. There was a melon-seller right next to the man in his dying agonies, but nobody was bothered. Helped with custom, apparently. Then there was this Khan, didn't like people smoking. If he caught them he had their mouths slit to the ears, so they went around with this permanent grin.'

'Like so.' Zach stretched the corners of his mouth grotesquely. The others laughed, though not for the reason Zach supposed: the face he'd made was a mere extension of his usual expression.

'Then there were the guys who made a meal of their enemies', the American took up. 'Literally. Breasts of captured virgins a delicacy reserved for senior officers. Lower orders got the dugs of old hags. You have to admire them, these were inventive people, with a great line in victory feasts. They put boards over vanquished leaders then set the tables on top, so when they sat down to eat their enemies got crushed to death. Only reason they gave it up was they had to talk too loud to drown the screams.'

'That was the Mongols', Alyosha specified.

'Sure?'

'Totally.'

'If you say so', Zach conceded. 'On Mongols we defer to you. Which reminds me of Baron Ungern-Sternberg, another fucking sadist. Asian adventurer and specialist in death *in varying degrees*, as he called it.'

'A German', Alyosha said quickly.

'Never said otherwise, though he worked for the Russkis as I recall. What's your problem, Alyosha my friend? Think we're saying you're a bunch of savages?'

'Try it and I'll bite your head off.'

'Break your teeth if you do. I got a neck like a baboon's. Tough and stringy.'

And so it continued as they ambled along the path in the sun, the jokes barbed, the clowning mirthless. Tony fell behind, left them to it. Nothing ever stopped them. A few days back he'd come across them on a sofa in the bar late one evening, boozed up to the point where they'd collapsed into each other's arms, pretty much, but still sniping away.

*

Osman stared from the window as the coach to Turfan passed through the ragged edges of the city. At this point the cheap blocks thrown up in the last few years gave way to half-ruined remnants of mud-brick houses built around walled courtyards, where indigent figures shambled around the crooked streets, as if searching for a way out of destitution. Soon every trace of the area would be gone as the Hans swelled the city. Squalid as it looked, he decided, the Uighurs would have been better-off where they were; the kind of four or five storey flats they'd be shifted to resembled cantonments, more salubrious perhaps but also easier to police.

Later came the main route south, a broad new highway built through a desert of stones. Here and there camels grazed on a few sparse bushes or sprigs of grass, their silhouettes incongruous among newly erected wind farms. Pylons marched from one horizon to another, disfiguring the unlovely landscape further.

To escape the barren ugliness his eye settled on the Tian Shan range, white with snow and somehow promise, if only because it marked a limit to this wilderness. Instinctively his gaze avoided the uplands in the mid-distance. Crisscrossed with dusty roads hacked from some hillsides, it was here that the mines, quarries, oil and fracking explorations were located, excavations of every sort destined to make the province – or rather the Hans – rich.

When the railway track wove into view he watched for military trains. The two he spotted were headed for Urumqi: a little late in the day for Tang and his men, but from his personal viewpoint a good sign. The Uzbek's strategy was working to perfection, the guns creating the necessary diversion of forces south to north.

To get to where he needed Turfan was the only route and the coach the safest means of travel. Not that he could afford to relax: at the coach station there'd been a moment's alarm. Soldiers ringed the building, singling out young men for papers. Crossing the concourse under their eyes he'd walked not too fast – mustn't appear hurried – or too slow; the foot was still giving him hell, but a limping man stood out in a crowd. He'd rest it on the journey, and apply more of the balm Hamid had given him.

He bought his ticket, made his way towards the row of buses. His coach started late – a hold-up while they searched an ageing Uighur's luggage, then set a dog on him to sniff for explosives: it snarled and put its paws to his chest, terrifying the old fellow. Catching the Chinese dog-handler's eye, he sniggered. You had to play your part.

The first on board, he'd gone for a place at the back. It was a three-hour trip, a rear seat would mean a bumpier ride, though better to look at the backs of people's heads than for them to stare at his. Soon the coach's undulations on the near-empty road eased him towards sleep. It was when he was on the edge of consciousness that he felt someone's eyes on him. Jerking awake, he saw who it was: a heavily built man sitting behind the driver had stood up, moved into the aisle, and begun surveying the passengers.

Chinese. A plainclothes man by the look of him, and with no more than thirty people aboard he'd have ample time to check everyone out. He watched as he went to work, squeezing his bulk between the seats then standing with out-stretched hand and surly face next to a Uighur couple, brusquely demanding tickets and papers. Osman took out his Chinese newspaper, keeping an eye on the man's progress over the top of the page. The fellow was taking his time, less from thoroughness, it seemed, than from the slowness of his wits. Observing the dull face and ponderous manner, he felt better.

The paper had a giant headline: *Our Heroes Hunt Down the Criminals*. A picture showed a soldier, his expression a mixture of truculence and resolution, like a Mao era poster, herding a group of Uighurs into an army truck, their heads bowed in exaggerated submission, as if they too were posing for a pro-paganda film. Turning the page in disgust he glanced along the bus.

The fat man was still taking his time. Eight more rows to go. Then six, four, three. He felt suddenly twitchy. The man had been singling out Uighurs but now he'd stopped before a young Chinese woman, his hand outstretched wordlessly. After finishing with her the cop amused himself by giving a couple of Uighur lads a hard time – one had left his identity papers in his luggage.

When he was two rows from the rear Osman flipped to the front page of his paper, so the football headlines and photos faced the fellow. Reaching the back seat, he stopped and stood in silence, engrossed in the sporting news. And when he finally pulled down the top of the paper for a glimpse of the face behind, something in the eyes that looked up from beneath the cap – a haughtiness close to contempt – made him sway back a fraction.

Dui bu qi, the man grinned awkwardly, *ni kan bao ji*, (sorry, you're reading the paper). Then turned and headed back to the front of the bus.

*

Before driving back to Urumqi, Alyosha took them to see the only first-rate sight Turfan had to show. The Emin minaret was something: eighteenth century, 44 metres high, a tapering tower of reddish bricks, intricately patterned. The full delicacy of Islam, Tony thought, shielding his eyes as he gazed at its lace-like fabric. And for once, according to their guidebooks, it hadn't been a scene of brutal slaughter.

With the tourists scared away they were alone in the square next to the tower. The short round women with long bright dresses and sad eyes whose stalls lined the space – pots, brass, artfully antiqued scrolls, silk scarves, daggers – as always, plenty of those – were the more clamorous for their custom. To escape their badgering ('You look, old picture, very old, you look') the three men stood with their guide in the sun-carpeted middle. Alyosha moped about, his head uncovered in the heat, picking at a bunch of grapes he'd bought on the way in. The Russian was in a poor mood: the Landrover's engine had begun stuttering – Chinese petrol, he swore – and he was worried they wouldn't make it home.

Zach and Tony, in straw hats, were listening to the guide, a pretty young Uighur with long dark hair who had dispensed with a headscarf.

'I read Marco Polo passed this way', Zach threw into a gap in her presentation.

'No, not here', the girl said. 'We think it was in Loulan, further south, across the Gobi Desert. Its burial site is better than here. It has manuscripts, wooden documents, and a rug with a swastika design. Many were taken abroad by Sven Hedin, a famous Swedish explorer and punderer, but there are still many left.'

'Plunderer', Tony said quietly.

'Sorry, my English is no good.'

'It's very good', said Tony. The girl seemed pleasant and intelligent, with a good figure, though he was sorry about her teeth.

'Sounds like we should go there', Zach said. 'Folks at home will say you went all that way and you never walked in Marco Polo's footsteps?'

'In old times it was a military town, to guard the Silk Route. Today it is still a military area. It is close to Lop Nor.'

'Now that I've heard of. What goes on there?'

'It is where the Chinese have a base. At Malan. It isn't on the map' – she gave a nervous smile – 'but everyone knows it's there.'

'A military base?' Zach's entire face seemed to wink at Tony, 'in the desert? Now what would they need that for?'

Tony looked at him hard, as if to say *come on, she's a nice girl, don't do this to her.*

'They have nuclear testing.'

'You're kidding! The Chinese have nuclear weapons?' He turned to the others. 'Now what in hell's name would they do with those?'

Embarrassed, the girl looked down:

'I don't know. For Americans. For Japanese. For Russians maybe.'

Zach glanced across at Alyosha.

'I see about the Americans and the Japanese, but the Russians? What has China got to fear from Russia? They're old friends, aren't they? I mean Mao and Stalin and all that.'

'The Chinese say the Russians take their land. Long ago.'

'But they're pals now, aren't they? I mean Putin's a great fan of China I read. Spends half his time in Beijing signing deals with his buddy Xi Jinping. So on the land business why doesn't he just say sorry, it's something we grabbed in our bad old imperialist days, and give it back? I mean the Russians have got plenty.'

Alyosha looked studiously away. The guide looked puzzled.

'The lady is a guide', Tony put in, 'not a politician.'

'And a very pretty one. But you can't like having all this nuclear stuff around. Not good for your health, is it?'

'My father says it is bad. He says many Uighurs have become sick.'

'With radiation?'

'From testing bombs, they used to do that. My mother used to work near the base, as a cook, until she fell ill. But they do not live there any more, and I am not involved with politics.'

'We understand', Tony butted in. 'Give your mother our best wishes for her health.'

Bored with the game and bothered by the sun, Alyosha was moving away when Zach called after him:

'Hey, Alyosha, Lop Nor, you remember don't you? Isn't that the place you asked Nixon to let you take out when you had your border war with Mao. '69, wasn't it? And Nixon said no.'

'If you say so', Alyosha called back, unsmiling. 'We always do what the Americans tell us.'

'Nah, you should have gone ahead and done it, if only out of charity. Then there'd have been fewer Uighur babies with cancer.'

Giving him the middle finger, Alyosha turned and made for the shade.

'Oh Jesus', Zach grinned. 'Now I've upset him. So thin-skinned, these Russians.'

*

After picking up speed on the deserted highway Osman's bus

arrived on schedule. Two hours to kill before taking his train south. Rather than dawdle under the eyes of the police in the town centre he looked for somewhere to pass the time. At a newsstand (*Eternal Loyalty to Our Province!* the headline on the local paper proclaimed) he picked up a travel guide. It came down to two choices: the museum, or the Emin minaret. The museum was too close to the centre. At two kilometres from the town and a Muslim gem, the minaret looked ideal.

He hailed a taxi, told the Uighur driver where he was going. After looking him up and down the man named a price. Two kilometres – 100 yuan. The man must take him for an overseas Chinese... All to the good. After a show of indignation Osman accepted. The driver shot him a glance of triumph mixed with malice.

At the minaret he seemed the only visitor. Telling the taxi to wait – on no account must he miss his train – he walked to the ticket office. No one there. It was while he was waiting that his eyes fell on a group in the square, beyond the turnstiles: a nice-looking Uighur girl surrounded by three middle-aged Western men. They'd come to the end of their tour, it seemed, and the short one with a wide grin was tugging a wallet from his pocket. Selecting some notes he held them out to the girl.

Stepping forwards to take them she looked down at the man's hand, frowned and shook her head. An American tight-wad, Osman thought, short-changing a local girl. Next thing a shy smile lit her face, her hand went out and she seemed to be making appreciative noises as she took the bundled notes. A Yank flaunting his cash, he decided, before a young and impressionable native woman.

The oldest of the three men averted his eyes as if embarrassed, and when his face turned Osman's way he saw who it was: the M15 man, Tony Underwood.

'Don't you want ticket?' the girl who had appeared in the

office shouted after the retreating figure. 'You go in, you need ticket!'

Osman didn't reply, and jumped into the taxi.

'Too much to see', he explained to the impassive driver. 'I don't think I've got time before my train. Take me to the station.'

He chided himself for his stab of apprehension. Why worry? There was nothing sinister in the encounter; on the contrary, it was an excellent sign. Underwood and his friends must have given up hope of his recapture and gone off on a tourist jaunt. How else would the M15 autodidact use his time than by sucking up a bit of Eastern culture to set alongside his quotations from Yeats and Montaigne?

Arriving at the station early he bought his ticket, then discovered that his train was running late. And the police were busy. Concentrating on Uighur-looking passengers leaving for Urumqi, they were stopping one in three to show their papers, as if working to a quota. For everyone else they confined themselves to lingering, insolent stares.

He went to the newsstand, the waiting room, a café, checked again on the train. Twenty-five minutes late now. Beginning to feel exposed, he found a toilet and stood for fifteen minutes in a filthy cubicle. Hearing a train pull in he was about to come out when an American voice rang out:

'Of all the fucking luck! Landrovers! Supposed to be the best of British! Don't care for the climate I suppose. Alyosha'll have to stay till they fix it. Rather him than me. Dump of a town... Ugly women too, though that guide had something. See her face when I paid her off? Like it was Muslim Christmas.'

'I did', an English voice answered.

Then the American again:

'Can't even guarantee a seat, they said. Trains all to hell. Troop movements I suppose, still pouring 'em in. Bit late in the day I'd have thought.'

'Uh-huh.'

The pissing sound continued – the troughs were metal – then a grunt.

'Looks like they don't go in for basins. Ritual ablutions, yes, taps and towels in the toilets, never.'

Osman checked his watch.

The throb of a diesel engine invaded the toilets as the door opened and the men went out. Leaving his cubicle a minute later he bolted into the station and, careless of his foot, dashed for the platform of the departing train. The three-minute sprint was torture.

16

Back from his Beijing trip Captain Tang left Tony a message asking if he'd call on him at six the next evening. A girl at reception wrote out the address in Chinese. Tony showed it to his taxi driver, an elderly Uighur whose gaily embroidered *doppa* contrasted with a dour, resentful face. His response to the Han script was a resolutely shaken head. After asking another driver's help he took off like a rocket along one of the city's characterless avenues, enlivened only by florid adverts in the evening.

'Man-mande!' Tony called from the back when the cab hit seventy. *Man-mande!* – Take it easy! – was one of the three most useful Chinese phrases, Alyosha had assured him. The others were *mei banfa* (too bad) and *tamade* (fuck you). Three words, the Russian assured him, that summed up life in this tense, nervy city.

His shout did nothing to slow the driver, busy at that moment overtaking a truck on the inside lane. It was crowded with PAP, as sullen-faced under their helmets and goggles as the cabbie himself. Police, soldiers and civilians, Chinese or Uighurs – everyone in this place seemed angry.

With the driver's racing speed and the thin traffic he arrived early. He didn't offer him a tip, not in protest at his crazy driving but because in Xinjiang it wasn't done, and would have been taken as an insult. Even tips made them angry. With half an hour to kill he ambled along the quiet street, looking up at the smart new twelve-storey sandstone blocks. Outside the Captain's building there was a pill-box, and the eyes of an armed guard followed him as he passed. A temporary Public Security HQ, perhaps, though it didn't look like offices – it looked like an apartment block.

He did a circuit of the area, the Belgravia of Urumqi it appeared. When he came back the guard let him in grudgingly, after peering at his passport for several minutes (not surprising – he had it open at a Chinese visa rather than the photo on the back page), and conversing with an entryphone even longer.

Inside the spacious hall the first sound he heard was a child crying from beyond a ground-floor door. These were apartments all right, a softly carpeted mansion block complete with an American-made lift that whooshed him silently to the eleventh floor. He thought about Tang's private life as he rode. Did he have a wife, children? Somehow he didn't associate him with domesticity.

An assistant (or maybe servant – his silence and deferential manner suggested the latter) waiting outside the lift showed him into Tang's apartment. The drawing room where the servant left him was traditionally furnished – bird and flower scrolls on the walls, heavy rosewood pieces – though with modern touches: a fancy glass table, stylish lamps, a vast television. Was this his new workplace, or an official residence? Either way the Chinese security people took good care of themselves.

Through an open door into a study he could see Tang at his desk, writing. Hearing him arrive the Captain came to meet him with an expression of something more, Tony fancied, than official courtesy: the fingers that grasped his arm as they shook hands suggested he was genuinely glad to see him. The absence of Zach and Alyosha was reassuring too; he'd feared that the meeting might turn out to be a final collective briefing, followed by a flowery speech thanking them for their visit and telling them their presence in Xinjiang was no longer required.

'A handsome room', he said. 'Your new office?'

'My office is in a hotel we have taken over. But there is nothing there. The fire liberated me from my papers. So I thought, better to have a drink at home.'

The servant came in and set out two glasses and a bottle on the glass table. *Medium amontillado,* Tony read on the label.

'I hear the English like sherry. My daughter knows about wine, she gave me some to try. It is a little like rice wine, so I understand why the English like it.'

No Englishman he knew, Tony thought, as Tang went ahead and poured, and they drank. Or in Tony's case, sipped gingerly. He had a particular aversion to sherry.

To his relief – it meant he could treat himself to a cigarillo – Tang lit up. He smoked in a way he had noticed a number of Chinese doing: nervily, with frequent drags, a foot tapping, as if the nicotine, instead of soothing them, fired them up.

'You've been away?'

'I have been to Beijing to see my boss. He is not happy. I don't have to tell you why.'

Tony signified that he didn't.

'He also has some, how do you say, old-fashioned thinking about foreigners.'

Ah, thought Tony. So it *was* a farewell drink.

'I explained the importance of our cooperation and he agreed we should invite you to stay on until we recapture Osman. I hope you are able to accept our hospitality for some time longer. I am sending a message to your American colleague. Colonel Benediktov, as you know, is stationed here.'

'I'm most grateful, Captain. I'm sure I'll be authorised to stay on.'

He asked about the aftermath of the revolt. 242 Uighurs dead and 365 Hans, Tang said, police and troops included. 'Like last time, you see, Mr Underwood, we Chinese have suffered most.' And as in 2009 there'd been atrocities. 'The details

I will spare you because they are – well, atrocious. Again it is like last time, only worse.'

Then there were his prisoners. Over two hundred had escaped when the building had gone up and to date less than a third had been recaptured. With the number of troops flooding into the capital he was confident the rest would keep their heads down. Meanwhile new leads were being followed, new suspects rounded up.

'The police are debriefing them', the Captain added.

Debriefing? A euphemism – or a lapse of English? Either way God help the poor devils.

'I apologise once again for your, ah, troubles on the way to your hotel. The killers of our driver and his guard – we have found them. It is a sad case. The young men were new recruits, only a few months in their work. The driver's mother, I know her, she works for me, in my office. A fine woman, so I am pleased we captured them. She is pleased also.'

'You know that teacher saved our lives, don't you? Me and Zach?'

'I know. It was not him, it was an accomplice in his group who shot them. The man was a worker from the Uighur meat market. A butcher in every sense.'

'You want us to testify? I mean I'd be happy to write something for the trial, so we can confirm it was him and not the teacher.'

'That will not be necessary. The teacher, he saved you and Mr Boorstin, but not the Chinese. It is a serious crime. The bodies were – what is the word? Parts cut off…'

'Mutilated.'

'Yes, mutilated, badly. The mother, we have not told her.'

'So what will happen to the teacher?'

'He was the organiser of the group. A group with arms. And the weapon that was used in these murders, we have established, was from Osman, one of his earlier trips. Under Chinese law – not just Chinese but the laws of other countries I believe – in such cases there is joint responsibility.'

'So the teacher –'

'– he has been executed too.'

Tony took a shot of sherry. It tasted sickly in his mouth.

'And Osman? How are things going?'

'Nothing to report', Tang said curtly.

'Did you get anything out of his friend? The driver who brought the truck in with him?'

Tang looked down at his drink.

'He was a Kirghiz and a fanatic. They tell me he was stubborn. So no', he looked away, 'they got nothing.'

The past tense and the Captain's unease told their story. The Kirghiz driver, the teacher – what chance would Osman have if they got him?

'There's nothing in the Chinese or Uighur media about Osman's escape, my Russian colleague tells me. Is that deliberate?'

'Personally I would have preferred to publish something. We could have released a photo, so the public would be vigilant, and if we had put something in the paper when we caught him the people he works with would know we had him. They would have spread the word in a hurry, to warn each other, and' – he raised his eyes skywards – 'we could have picked something up. But I was overruled. My seniors, they are against publicity, always…'

'And why's that?'

'Afraid for China's image.' The Captain pursed his lips. 'If the public heard we had captured foreigners distributing weapons they would be afraid. And if we said we had lost him we would appear incompetent. So we obeyed orders. We said nothing when he was captured and nothing when he escaped.'

He gave a sour smile. 'It is logical.'

He refilled his glass – his sherry was subsiding at treble the rate of Tony's – and drank in small gulps.

'I collect DVDs', he announced suddenly. 'Films mostly. You like them?'

'I have some at home, yes.'

'So I will show you my collection.'

He took him to his study and there they were, hundreds of them, meticulously arranged on shelves. Tony had a quarter the number. For him it was crime and comedy, for Tang old films by the dozen, American mostly. Inspecting them out of politeness, row by row, he alighted on an entire shelf of Doris Day. Tang must have registered his surprise.

'Such a pure, happy face.' He took one out and gazed at a picture of her like a man in love. In an odd way it made sense. For him the idealised photo must be a symbol of innocence, an antidote to what he must have seen in his career.

'I see you're a Tom Jones fan too.'

Five CDs. The cheery Welshman seemed another favourite.

'It is my daughter who gave me these. At first I thought, very loud, very noisy! But now I like him. It is good to have things that fathers and children can like together.'

Leaving the DVDs his eyes ranged over the books in English. One was Jung Chang's *Wild Swans*. He pointed to it.

'A great story.'

'A true story', Tang said, sternly. 'To my family, things like that happened in the Cultural Revolution. We Chinese have a lot of stories to tell. Unfortunately many of them sound the same, the same because it was Mao Zedong who wrote them all. But now we have his story too.'

Removing some books he reached into the back of the shelf. Concealed behind *Wild Swans* was a battered-looking Chinese volume.

'Here is one even better. Her biography of the Chairman.'

This one too Tony knew: he'd bought a copy in London and brought it with him. He was three quarters through, getting towards the endgame, where Mao was refusing to allow Zhou Enlai an operation for cancer to ensure his Prime Minister died before him.

'I heard it was banned in China', he said.

'Mr Underwood, many things are banned, but today Chinese people do not live in a cage. They travel, they bring things back, and many people can read a single copy of a book. I am aware of my country's past mistakes', he went on, suddenly earnest. 'Officially we say the Chairman was seventy percent right and thirty percent wrong. Personally, I would invert that. Seventy percent wrong is a better figure. Better because seventy million Chinese died under him.' He looked down again, gravely, at the book. 'How many people are there in Britain?'

'Sixty million, I suppose.'

'Imagine they had all died. From hunger, hard labour, purges, beatings, torture… I see you are surprised to hear me say this, a Chinese intelligence officer. You are new to my country, and I want you to know that whatever foreigners believe we Chinese are not insects, or machines. We are individuals, with our own thoughts. The Chinese people are not as – how do you say? – compliant as they were. Even people in my work.' He gave a sardonic smile. 'And for my work I need to read books like this to know what our dissidents are reading. Jung Chang I like especially. She writes with a strong voice. Her own voice, that is strong too.'

'You've met her?'

'I have heard her speak. She is very intelligent, very persuasive.'

'I thought she lived in London.'

'It was before she left that I heard her. She addressed a meeting.'

'You were invited?'

'Not invited exactly.' The Captain smiled. 'It was a private meeting. But I heard.'

'I see. You're lucky. The only recordings I've got to hear these last few years are by Islamist crazies.'

'We have those too, but for you it will soon be over. You are retiring, no?'

'That's the plan.'

'You don't sound happy. If somebody said I must retire I would be happy. With a small pension, naturally.'

'But you're young.'

'In our work we age quickly. Our hearts' – he tapped his chest – 'wear out. So we become heartless.'

Pleased with his English pun his face, red from the sherry, reddened further.

Back in the drawing room he poured more, and drank quickly.

'You like Urumqi, Mr Underwood?'

'I haven't seen too much.'

'I will tell you. You are lucky not to live here, even when there are no riots. The Chinese settlers, they can be difficult people. People without culture, looking for easy money. And the Uighurs…' He winced, as if at his own thoughts. 'Of course they have problems, problems from history… But their culture, their religion…' He looked at him as if testing him out before going on. 'I am not an admirer. I understand them but I do not admire them. You know what I am saying, Mr Underwood?'

Tony half-nodded; he would have preferred not to know what the Chinese was saying.

'They have grievances, they remember the past, they are

bitter. It is all they remember. It is what they live for. And we Chinese, we give them more reasons for bitterness. So they hate us.'

Again Tony nodded, and reached for his glass. He felt a need for whisky, something strong and sour. Tang was confiding in him in a way that made him uneasy. Instead of shrinking the gap between them – their backgrounds, their experience, their situations – it seemed to grow as the Chinese spoke. By now he liked the man, and he was afraid for him.

It was half past seven and he felt an urge to go.

'I'm sure it will work out', he said with a smile whose vacuity he could feel himself. 'And when it's over you'll have a big office in Beijing.'

'You believe I aspire to a bigger office? More responsibility, harsher decisions?' He paused, as if questioning himself. 'And how will I get away from Xinjiang? When will our problem here be over? People say it is something left over from history, but the passions between the Han and the Uighurs go deeper than politics, deeper than religion. It is' – he tapped an arm – 'in the bone.

'Even in my daughter I see it. She says the Muslims are backward, dirty, ugly, superstitious people. She mustn't talk like that, I tell her. She says why shouldn't she, all her friends think that, and it's true, so why not say it? Why don't they all go to Kirghizstan, she says, with their own people, and leave Xinjiang to its rightful owners? It has always been ours, she says, never theirs. Excuse me', Tang smiled, 'but her history is not good... And I say to her don't say that, it is not appropriate, it doesn't help. We need greater understanding.'

Oh dear, Tony thought, he's going to revert to script. But the Captain didn't.

'We give them mosques, though I don't like seeing people beat their heads on the floor saying we humans are nothing. If you are nothing, nothing is worthwhile – except to explode yourself. If you are nothing, then nobody else is anything either, so you can do what you want to them. Call them infidel pigs, kill them like pigs.

'It is not just ISIS and Al Qaeda. Mao Zedong too, he thought our lives were nothing. We had to bow our heads to the floor, worship him like a prophet. That is another kind of religion, but all these religions that say we are nothing are wrong. We are something, Tony, human beings are something.'

'Absolutely', Tony said, looking glazed.

'To help my daughter understand these matters I want her to study. At present she is rather interested in enjoying herself. Nothing else.'

'It happens', Tony sighed. 'Though if she's abroad the risks of her enjoying herself too much –'

'– I know, I know. This is the problem China faces. Either we close the doors to keep out the world. Or we open them wide and join it. But if you close the doors the world comes in the windows. If we join it we get good things and bad. I personally believe we must take the risk.'

'Even with your daughter?'

'That is correct.'

'So where were you thinking?'

'Maybe Britain. There are good universities in Britain.'

So Tony had heard. He'd never been to one, though his daughter had. Bristol, sociology. It lasted less than a year and cost him £14,000. After ten months she'd met someone, got into drugs and dropped out. And university was just the beginning. Rehab, mortgage payments, a fatherless child – the heartache and the costs had mounted ever since.

'And expensive, Captain, very expensive. I had a daughter at university.'

'Yes, too expensive. But I read there can be scholarship, for

Chinese people. To help us understand each other better.'

'I would hope so, I would certainly hope so.'

He was talking like a diplomat now, Tony told himself. How tedious, he thought, to be a diplomat.

'And your wife, Captain. She agrees?'

'My wife did not want to come to Xinjiang.' A non-sequitur that put an end to Tony's fishing. 'Maybe I visit England, to see universities. Or maybe I am invited, for exchange visit. Mutually beneficial. You will make enquiry?'

'I will certainly see when I get home. It would be good if you and your daughter could come over. Does she live with you here?'

'No, not here. She has her flat, a small place, she wanted to live alone. She too met someone, a Frenchman, working in oil. She doesn't think I am aware but we know things we fathers, don't we? Her French boyfriend was a bad influence, his English was not good I heard. Now he has gone she wants to go abroad. But not to study.'

'So what does she want?'

'She wants to become a model.'

'She models? Here?'

'No, in Xinjiang there are no opportunities. For the moment she is working in a hotel. A good one', he added quickly, 'a new hotel.'

'Ah, which one is that?'

'Your hotel, she is in your hotel.'

'Really? I must look out for her. Does she look like you?'

'She is taller, very tall. If you see her you can say you know me. Maybe you could talk to her, persuade her to go to British university?'

'I'll try, certainly, though it's difficult. Young girls nowa-days...' he felt himself waffling, 'at least you have a tradition of respect for elders.'

'Today it is Western song stars they respect. Not their parents.' Tang's smiles could be regretful, but this was the most melancholy he'd seen to date.

'Well I'm sorry if it's our influence.'

'It would have happened anyway. Before there was no freedom, now too much. So young men and women, they go too far. Especially women. They are too, ah, too strong in the mind.'

'Strong-minded.'

'Yes, that is it. Strong-minded but with weak wills. They are strong with everyone except themselves. Not just clothes and money, they get drugs, here in China they get them, in Xinjiang as well. Too many frontiers. And there is sex. Twenty years ago they talk about it, laugh about it, now they do it. Drugs and sex, yes.'

'Well I'm sure your daughter — what is her name by the way?'

'She is called Ling-Ling. It means silk, a kind of silk.'

It took a moment to register: the big eyes, the exquisite legs on the bar counter. Model material alright.

'Does she work at the bar?'

'Yes.'

'Then I've seen her, of course I have. She's a good-looking woman, and her English seems excellent.'

'But I want her not just to speak, to be good-looking, but to study. To have degree, not be model. Your daughter, Mr Underwood, she studies?'

'She's older than yours.'

'And married?'

'In a sense she was.'

'She has children?'

'One. With a man she met at University.' There was nothing more to say, not least because Tony had never met him.

'Excuse me, but you are not happy about your daughter, I can tell, because I am not happy about mine. So I will ask for your help. Talk to her about a Western education, as if she were your daughter too.' The Captain gave a wan grin. 'It is not just ISIS and Al Qaeda we have in common.'

17

His foot was on a chair, his shoe by his side while Kul massaged ointment into the swelling, and applied cream to his heel: the outsize trainer had given him a vast blister. Osman watched him at work. Graying, well-ordered hair, beardless, nondescript Western clothes – nothing about the man tending him suggested a jihadi, with no hint as to what lay behind the beatific face. For the moment he was all solicitude. The man who would soon be dead by his own hand and take God knows how many with him had a gentle touch, would have made a good nurse.

The room was stifling and for a few moments his eyes closed. On the train from Turfan he'd slept an hour or two, enough to make him wake up groggy. Getting here had been a business. Little more than a dozen kilometres outside the exclusion zone surrounding Base Twenty-One, the small town was remote and hard to access, with a long bus ride after the train. The travelling was wearing him down; he'd be relieved when it was over. Just the journey back now, and that would be it.

Meanwhile a drink was what he needed, but no hope of that in this dismal hole. The small, square structure behind the town's main road had a Puritan simplicity: adobe walls, few windows, little furniture, a table with bowls of dried fruit and nuts, the single luxury a tapestry on a wall depicting trees and flowers. The only thing that distinguished it from others in the street was a rickety-looking extension that raised it above its single-storey neighbours. In Kashgar the Chinese were tearing down whole areas like this, erasing their identity, the Uighurs complained. In the abstract Osman sympathised, though no one would miss this place.

It was a bad feeling and he'd done his best to suppress it, yet his meetings with Kul had become painful to him. The way he'd drawn him to himself when he'd arrived, like a brother, his odour of sanctity and that strange, primal staleness – the truth was that almost everything about the man was distasteful to him. The fact that he *was* his brother – a fellow Tungan, a man of faith and a martyr in the making – made things worse.

The thought of his half-crazed grandmother upstairs didn't help. She lived in the extension, he assumed, though the idea that a ninety-year-old White Russian was up there seemed suddenly implausible. Why had he taken Kul at his word about her? What if she was a part of the story of his Muslim ancestry, and the story was a mirage? What if there was no one upstairs at all?

When Kul finished his foot, Osman put the trainer back on and looked around:

'So your grandmother shares the house with you.'

'Yes. She has her room upstairs.'

'I shall need to see her.'

'That will not be necessary.'

'Oh but it is, for me it is.'

'For what reason?'

'Security. A technical requirement. To see whoever's in the house.'

'She is asleep.'

'I won't wake her.'

'But she has no idea you are here. A stranger might frighten her.'

'Not if she's asleep. And if she's not in her right mind what harm can come from meeting her?'

'She could develop nonsensical ideas about why you are here.'

Shyness? Modesty? Disgust at having an infidel for a grand-mother? The more Kul resisted the harder it was to fathom the roots of his obstinacy. Assuming of course there was anyone there.

'Sorry, those are my instructions. Nothing can be taken forward till I've seen her. Does she have a mobile?'

'Of course not.'

'Does she see anyone? Anyone at all? You mentioned a cleaner.'

'Yes, the cleaner feeds and washes her.'

'How old is she?'

'Seventeen.'

'Nationality?'

'Uighur, and a Muslim. My grandmother talks to her in Chinese. If you see her she may say something to the girl.'

'I'll take the risk', Osman said, and stood up.

Kul bowed his head and held out a hand, sorrowfully.

'This way.'

He led him to the narrow stair. At the top the ceiling was so low he was obliged to stoop. Kul opened a door and stood back, looking at him silently as he passed as if to say, you asked for this.

Osman took a step into the room, and stopped. It wasn't the stench that took him aback, so much as the violence of the perfume that overlay it: a scented spray he guessed, roses it seemed. He looked towards the bed. There was someone there alright, but the curtains of the single window were half-drawn, the room in shadows, and it took a moment to make her out.

The figure was propped against a pillow, her head to one side, her stark white hair falling raggedly down her face, in a caricature of ringlets. The neck of her nightdress was loose, its ribbon dangling, as though she'd begun to tie it then given up and fallen asleep. If she'd been dead, it occurred to him as he gazed, she would have looked no different.

Yet the old woman was awake, the eyes fixed on him troublingly alert.

Without moving, she spoke:

'Nakonyetz! Nakonyetz vy prishli!' – so finally you've come!

He was about to murmur something in reply, but stopped: Kul's waving finger signalled that silence was the best response. Now the old woman was trying to move, twisting and groaning, a frail white arm fishing beneath her bedcovers. Locating something there she pulled it out: a small Russian icon, six inches square, its gilt frame chipped and crooked. Holding it to her face and closing her eyes in rapture for a long moment she kissed it.

'*On mne nye razreshayet! A vy, svyashchennik, skazhitye yemu, on dolzhen razreshat!* – He doesn't allow me! But you're a priest, you tell him he must!

Agitating the icon feebly, her eyes wide now and mocking, she went on in Russian:

'He's afraid of it, afraid of the true path! Never mind what he tells you, he's Orthodox, a Christian I'm telling you! Of course his grandfather was Muslim – a great man the Lord be with him! But look at him in his Western clothes, what kind of Muslim is he? He's pretending, just pretending!'

'*Pozhaluista, spokoityes! Niet problemy*', Osman said before Kul could stop him: please be calm, there's no problem.

'Of course not!' The woman gave a withered smile. 'Now that you're here I can die!' She patted the bed. 'Come and sit here and say it, say my absolution!' In a high, tremulous voice she began chanting: *May Our Lord and God, Jesus Christ, through the grace and bounties of His love towards mankind, forgive you, my Child, all your transgressions.* Come on, what are you waiting for? Say it! Say it so I can die!'

Without a word Kul took his arm, led him from the reeking

room and closed the door. They went downstairs.

'Nearly twenty years like that', he said, smiling. 'It is what happens to infidels late in life. I have studied this, I have noticed. It is as I said: her religion has made her mad.'

'So what will happen when you're...not here. Would you like some cash so the girl can go on taking care of her?'

Kul shook his head, vigorously.

'Money will not help. And they will take it, afterwards the police will take it. Why do you want to give money to infidel police?'

'And why do you want to leave her here? What if they, you know, pressure her, make her talk?'

'They'll get a lot of idiocy, won't they? She will say what she said to you. That an Orthodox priest came to say her absolution. Is this something that should trouble us?'

Troubled already, Osman persisted.

'What if she's only intermittently crazy? What if she's picked something up? Or remembers my visit, and describes me?'

'I told you it was better for you not to see her.' Kul considered. 'Perhaps she should die before? Maybe that is what you prefer?'

His face showed no emotion. It was a question, a neutral enquiry.

'That's not what I'm saying.'

Osman was angry with himself. It was stupid to have seen her.

'It is easy, she takes medicines. Every day she must take them. I can forget...'

'I've told you, I'm not asking you to kill her.'

'As you wish.'

'I have some points I'd like to run through, and some questions.'

They sat at the table. The martyrs, the truck, the passes Kul would arrange to get into the complex – one by one they went through them. It was only days since he'd seen him, yet as he answered his questions Kul seemed to have aged, his head inclining to one side, his voice tailing away mid-sentence. He seemed weary, exuded a sense of detachment. Watching him Osman felt his irritation returning: if the man's mind was on paradise already he was a little premature. There were things to be done.

Yet it seemed that Kul had everything in hand. The martyrs, he explained, he had found without difficulty, from within his circle.

'You managed that pretty quickly,' Osman said, frowning. 'You sure you didn't take any risks?'

'I approached only two, and both agreed. They have talked of doing something before. I was convinced they would accept.'

'Tell me about them. You have photos?'

He smiled: 'I knew you would ask, so I took them.'

Going into a back room he returned with snapshots of the men. The older one – forty he said – was a driver and mechanic. He wasn't new to the area, Kul assured him, he worked at a garage on the fringes of the base, so his face was known.

Osman studied the photo. Sensitive to mixed blood, he put him down as a Chinese-looking half-caste; his eyes sloped like a Han but he had more defined features. Uighur, Kirghiz, Uzbek, Mongol – the other half could have been anything. As for his expression, there was nothing striking, except something dead in the eyes.

'He looks sort of…blank. But determined.'

'There is a reason. He has a son who was damaged at birth, by radiation. His brain. An only child. He is grown up now, but an idiot. He won't live long. So yes, his father is determined.'

The younger one, more Uighur-looking, was a builder. Square-faced and heavy-browed, a lugubrious-looking type. He lingered over his picture.

'I know what you are thinking – that he appears a little simple. It's true, he is not bright, but together they make a good pair. One has strength, the other is intelligent, so there is no conflict about who is leader. And both of them are true men of faith. I have known them many years, we pray together.'

Osman stared on at the photos.

'Perhaps you would like to meet them? I have told them to stand by, in case you wanted, they can be here in minutes.'

'No need.'

He spoke quickly, without thinking. He'd promised to check them out personally, though now that it came to it, it seemed risky. What if Kul had made a bad choice? What if one of them was caught, and told them about his visit? His fear for himself was real, yet there was another reason: the thought of meeting them face to face filled him with revulsion. The older man especially, with the idiot child and those death-desiring eyes, a death he was helping to organise... What would he say to him?

'The photos are enough. We don't want a whole crowd at your house, people might notice. You say they're reliable, I'll take your word.'

'As you wish.'

The mechanic had been to the Russian showroom and tried out a *Ural* truck, Kul explained.

'He says it is magnificent. Like a tank, even the smaller one he drove, even without the reinforcement. It will get into the secure zone without difficulty, he says.'

'And what do they keep there?'

Kul shrugged.

'Research facilities, offices.'

'So no testing?'

'I told you, in 1996 they stopped.'

'So what happens now?'

'In addition to the research facilities there is a storage depot. A big one.'

'Storing?'

'That I cannot say. What is there is secret, but there are rumours…'

'Saying?'

'That there may be warheads.'

Warheads? No one had said anything about warheads. Was this why Salih and the Turkman refused to tell him about the target?

'Are they' – he hesitated, it seemed a stupid question – 'dangerous?'

Kul rocked his head, his smile serene as ever.

'Only a rumour. In this part of the world always there are rumours, because it is so secret. Even a rumour that now the testing has stopped, soon they may close the base down and turn it into a tourist centre. Tourists, in a place that has caused so much death and sickness!'

'I'm asking what goes on there now.'

'From my job I know about some deliveries to Malan, technical things. But no, not the storage. What they store there is delivered by special troops, with a special entrance, so I never see. People say there are warheads that they will soon begin to transfer to more secure places. To Qinling mountains, near Xian. You know Xian, where they found the terracotta warriors? Now there will be new warriors buried there: missiles, warheads, deep underground, inside the mountains, protected by granite. Base Twenty-Two it is called.'

'Meanwhile they could still be here?'

'The warheads?' He shrugged. 'Maybe. That is why there are

rumours they may be moved. Maybe they are afraid they are not safe here.'

A sound like giggling escaped him, and he found it hard to stop. Osman frowned.

'So we don't really know what's there. And if they're hit... There could be explosions, fall-out. Couldn't there?'

'I am not a scientist, professor. I heard they store things separately, for safety, but I don't know.' Again Kul shrugged, his smile verging on a grin. 'Maybe *our* explosion will bring the two parts together!'

More giggling.

Osman looked back at him sternly.

'So there could be radiation.'

'People in Xinjiang, they have suffered contamination already, I have told you. They may suffer more but then it will be gone, destroyed forever. And they will not dare build Base Twenty-One again. Not here, not in Muslim Xinjiang, no, never.' He stopped and gazed at him, his eyes dreamy: 'Everything will go in the explosion! It will be magnificent – beautiful! The new Loulan Beauty!'

Pleased with his phrase, for the first time since they'd met he laughed.

Osman was silent.

'The Loulan Beauty, you know of it? A mummy of a woman in Urumqi, in the museum. They found her in Loulan, not far from here. The Loulan Beauty is famous, so well-preserved, with her good looks and her hair. The most beautiful mummy in the world.'

'Of course I know.'

'But have you seen her?'

'I'm not here as a tourist.'

'I understand, but one day you must see her. She is a great mystery, but I have studied this question, because the truth about the Uighurs lies in the answer. The first mystery is, how old is she? It was in 1981 that they found her. At first they thought 6,000 years, but now they say 3,000 only. Such a big margin! Why are they so unsure?' His smile hardened. 'It is because of the Hans, and their atmospheric testing.'

Osman failed to disguise his incredulity.

'You think that is strange? But it is true. Loulan was like Pompeii. After a thousand years, in the seventh century it disappeared, in a giant sandstorm. It was a center for trading silk, tea, fruit and jewels, so today they are always finding things. How can they know how old they are? By radiocarbon dating. Now they have to think again, because these pots, this jade, these relics and old bones, sometimes they lie only a metre or two beneath the surface. Which means they could have been contaminated by nuclear tests. Even Chinese scientists admit it. So for the mummies they say 6,000 years one day, then 3,000 the next.

'The second mystery is her brown hair and her nose – a nose more like yours, like mine, not too Chinese, a little perhaps but not very. So she is not a Han. And if she is only 3,000 years old she could be Uighur. It wasn't just her, a number of the mummies they found in the same area were brown-haired too, sometimes a little red. Now you see them everywhere, you have noticed?'

'So what are you saying?'

'I am saying that today the Loulan Beauty would be a Muslim, a servant of Allah, her lovely face veiled from the corrupt desires of men!'

His eyes were wide, triumphant.

'You see why it matters, professor? Because it proves what we always knew: that Xinjiang is not Chinese, it is ours! And if the Jews could be given back their homeland after two thousand years, why not us? But the Hans tried to destroy the evidence, contaminating everything. It is not just the present generation they have made sick and deformed with their radiation, but the past as well. The very bones of our ancestors they have poisoned.'

Osman listened, impatiently. He knew something of the Loulan mummies. Knew there'd been a dispute about them, though the latest he'd seen was that they'd been neither Han nor Uighur, but migrants from Central Europe who had intermarried with Turkic or Mongolian peoples. For a moment he was tempted to put the old man right, but why bother? There was no reasoning with him, he was half-deranged.

'Fascinating', he said briskly. 'I'll make a point of seeing her one day, though for the moment we have things to do.'

'Everything is prepared', Kul said, businesslike suddenly. 'The delivery documents and the passes, I have made them out, they are ready. All they need are the number of the truck, and the date. The date is my main problem. With my retirement approaching it must be soon.'

'I know. It's why we are meeting so often. To push things forward.'

'All this travelling,' Kul looked fretful, 'I am afraid they might capture you. Though you would never submit to the Hans, professor, you would tell them nothing, because you are a Tungan! A Tungan and a true servant of the Prophet, prepared for sacrifice. So you will never betray us. When they said you were coming again so soon my heart lightened, because it means that my entry to Paradise, that too is coming. Now all we need is the time, the signal.'

'You'll get it', Osman said. 'Very soon.' Though not from me, he was thinking. One trip here was enough. And if the target was what he thought... 'For the moment you must wait, and take this.'

He took the envelope from his pocket, handed him the 30,000 yuan.

'What is this? For my grandmother? I have told you –'

'– no, for your men – your martyrs. Ten thousand each. The other ten, I don't know, for things you may need.'

Kul stood looking at the money, then made to give it back.

'I don't like this money. Money I do not need. Why are you giving it to us? Because you have doubts? I have told you, you can meet my brothers if you want. And martyrs don't need money.'

'For their families they do. Tell them it's for their families. They both have children, I assume?'

'Wives and children, yes. The mad son, I told you, the other one, he has two daughters.' He pondered a moment. 'You are right, the money will be good for them, if they become ill.'

With contamination maybe, Osman thought, God help them.

'I have pictures of their families too, I can show you.'

'Never mind', Osman said quickly.

He wanted to get this over, but there were details, always more details, and for nearly an hour he did his best to drill them into Kul's head. Unsure how much those blank-looking eyes were taking in he did it point by point, sentence by sentence, leaving him time to chant out the lines several times, like passages from the scriptures, till he'd got them word for word.

When it was done, he stood up.

'Well then, it looks like everything's in order.'

'One thing.'

Kul was looking apprehensive.

'And what's that?'

'Last time we met you said you would bring something for me. Just in case...'

With a piteous smile he raised two fingers to his head.

Osman's eyes dropped. He'd forgotten the revolver. He prepared to explain in the nicest way that Kul shouldn't fret, that the force of the explosion meant he had every chance of being blown to bits together with the others, but held back. Sensing from the face looking up at him in supplication that for Kul this was an absolute, and that without the certainty of death...

He slipped a hand under his jacket – and hesitated. If he gave him his own gun he would have to make his way back unarmed. Would it matter? If he was challenged, if something happened, would he use it? On them – or himself?

The scene outside Tang's office in the burning Security Bureau came back to him. The guard, surrounded. The Uighur handing him his gun, smiling. The guard's eyes swelling with incredulous horror as he began gabbling wildly, reverting in his last moments to some incomprehensible dialect. And him enjoying the man's terror, taking the gun willingly, to avenge himself for what he'd made him feel down there in his cell, for his hidden fear.

Then handing it back, awkwardly, with a shake of his head, as if the weapon was unfamiliar. In fact, he knew the model well, it was the type he'd trained with, the kind he'd smuggled in. Though he'd never killed anyone, so in that sense it was true, he didn't know how to use it.

'It's Chinese', he said, pulling the revolver from the back of his belt and handing it to him. 'You know how it works?'

From the way Kul held the weapon – in two hands, looking down at it with a kind of exalted timorousness – it was clear he had no idea.

'Here, I'll show you.'

He did it patiently, as if explaining to a child: the magazine, the safety catch, the trigger. When he'd finished Kul gave him a look full of wonderment and gratitude.

'Thank you, professor. From my heart, thank you. No gift can be greater.'

Cradling the weapon, he got up. For a long moment he stood there, looking round, wondering where to put it, before stowing it in a low cupboard next to the table.

He came back to him, beaming.

'Now we are ready. For the great day we are ready! Allah be with you!'

'With both of us.'

When they embraced Osman was the first to disengage. The smell…And today there was something extra: an odour of death and roses that seemed to leak from the top floor to where they were standing.

'It's late. You're sure you wouldn't like to stay the night?'

'No thanks,' Osman said with an inward shudder. 'It's better to go while it's dark.'

Walking away from the house he breathed in the clear night air. Then pulled a miniature of whisky from his pocket, stopped in a darkened doorway and glugged it down. He'd bought it at the station, in anticipation.

18

Licensed by her father to take an interest in Ling-Ling's future, and with little else to distract him, Tony took the earliest opportunity to make his number. This was a side of Anglo-Chinese cooperation he was more than happy to pursue. Choosing a rare moment of Zach's absence from the bar, when the girl came across to take his order he told her he knew her father, and that he'd asked him to discuss her education with her.

'So it's you!' she said with sudden enthusiasm. 'He doesn't like me seeing too many foreigners, but he said there was an Englishman I should meet, that you were a friend and you have a daughter in England. It would be nice to discuss with you.'

'For me too', Tony replied with awkward gallantry. 'Maybe we could meet outside of the hotel? The museum's re-opened I heard, and I'm thinking of going in the next day or two.'

She had a half-day next morning and they met at the entrance. The sight of her outside working hours was a surprise. She'd dressed down for him, he noted with a twinge of disappointment. Gone was the hotel glamour girl: with her long legs piped in denims beneath a short, plain jacket, now she looked like a secretary, or young housewife. The kohl-rimmed eyes turned out to be reserved for hotel customers too, though they were lively enough, even unembellished.

He bought tickets and they went into the museum. A grandiose, domed structure with an elaborate façade, it was part of a drive to boost the status of the town and make a virtue of its many ethnicities. Ling-Ling had been before – her father had taken her – and proved a brisk guide, especially when it came to displays she didn't care for. Which included the whole of the first section, where the rooms introduced the visitor to the minority cultures of the province.

Moving swiftly from one idealised tableau to the next – Mongols in their yurts, Russians on horseback, Kazakhs fur-hatted and booted, dolls' house women in spotless ethnic dress milking cows or baking bread – Ling-Ling waved them aside and did her best to hurry him through. Before a display of homespun Uighur women in scarves and gaily striped dresses she stopped for a moment, smirking.

'In small towns you still see them dressed like that, and some of them are veiled. It's as if we Hans still went round with bound feet. They're backward, like the Tibetans. Why can't they be modern? I'll tell you. It's because of their religion, those mosques where they practise their stupid customs. *And* they're drug-takers. Nearly all the people in Xinjiang with Aids are Uighurs, you know that? *And* they smell, it's terrible how they smell! They eat so much mutton they smell of sheep!'

She strode on, a slender hand dismissing the tableau as if it were not worth her anger, her casual detestation.

Tony lingered before catching up.

'Maybe it's just Urumqi', he said, 'but a lot of the ones on the streets seem modern enough to me. I mean you see plenty of Uighur women in short skirts, smoking, and plenty of the men drinking beer. Sometimes it's hard to believe they're Muslims.'

'But that's the point!' Ling-Ling turned to him, animated now. 'Because the modern ones hate us as much as the back-ward ones! And the women, they pretend to be so virtuous, but they're not, they sleep with men.' She giggled and put a hand to her mouth. 'You know what they do when they get married?' Her hands made sewing motions. '300 yuan and you're a virgin!'

'But you have to admit they've got problems. They can't get

jobs, I heard. I don't see many of them in the hotel. Everyone seems to be Chinese, even the cleaners.'

'That's because you can't trust them.'

'Don't you have Uighur friends?'

'Why should I, if I don't like them? How can you have friends you don't respect? And how can you respect people with primitive beliefs? I know what you're going to say – what my father says: that we should help them modernise, spend more money, educate them, build them houses. But we've done it – and they still riot and kill us! But my father says we should respect them.'

'He's a wise man, your father.'

'Wise enough not to believe our government's propaganda!'

This wasn't a good start, he was getting nowhere, and wanted to let it go, but Ling-Ling wouldn't. They were in another gallery, admiring a group of Tang burial sculptures – pottery horsemen and their equerries, exquisitely fashioned – when she said:

'They're Chinese of course, not Muslim, they don't have things like that. All they have is their mutton and their hatred. But I don't have to tell you, you know because you work on terrorism, don't you? My father said it was why you were here.'

'It is, but it's. like his job. I don't talk about it.'

'Oh I know, I know. All the time he reminds me not to tell anyone, and I don't. If people knew he was my father I'd have no friends. It isn't just Uighurs who don't like the police! Anyway I don't agree with him about Muslims.'

No more Uighur talk. He had a job to do, for her father.

'You want to study abroad, I hear.'

'Maybe I will. I like working at the hotel but soon I must move on. You know what it's like, hotels. The foreigners think we – well, you know what they think. One of your friends – I won't say which one – wanted me to come to his room.' She made a face. 'But he's not good-looking.'

'Not the only reason you didn't go, I hope.'

'Of course not! He asked me to teach him Chinese writing. He was joking about being lonely without his wife, so I told him I knew someone who could help him. Someone who brings in women for foreigners. Young ones, nice-looking and healthy, with no risk of – you know what. Though of course it's expensive.'

Startled by her frankness, he found himself asking:

'And who takes care of that?'

'Someone in the hotel.' A giggle, a moment's pause, then: 'Shall I tell you? Maybe you need him?'

Her tone had gone from joking to matter-of-fact. What she was suggesting, without the slightest sign of inhibition, took him aback. He'd had his share of honey-traps over the years – twice the KGB had made a set at him in London, once with a Russian girl, once with a beautiful Hungarian – but the daughter of a Chinese counter-intelligence man, offering to fix him up with a call girl? This was new. Maybe he was being naïve, but he wasn't sure the Captain would have approved.

Ling-Ling must have caught the surprise in his eyes:

'Don't look so amazed! It's nothing special. You just have to say, it's no problem.'

'Well, thanks, but tell me something. I thought Chinese girls were very modest about sex. And very moral.'

'Under Mao Zedong they were – they had to be – but now they want to have their own lives. I mean it's not immoral to watch yellow films, is it? I hope not because I've seen some with my friends, they're so funny! My friends aren't bad people, but they're not saints. They're just – how do you say – amoral.'

'I'm not sure that's what you mean. Amoral means, well, being indifferent to morality.'

'That's right, that's what I mean.' She shrugged. 'That's what

China is now. People making money, corrupt people in the government, people having sex when they want it – in China everyone is amoral now. Maybe it isn't right but it's the way things are and people are happier than before. So if you need a woman…'

'Actually, I'm married.'

'The men at the hotel are married too – at least they look as if they are. I don't see the problem. If I were a man on my own in a foreign country, and I could afford it… And after all, your wife will never know.'

'Well, there is this thing about loyalty.'

'But that's the point! She'll never know if you've been loyal and she won't know if you haven't!'

She laughed, enjoying her own teasing, if that was what it was.

'Maybe you don't like Chinese women?' She affected a model's pout. 'Maybe we're too skinny for you?'

'It's not that, they're very attractive. I told you, I'm married.'

They moved to a new gallery, a display of carpets. Tony was as interested in carpets as Ling-Ling, and they stood in the centre of the room, talking.

'My father doesn't have a wife now', she went on in a confidential tone. 'It's why he's always so worried about me. He thinks he has to be father and mother.'

'They're divorced?'

'Yes, when I was young.'

'That must have been difficult for you.'

'For her it was terrible, she lost a good man. For me it's not so bad. I never really knew her and my father never talks about her. He got married again but his wife refused to come and live in Urumqi. Anyway I don't like her. She worked with him in intelligence, she was a translator, strict and bossy. She taught me good English, though it was better she didn't come. With no mother to nag me and a father who was always trying to make up for her not being there I got used to having my own way. Until I grew up. Now he worries...'

She played with a strand of hair.

'I tell him he should divorce again and work abroad, then I could study. Maybe fashion, in England. Will I need a visa?'

'A student visa, yes', he said, adding before he knew it as her lively, expectant eyes met his, 'there are ways.'

He broke off. They'd come to the museum's largest gallery, *The Mummies of Urumqi*. There were over twenty in all, a superb collection. He began looking round, enchanted: a 3,800 year old baby wrapped in swaddling clothes, a couple who'd died at different dates but had been buried together, a distinguished elder, pompous-looking even in decay.

Ignoring them all Ling-Ling took his arm and guided him to the middle of the room.

'Never mind them. You have to see the star. The Loulan Beauty.'

Tony gazed down at the 3,000-year-old figure. After that first glimpse of her on TV the night of the attack on the Bureau he'd read about her in his guidebook, and here she was: the large eyes, the abundant lashes, the astonishing hair. The structure of the face staring up at him between the blanket covering her torso and a conical fur hat was that of a woman who must have been extraordinarily attractive. On her feet were leather and fur sandals, quite coquettish, and by her hand a small purse.

'A typical Chinese beauty', Ling-Ling said with satisfaction. 'You can tell by her cheek bones. She died when she was forty. I hope I look as good as her when I'm that old.'

Chinese? It wasn't what his guidebook said: it said her ethnicity was undetermined. He looked harder. The cheekbones didn't strike him as right – not high enough – and so far as he recalled there weren't any Chinese in Xinjiang three thousand years ago. He looked at the English label: *Indo-European ethnicity*, it said.

On the question of who owned Xinjiang and when, the mummy proved nothing. She lay there, contented-looking (he could almost imagine a Mona Lisa smile), secure and indifferent in her knowing beauty while the hatreds and the killings continued around her.

He glanced at Ling-Ling. She was still staring adoringly at her face. She clearly hadn't looked at the label, though it would have made no difference. Like Xinjiang itself the mummy had to be Han, and that was that. No point in disappointing the girl or sounding like her father, who must have told her the facts. The race thing meant a lot to her, clearly.

It was when they were moving on to the next room through the almost empty galleries that he saw Zach. He was standing at a display case, his busy back inclined before some porcelain he was inspecting. An unfortunate encounter. To hurry their exit from the room before the American saw them, he took Ling-Ling's arm and drew her, wordlessly, towards the next gallery. And that was how Zach, turning at the sound of her clackety sandals on the wooden floor, caught them in the doorway, arm in arm.

'Hey!'

Tony turned slowly, forgetting to let go of Ling-Ling as Zach approached.

'Well now! You don't look like you did at the hotel but we don't need introductions. Your day off, is it, Ling-Ling? We got plenty of those, eh Tony?'

'We bumped into each other here', Tony said, 'and Ling-Ling's been showing me round.'

The girl nodded in confirmation.

Zach smiled knowingly.

'It's getting towards lunchtime. Why don't the three of us go for a meal? I'm sure Ling-Ling knows somewhere good and local.'

'I have to go to work.' She turned to Tony. 'It was so nice to meet you here, so unexpected.'

'I'll see you out.'

'That is your funny friend I told you about', she whispered on the way to the door. 'You see how he looked at me?' She grinned, more proud than indignant. 'Never mind, I think my friend at the hotel is helping him have a nice time in our country!' She turned to go, then threw over her shoulder: 'You too, you must have a nice time.'

19

Collinson was due out from Beijing again the next day, God knew why. Delivering another pointless telegram from Thames House, probably. Then came a message saying he was tied up and couldn't make it. A relief – till a second one arrived saying a First Secretary in the Embassy's commercial department who had business in the area would be acting as courier in his stead, and was coming the day after.

Toby Sanderson turned up after the usual delay – troop movements at the airfield. The fact that Tony hadn't met too many embassy folk in the course of his career didn't prevent him having his preconceptions and Sanderson seemed to have done his best to satisfy them. Mid-thirties, brown-brogued, cream-suited and with a supercilious air, there was no problem picking him out from the foreign business crowd in the lobby when reception called him down. A pink carnation in his lapel seemed all that was missing.

Tony proposed they dine outside the hotel. He had in mind an up-market Chinese restaurant, which meant switching from his casual clothes into shirt and tie. Back down in the foyer he found Sanderson waiting in sweat shirt and jeans. Seeing Tony he said:

'Ah, you were thinking of somewhere formal. Sorry to mess up your plans, but it's my first time out here. Would you mind terribly if we ate in a Uighur restaurant, so I can get a local feel?'

'Why not?' said Tony, disguising his irritation. Too bad, he preferred Chinese food. The concierge cancelled the reservation, and recommended a Uighur replacement. 'No need to reserve,' he assured him suavely, and Tony went back to his room to dress down.

By now it was well after eight. Going to Uighur areas after dark was not recommended, on the other hand they were intensively policed. After a half hour journey to the south of the city the driver branched off from the main road, immersing them in shadowy streets, where the only signs of life were police hanging around corners with shields and batons, before drawing up in front of a humble-looking eating-house.

'You haven't reserved a table, have you?' Sanderson asked as they got out of the car.

'No I haven't. Doesn't look like the sort of place where you do, does it, and I was told it wasn't necessary.'

'So we're not expected.'

'No.'

'Good. Means we can talk more freely.'

If it was an ethnic experience Sanderson was after, Tony thought as they entered, he couldn't have done better than this. The place seemed to consist of a single room, reeking of boiled mutton and roasted meat sticks and with only a dozen or so tables. On a stove a variety of soups, thick and murky, simmered. Behind a counter an old man in a blood-stained apron sat threading skewers with hunks of lamb, bare-handed, while behind him steam rose from a great vat of *polo*, a rice dish with carrot and yet more lamb.

'Looks splendid', Sanderson exclaimed.

There were no other foreigners. As they came in every pair of eyes was raised in their direction, with the exception of two men engrossed in a game of chess. The younger one must be a rank beginner, Tony noticed as they took their seats at an empty table close by: they were still in their opening moves but his opponent had already taken his queen.

It was after he'd ordered their tea – the place didn't serve alcohol – that Sanderson intimated, in the turn of a phrase, that he was from a brother service: an M16 'friend' in commercial clothing.

Tony nodded, unsurprised.

'You have business here? Real business I mean.'

'Absolutely. Export credits guarantee stuff for UK oil drilling equipment. Not that my presence was urgently required, but it seemed a promising moment for a trip.'

Vaguely displeased, Tony said nothing. What was this about? If the purpose of his visit was no more than to keep an eye on events in the province what could M16 accomplish that he couldn't?

'And I'm a genuine courier too. Here.' Sanderson fished in a back pocket, 'I brought a message.'

It was an extract from a security service telegram, a single sheet of paper, topped and tailed, marked *personal for Underwood*. They'd been preparing to send out someone familiar with the area to relieve him, it said, though now that Osman had escaped they would await further developments. Meanwhile would he be good enough to go on holding the fort, and keep an ear to the ground? They were concerned about what Osman might get up to in the region now he was on the loose, and unsure that the *Guoanbu* would keep them informed. So could he transmit via the Embassy anything he picked up from the local Chinese security people.

Meanwhile more material on Osman had become available, the telegram continued, though most of it could not be shared with the Chinese, to protect the sources. The gist was that his main field of action appeared to be Central Asia, though if he got out of China he appeared less likely to return to the Fergana Valley than to make for the tribal areas of Pakistan. Hence their worries.

That was all. Like a lot of supposedly secret stuff it amounted to little more than common sense. His impression

that Sanderson had used the routine telegram as a pretext for a
visit increased. He returned the page to Sanderson without
comment.

'So how're things out here?' the M16 man enquired.
'Quietened down, has it?'

Tony described the tensions, the arrests, the disappearances
to places outside Urumqi from where, Alyosha had told him,
people generally did not return.

'And Osman? Still no joy?'

'Not that I've been told.'

To flesh out his lack of information he began giving his
impressions of Captain Tang. For the first time, Sanderson
showed interest.

'Collinson said you get on well.'

'We do.'

'And that he's a bit of a maverick.'

'I wouldn't overstate it. He sticks to the official line but he's
an independent-minded sort who's pessimistic about the
prospects here.'

On the point of telling him about the Captain's frankness
during their conversation at his apartment, he thought better
of it. His mind went back to Tang in his study: his pride in his
DVD collection, his warm words about Jung Chang, the conflict that was evident between his patriotism and his awareness
that things must change. To hold back information about
someone from a colleague simply because you liked them was
unprofessional, but so be it, and the fact was he had taken
against Sanderson. Though feeding him a few tidbits would do
no harm.

'He also has personal problems.'

'Such as?'

'He's estranged from his second wife and has a daughter
who's playing up a bit.'

'In what way?'

'She wants to be a model, he wants her to go to university. No big deal. The story of most girls' parents.'

'Tang is not most people. He has a promising career, one of the younger, smarter breed taking over. And for once he's not a *fils à papa.*'

'Sorry?'

'Daddy's boy. Princelings they call them here. Tang rose through the ranks, so he's probably got views on some of his older and thicker superiors.'

'Losing his Category One prisoner won't do much for his prospects.'

'Finding him will. And if he doesn't and his career goes downhill, who knows?' Lowering his voice Sanderson leant towards him. 'He could get disaffected. Either way there could come a point where he might be of interest. Which is where your ties with him could come in useful. You know the daughter?'

'She works in the hotel bar.'

'You must point her out. If she's keen to go abroad perhaps we could help. Get her invited onto a course, smooth the visa, arrange for a scholarship perhaps.' He smiled. 'Fathers will do anything for daughters, and once she's established he'll want to come out to visit. We could facilitate that too. At which point maybe you could put in an appearance and, who knows?'

Smiling, he reeled in an imaginary fish.

Tony frowned.

'Not sure I get you.'

Sanderson shrugged.

'Sorry, I'm running ahead of myself. Just a thought.'

Tony contemplated his mutton kebab without relish. So this was the reason for his visit. The idea of Tang working as a British agent was outlandish, though not so improbable as the notion of Tony being instrumental in his recruitment. On that side of things he'd had problems before.

It happened six years earlier, when he'd worked on counter-terrorism. They'd put him on the infiltration side of the business and for a while he'd enjoyed it, and got results. Something about his quiet style. There'd been an element of blackmail in the work – recruiting a pious Muslim *pater familias* with a Christian mistress, or arranging for a business fraud to be overlooked if the fraudster reported on a suspect – but that was part of the job. It was terrorists they were after, lives could have been at stake, and his conscience had rarely troubled him. Though one memory had been hard to shake off.

A young Muslim teacher he'd signed up to penetrate an Islamist group in Liverpool had committed suicide. A closet homosexual with a fragile temperament, he couldn't take the pressure. It wasn't Tony's fault – he hadn't threatened to expose the boy – yet he'd been his handler when it happened and felt guilt about his death. It wasn't even as if he'd been of value as an agent: the group turned out to be little more than a Muslim talking-shop and M15 had learned nothing of interest from his reports. A botched operation from start to finish, which thank God had never come to light. Feeling none too proud of himself he'd taken the next opportunity to move on from the infiltration business.

He was tempted to tell Sanderson the story, but a glance at the man opposite – the smoothed-back head of hair and self-satisfied eyes – changed his mind: he'd see qualms about agent-running as weakness. Maybe it was, yet for Tony an approach to Tang was out of the question. He would have no part in it, he told himself – not least because of the risks for the Captain.

Even if he declined the invitation, which seemed more than likely, it wouldn't end there. Tang would have two choices: he could report the approach to his superiors, or stay quiet. If he told his bosses they would conclude that he must have given signs of being open to an approach. And if he didn't, and they found out later, he'd be arrested.

Why should he care? Because of an unspoken bond that was forming between them. Since their first talk together Tang had invited him to lunch at his apartment twice more, not for business but because he seemed to enjoy his company. And now that he'd found a way to intimate that he was a whisky man and the sherry was reserved for the Chinese, the sessions got longer, the bottles drained faster and the talking became franker.

The better he got to know him the harder it became to think of him as an enemy. Was Tang cultivating him with an eye to recruitment? Unlikely: it wasn't their style. The Chinese were not the Russians. The *Guoanbu*, his colleagues at Thames House told him in their briefings, got most of what they needed from the world-wide Chinese diaspora. The Captain had shown great trust in revealing his liberal views and discussing his worries about Ling-Ling, father to father, and Tony would not betray it.

The M16 man had stopped eating, watching him closely before leaning close again.

'So what do you say about Tang? Could we be in with a chance?'

'I wouldn't exaggerate my acquaintance with him. I suppose I've spoken to him half a dozen times in all. I'd need to know him a lot better to give you a useful answer, and I'm not sure I'll get the chance.'

'You like him?'

'Well, yes. I can't say I find him easy to read, but then he's the first Chinese I've had dealings with so that's not surprising. All I can say is that compared with what I was expecting I'm rather impressed. He's a sophisticated fellow.'

'Ah yes.' Sanderson gave a knowing smile. 'The Zhou Enlai syndrome.'

'You've lost me.'

'Mao's Prime Minister. Another sophisticate who did what his boss told him. Killed God knows how many millions in the Great Leap Forward on the Chairman's orders and had the Western world grovelling at his feet. The Captain's a civilised-sounding fellow, by all accounts, with excellent English I gather and a courteous manner, and when the Chinese switch on the charm we're suckers for them. Five thousand years of culture and all that. I'm not saying he's a mass killer – he's too young for that – but you don't work in his world without bloodying your hands.'

The younger man gave what seemed to Tony a patronizing smile before going on:

'Central Asia is a strange part of the world, Tony, and it does strange things to people. All that buried history that won't go away. Don't be taken in by the stuff about the new China. In these parts, when it comes to cruel and unusual behaviour, the beat goes on. Though I have to say there are times when you've got to sympathise with the Han. On the locals I mean. They're not exactly an engaging lot, are they? Look around you.'

Tony did. With no drink, the place seemed mournfully quiet, and the mostly male Uighurs who filled it a disconsolate crew. The contrast with the posters and placards plastering the city depicting them as exuberant folk in colourful national dress, dancing and singing to *dutars,* their two-string lutes, was poignant. The chess players looked especially morose, sunk in their game and ignoring their food. The beginner had made a startling comeback, Tony noticed: by now he'd taken a rook, a bishop and several pawns to offset the loss of his queen.

'Jolly bunch, aren't they?'

'Not a lot to be cheerful about', Tony said, 'the way they're treated.'

'Anyway, back to friend Tang. There can't be too many senior Chinese intelligence men like him.'

Tony ruminated for a moment.

'Let's imagine you make a play for him. Supposing he came across. How would it benefit us exactly?'

Sanderson stopped eating, puzzled.

'I don't get you.'

'I mean what exactly do we need that he could tell us?'

'What he knows best. Counter-intelligence.'

'So your lot can operate more freely.'

'Among other things, yes.'

'So we collect more information?'

Sanderson looked at him as if Tony was questioning his right to life.

'Of course.'

'But if he's a man with enlightened views and a promising future, wouldn't it be in our best interests for him to stay on here and do well in his career?'

'He could do both. Get to the top and work for us at the same time. I'm not suggesting we get him to defect.'

'I don't recall too many precedents for that.'

'Always has to be a first', Sanderson said breezily.

To that there could be no answer. They went on eating, then Tony looked up.

'You're a specialist on the country, I'm not. You see China as a threat?'

The M16 man gave him another of his quizzical looks.

'Of course. I'm not saying they're congenitally evil. It's just that with the best will in the world – which in China it would be rash to assume – they can't help it. It's their size, Tony, and their history. It's not complicated, there's no mystery. They spent centuries deluding themselves they were the centre of the world, now it could be for real. We kicked them around in the past and their memories are elephantine, so they're not going to be soft on us when it's their turn.'

More silence, before Sanderson returned to the charge. 'You and Captain Tang must have hit it off in a big way. Three weeks here and you're sounding like a panda-hugger.'

'A what?'

'A sentimentalist about China. You don't seem too keen on the idea of having a crack at your friend. I must say I'm surprised. The IRA, the Russians, the Islamists – you must have run plenty of agents in your time. Did you have qualms about them too?'

'Once or twice, yes. It's normal, isn't it?'

Sanderson was eating a dish of *polo.* He began poking about among the rice and carrots in a desultory way, avoiding Tony's eyes.

'You've been in this game a lot longer than me', he said, 'so forgive me asking, but have you ever had the feeling you're in the wrong business?'

'Oh many a time. Haven't you? Doesn't everyone?' He enjoyed Sanderson's frown at his avuncular smile. 'Anyway I'll be out of it soon.'

When the bill came he let Sanderson pay. It wasn't much, but he didn't seem too happy about that either.

*

Tony went to bed ruminating on the evening. He didn't blame Sanderson – a greenhorn by the look of him with a career to make – for having a go. He just felt disinclined to cooperate. And if the M16 man complained about him, so what? He was surprised at his own indifference. It wasn't the first time these last weeks. Since coming out here he'd begun feeling strangely disengaged from a world where he'd spent his life, as if mentally on the outside already. For somebody with a sense of duty as compelling as his own it was a disconcerting feeling.

Was this the beginning of some sort of depression, he wondered, brought on by the spectre of retirement? The sense of purposeless he felt coming on, not to speak of the money problems that were looming, and his troubles with Jean and Penny?

He didn't *feel* depressed – rather the opposite. Now he was as far removed as he'd ever been from the obligations of work and family, what he felt was a sense of liberation. Including from people like Collinson and Sanderson, who seemed like intrusions from a past life. Sanderson especially. The more he thought of his behaviour the more annoyed he felt. To judge by his self-important chatter about his previous posts, the stripling who hadn't hesitated to give him the benefit of his wisdom over dinner had achieved nothing in his life to date. Which didn't prevent him oozing the confidence and sense of entitlement characteristic of his type. A type all too familiar in M16, though he'd spotted more and more Sandersons in his service.

It was people like him who seemed to be taking over, he told himself, not just in the intelligence game but wherever you looked: the smoothies in government, the media, the City, all of them cocky as ever as a whole new world came into being and their country shrank around them. Even some of the terrorists were coming from the upper reaches of society nowadays, like Osman, another cocksure bastard. And somehow the bastards got away with it, as Osman appeared to be doing.

To find himself thinking like this was troubling. Politics and the state of the nation had never been his thing. Was it because after all these crowded years for once he had time for contemplation? Or because for the first time in his life he found himself in a new world, on the far side of the globe, from where things back home looked so much smaller than before? As did the consequences of his actions, or inaction.

What was he doing here, a lone M15 man in a post-imperial outpost from which we had been ejected almost a hundred years before, powerless to influence anything one way or the other? What difference could his presence – or absence – possibly make? So why carry on going through the motions? Why not free himself, finally, from this gnawing sense of duty?

The Chinese had a word for it, he'd seen somewhere in his recent reading: *wu wei*, a Taoist term meaning a kind of non-resistance, of going with the flow. If that's what he'd begun doing, it wasn't a disagreeable sensation. He went to sleep wondering where this new detachment, this drifting with the current, might take him.

20

Back in the capital Osman was feeling used up, empty. The journey north to Urumqi had gone by in a haze. Partly it was the drink. He needed it to keep his wits about him, he told himself after picking up another bottle at the station, though the truth was that he was reaching a point where he needed it, full stop. And it was making him careless. Controls on travel from the outback to the capital were strict, yet on the train he'd allowed himself to drowse, then lapse into a fitful, dream-filled sleep, in which images of Kul filled his mind.

First he was smiling placidly, then spreading his hands and puffing out his cheeks, the way a child simulates an explosion, chanting again and again in a soft, caressing voice *look how beautiful – the Loulan Beauty!* Then came the image of the mummy itself, with its vestigial body and sunken skin. A dusty human shadow, an irradiated corpse.

For the rest of the journey he'd drunk bottled water, eaten nothing and done his best to stay awake, as much as anything to avoid the dreams.

*

The train had been delayed, and the shop door took longer to open after he'd checked for the chalk sign and rapped on the shutter. Looking up and down street nervously as he waited and despising himself for it – the area was empty as always, why be nervous? – he rapped again, harder. Finally he heard the click of the bolt, pushed in and shut the door.

'You're late.' The voice behind the curtain was querulous. 'It's lucky I'm still here.'

'And you're lucky I made it.' He fell into a chair. 'I've scarcely slept for three days.'

'Tough. Tell me how you got on before you drop off.'

When Hamid brought a glass and bottle he waved them away.

'Well now,' the Turkman's voice was sardonic, 'that's a first.'

'Some food if you have it.'

Hamid brought bread and some *pora,* fried meat pie stuffed with herbs, before absenting himself, as before. The pie looked old. Osman eyed it, grimacing.

'So how was Kul?'

'Fine', Osman said through a greasy mouthful.

'He's up to the mark? Not twitchy, is he?'

'Calm as they come. His only worry is whether he'll get to die.'

'Exploding himself, a problem? He'll go up with the others. I thought you said we'd got the right man. Now you're saying we have to tell him how to die.'

'It seemed important to him, a make or break issue, so I gave him my revolver. I'd like a replacement if you don't mind.'

'Hamid will fetch you one. So tell me, how were his martyrs?'

'He got the first two he asked. A mechanic and a labourer, a well-balanced pair. The mechanic's already had a go with a *Ural* truck. Said it drives like a tank. One way and another they seemed OK.'

'You met them?'

'Kul said it would take too long to get them round.'

'You *didn't* meet them?'

'I just told you.'

'So we go into this with a couple of unknowns?'

'I grilled him about them, saw their pictures. There's a limit —'

'– to the number of risks we can afford to take. All that way and you didn't see them. And the Russian granny, you saw her I hope? Or was she unavailable too?'

'I saw her, and she's weird.'

'Weird I do not like. Weird Russians especially.'

'She's delusional, thought I was her Orthodox priest. Been waiting for one for years. He won't have one in the house.'

'So she's off her head.'

'Absolutely.'

'And you told Kul to beef up her medicine?'

'We talked about it. He's not sentimental about her, that's for sure.'

'At least you saw her. Any more problems with Kul?'

'Apart from getting himself killed the only thing he seemed worried about was timing. He's keen to get on with it, says his bosses have got a replacement lined up. So when are you going ahead?'

'You need to know?'

'Not exactly, but –'

'– so why are you asking? At this point we have no date. How could we, till you were back?'

He went on eating. Raising the real problem on his mind – what Kul had said about warheads – would be pointless. The Turkman and Salih must know about the storage and research facilities and what was in them. Or else they didn't know and didn't care. Either way it was a taboo subject, and if he probed them about it they'd suspect him of having qualms. Too late for that now.

'So that's it,' he said. 'You won't need me for another trip.'

'Correct. When it's time to push the button we'll get the word to Kul directly. No more overnight trains, so now you can relax. You've done your stuff, for you it's over.'

'Just one thing.'

'And what's that?'

'It would be nice to be out of the country before it happens.'

'That I understand.'

'So how do I get away?'

'Say the word. We could help you out into Kirghizia, same way you came in.'

Kirghizia was not where he wanted to go. First he needed to get to Kiev, to see his mother. A year ago she'd gone there, to her home town in the west of the country, where it was relatively safe, to visit relatives, then fallen ill and stayed on in a sanatorium. The last he'd heard her mind was failing. The years of abuse by his father, the loss of contact with her son…. Not something he could explain to the Turkman.

'So where is it you want to go?'

'I'll sleep on it,' Osman said.

At that moment the door opened and Hamid returned. 'OK,' the Turkman growled, 'we'll leave it there. Hamid will be along in the morning. Meanwhile don't move a step. Just sit tight and wait.'

The usual hocus pocus with the lamp, and they were gone.

Osman locked the door, stowed the key, said his prayers, fell into bed, and for a long time lay awake. His stomach hurt. The cold pie he'd wolfed was doing terrible things. Indigestion made him dream, his dreams had a habit of recurring and he'd seen as much as he needed of radioactive mummies. When his eyes closed at last he dreamt so vividly of Kul that he woke up and never got back to sleep. At nine he got up and washed as best he could. Bottled water and the nans left on the table, stony now, were his breakfast. Nibbling without appetite – his stomach still wasn't right – he pondered the best route out of the province, then to Kiev.

Eleven o'clock. With the shutter down it was hot in the

room, and as the sun rose higher the stink of rotten vegetables grew. He listened for footsteps in the road, but as always there was nothing. Sit tight and wait, they'd said. Sit how long, and wait for what? Till Hamid arrived, to ask him where he wanted to go? Or till it was done, and Tang and his men came for him...

Remembering he hadn't prayed that morning he dragged a scrap of carpet to the centre of the room, took off his shoes, and knelt. It was a real prayer this time, filled with genuine submission, a prayer that beseeched Allah for help and guidance.

Twelve o'clock. By now the atmosphere was pestilential. By noon the sun fell squarely on the metal shutters, the place was sweltering and he was parched. Beneath the counter was a stock of water, he drank off a whole bottle and sweated more. One o'clock. The sun was still stoking the furnace in the shop, and still no Hamid. This morning, the Turkman had said, so where was he?

An urge to get out overcame him, if only to walk a few paces, breathe some air. He fetched the key, went to slide it into the lock. It wouldn't go. Thrusting harder he yanked it sideways, upwards, then took it out and peered into the keyhole. No daylight, something blocking it: metal. Hamid must have locked it from the outside, overnight.

To make sure he stayed? But he wanted to go, get out of the country quickly, because whatever date they decided there was no need for him to be here longer. If Hamid came back, would it be to tell him to remain where he was – keep him locked up? What if they just left him – waited till it was done, then left him. Either way there was a logic, one he didn't like. The logic of *for you it's over.*

He went through the curtain to the storeroom and threw aside crates and boxes till he found a toolbox with what he needed – a hammer, a wrench – and went to work on the door.

The wrench was strong but the hefty door sat tight in its frame, so tight that when he worked it in near a hinge and got purchase it wouldn't budge. He gave up, went back to the storeroom and stared around. Hopeless: a window looked onto a back alley, but it was small and newly barred.

He came back and checked the shutter. It was solid but old, the bottom inch red with rust. Hammering the wrench into the gap between its base and a lip of concrete, he stepped back, and jumped on it.

Nothing gave. Now he balanced both feet on the rigid wrench and, his hands on the shutter, began bouncing, gently at first then rhythmically with all his weight till the wrench collapsed beneath him and he sprawled backwards. The bolt clamping the shutter to the floor had given.

21

Tony thought he'd seen the last of his M16 man, but he hadn't. Sanderson got back from his jaunt to his oilrig after ten in the evening and rang his room to propose a late-night drink. When Tony prevaricated he insisted, and it was soon clear why.

The moment they sat down in the bar he turned the conversation to Tang, asking which of the girls serving was his daughter.

Tony looked round with an abstract air.

'Off duty, it looks like.'

Ling-Ling was at the far corner of the bar, in conversation with Stewart Handler, a *New York Times* correspondent and a buddy of Zach's, but so what? In his new detachment Tony was damned if he was going to play along with the man. The thought of him using her as a line to Tang after he'd gone home, perhaps over the scholarship business, was suddenly intolerable to him. Luckily Sanderson didn't stay long. Tired after his day's travels and with an early start next morning he had his brandy, delivered a few words of wisdom about prospects in Xinjiang after his 36 hour stay in the province, and that was that. Wishing him a pleasant return journey and hoping he wouldn't be back, Tony turned in for an early night.

He'd finished brushing his teeth when there was a knock. Sanderson again, sod the man. He opened the door but it wasn't him, it was two girls. On the point of telling them they'd got the wrong room and closing the door smartly, he saw that one was supporting the other, who looked unwell. There seemed to be a trickle of blood under her nose.

'What's the trouble?'

'My friend, she has face bleed', the one holding her said.

'You help her, please?'

Not much of a bleed, he thought, inspecting the scarlet dribble on her upper lip more closely. Some sort of con more likely, but by now they had a foot in the door and at the thought of pushing them out, he weakened.

A nosegay of perfumes was his first impression as they entered the hall, one still with an arm round the other. His second was that the girls, in cheongsams, were young, attractive, and not in the least whoreish-looking.

'Can we use bathroom?'

It was a few steps along the hall. He led the way and switched on the light.

'Thank you, Sir.'

The girls went in and shut the door. The sound of whispering and a running tap reached him. Moments later it opened. The blood was gone, the smell of scent stronger, the girls smiling. As they came out and walked towards him, the game was clear: he had seconds before they reached him to invite them to leave, but he didn't.

'Thank you. You nice man.' A joint giggle. 'We nice girls. You want we stay?'

Officially the answer was *not on your life*. Though personally...

Tony knew as much about oriental women as the average Western male – their delicacy, their beguiling slenderness – and that was all: carnally he knew nothing. It wasn't through lack of interest. His taste in feminine types was broad, there was something to delight him in women of every race, so in that sense, if in no other, he was a true cosmopolitan. It was the action that was lacking.

In matters of sex Tony's perfect world would have been the opposite of the one he'd experienced: one where he would have used to the full the freedoms of the Sixties and Seventies before he'd married, which for reasons of excess timidity coupled with lack of cash, plus the constraints of his job, he most definitely hadn't. Except for a youthful interlude with a Caribbean girl he'd met at a dance before his career in M15 began and the dancing stopped, then a drunken episode with a Russian in his mature years that was best forgotten, his attraction to exotic women had remained just that.

The idea that sex and espionage were inextricable mystified him. Tracking KGB smoothies, Irish bigots or Islamist crazies had never struck him as erotic. Maybe M16 was different (all that foreign travel) but the ethos of his own service required a level of self-restraint beyond the average, and in his more honest moments he felt it as a loss.

Oriental women he found especially appealing, and their allure had grown with the years; something to do with the placidity he saw in them, perhaps, in contrast to the endlessly fretful Jean. And now here he was, with his secret yen, kicking his heels in a swanky hotel in China at an age when men of his self-denying disposition begin lamenting that they had denied themselves quite so much.

It was a situation that seemed unlikely to recur, and the idea that he would die without having enjoyed the embrace of the most numerous and (as he imagined) most pleasing species of femininity the world offered seemed unjust. It was not something he dwelt on, and in the many disappointments in his life it didn't figure large; it was just that it seemed an unnecessary abnegation for a man to suffer, and in the last weeks he had begun to find the parade of available-looking women visiting the hotel in the evenings (some of them turned up with their patrons for breakfast) a challenge to his self-restraint. An excess of conscientiousness, he'd begun telling himself, was the story of his life, in his marriage as well as his work, and as a dutiful husband of over thirty years he'd earned some reward.

'I think you'd better go', he said.

'Why we go?'

'Because I'm tired.'

'No problem, we make show. You like show?'

Entrapment? Unlikely. And if a fifty-nine-year-old on the brink of retirement were to succumb, what was the worst the *Guoanbu* could do? The pair of them were in his room, throwing them out could cause a fuss, so let them put on their show, pay them off, and leave it at that. *Wu wei,* go with the flow.

The girls, meanwhile, were making themselves at home, sitting on his bed chattering and laughing, with pretty looks in his direction. Persuading himself that he had no choice in the matter, with a resigned smile he sat down in an armchair.

'So you want show, OK?'

He nodded and the chatter stopped: two minutes and the cheongsams were off and their arms were around each other as they kissed, languidly. Then the familiar sequel. He didn't feel too good about what was happening a few feet from his eyes, but then neither did he look away. When the sighs and moans subsided he poured himself a whisky, neat. Instantly the girls were perched at the edge of the bed.

'And us? We thirsty too!'

He indicated the mini-bar.

'Help yourselves.'

Scrambling from the bed they crouched before it, their slender backs turned to him as, like hungry schoolgirls, they selected their nuts and chocolate bars and tins of Coke. When they climbed back onto the bed to enjoy their spoils he stood up.

'I think it's time to go.'

A hand patted the bed.

'You don't want come with us?'

'No thanks.'

'Sure?'

'Sure.'

They dressed swiftly, amidst more chatter. Whatever the usual rate for the job, to judge by their grateful looks and lack of haggling, he had overpaid. Tucking the wad of yuan into her bag with a nod and a smile the first one made for the door. As she gathered their sweetmeats from the bed and went to join her, a step before she reached it the second girl turned.

'It's true you nice man.'

It was the younger of the two, the one who had shown some embarrassment at their performance. No more than twenty years old she had a fringe and a kind smile.

'Wait a moment.'

He walked past her, said goodbye to her friend and locked the door. Then turned and held her face in his hands.

'What's your name?'

'Meili.'

'Well, Meili, it would be nice if you stayed the night.'

*

Next evening the three security men were due to meet at the bar for one of their late-night sessions. By now they'd settled into a routine, getting together every third evening to exchange information, or more often to lament the lack of it. Conflicted by the feelings unleashed by his night with Meili Tony had spent the day brooding about who could have sent him the girls, and by now he thought he knew.

He arrived at the bar on time. Due back tonight after a day conferring with his Embassy in Beijing, Zach would be joining them later, but Alyosha was there with his vodka.

Tony ordered his whisky, lit a cigarillo and said:

'Thanks for the girls, Alyosha.'

'Girls?'

'The ones who came to my room.'

'Ah, them. No trouble. A gift from a colleague, like a bottle of Armenian brandy.'

'Why did you do it?'

'Not my decision.' Alyosha pointed up. 'Higher authority.'

'Sorry not to have provided a photo opportunity.'

'Think nothing of it. We can always mock them up.'

'Feel free.' Tony forced a shrug. 'You're behind the times. No one gives a damn any longer about who sleeps with whom except your lot. I thought this was an exercise in cooperation? Maybe the word means something different to you.'

'We're professionals.' The beefy shoulders went up, the baby face wide open in a lop-sided smile. 'To come to an encounter with an M15 man without setting a honeytrap would be unprofessional, and you wouldn't want to cooperate with non-professionals.'

'And Zach, you've set him up too?'

'No need, he does it himself.'

Suddenly the Russian threw his head back with a huge rumbling laugh.

'Tony, you won't believe this, but I didn't send them! And neither did our hosts I'd bet. This is China my friend, not the London Ritz, the girls just come! Or maybe it was Zach's idea of a joke.' He imitated Tony's downturned mouth. 'If it was you don't seem to see the funny side. I hope you threw them out. If they were Chinese I would, I can tell you!'

At that moment the American arrived, slumped into a chair and got himself a drink.

'We were talking about Chinese women', Alyosha went on. Tony shrank in his seat, prepared for the worst. 'I was saying they do nothing for me. The idea that anyone could prefer them to Western women is crazy. I'd rather jump over Satan.'

'You *what?*' Zach stopped in mid-drink.

'Jump over Satan. It's Uighur for' – the Russian made a masturbatory gesture. 'Nice metaphor, eh?'

'Chinese girls don't grab you? You don't think they help bring a little, you know, grace to the world?'

'Let me tell you. The first time I saw Chinese women was when my father worked in the Soviet Embassy in Beijing. It was the late Sixties, the Cultural Revolution, and the girls used to go about in these boiler suits and military caps, so they looked like men. Nothing upstairs, or down. Our Embassy was besieged by bitches like that for months on end, marching up and down screaming their stupid fucking slogans. A regiment of hysterics having collective orgasms it sounded like. I was an adolescent at the time and it put me off Chinese women for ever.

'Now they've gone to the other extreme, tottering about on high heels and the rest of it, but for me they're just as unsexy as before. Stick legs and poky little arses, know what I mean? Incredible to think there are people who love having those parcels of skin and bone next to them in bed.'

'Me for one', said Zach.

'Well each to his tastes, but Chinese women? Isn't that bordering on perversion? You know, men who would really prefer a boy –'

'– oh come on, now I'm a homosexual 'cos I like Chinese girls! Same way I go for, I dunno, marmalade on toast once in a while.'

'You said it!' Alyosha roared. 'Toast and marmalade! Dry and bitter! That's what they are. Know what we call the Chinks in Russia? *Limonchiki.* Little lemons, all yellow and sour.'

'You got a woman in Moscow, haven't you?' Zach asked.

'Worse, I got a wife. Or rather she got me. Too young to protect myself. Now I know better it's too late.'

'You're divorced?'

'She's too smart for that. We live together, we go our separate ways, and both ways I pay for. I want a girl, I have one. And she has her men.'

'They don't mind that? Your service, I mean?'

'Before they would, in the days of the KGB, but things have changed. It's like you said, Tony, no-one gives a fuck.'

'And you?' the American looked at Tony. 'Wait – don't tell me! I know what you're gonna say. You'll say you have a wife of forty years and three grown-up children who are doctors, civil servants or airline pilots, and you've never so much as glanced at another woman, Asian, Caucasian or whatever.'

'Well, it's nearer thirty, and Jean and I, you know...' It seemed an age before he got out: 'We have our lives.'

'And the children?'

'One. A girl.'

'A doctor?'

'She's in the music business.'

It was a generous description of Penny's career. The truth was that since dropping out of university she'd worked off and on in a small-time music distribution company, for a pittance.

'Kids...' Alyosha nodded, ruefully. Slumped in his seat and with God knows how much vodka under his belt already the Russian was in a lugubriously communicative mood.

'In the Cold War we used to think we were keeping them safe from Western degeneracy. Now we keep them safe so they can piss around. And there's no fathers-and-sons conflict any more, because now we've got the inter-generational dialogue, right?

'I got a boy in music too. Singer, he thinks. Also thinks he's gay. Thirty years back it would have been suicide, today he comes to me when he's nineteen years old and he says dad, I think I'm gay, what should I do about it? And I tell him see here son, don't give it another thought, because we've moved on. He says what do you mean, dad, and I say well son science has told us it's in the genes and there's nothing you can do about it, so why worry? And he says that's right dad, that's so right. Then I hit him with it.

'You can't be gay, I tell him, 'cos if it's in your genes I'd be similarly inclined, and I swear to God I have never looked at another guy that way, not even for a locker-room moment. I like women. In fact I have problems about how much I like them, ask your mother. And finally I tell him that the real reason he couldn't be a faggot is that if it was passed down in the genes he wouldn't exist. So don't give me that shit about how you're born gay.'

Tony said: 'So is he?'

'Been living with his dancer boyfriend for a year, so he's giving it a try. Or maybe he's going to all that trouble to spite me, 'cos what really happened when he told me was we fell out, big time. Least we don't have arguments any more, 'cos I never see him.'

Alyosha did his best to smile. It came out so melancholy that not even Zach had the heart to rag him.

'You ever have a Chinese woman?' Zach asked Tony. 'You seem to have a thing for Ling-Ling.'

'No comment', said Tony.

'If that's a no you missed something my friend, I'm tellin' you. I was lucky. Had this year out East when I was young, internship with the Singapore Security Department, working against Captain Tang and his outfit when they still counted as commies. I wasn't married and it was paradise. 24 years old and the Chinese guy in charge took a fatherly interest. Showed me the eateries, the race courses and the girls. Fatty Sung they called him, great big slob he was, piggie eyes an' all, didn't look like no ladies' man but he went for them big time.

'There was one high-class joint, Chinese, Malays, Indians,

Indonesians – they had 'em all. Perfect place to keep an eye on the ethnics, my Chinaman used to say, the madam was the source of half his stuff. A two-at-a-time man he was, racially mixed, always. I had my fill too, I can tell you, and you should have seen the quality. Know what it's like with Asian food? You gobble up as much as you like and still feel peckish. It was like that. Plus we got preferential rates.'

Tony gave what he hoped was a knowing laugh.

'But here's the story', Zach went on. 'Few years later I heard what happened to Fatty Sung. Soon as the Chinese began opening the country up he trots off to Beijing to see relatives and doesn't come back. Turns out he's been working for Beijing all along. Recruited in the Seventies. God knows how much FBI stuff he passed on over the years. Our friend Tang will have a file on every fuck I had that year. Not that I'm complaining. Means there's no harm beefing up my score a little while I'm here.

'So there you go, on the women side I'm a free agent. What they gonna do? Set me up and recruit me? I don't think so. They'd never trust us, or you Tony, or the Russkis, 'cos like everything else with them it's a racial thing. They want agents they keep it in the family, and the Chinese have got family across the whole fucking globe.'

Unsure what he had to contribute, and remembering Ling-Ling's teasing, Tony remarked on how matter-of-fact the Chinese seemed about these things.

'You bet. If sex was a Chinese stock you'd put money in it. It's getting to be like our nineteen sixties, on a monumental scale. Another few years it'll be same as it is with us, like brushing your teeth: up and down, up and down, thinkin' of somethin' else. They'll go at it like rabbits now they got the chance 'cos when Mao was around no one was allowed a hard-on outside marriage, 'cept the old bastard himself. So they got a

60-year backlog to get through.

'You should help 'em out, Tony. Do your bit. The white man's burden. Do nothin' in a place like this and they'll put you down as a faggot. And come the Chinese democratic revolution they'll open up the files like they did in Russia, and it'll say *Tony Underwood, M15 man and a faggot.* You don't look like one, the way you ran your eye over that woman in the little green number over there. You didn't drool exactly but you know what your eye did? It licked her. I never saw you do that. Something got your pecker up?'

'Shut up Zach, for Christ's sake.'

'Whoa there! Sore spot, Tony?'

'I'm going to bed.'

'Me too', Alyosha said, pouring and downing the last of his vodka and stumbling to his feet.

'So am I.' Zach's eyes went back to the girl in green. 'Eventually.'

22

'Tony, you have to believe me. On my mother's grave I swear it wasn't me.'

The article Tony had set before Zach over breakfast was from *The New York Times*. The heading was 'FBI AND MI5 LEND A HAND IN CHINESE XINJIANG'. Datelined Xian four days earlier, it was signed Stewart Handler, Zach's journalist friend, who must have gone there to file it. The newspaper had arrived at the hotel at eight that morning, special delivery, addressed to Tony, compliments of Collinson, no comment.

It could have been worse, Tony thought as he scanned it, then discovered that it was. The piece named both him and Zach, as well as the hotel. Plus there was a picture: a close-up of the pair of them passing through the revolving doors. The camera had caught them walking swiftly, heads down, hats tipped over their brows, enough to make them spooky-looking though not low enough to hide their faces.

The effect was comically mysterious, a point not missed in the caption underneath: *If working with Chinese security is as open and above board as our authorities claim, Western intelligence ought to inform their operatives in Urumqi, who go about like actors in a spy melodrama.*

Never easily provoked, Tony was an angry man.

'Not you, you say? How do you expect me to believe that? You know him, you talked to him. I saw you, there', he pointed to the end of the bar, where Ling-Ling was sitting on her own, out of earshot, looking prettily bored.

'Obviously we talked, he's an American for Chrissake! He was here when we got here. Hears me ordering a drink, sees I'm a fellow countryman, says he's from the *New York Times*, offers to roll up the order with his. What am I supposed to do? Tell him to fuck off home?'

'That's not what I'm saying. There've been Brits here too. A *Telegraph* man, I told you about him. We had a drink but I stuck to the line – that I was out here on a private security contract. And that stuff about us looking like actors in a melodrama. Not exactly friendly, is it?'

'He's not responsible for the captions. And Tony, you have to believe me, I didn't say a word about you. Someone else must have done it. Tang, you reckon? They wanted to announce our visit to the world at the beginning, remember? Maybe they just did?'

'I don't think so. It doesn't read like that, not at all.'

'What's the big deal? So Al Qaeda know we're cooperating with the *Guoanbu*. It's old news, Tony, we've had an FBI guy at the US Embassy declared to the Chinese for years, same as you. I've just been there, talking to him, and your guy comes out to see you. The *Times* just put a new face on an old story.'

'They certainly have.' He jabbed at the paper. 'Yours and mine. Here we bloody are.'

'The trouble with the Brits', Zach came back, '*if I may say so,* is that you guys are neurotic about the press. It was only a few years ago you stopped pretending you didn't exist, as I recall.'

'You're showing your youth, Zach. We gave that up thirty years ago. And it wasn't M15, it was 6. Non-acknowledgement it was called, and to my mind it made sense. Better than flaunting your dirty washing all over the globe.'

'Come on Tony, get modern. Try telling America the CIA doesn't exist. Anyway you were blown, weren't you, in your dirty bomb case?'

'I wasn't, as it happened. The court had the sense to stop the press publishing my name and let me give evidence behind a screen.'

'Amateur dramatics.'

'Common sense', said Tony.

If he was making heavy weather of the article there were reasons for it, ones it would have been hard to explain to Zach. The leak upset him as much for personal as for operational reasons. Publicity of any kind he abhorred; he felt more comfortable in the shadows, always had. Operationally, his fear was that his bosses would blame him for the leak, think he was getting careless, demob happy, and order him back to London at a moment they might otherwise have begun to forget he was here. Which would have suited him fine, not least now that he had an arrangement with Meili.

A tall, gangling man wandered into the bar at that moment and headed in their direction. Too late Tony recognized Handler. He put the *New York Times* away quickly.

'Stue!' Zach leapt up. 'How's it going?'

'Better than for you, Zach, I imagine. Sorry 'bout that piece, but –'

'– I know I know, you gotta job to do. Forget it, no problem. This is my British other half. You'll recognize him from your photo.'

Tony gave a frozen nod.

'If it's any consolation, Mr Underwood, Zach here was not my source.'

'I accept your assurance', Tony said stiffly. 'On the other hand if you never comment on your sources –'

'– what's my assurance worth? It happens to be the truth. Maybe I could buy you a drink sometime? Smooth things over.'

'I'm sorry, you'll have to excuse me. I too have a job to do,' Tony smiled, not too nicely, 'and in our trade we don't give interviews.'

'Fair enough', the American shrugged, and fell into conversation with Zach.

Seeing Ling-Ling on her own he got up and went towards her. At his approach she looked up, girlishly excited.

'My father told me you were in the paper', she whispered. 'Is that it, in your pocket? Let me have a look.'

'It's nothing, it's silly.'

'So why are you upset? Nobody reads American papers here, you can't get them. So come on, show me.'

With a resigned look Tony took it out for her to see. While she read he glanced back at Zach and Handler. The pair were making for the revolving door, and as he waited for Zach to go through Handler turned and saw them: the bar girl deep in the spread-out *New York Times*, Tony standing over her. For someone complaining about publicity it didn't look good. When he joined Zach outside Tony could see their smiles through the glass.

Ling-Ling had finished reading and looked up at him, laughing.

'It's very nice – even the hat. Very young style.'

When he reached to take the paper back she put it to her chest, teasingly.

'Maybe we put it with the others?' She nodded to a board of celebrity customers behind the bar, Chinese actors and singers he didn't know, glamorous-looking Westerners he'd never heard of.

'I'd rather you didn't.'

Irritated, he leant across the bar to snatch it back. She was holding it close to her chest and his fingers touched her throat, like a drunk making a grab. That didn't look good either.

*

Next day a Uighur paper picked up the *New York Times* story, complete with photo. A disaster, Tony thought when Tang phoned to warn him. The whole of Xinjiang would know who they were, the hotel they stayed at and why they'd come. Any one of the bar-fly correspondents could pester them and, more to the point, any Muslim crazy could track them down.

Tang said he was sorry and promised the paper involved would be closed. When the Captain offered him protection he said not to bother, he'd be fine. Best concentrate on Zach; as an American he'd be most vulnerable. To change the conversation he asked about Osman, and got a clipped reply:

'Nothing new, and nothing in prospect.'

The Captain seemed a bit down, it struck him.

'Well I'm sorry to hear it. Not least since the *New York Times* will get my people wondering whether it's worth me staying on.'

'Maybe you should use the free time to see more of our country,' Tang suggested, a little mournfully. 'I will tell my secretary to arrange a travel document, so you have no problem moving around.'

'That's good of you. Maybe I will.'

By the time they rang off it had begun to sound like a farewell call.

The thought of leaving was depressing. He'd bought a DIY book on the language and was looking forward to learning some ideograms, courtesy of Meili. A time-honoured arrangement, but it had been her idea; she'd be uncomfortable, he sensed, with the simple exchange of cash for sex. And if they were going to pull him out he might as well take up the Captain's suggestion, use up some of his accumulated leave for a swing around China before he left. For that he'd need an interpreter, and who better than his new language teacher?

It could be his last trip to the Orient, he suspected. Jean wasn't keen on holidays outside Europe, Cyprus was as far east as she was keen to go. Plus she had a thing about China and the

Chinese. Spooky was her word for them, and so what if they were going to take over the world? The way things were going they'd be welcome to it, though preferably not while she was around. She didn't go for Chinese food either: *you never knew what was in it* – she'd actually said the words.

It was part of a change he had noticed in her as she aged, a kind of battening down, a closing of her mind to the unfamiliar, a process he'd watched these last years with the feeling that their future would be bleak and narrowing. Another reason for not hurrying home.

*

That afternoon he kept away from the lobby, to avoid running into Zach or Handler. Resigned, by now, to a summons home he stayed in his room, reading, dozing, waiting for the worst.

At around four o'clock a message came, though not the one he'd been expecting.

Dear Mr Underwood, the letter slipped under his door said, *I have saw you in Uighur paper. You need know Uighur people view. Please to come to the Grand Bazaar at 10 tonight. A Uighur friend.*

Reading it he sighed to himself. Another of Zach's practical jokes, to inveigle him into a drinking session at some new joint he'd discovered, maybe with Stewart Handler in tow. He crumpled the note up and threw it in the wastepaper basket. The last thing he needed tonight was another of Zach's benders.

He lay down for a nap – lunchtime beers did that to him – woke up at five, settled back into his book. Ordering dinner from room service two hours later he had a drink from the minibar and began wishing he'd set up Meili for the evening. The meal came promptly, but his appetite was gone. He went back to his book, read for half an hour, put it down. Sitting around reading wasn't much of a way to spend what could be his last night in China. Retrieving the note he read it again. Was it Zach? He checked the writing against the comments the American had scribbled on the *New York Times* piece: a different hand, no comparison.

He took the lift to the lobby.

'I got a message in my room, a few hours ago. Do you know who delivered it?'

The receptionist went off, made enquiries, came back.

'A taxi driver.'

'Thanks.'

Could it be genuine? Somebody who'd got his name from the paper and wanted to talk? The security situation and the language problem had been a barrier to even casual contact with Uighurs. Maybe this one might have something interesting to tell him, so perhaps he should go? It was getting dark, there'd be a risk, but there'd been a time when he'd enjoyed them.

He went onto his balcony, looked down. A pleasantly warm evening had drawn more people onto the streets. If things looked nasty there'd be plenty of folk around in the market area, and no shortage of police.

He took the lift down and, careful to keep out of sight of the bar, set out for the Grand Bazaar.

*

His taxi pulled up in the street bordering the market square. Except for some kids playing around the fountain, it was empty. The gates of the Bazaar itself were closed, the lights out, the whole place barred and shuttered. The reopening of the market after the riots, he realised now, must have been limited to daylight hours.

A waste of time coming, yet it was only a few minutes after

ten, and now he was here, what had he to lose by waiting? When he got out of the taxi and paid, the driver gave him an enquiring look. Gesticulating round the empty square he said something in Chinese, then Uighur, before shrugging and driving off.

He wandered around, waiting. A couple of tourists passed, German it seemed, the woman sounding as if she was upbraiding the man for not knowing the place was shut. At the entrance to a side street a girl in low-cut blouse and jeans called out as he passed. Further along, in the doors of pink-lit entrances, there were more. He drew back, stuck to the square.

Twenty past ten and still no one around, time to call it a day. He walked back to the main road, where a taxi was parked. He waved, walked towards it, and it drove to meet him.

The rear door opened.

'Share my cab?', an accented English voice said.

'Thanks, where you going?'

He glanced in. A man sat in the back, his face obscured by a cap.

'Downtown.'

'Fine.'

He climbed in. The man spoke to the driver, urgently, in Chinese, and the cab lurched forward. At the same moment he leant across, snapped shut the lock on Tony's side, and turned towards him.

'Mr Underwood.' The voice had lost its accent. 'Good of you to come. Would you mind if we resumed our conversation?'

When the cab slowed at a red light he got his fingers on the door lock. And that was all. Feeling the point of a knife in his ribs through his casual shirt, he let go.

23

'It is putting a high price on one's conjectures to have someone roasted alive on their account.'

'Good memory', said Tony.

'Good quotation. Except it was me who nearly got roasted.'

They were in a late-night café in God knows what part of town, a hole-in-the-corner place of scrubbed wood tables and plastic chairs. Except for themselves and the owner, an ageing Uighur with necklaces and plaits to her waist, like some super-annuated hippie, it was empty.

Before she had time to bring their beers Osman took a bottle from a pocket, downed a mouthful and thrust it back. Whisky fumes, Tony remembered, had filled the taxi: the darkness, the knife and the smell of booze made a nasty combination. Hence his decision to do nothing impetuous. In the light of the café Osman's limp and drained-looking figure and drink-glazed eyes robbed him of his menace.

The woman shuffled up with their beers.

'Well, cheers.'

They drank. Tony let Osman fill the silence.

'Why do you think I wanted to see you?'

'I have no idea.'

'It's not to hand myself in – don't think that.'

The café door opened at that moment and a Uighur couple in their twenties entered. Selecting a table on the far side of the room, they sat down.

Tony spoke softly.

'You're taking a hell of a risk. What do you want with me?'

'What do I want?' Tony motioned him to keep his voice

down. 'A consultation is what I want. With my surrogate Consul.'

It was said with a crooked grin.

'I need to get out of the country', he went on, his voice lower now, and steadier.

'I can well imagine.'

'And you can help.'

'That I find hard to see.'

'You've no choice. You have to. It's your duty.'

'Explain.'

'You told me we don't have an extradition treaty with China because *habeas corpus* doesn't translate into Mandarin, correct?'

'Roughly speaking.'

'So we could never send anyone here for trial because we don't trust their interrogation methods, or their courts.'

'That's the theory.'

'So if I make it to Britain I can't be sent back. And now I'm out of that cell you can't turn me in, for the same reason. They executed a drug-runner from London not so long ago, so a gun-runner wouldn't stand a chance.'

You should have thought of that before Tony forbore to say.

'That's my understanding,' he agreed. 'Especially since the Chinese think you've got something else lined up.'

Osman took a slow swig of beer.

'Let's assume they're right, and there's something about to happen. What will be their priority? To pick me up – or stop it?'

'Both. If they catch you they'll hope to persuade you to come clean.'

'Torture me is what you're saying.'

'This isn't Britain. You chose to come.'

'And capital punishment? It doesn't worry you?'

Officially, yes, personally not so much, was Tony's private view. The only argument against executing jihadis, he had long believed, was that death was what they wanted. Though evidently not this one.

'I seem to be left out of your calculations,' he said. 'If I helped you leave the country – though Christ knows how – and you have something else planned, in Chinese eyes I'd end up as an accomplice.'

'And if I tell you of the event in question after I'm out?'

'So it doesn't happen?'

'Correct. If I get back home they can charge me with whatever they want. But if I were to prevent something bigger than gunrunning – a lot bigger – maybe I could expect a little clemency?'

'Maybe.'

'Don't look so surprised, Tony – if I may. It was your idea, remember? You said I should offer the Chinese a deal: I tell them anything else we may have planned, they let me go home. I didn't take it seriously because it's the Chinese we're dealing with and I don't believe they'd stick to it. Now the position has changed. This time round I'm out of their hands, and ready to trade.'

Osman gulped at his beer then slugged down another shot of whisky. It was doing him no good. He looked in a poor way, and as it lifted the bottle his hand trembled. This was no longer the Osman Tony had met in his cell: behind the studied arrogance he sensed a man breaking up.

'You have a cigarette?'

'Only a cigarillo. Didn't realise you smoked.'

'At times of stress.'

Drink, and now cigarettes. Some Muslim... Tony gave him a cigarillo, took one for himself. Lighting a smoke for a man who'd brought him here at knifepoint felt excessively sociable, but he did it.

'Just one thing,' Osman said. 'I'm not going to trade directly. Fair play is something else that doesn't translate into Chinese, and if anything went wrong', he took a long drag of his cigarillo, 'a lot of people could suffer. Never forget that. But there's another way.'

'Which is what?'

'There's nothing in the media about me, have you noticed? Which makes things easier. If there's no public hue and cry and no pictures in the press it means I could try my luck getting on a plane. And once I'm gone you could tell them when and where the event in question is due to happen.'

Drawing too deeply on the cigarillo, he coughed.

'I don't follow. You've got no passport. I saw it in Tang's office.'

A hand under the table, Osman fumbled with a dirty white and gold trainer. Reaching inside he brought out a passport with its corners bent.

'Collected it on the way out of the Bureau, from the Captain's drawer. And look – a nice new name and photo.' He opened the back page. 'Like it?'

The picture Tony had seen in Tang's office of the racially indeterminate youth with long hair and fashionably threaded scarf had gone. Now he was in jacket and tie. The effect was to make him that much less Asiatic. In his baseball cap he looked Chinese, in the photo Caucasian, pretty much. Uncanny.

'And if there's a stop on the passport? If they pick you up at emigration?'

'That's where you come in. You'll be the failsafe. I'll tell them to contact you, my DIY Consul. Because you'll be on hand, at the airport. Then you can broker a deal with the Chinese if things go wrong. That way I get two chances. What do you say?'

'I need time to think.'

'Go ahead then, Tony. Think.'

Looking suddenly paler Osman stubbed his cigarillo then made for the toilet, walking stiffly.

Tony eyed the café door, half got up – and subsided into his seat. Out of the question. If he got away from Osman what could he do? Turn him in? A non-starter. Though if he didn't… Had his weeks on the run brought a late conversion to sanity? Or was the whole thing a bluff, a trick to force him into helping him get out of the country, when he had nothing to offer at all? And assuming there *was* an operation, did he intend it to go ahead after he'd helped him onto a plane?

It took a moment to realise he had no choice. If there *was* something waiting to happen he would have to go along with Osman's plan, and if Osman was bluffing, given the risks, he could do no other.

The thought angered him. God how he despised Osman and his kind. Rich kids toying with mass murder, dabblers in jihadism who screamed for their rights when the going got tough. What sort of perverted human type was this? But then in the terrorist game nothing was new. Russian nihilists, the Baader-Meinhof gang, the Japanese Red Army, the Italian Red Brigades – who had they been? The offspring of the bourgeoisie, all of them – though nonetheless fearsome. More vicious than the working-class revolutionaries whose cause they had adopted. In the past it was politics, now it was religion, so you could multiply the viciousness, the hatreds and the corpses a hundred times. *An intellectual hatred is the worst…*

And invariably the press portrayed the security forces – people like himself – as fumbling incompetents effortlessly out-witted by their social superiors. Though there was another way to look at it. In the long run it was the revolutionaries who killed and died for nothing, and the plodders who held things together.

*

Osman came back wiping his hands on a handkerchief with a disgusted look.

'Filthy, these places. My cell was cleaner.'

So fucking fastidious – Zach's words came back to him – *these mass killers.*

Before sitting down he stood at the café window, peering out at the empty street. Back at their table he faced Tony squarely, the rim of his cap lifted an inch, his head straighter on his shoulders, his blank eyes as if staring through him. He's thrown up, Tony thought. The cigar on top of the whisky must have done it. A man who claims to be planning mayhem, and a bit of cigar smoke turns his stomach.

'How do I know?' he asked when Osman had ordered more beer for him and a Coke for himself, 'that your operation isn't a fantasy? No more than a bargaining counter to get yourself out?'

'If you're on a fishing trip, Tony, you're wasting your time. Feel free to doubt my word, but if you do there could be con-sequences – for you included. They won't be able to keep this one out of the press, I can tell you. Think how the media reports will look for you. *It is believed that Osman and the Chinese had been close to a deal,* is what they'll say, *but the M15 go-between refused to take Osman seriously. As a result…*

'OK, so let's assume it's true. That there's a real attack planned and that as a would-be martyr you're prepared to sell out your Uighur friends to save your skin.'

'Martyrs exist for martyrdom. They're a different caste. Maybe I'm not one of them.'

He stopped, a frozen look in his eyes. What Tony could not know was that an image of Kul had swum into Osman's mind.

Kul with his beatific detachment and lust for death, a martyr to his own cause who didn't care if the explosion rained down radiation on his own people.

'In any case it's no more than a tactical retreat', Osman continued. 'Whatever happens to me the situation is not going to go away. The more the Chinese kick Muslims around the harsher the retribution when it comes. Ancestral hatreds, Tony. Imagine the Arab-Israel dispute, Syria and Iraq fused into one. That's what the Chinese can look forward to in Central Asia.'

'I'll take your word for it,' Tony said sharply, privately doubting. 'Another explanation of your selling out is that you've got doubts about your commitment to the cause. You know how people say they discover things about themselves in a war? Is there some of that? Did you discover things about yourself in that cell? I'm not saying you're afraid' – Osman was looking indignant – 'just that it's one thing to plan things in your head, another to confront the bodies ripped apart.'

'They wouldn't be,' Osman said quickly.

'Ah. So what are we talking? Drowning, gassing? A dirty bomb, radiation, children with cancers? I don't suppose you'd relish that.'

'You misunderstand. I'm not acting from pity. Pity is weakness. You think I'm weak?'

'Absolutely not, otherwise you wouldn't be here. And don't worry, I'm not accusing you of pity. So why are you pulling out?'

Osman leant closer.

'Are you a believer?'

'I believe', Tony spoke guardedly, 'that I'm an agnostic.'

'Ha! Typical British cop-out!'

Tony grinned, but saw no answering smile. Osman had fallen back in his seat, his eyes closed, the tension in his face gone suddenly, as if he were in a profound sleep. Like this he looked even younger than his age, and watching him Tony tried to imagine him as a child. A child with a soft, oval face but with sharp, clever eyes. There'd have been nothing winsome about him, and with his background he'd have been spoilt from his earliest days. Willful, cocky, imperious beyond his years, marked out even then as trouble to come.

After a full minute the eyes opened as Osman said:

'Why shouldn't I tell you? Your friends at M15 will know by now. Because of my Kirghiz background I trained in the Fergana Valley. I've seen jihadis after an operation. When they come back and watch the TV shots of the dead and injured you should see the rapture on their faces. They turn their eyes to heaven. A kind of…spiritual ejaculation.

'I tried to think myself into their minds, to imagine what the sight of hundreds of dead Chinese would do for me. As I said I wouldn't pity them – don't think that – but then nor would it give me pleasure. Nothing. Just more human meat to offer to God.'

His lids drooped again.

'You said about people discovering things in war. Well for me this war is personal, so I've discovered more.'

'Such as?'

He gave a sour laugh.

'That I couldn't let it happen.'

'It?'

'Our spectacular. That's what the press calls it, isn't it? What they secretly long for? A spectacular. Well I'm going to disappoint them.'

He was staring directly at him. On his face there was no regret, no contrition. Even his failure Osman announced defiantly, with pride.

'I'm glad to hear it.'

The words felt fatuous, though what else could he say? Was

this a crisis of faith – or fear? A man brought up to think himself invulnerable, then the discovery in that cell that his charmed life was over, that neither his money or his brains or his country could do anything for him. In China there'd be no expensive lawyers to portray him as a freedom fighter, no impressionable juries or successful appeal. All there'd be to contemplate as he sat in his cell waiting was the certainty of a swift, anonymous death.

'I had nothing to do with planning the operation, or the target – especially the target. I was the link man, that was all. They sent me to make contact because I'd lived among Tungans and Uighurs in Kirghizstan, knew their history.'

'I still find it hard to imagine how you got yourself in this situation.'

'Maybe it's your imagination that's at fault.'

Patronizing bastard, Tony thought, even when he's throwing in the towel.

'I told myself I was on the Muslims' side, and I was. Chinese settlers flooding in by the day, extinguishing an entire culture! Fouling up historic landscapes in their grab for oil and gas and gold, smashing up old towns, despoiling the whole region with their hideous streets and buildings, so they're like any Chinese city, stamping out its character, its language, its beliefs! But this is Muslim land – my land, once.

'Then I got here. My first visit. I'm no romantic, I knew the lives of Muslims in this part of the world would be debased but – well, look.'

He nodded towards the couple who'd come in after them. The man, Uighur-looking though with no *doppa*, was in jeans, gaudy trainers, a T shirt with some kind of Arabic inscription, and a baseball cap, backwards. The girl wore no headscarf, her long, hennaed hair tumbling free over well-defined breasts. Both were smoking, drinking beer, laughing. As Tony glanced their way another young group came in, similarly dressed.

'Not sure I get you. What worries you about them? Is it the drink?'

His eyes fell to Osman's glass – he was back on beer.

'I know, I know. I was dry for nearly a year – till I got here. There too I've failed. But the Muslims of Xinjiang say they want to live in their own country, free to practise their religion. Bullshit! How many are true believers? Watermelons, most of them, green for Allah on the outside and red like Hans inside. Freedom to booze and take drugs and for women to wear skirts to their thighs – that's the freedom they want – and they can get it in China! So where does that leave their struggle for independence?'

Tony looked back at him, marvelling: twenty-nine years old and the one-time playboy was sounding like a finger-wagging *pater familias*. Amazing what a dose of Islamist ideology could do to you.

'Look at my father, a Muslim with a wife who converted to please him. Then he goes West and throws her aside along with his religion and puts a Czech whore in her place. I was six years old and I remember looking at her, admiring her, thinking, she's beautiful. But she's not my mother, and I hate her.' He jerked his head at the youngsters round them. 'Am I supposed to risk my life for a bunch of Muslim fornicators and apostates, like my father?'

'And your real mother?'

'She went back to her family, in Kiev.'

'And now?'

'She's…' Osman looked down, 'in a bad way. She was never a money-grubber, the kind to go for an expensive divorce. She just couldn't face up to him. Being cut off from her children damaged her, made her… psychologically unwell. I need to see her…'

The feeling in his eyes seemed uncontrived, but Tony was in no mood for condolences.

'Can we get back to your operation? You make it sound like this whole thing was a kind of psychological experiment, to see if you could do it. And it turned out you couldn't.'

'Except with the guns', Osman came back smartly. 'We got two loads through – it was the third when they caught us.'

His face alive again, for several minutes he recounted his gunrunning triumph: the Turkish middle-man who had supplied the weapons, the truck he'd bought, the night trips over mountain roads on the frontier. As he spoke his eyes lit with pride.

'And that I don't regret! You should have seen the gratitude on those guys' faces when we delivered! Suddenly they had something to fight back with. Chinese guns, good quality, I made sure of that, it was my own money. So with the guns I succeeded.'

'Except you were caught. Somebody rat on you?'

'Not your business.'

Tony glanced round. Another group had come in, the tiny place was getting crowded. He turned back to Osman.

'Can we talk practicalities? You're going to try to get out, and I can't stop you. But what guarantee do I have that you'll tell me about your spectacular before you go?'

Leaning forward, Osman said quietly:

'You have my word.'

Tony rocked his head.

'You doubt it?'

Feeling for his back pocket Osman reached out a small volume. The cover was in leather with an elaborate red and gold design. A medallion in the centre was inscribed with Arabic script. A moment later the Koran was obscured by the flat of Osman's hand.

'Something else I got back from Tang's desk in the Bureau! Don't look so surprised! It's as valid as the Bible!'

Not if you've lost your faith, Tony thought. When Osman put his pocket Koran away he said:

'So where will you go from? Not Urumqi I imagine? And how will you leave me the information?'

'So you agree to our deal.'

'I'm not happy about it, any of it, but no alternative occurs to me. We need to work out some contingencies.'

'And I need air.' The atmosphere in the café was heavy with smoke and Osman had begun looking unwell again. 'We'll do it outside.'

They got up and made for the exit, Osman leading. As he leant for the doorknob his jacket rode up over the handle of his knife.

'*Suan zhang!*'

Tony jerked round. Plaits and necklaces swinging, the proprietress flew down on them and grabbed his arm. Fearing she'd seen the knife he did his best to block out Osman's back, but he swivelled round, smiling, and spoke to the woman.

'She wants us to settle the bill', he explained.

Relieved, Tony reached for his wallet.

Out in the silent street they finalised the details. As they parted Osman reached out his hand. Tony wavered but Osman insisted. They shook.

24

When he came down for breakfast next morning there was a buzz in the hotel lobby, and it was soon clear why. Telephones and the Internet were on again, receptionists were brightly assuring the guests, permanently this time. For more than a month businessmen and correspondents waiting out the end of the emergency had talked of little else, and the authorities must have caved in to their complaints.

For Tony the phone lines were of little use. He could get through to Collinson directly, but what could he tell him? For the rest of the morning he fretted before concluding – nothing. He'd be speaking on an open line, though even if he wasn't what could he have said? That he was colluding in Osman's escape from the country, for the best of reasons? Not getting clearance for so important a decision went against all his instincts, but then referring the decision upwards would cause panic in high places.

Secret meetings with a fugitive prisoner behind the backs of the Chinese? Doing unauthorised deals with a British-born terrorist? And all this after getting his name splashed across the press... They'd think he was out of his mind. Thames House would burn up the lines to the Beijing embassy, ginger-top would show up at the hotel next morning and march him onto the next plane out.

Then there was Tang. He'd thought it through during the long night, endlessly, and come to the same conclusion: there was nothing he could say. The fellow-feeling he'd developed for the man made him want to take him into his confidence, but it couldn't be done. Sophisticated as he was, the Captain was a prisoner of his culture: the idea that a counter-intelligence officer could decline to turn in a terrorist on the run for fear of what the press might say about his right to an open trial would seem to him outlandish. And even if Tang agreed that letting Osman go was the only option, he'd get no backing from his bosses.

He'd be bound to alert his superiors, who would step up surveillance on airports, and if they caught Osman at immigration Tony wouldn't be there to do a deal because by then they'd have thrown him out. So that was it. There was nothing he could do, nothing at all, except sit tight till Osman got in touch.

*

About six that evening there was a soft knock at his door. Osman – in the hotel? The thought of him waiting in the corridor in some new disguise propelled Tony urgently from his armchair to the door.

It was Ling-Ling. Gliding in without a word she closed the door quickly.

'You knocked so softly I hardly heard.'

'There was a maid nearby, and I didn't want the world to know about our rendezvous.'

Rendezvous was putting it strong. She'd got into the habit of dropping by now and again when her shift was over, or she got off early. The company of a lovely young woman who treated him with easy familiarity could be agreeable, though it was someone he could never allow himself to covet. She came by for nothing more than a drink and a chat. As always the drink was Diet Coke ('I read that models don't drink alcohol in the West, they do drugs, it keeps them thin. Maybe I'll try some if I go, my dad would be wild if I did it here'), and her chatter was gossip she'd picked up in the bar. This time it was soon clear that she'd come to talk about her preferred subject: herself and her future.

'You know that American journalist?'

She was sitting on his sofa next to him, her legs stretched out before her. As she spoke she adjusted her hem upwards, experimentally, as if he wasn't there.

'Stewart Handler?'

'Yes, him. Is he in the same job as you and my father?'

She said it with an innocent look, though if she'd been fishing, it occurred to him, he would not have known.

'I wouldn't know, I'm British not American. As far as I'm aware he's just a journalist.'

'He's not bad-looking, is he?'

She seemed uncertain, wanted his assurance. Seeing what was coming, he gave it.

'I suppose not.'

'He was flirting with me again today. He wanted me to go for a drink in his room when I'd finished, but I said I had a date.' A giggle. 'Don't worry, I didn't say it was you.'

In a gesture of playful intimacy, a hand went to his knee. She did this from time to time. It was a pleasing sensation, though at the same time painful, emphasizing as it did her safeness in his company, and today he was in an un-playful mood.

'Don't tell me he said you were pretty enough to be in fashion magazines or on TV', he said sourly.

'He said that about me? To you?'

'No,' Tony laughed, 'It's just that it's a pretty standard way to pick girls up.'

'Anyway he told me in America the scholarships to study were more generous, especially for Asian people.'

'I think that's for scientists and computer folk.'

'But if I go there I won't have my English uncle to take care of me.'

The hand was on his knee again, this time pinching.

'Can I give you some advice?' Tony removed the hand. 'Don't get too hung up on this model thing.'

'Hung up?'

'Determined.'

'But I *am* determined! You don't think I have a good figure?'

'That's not what worries me. It's just not an easy career. It's very unpredictable. There are thousands of disappointed girls out there, and it's a long way to go to be disappointed. Maybe you should study something more, I don't know, more...'

He tailed away. His mind was not on what he was saying. And who knew, someone with her steely delicacy and vivacious temperament might make it as a model? To him it seemed strange that all models weren't Chinese.

Ling-Ling had given up listening. Her Coke was gone and she'd got up to fetch another, stopping for a second with her back to him to wriggle her dress down where it had ridden up. Now she was ranging around his room, as she often did, inspecting everything: his alarm clock, his clothes, his books.

She'd stopped to look at the cover of a thick volume lying on his desk: it was Jung Chang's biography of Mao, the book he'd finally finished. Grimacing, she snatched up another volume and covered the Chairman's face.

'I read *Wild Swans,* my father said I should. It was all right, but I'd heard so much about the Cultural Revolution. Too much. That's what parents do in China, always telling their children how terrible it was in the past and how lucky they are now. You feel sorry for them, sorry for their generation and their suffering, but the stories are always the same. I don't want to know any more about that time. So many dead and starving people! So long ago! It must be a gloomy book. I prefer lighter things, more modern.'

'I can understand.'

She stood before him, sipping from her can, then checked her watch.

'I need to fix my hair. Can I use your bathroom?'

'Of course. Though it looks fine to me.'

A few minutes and she came out, all primped and newly powdered. The skirt, he noticed, had gone up an inch.

'You're off on a date?'

'Perhaps.' A smile. 'Are you jealous?'

His laugh was brief.

'The last time somebody asked to use my bathroom,' he found himself saying, 'it was a trick. They turned out to be what we call good-time girls.'

'And was it a good time?'

She was facing away from him, tinkering with her hair in a mirror, but the grin he glimpsed in the glass told him everything.

'You sent them!'

Ling-Ling turned from the mirror, smiling sweetly and making a pretence of hanging her head.

'Don't be angry, uncle.'

But he was. The thought of them telling her how he'd spent the night with Meili...

'I thought you might be too shy to ask. It was just a present.'

'From you?' he said, adding before he could stop himself, 'or your father?'

'Oh not him! He wouldn't approve – not with you.'

'And you've told him?'

'I don't tell him everything! And don't worry, they weren't prostitutes, they were students. Some of them go with foreigners because they need the money for their studies, or to travel. One of my friends does it sometimes. I said to her, how can you do that, and you know what she said? She said I don't do anything dirty, so what's so bad about it? And foreigners are more respectful, she said. Does it happen in Britain? With students I mean?'

For him it was a painful question, forcing his mind back to a scene he'd tried to obliterate from his memory. It happened during his daughter's second term at Bristol, the time when he'd found out about the drugs. It was soon after the 7th of July Tube bombings, his work was eating up every hour of the day, he was seeing nothing of her, a pattern of alienation was building up and he blamed himself.

When the showdown came he'd handled it badly. She'd piled up bills, she was out of cash, and the bank had pulled the plug. Not a penny from me till you kick the habit, he'd said. Rehab he would pay for, but nothing else. Well she'd have to get it any way she could, she'd spat at him, the way some of her friends did. And it wouldn't be stacking supermarket shelves.

It was late at night, she'd been drinking, yet to be accused by your daughter of forcing her into selling herself was something that had incised itself in his mind. There was no reason to think she'd meant it, but he'd come up with the cash, smartly. And the drug-taking got worse.

'It happens in every country, I suppose', he said.

'I don't think it's so terrible. If they're nice people, and not too old or ugly, what's the problem?' She gave a mischievous smile. 'You're not bad-looking, Meili said.'

Oh God. What else had Meili told her?

'She's a film student, did you know that? She thinks you look a bit like Stewart Granger in *The Prisoner of Zenda.*'

'Oh come on!'

'My dad has a DVD of it, so I can see. You don't look like him?'

'I'm just not that old. He died twenty years ago. More.'

'Film stars are always young because they stay in people's hearts. So you will always be young too.' She smiled, cajolingly.

'My friends said you were very generous, they liked being with you, so don't be sad. Remember you've helped with their education!'

And they with mine, Tony mused.

She turned back to the mirror and went on fussing with her hair. Suddenly irritated, he wanted her to go.

'Drop in again. If there's any way I can help...'

He petered out. Help with what? And how? He would never persuade this girl to do anything she didn't want.

'Thank you, foreign uncle', she said, and pecked his cheek. 'Maybe I'll go to London, and meet your daughter? Dad says you have one about the same age as me.'

'Maybe.'

'Well, I'll come again soon. My dad keeps saying I'm not to go to people's rooms, but I knew I'd be safe with you!'

*

Next morning Tony came down late in the hope of a quiet breakfast, but Zach was still at his table, on the dessert course of his breakfast to judge by his plate of assorted pastries. Engrossed in a book, he looked up when Tony sat down opposite.

'Bad news. Looks like my Central Asian vacation is coming to a close. Message from the boss overnight, soon as the Internet got working: "Happy as we would be to have you out of the country indefinitely, we'd be grateful if you could see your way to getting the hell back at your earliest convenience and lending a hand." Or words to that effect.'

'Sorry to hear it', said Tony.

'I tried 'the recapture of Osman seems imminent' bullshit but they said forget it, you boys had a bigger stake than us, him being a Brit and all. If you get to interrogate him again they figure your people will pass on a copy of anything new. So there we go. I'll be sorry to leave. Getting a thing about the place. Been reading that book you lent me, 'bout China in the 1930s. Thing by Fairbank, the Harvard guy. Remember this bit?' He found the page, and read:

Even the most undistinguished American citizens – dead-beats escaping their failures, remittance men sent abroad for their families' sakes, stowaways and adventurers – once they disembarked at Shanghai had upper class status thrust upon them. Like the Chinese gentry, they were set above the masses, not subject to local police coercion. Embarrassed at first to be pulled by a human horse in a rickshaw, the average American soon accepted his superiority and found Oriental life and its inexpensive personal services enjoyable.

'Bit like it feels here, right? 'Cept for the rickshaws. So how 'bout it, Tony? Whaddya say we defect? Set up a security advisory outfit, Islamist atrocities a specialty! Think of the money we'd make! And the life! *Personal services* is the bit I like. You never been tempted by a personal service or two?'

'Haven't see our Russian friend around,' Tony said, diverting the conversation.

'He's off for the next coupla days, I gather. Family issues or something. Soon be on your ownsome, way things look. Out here in the Gobi waiting for Godot till you retire. By the way, the NSA ran a check for Osman on the Afghan-Pakistan border, see if there was any chatter 'bout him there, but no joy.'

And so on he went, throughout breakfast, which suited Tony fine since there was nothing he could or wanted to say.

25

The note to his room was on the same plain white sheet as the first. This time there was no writing, only numbers. It was the code they'd scrabbled together outside the cafe for when and where they'd meet.

0086-4-1255-27, and that was it. Not too clever, but secure enough for the purpose. 0086 was the dial code for China, to make it appear like a phone number. 4 was the last on the list of four regional airports that Osman was considering using to make his getaway, none of them in Xinjiang: Chengdu, Qinghai, Gansu and Inner Mongolia. 1255 was the take-off time, and 27 the date. So *en clair* the message read *expect you to be on hand when I fly from Baita International Airport, Hohhot, Inner Mongolia, take-off time 12.55, Thursday 27 June.*

Four days time – enough for him to pick up the internal travel papers Tang had offered. But Inner Mongolia? It sounded distant and exotic, and a long way round to Kiev, though when he checked the hotel's travel guide he saw that Hohhot was a shrewd choice. Its only international link was a daily flight to Ulan Bator in Mongolia proper. Which meant that its immigration facilities would have lighter security than airports serving the countries of Central Asia, many of which had terrorist problems of their own.

Whichever airport he chose, Osman had said, he would travel by a mixture of car, bus and rail. For himself Tony decided on an overnight train to Hohhot: more anonymous than a flight, less vulnerable to delays – and a long-awaited chance for a glimpse of the Gobi Desert. The trip was 30 hours, tomorrow was the 24th, so the timing was good.

Meanwhile he had an evening of Chinese lessons with Meili to look forward to.

*

He woke with the memory of Meili lying beside him, her soft voice schooling him in the four tones of Mandarin till after midnight. The weather, together with thoughts of Osman, swiftly dissipated his mood. For the first time in weeks mist and pollution blocked his view of the Tian Shan range that rose beyond the city, shrouding the tall new structures around the hotel so they seemed shifting, ephemeral, like imaginary buildings seen in sleep.

His train was not till late morning, but to avoid running into Zach he'd decided on an early start. He could put the spare time to use by running through a few counter-surveillance drills on his way to the station. His travel documents from Tang's office, copiously stamped and signed, lessened the chances that he'd be followed, but for all the Captain's benevolence, this was China.

Downstairs he left a note for Zach:

Dear Zach,

Had to fly to the Beijing Embassy at short notice. Sorry to have missed what would have been a great send-off. Hope you may still be here when I get back. If not, give me a ring when you're in London. There'll be plenty to reminisce about, I suspect. Great meeting you,

Tony.

He left the hotel on foot with no luggage, only a briefcase with a book, his toilet bag and a change of shirt and underwear. It had begun to rain and soon after seven the pavements were an undulating mass of umbrellas as people headed for work. Holding the one he'd borrowed from reception low, to disguise his height, he set out on a leisurely, loping walk to the station, reversing direction from time to time to see if anyone showed a sudden interest in a shop window at his approach. Then into a supermarket or two and out the back, pausing on the other side to see whether anybody copied his oddball behaviour.

A couple of hours of this and he arrived at the station, with no tail so far as he could see. Police hovering near the ticket office showed no interest in the damp-looking foreigner, and getting a sleeper on the train was no problem: there were few takers that day for the trip across the empty and arid roof of China, and he found himself in sole possession of a four-berth, air-conditioned soft sleeper compartment.

It looked comfortable, which was fortunate because the train's departure was delayed for several hours. There were no announcements. 'Soldier go back Gansu. No room on line. Soon we go', was the best he could get from his attendant. Lucky he'd left a wide margin.

It was four thirty-five before the train pulled out. At eight he made his way towards the dining car, but never got there: an overpowering smell of *polo* and hot fatty mutton drove him back. Running into a vendor in the hard sleeper carriage on the way he bought a cold pie, grapes and black tea for his supper. Lulled by the train's unhurried rhythm he fell asleep early.

He woke to vivid light leaking through the shutters. His first thought was of Osman: to get there on time he would have had to set out before him, though if his trip included a stretch by train, would he too be delayed? And if he couldn't make it on time, would he show up at all? Or give up trying to get out and...

He drew the shutters over the window and in an instant his anxiety fell away. Breakfast forgotten, he gazed at the wilderness unfolding like a scroll before him: gravel plains with nothing but thorn bushes and stunted trees, grasslands balding where the thin soil crust had been whipped away by wind, or sheep had eaten it bare. Then giant dunes stacked against a sky of endless blue. Wherever he looked evidence of life seemed on the retreat, the sun and wind shrivelling the land, the soil drying, the desert advancing. The desolation of the Gobi, he had read, could induce a man to hang himself, if only he could find a tree.

As the day went on remnants of life appeared: a herd of gazelles, fragile as a mirage, or a clutch of long-deserted yurts, their covering stripped by the storming sand, leaving nothing but a lattice framework. Then there were sheep pens, their perimeters draped in felt rugs, all that protected the lank-looking, scrawny beasts from desert wolves. Later came distant glimpses of the Great Green Wall – orderly rows of trees and shrubs the Chinese had planted as a barrier to the scouring winds, to stabilise the shifting land.

The train made up time and by early evening Hohhot was approaching. The road bordering the track was busy with cars and trucks, their paintwork blasted by sandstorms, and swarms of bicycles and mopeds, the riders masked against the enveloping dust, like raiders. Then slummy-looking suburbs, and finally a large new railway terminus approaching completion, with posters displaying the high speed train that was planned to link Hohhot with Beijing.

Urumqi had taught him not to expect too much of remote provincial capitals, and at first sight Hohhot ('the green-blue city', his guidebook promised) appeared less beguiling than its history and less amusing than its name. A giant central square, concrete mostly, like a parade ground, recalled its origins as a garrison town, and there seemed not too many Mongol faces, he noticed; here too the Hans had become the predominant race.

He took a taxi to the Holiday Inn, near what remained of the old town. Modern, middle range and anonymous, it seemed the right place for his needs for the night. Waiting at reception – a French tourist couple were taking an age to fill in forms – he glanced around for watchers. At the same moment a man entered the lobby and lounged by a pillar, waiting. Dark blue suit, no luggage, moderate height, middle-aged, Asian but of nondescript race. To test him out he did his best to make eye-contact, but the man avoided his gaze, and lit a cigarette.

He turned back to the desk, wondering how he would shake off the blue-suited fellow next morning. The French couple had gone and, displaying the imposing papers furnished by Tang along with his passport, he booked in quickly. Key card in hand he turned for another look at his man by the pillar – in time to see him greeting someone as hard to classify as himself. The pair of them smiled and bowed at one another in greeting – and burst into a loud torrent of Japanese. Feeling foolish, he made his way to the lift.

He was famished but it was too late, the hotel restaurant had closed. Disinclined to walk the streets he settled for a sandwich and a beer from room service. He had dozed on the train, sleep was long in coming, but there was plenty to occupy his wakeful mind.

He wasn't happy about the arrangement for passing the information before Osman flew off. Without knowing the lie of the land, the gunrunner and the M15 man had finally settled on the time-honoured toilets as the place where Osman would leave his message: whichever was closest to the check-in counter for Osman's flight, third cubicle from the entrance. Assuming there was a single row.

The room was horribly hot, his mind was blurry but his subconscious wouldn't let go: after falling asleep he dreamed he was walking around an airport, bursting to take a leak, but finding all the toilet entrances he approached barred by square-shaped Mongolian women in masks and rubber boots standing in pools of water, waving their mops at him and shouting in immaculate English, 'No entry! Absolutely no entry!'

*

Baita airport was a half-hour ride from the city centre, and he arrived well in time to check the layout. Sure enough there were two toilets, equidistant from the check-in counters. He walked past one, with a quick look inside before entering the second. A single row of cubicles in each, and no squat Mongolian ladies in gumboots to be seen.

Between monitoring the lavatories he booked a flight on a 2.35 plane to Urumqi – a ticket he might or might not use, depending on whether he could contact Tang on his private line to relay Osman's information. If everything went to plan he would need to be in touch, pronto. If it didn't, and Osman was picked up, he'd need to get onto him just as quickly. And should Osman double-cross him and take off without leaving anything…he'd think about that later.

At the bookshop there was nothing in English except a Lonely Planet book on China. Selecting a table in a café overlooking the main entrance, he passed up on the cakes and buns and ordered the dishes Mongolians around him were eating. One resembled overblown cheese puffs, the other was *shaomei*, a not too delicate-looking delicacy consisting of steamed dumplings filled with mutton.

Ten thirty, two hours till take-off: at check-in, nothing happening. He flipped through the guide book, which set out in startlingly arid photos the dismal environmental facts behind the sights he'd seen from the train. Drought, deforestation and overgrazing – Mongolia, the dairy capital of China, seemed headed for desertification. As a piece of anti-tourist promotion the guide was a masterpiece.

Eleven o'clock. Parties of Mongolians were arriving for the Ulan Bator flight: cheerful, round-faced folk lugging their Chinese loot – clothes, CD players and laptops he supposed – in bulging red and white chequered bags. Eleven thirty. The Ulan Bator flight had a single check-in counter. The queue was building and they weren't all Mongolians now: mixed in with the crowd were a few groups of Chinese and the occasional Western tourist. His eye sifted through the line for lone figures. Only one, of indistinct nationality, about sixty, in a skullcap, with a rucksack on his back. Not even Osman could contrive that transformation.

It was a small airport, he could see the runway from his table, and at that instant an Airbus A310-300 with *MIAT* – Mongolian airlines – in blue on the tail was touching down. Good. With so few planes the turnaround time would be minimal, the chances of delay fewer.

Then he saw him – at least it seemed like him, with Osman you could never be sure. The figure who came in and began crossing the concourse in a leisurely manner was a slim, dark-haired man in business suit and spectacles. Severe rather than stylish, tinted rather than dark, the glasses were not the kind to prompt an immigration officer to wonder what was behind them and ask him to take them off.

Behind he was towing a suitcase. What could a man on the run have in there? Part of his businessman pose, surely – though it raised a question: he'd left prison destitute, in pyjamas, so who had given him money for the suit, the smart-looking case, the glasses, the air fare? Something else he hoped to discover shortly.

The figure was still crossing the concourse, the two toilets to his right and left. Deviating from the direction of the check-in counter he turned suddenly right – and made his way to the newsstand. Minutes later he emerged with something pink under his arm: *The Financial Times,* presumably, Chinese edition, in keeping with his Eurasian businessman image. A nice touch: his man was playing his role like a pro.

Though what was this? He was heading back towards check-in. Then half-way there he stopped, looked up at a departure board – the Ulan Bator flight was on time – contemplated the queue, glanced at his watch and – thank Christ! – veered left and disappeared into the toilet entrance. Minutes later he came out, stopping to tuck a pen into his inside pocket. A tantalizing gesture designed no doubt to reassure him. Tony felt reassured.

Now the figure joined the queue at check-in. The deal was that Tony would wait till he was airborne before looking for the message. Why should he do that, he'd asked when they'd been finalizing details outside the café? A question of honour, Osman had replied gravely. *Osman? Honour?* To hell with that, he thought now: he'd be in there the moment he was through immigration and out of sight.

The queue was edging forward. From his table he agitated a hand for his bill. No response: the girls behind the counter had gone into a gossipy huddle, ignored him. He glanced back at the queue. Osman was checking in, his case on the weighing machine. The check-in woman was pointing to the dial, smiling. *Very light!* She must be saying. Cool as ever Osman was smiling too. *Short stay,* he must be explaining, *no time to shop.* Then he was taking his boarding card and passport from his pocket, making his way towards departures, his back towards him.

'The bill!'

Tony was at the counter, leaning over it, calling out to the gossiping girls, agitating his hundred yuan note. Finally one of them turned.

'What you eat?'

He gesticulated, wildly, to his table, where the cheese puffs and the *shaomei* were intact.

'*Ahh.* OK.'

Not OK, Tony signified with a frown, get on with it! After a parting giggle with her mates she wandered towards the till. Tony glanced round. At departures Osman was holding out his boarding card. The official made a sign. Osman produced his passport.

'*Change Sir!*'

Tony turned to take it, then looked back. At departures a queue was building, obscuring his vision. Was it Osman, holding things up? A problem with the passport? Or perhaps he was through, and it was something else? He couldn't be sure. Either way his man was out of sight.

He set off towards the toilets.

'Mr An-de-woo?'

Two men had materialised next to him, one either side. He turned to the first, then the second. Something familiar about them. Ah yes, the pair who'd greeted one another in the hotel lobby, effusively, in Japanese. In grey suits now, rather than blue.

'Yes. Is there a problem?'

The men were silent, disinclined to say.

Well, that was clever, he thought as his shadows led him away. Bloody clever, you had to admit.

26

The office they ushered him into, deep in the recesses of the airport, was distinguished by its many absences: no sign on the door, no windows, bare walls, no telephone, a naked desk. Even the Mongolian behind it seemed a negative presence: silent, expressionless, his plump features static, as if mummified. The only thing that struck Tony about the room was its stench of old tobacco. It must spend a lot of time occupied, with the door shut. An unpromising sign.

The pair who'd taken him in stood behind him. Lifting his head higher the Mongolian at the desk began inspecting him in frozen contemplation. The effort seemed to tire him. After a minute his fleshy eyelids began drooping, to the point where he appeared to be falling asleep. As the moments passed Tony glanced at his watch, an ear cocked, avid for announcements of departures. It was twelve twenty-five. Thirty-five minutes to go.

The Mongolian's eyes had widened a fraction, examining him not as an individual, it seemed, so much as a species. Insofar as his expression had evolved it was in a disapproving direction. It began to seem a long moment since they'd brought him, and Tony felt a need to assert himself. Receiving no invitation to sit he selected the only chair available, opposite the immobile figure.

The Mongolian spoke. From behind, one of the men interpreted.

'You arrived yesterday?'

'I did. From Urumqi, by train.'

The Mongolian brushed some air aside.

'We know it.'

Sitting straight in his chair, Tony assumed a dignified air.

'I assume I am addressing a member of the security author-ities of the People's Republic of China.'

The Chinese interpreted. The Mongolian didn't react.

'If so', Tony smiled, 'I am honoured to meet my Mongolian colleague.'

The immobile face seemed to freeze further.

'Perhaps I should explain who I am. My name is Anthony Underwood and I am a member of the British security ser-vices. I have been invited to China on a mission of counter-ter-rorist cooperation in Xinjiang province. At the moment I'm doing a little tourism.'

The Mongolian stared. Incredulity didn't come any blanker.

From his briefcase Tony drew out a copy of the *New York Times* story, pointed to the article, then to the picture of himself:

'This is me. And these,' he produced the document Tang's office had given him, 'are my internal travel papers. If you tele-phone Captain Tang Luming, the chief representative of the Ministry of State Security in Urumqi, he will confirm.'

The Mongolian was more interested in the *New York Times,* staring at the picture before passing the article to the goon who spoke English. While he laboured over the translation Tony tore a leaf from his notebook, wrote down Tang's name and private number, and handed it to the Mongolian. Who passed it to the translator and, giving Tony a kind of holding look, said something curt. The man felt for his mobile, dialled, spoke briefly, stopped. From behind him Tony heard a heightened version of Tang's low-pitched voice: the Captain wasn't angry, it appeared, he was furious.

Turning to glance at the fellow with the mobile he saw that he looked unhappy. Putting his hand over the receiver he spoke to the Mongolian at the desk, urgently, before thrusting the phone at him, as if glad to be rid of it. Tang's voice reverberated round the small room, louder now. Listening to it the Mongolian stood up, nodding deferentially at the mobile as though it were a person. Extinguishing it he thrust it back at the translator and, a smile widening his broad face further, held out a hand in greeting.

'Mister An-de-woo! I am Batbayar!'

They shook, and on he went. His words interpreted in spasms, he was saying that Captain Tang had informed him about the position fully and that he was sorry, supremely sorry. His service had orders to keep a watch on arrivals from Urumqi – the riots, Mr Underwood, the terrible riots – and unfortunately they had been given no notice of such a distinguished visitor. So much trouble, Mr An-de-woo must be thirsty, would he like a drink?

Tony hardly listened. Above the litany of regrets and apologies he had half-heard an announcement, first in Chinese then in crooked English. *The 12.55 flight C42 to Ulan Bator is delayed.*

'Mind if I smoke?' he asked.

'Me too', Batbayar exploded in English, nodding, 'Me too I like smoke!'

Producing an ashtray from inside a drawer he pulled a pack of *Double Happiness* and a lighter from his pocket, holding the flame to Tony's Davidoff cigarillo.

'Captain Tang tells me you are a welcome guest in Xinjiang, and to treat you as a guest in Hohhot. We are interested in cooperation with all countries. I myself have been abroad, many times, to Moscow, Ulan Bator.'

A prisoner of courtesy now, with sinking heart he watched as orders were given and tea was brought, together with two glasses and a bottle. At the sight of it he gave an inner sigh, but there you were, nothing could have stopped it.

'France brandy!'

Tony smiled and nodded. Batbayar glowed, pointing to the

label insistently till, leaning forward, Tony read:

Dynasty Brandy. The spirits are aged for a number of years in oak barrels imported from Limoges, France.

The Mongolian began pouring. Reflecting on what might be happening to Osman at departure Tony decided he could use a drink, of whatever vintage and whatever barrels. Affecting to savour the taste he swallowed quickly. It was strong, it burnt its way down, all he needed.

His cheeks instantly afire with alcohol the Mongolian was getting personal, confiding. There were indiscretions about airport security, of which he announced himself in charge. Not too many terrorists in Hohhot, thank heavens, they're all in Xinjiang, and they're welcome to them! No crazy separatists here either, we get on well with our Han brothers, as well as with our Mongolian friends across the frontier. All brothers! So it's a comfortable position, Mr Underwood, not like England, he imagined, all those bombs.

Tony said it was a handsome airport. A new one, Batbayar explained, and very modern. An international airport too I gather, Tony probed. Absolutely, the Mongolian said with pride: a connection to Ulan Bator, once a day. So not too much security, said Tony. Just routine, Batbayar shrugged, to protect the motherland. Drug-runners, criminals, smuggling – you had to be careful nowadays.

Conversation stopped while a plane roared overhead. Landing? Taking off?

You get many delays? Tony asked, what with the strange weather we're getting? Not too many, said Batbayar, though the Ulan Bator flight was late leaving today. Weather? Tony enquired. Security, Batbayar replied. Ah, Tony nodded, sipping his brandy faster and wondering when the hell he could get away.

A knock, and a uniformed official entered. Frowning,

Batbayar said something sharp. The official explained himself, the Mongolian listened and turned to Tony.

'You must excuse me. Business....'

'Security?'

'Immigration', Batbayar sighed. Looking embarrassed, he added: 'A British passport.'

'Oh dear', said Tony.

A wave of fatefulness came over him. He could see what would happen, every stage. They'd bring Osman here. Tony would phone Tang, explain the situation, enquire about the possibility of a deal. And the Captain would be shattered, incredulous, tell him he could do nothing without consulting higher authority. And higher authority would say 'detain the Englishman, put Osman back in his cell and beat the details of the operation out of him.' Exchanges which would entail many hours with Batbayar and his goons, in a less convivial atmosphere.

Finished grilling the official, the Mongolian turned to Tony.

'One flight a day, and they come to me with problems! And the passenger, he's not even entering the country – he's going out! You know what I said to him? I said, you see this man? He is an officer of the British security services and a guest of the Mongolian people! And you want me to hold up a plane because of a British passport.'

He turned to the official.

'Show our guest the passport! He'll tell you whether it's good or not!'

The man took it from an envelope and handed it to Tony. He flicked through, made as if to inspect the last page. The photograph Osman had showed him in the café looked back at him, cocky as ever. Something permanently derisive, now he saw it again, about the man's mouth.

'Of course I don't know Mr' – just in time he checked the

name on the passport – 'Mr Lang personally.'

'But it's all right, isn't it?'

Batbayar was impatient. With a shrug, Tony said:

'Seems fine.'

'It is genuine passport, but about the name we not happy', the immigration man said in English, before continuing in Chinese: 'We could run a detailed check, though unfortunately our computer –'

'– and keep a planeload of people grounded while you fiddle with your computer!' the Mongolian exploded. 'Let it go, just let the plane go!'

'With the passenger?'

'Of course with the passenger! If there's a problem they'll find out soon enough in Ulan Bator! Why do we want to keep a problem to ourselves when we can make a present of it to them! And up there maybe they have computers that work!'

Turning to Tony he explained what he'd said, adding:

'You see, Mr Underwood, the way I see it security must take account of the travellers' convenience. If immigration had their way no one would be allowed in or out of the country.' A plump fist banged his knee. 'Not even me!'

'Not even you!' Tony echoed with incredulity, pointing at the Mongolian.

Cacophony broke out in the room. Batbayar was heaving, his men joining in, Tony too. Laughter came from release from fear, the psychologists said, a thought that made him laugh the harder.

Unamused, the immigration man went his way while Batbayar poured more drinks. The interpreter and his colleague received a splash, gratefully, in their empty tea-cups. It was looking like a long session.

Batbayar was in mid-flow when a Tannoy announcement began. Tony strained an ear, couldn't make it out.

'That must be the Ulan Bator flight going', he said.

Batbayar enquired of the interpreter. The man said he would go and see. In seconds he returned.

'It has gone, the 12.55 to Ulan Bator has gone.'

'Another non-problem solved', the Mongolian roared, 'let's drink to that!'

They drank. Tony stood up.

'Will you excuse me? Your tea and brandy are excellent, I've drunk too much, I have to go to —'

Batbayar signalled to the interpreter:

'Show Mr Underwood the washroom.'

'No need, absolutely no need! Your staff's time is precious and I've taken too much of it. It has been a pleasure to meet you, Mr Batbayar, a genuine pleasure. And I must compliment you on the professionalism of your officers', he turned to them, 'your Japanese-speaking officers! A very clever trick!'

When the translation came Batbayar's breast swelled.

'My idea! For foreigners, we use it for foreigners.'

The goons exploded in smiles. Tony gave them an appreciative nod. You could never have too many friends, the way the world was going, even in Inner Mongolia.

*

He went to the toilets, cubicle three, searched the usual places. On top of the cistern lay Osman's knife, but no message. He prised off the lid, peered inside: rust, dirt, and that was it. No envelope stuck above the waterline, or sealed condom, floating. He looked under the lip of the pan, the space behind it. He rolled out the toilet paper to the end. Nothing.

For a moment his mind emptied, leaving a blankness filled with rage. It was when he turned to unlock the cubicle door that he saw it. Osman's message was right before him, scrawled like graffiti in black marker pen, at eye level:

23 Kadas Street, Urumqi.

Kul. Despatch clerk at Base 21, Lop Nor.

The first address meant nothing. Though Lop Nor...

The tannoy interrupted his thoughts.

Will passengers on the 14.35 flight to Urumqi...

He strode towards the check-in counter, pulling out his mobile – then stopped. His plan had been to ring Tang, instantly. Now things seemed less simple. He pictured himself explaining from the middle of the airport concourse that he had just helped facilitate the Captain's Category One prisoner's departure from China, but not to worry, Mr Kul, a despatch clerk at the Lop Nor nuclear base would explain everything.

A lot to get across in a phone call. Better take the plane, do it face to face. Though it would be early evening before he was in Urumqi, and if the attack was imminent...

He rang Tang's number.

'Tang.'

The tone seemed more peremptory than usual.

'It's Tony. Tony Underwood.'

'Ah. I hope you are enjoying Inner Mongolia. I am sorry for the complications of your trip.'

'I have to tell you something, of the utmost urgency.'

A pause.

'Well?'

'Your prisoner. His operation. It's at Base Twenty-One, Lop Nor. Someone called Kul is involved. And an address you should know: 23 Kudas Street. That's Urumqi.'

Another pause, before the Captain said:

'Thank you. Is that all?'

'Well, there's some background I'd like to explain in person. I'm flying back this afternoon. When can I see you?'

'This is not a good day.'

'But it has to be soon. Can you make it at six?'

'Maybe later. At nine o'clock perhaps. At my apartment.'

The line went quiet. The Captain seemed to be in conversation with someone else.

'Hello, hello?... Ah, you're there. Maybe I ought to tell you more now. About Osman. You see –'

'– thank you, Mr Underwood, later will be fine. It is difficult to discuss on the phone, and at the moment it is not convenient.'

The phone went dead.

What was this, he thought, hurrying towards check-in. There seemed a change of tone. Was Tang angry that his guest knew something he didn't? Or perhaps it was a professional requirement never to appear surprised. Chinese face, it really was something.

27

Tang's servant welcomed him, wordlessly; a stiff, silent fellow who spoke no English, he too seemed frostier than before, and after signalling him to take a seat he disappeared.

He waited. Ten minutes passed, half an hour, an hour. The longer he sat there the gloomier the room seemed to grow. His first impression of the décor had been of a congenial East/West mixture; tonight the lighter modern touches seemed submerged, the dark Chinese tones dominating.

The journey from Hohhot had turned out to be a long one – airport delays, traffic jams in Urumqi – and he could have done with a drink. When the servant had appeared with a tray and glasses his hopes had been raised – till he returned with the sherry bottle, and no whisky, indicating that the guest should help himself. Tony signalled that he would wait.

It was well after ten before Tang arrived. Outwardly his greeting was warm, yet his mood was different: determinedly calm on the surface, but agitated beneath. As he lifted the sherry bottle Tony said:

'Captain, I'm going to do something impolite. In the past you've been kind enough –'

'– of course,' Tang said distractedly, 'you prefer whisky.' He summoned the servant and a bottle was brought. 'You must excuse me, I've had a difficult day. I just arrived back from a meeting, in Beijing. Yes, whisky is what we need, I will have some too.'

Both men lit up and for a minute they drank in silence, while Marlboro and cigarillo smoke curled and mixed. Finally, Tony drew a breath, and began.

'My phone call from Hohhot must have seemed strange. I

asked to see you because I have a long story to tell.'

'Excuse me, Tony. Perhaps I can make your story shorter. You see, these last few days we have been monitoring your movements. I am sorry, it is not polite, a guest of our country, but after the *New York Times* article appeared in a Uighur paper it was for your own safety. You refused our offer of protection, but from intelligence we knew that a jihadist group had an eye on your hotel. You would have made an excellent hostage, with much publicity and pressure to release Uighur prisoners in exchange for your life. Like you Mr Boorstin refused our protection, but before he left we monitored him just the same.'

'I see.' He hesitated. 'Does that mean you know about –'

'– your meeting with Mr Osman? Naturally. We could hardly allow you to wander about the market area alone at night. We thought you had been kidnapped, then discovered it was Osman. A British counter-intelligence officer and an escaped terrorist, also British, meeting in secret. My superiors would be indignant, see it as an operation against my country.'

'Absolutely not.'

'Of course not. I listened to your conversation. Our agents were present in the cafe. You remember the young couple? Mixed race, so they can be Uighurs one day, Hans the next. I am sorry Osman did not approve of their clothes and behaviour. They are married, in fact… They alerted me and I listened here, in my study, live. A directional microphone – the reception was very good.'

'I admire your efficiency.' Tony's mind scudded back to what he'd said in the cafe. 'I hope you understand I wasn't at liberty to say what I wanted. He had a knife.'

'I know, our agents saw it, when you left. I was afraid – but then they said you had parted outside the café without trouble, that you weren't a hostage. I understand the circumstances of your conversation, even though you did not tell me.'

'I was afraid it would have put you in an impossible position.'

'Your judgment is correct. I am not sure what I could have said, what I could have done.'

'And you knew about my trip to Hohhot?'

The Captain frowned.

'Only when airport security rang me.' He sighed. 'The truth is, our agents lost you here. They were in a car at the hotel, assuming you would get a taxi in the rain, but you walked away into a side street, and they lost you. Very unprofessional – though in a way it was a relief. If we had known where you were going I would have had to decide whether to allow Osman to leave the country.'

'So you let him go.'

'Personally I would have preferred if we had him back in jail, so he could be punished for his anti-Chinese actions. But you had done a deal...'

'And the message he left? About Lop Nor, and Kul? And the Urumqi address? I hope that meant something to you?'

'It was useful corroboration.'

'Corroboration only?'

'I knew about the operation before you told me.'

A moment's silence, before Tony got out:

'How?'

'Our source was Colonel Benediktov. About Osman and his terrorist contacts – the Colonel told us everything.'

Tony frowned. Bad enough to have wasted his time, but to be beaten to it by the Russian...

'How did he find out?'

'According to the Colonel he knew about the operation from intelligence the Russians had picked up in Kirghizstan.'

'Why did he only tell you now?'

'The Colonel said he had made some investigations, but

instead of telling us, he said he had taken over the operation.'

Tony caught a sardonic glint in his eye as he went on:

'It is very Russian to do that, is it not? I have read the history of their intelligence services, from the times of the Okhrana under the Tsars to the KGB. Things in Russia are not like other countries, so complicated. Sometimes it is impossible to know whether it was terrorists or the security agencies running a plot. Though the Russians are not alone. In the Second World War your British operations, they were complex too, I have read. You seem to have been running all the Germans' operations against you, with double or triple agents.' He affected a sigh. 'You British, you are so inscrutable.'

'Wait. On the Colonel, there's something I don't understand. He could have taken over the operation and told you.'

'He said he was afraid of leaks. He intended to tell us when the moment came, so he could discover the maximum amount about the operation.'

'So he was handling Osman, personally.'

'He said he had never met him, he was controlling him through Kirgizia.'

'And the operation was at Lop Nor.'

'Yes.'

'Jesus!'

'Kul was a despatch clerk inside the installation. A strange individual, with delusions about his past. He believed he was descended from Ma Zhongying, a famous Muslim general, General Big Horse they called him. I doubt this, but he was certain of it, a quiet fanatic. His religion appears to have made him mad. He was living with a dead woman in his house, a White Russian, his grandmother we think. Whether he killed her we don't know.'

'And he was working with Osman.'

'A perfect couple. They were both Tungans, you see. An

Uzbek from the Fergana Valley where Osman was training put them in touch.' Looking down to flick his ash, he added: 'According to the Colonel.'

Again, the sardonic look.

The dawning suspicion that Benediktov was behind everything ought to have left him astonished. Strangely he wasn't. Now he had a vision of him in his habitual pose: one hand dismissing somebody or something with contempt, the other raising a glass urgently to his lips. Whatever it was to be a nihilist – and Tony had never been sure – the Colonel was one. A cynic, a drunk – and an obsessive, especially about China. Even their women he appeared to loathe.

'What you haven't said,' he spoke softly, 'is whether you believe the Colonel. You don't think he was bullshitting?'

'I beg your pardon?'

'Lying. About taking over the operation.'

Tang rocked his head – and that was all.

'Why did he tell you about it at that moment?'

'Because he knew Osman was about to inform us about everything.'

'How could he?'

The Captain's face was pained.

'Because we told him. Yes, another mistake. By accident he saw the transcript of your conversation in the café with Osman.'

'Good God. How?'

'Someone sent it to him, from my service. A clerk. She wasn't being disloyal, she sent it to his office in Urumqi because we had been copying other material on Osman, under our cooperation agreement. She saw the name Osman, then yours, she tapped a key – one finger – and it was gone, to the Colonel's computer.'

'Ah yes, computers.' Tony shook his head, his Luddite

instincts gratified yet again.

'When there are mistakes in intelligence matters,' Tang sighed, 'people always think about plots, traitors, infiltrators. They do not allow for –'

'– Sod's law.'

'I'm sorry?'

'Silly mistakes. Cock-ups.'

'That sounds like the correct word.' The Captain waited before adding: 'Of course this does not prove that the Colonel was not telling the truth.'

'But what if he was involved in the operation himself, and using jihadis to carry it out –'

'– Tony!' The Captain's tone was one of mild reproof. 'A Russian intelligence officer, working against a friendly country? That is a grave suggestion.'

It was at that moment that something surfaced from the depths of Tony's mind: the personality report on the Russian he had skimmed at Beijing airport on Collinson's computer when he had arrived. The memory came back as a faint imprint, like a photograph waiting to be developed.

'Let me tell you something else about the Colonel', he said. 'Something I just remembered. You know about his record in Kirgyzstan, when he was in the Russian Embassy there?'

'No I do not.'

'Something our people got from a Russian source. Only a rumour, but significant in the context. Apparently he was suspected of having a line out to jihadis in Kirghizstan. Arms supplies, I think it was. Some kind of double game. The Russians wanted the Americans out of the air base the Kirghiz had given them – the one they used to supply their people in Afghanistan. The idea was to give the jihadis enough weapons to frighten the Kirghiz government into closing it down. Nothing proven, but he left in a hurry.'

'Ah.' Tang frowned. 'That the Russians did not tell us. If we had known we would not have accepted him here.'

'So where is the Colonel now?'

'He left, a few days ago.'

'Recalled?'

'He left,' Tang deadpanned.

'You didn't question him?'

'He had immunity. Now that Osman has gone too, we may never know more.'

'And Kul?'

'Kul is dead. Our people went to his house, to arrest him. They planned to do it at night, but I said no. They have explosives, these devils, and when we went in he might have blown himself up. We needed him alive, so we waited till morning, when he was at his table, eating. Our people threw in gas, but too late. There was a cupboard behind him. He reached in, took out a pistol and shot himself. Still, we have the martyrs he recruited. He had photographs of them in the house, and they are talking.'

I bet they are, Tony thought.

'And what was the plan at Lop Nor? A bomb, was it?'

'An explosion, in a truck. It would have been enormous. Large numbers would have died, perhaps from contamination.'

'So what was the target exactly?'

'Ah yes, the target. I hoped you would not ask. The installations there are secret, and anyway, nobody knows for sure. The martyrs were to be told at the last moment. All I can say is there is a weapons storage site, and some research.' He hesitated before adding. 'Research at a high level.'

Into miniaturised nuclear warheads, perhaps? It was something else he'd read about in his briefing, before coming. Russia and the West had them, and the Chinese were keen to develop them.

'The address I gave you, in Urumqi. Did you know about that too?'

'No.'

'So Benediktov didn't tell you.'

Tang shrugged: 'Maybe he didn't think it was important.'

'And was it?'

'We went, at once. It was an abandoned shop, a safe house I assume. There was a bed and some food. Also empty whisky bottles.' He smiled. 'Very good whisky, with *wu gui* on the bottles – it means duty free – and some dirty glasses. We took the DNA from the rims. It was old but in this climate things are preserved very well, for centuries. Like the mummies, or the hatreds...'

'So who had been there?'

'There was the DNA of Osman, but also of the Colonel.'

'I thought he said they had never met.'

'The glasses do not prove they were there together.'

A silence. Why was Tang so stubborn in defence of Alyosha? Tony had another go.

'Surely the simplest explanation is that the Colonel was behind the whole thing. If you're not allowed to say, for official reasons,' he gave a tense smile, 'I understand. But tell me, how did you get onto the guns? And why did you suspect there might be something else planned? It's interesting, professionally.'

'It was chance. Someone we were watching, a Uighur, a weaver. After guns were used in the riots we searched his shop. In his cellar we found weapons, under piles of carpets. He was a nervous man, very frightened.' He stopped to flip his ash. 'So he talked. When the weapons were delivered he told Ekrem, the driver, that there were not enough, they needed more. And Ekrem said he shouldn't worry, he had heard rumours there was something bigger coming. Much bigger. That is why I was at the scene when they picked up Osman.'

'There's also the question', Tony pursued, tenacious now, 'of communications. It seems to have been a complex business.'

'Not really,' Tang shrugged. 'There was a triangle. In Kirghizia there was Salih, the Uzbek in the camp where Osman trained. In Lop Nor there was Kul, and in Urumqi there was the Colonel. For communications the Russian had his cipher link to his Bishtek Embassy, the Uzbek had his courier from Kul to the Kirghiz camp, and Osman was the go-between with Kul. Six people, not so complex.'

'Maybe the Colonel's Embassy contact was an FSB colleague, acting unofficially, in the way our Russian friends do. Presumably you'll discover the truth from the Russian government.' He smiled. 'Assuming they were not involved.'

The Captain's expression, scarcely readable already, became more opaque. Taking an urgent puff on his cigarette he exhaled quickly, as if to retreat behind the smoke. As he did a foot began to tap the carpet – invariably a sign, Tony had noticed, that he was reverting to his official self.

'Even if what you suggest about the Colonel were true it would be inconvenient to say so.'

'Inconvenient for who?'

'For my country. I am being frank with you, Mr Underwood, perhaps too frank. Our government has discussed this matter. The meeting I have come from in Beijing – very high level – we discussed it there, for a long time, because the solution is not easy.

'Imagine you are right. Imagine we announce this plot, and say it was a Russian representative behind it. For my country it would be a national humiliation. We could not put him on trial – he has immunity. We could insist that the Russians try him, but...' He raised his hands.

'Whether he had official links or was operating as a rogue element I think you call it, would make no difference. They would deny he was involved. Remember what happened with your Litvinenko case, when it seemed that somebody connected to Russian intelligence circles –'

'– but this is so much bigger!'

'The principle, it is the same.'

'So what will you do?'

'It is better that the Colonel should disappear from China, quietly, which he has. Maybe he will be punished – and maybe not.' The Captain nodded, resignedly. 'You know the situation. When communism fell in Russia it was as if the KGB was privatised, like gas or electricity, and people could take a stake. Strange people sometimes, shadowy people, deniable people…Gangsters, mafia, ultra-nationalists…'

The Captain was looking uncomfortable again, his right foot tapping away.

'This case will have a bad effect on our leaders. Here is a Russian and a British Muslim working to bring terror to Chinese Xinjiang! For them it will be like an echo of the nineteenth century, a new episode of your Great Game. Except that this time the Russian and the Englishman were working together to weaken China by damaging its defence research and by the export of terror. For some of our leaders every obstacle we encounter is an attempt by foreigners to stop our national advance.

'At present Russia is a friend, but they see the rise of China and deep down they are afraid. *It was better under Mao. At least he kept the little bastards poor and weak. A few more years and they'll be staking a claim to Vladivostok.* That is something the Colonel said, I remember.' Looking annoyed with himself, he added: 'I should not have told you that. You must forget…'

But Tony remembered it too: something Alyosha had

blurted out in one of his late night drunken diatribes, in the bar.

He stared at the whisky bottle. It was low, he'd had too much, he was tired. He got up.

'Maybe I should go. You must be tired, Captain.'

'And you too, Tony. An exhausting day for us both.'

They had reached the door when the telephone rang in Tang's study. Excusing himself, he hurried to answer. Tony hung on to say goodbye.

It was a long call. Five minutes in Tang came to the study door, the receiver to his ear. Tony indicated that he was going. Frowning, Tang signalled at him urgently to wait. The conversation, animated it seemed, continued several more minutes before the Captain returned. If there is such a thing as a half-sad, half-exultant look, that was his expression.

'Please sit down', he pointed to his chair, 'there is something more we must discuss.'

With an unhappy feeling, Tony did as he was told.

'My telephone call, it was about Osman, and it concerns you. You remember the immigration official at Baita airport? The one who was ordered to let Osman's plane go?'

'I do. He was not a happy man.'

'He was a dutiful man. The passport, he saw, had been interfered with. So when the plane took off he telephoned his opposite number in Ulan Bator and explained the circumstances, and the man called in the counter-intelligence people.

'I have a friend in their service. It is he who telephoned. The passport wasn't right, and we distrusted his explanations, he said. It is up to you, my friend told me. Is it important for you? Should we let him go on to Kiev and give his silk to his mother – or send him back to China?'

Tony sat, rigid.

'He's still in Ulan Bator? At the airport?'

'Yes.'

'So what did you say?'

Tang took a breath.

'I said, yes, it is important to me. You must send him back.'

The incredulity on Tony's face stopped Tang for a moment. He went on, softly:

'Earlier you suggested that I had allowed Osman to leave China. That is not exactly the case. The truth is that he went because I did not do everything I could to stop him. There is a nuance. In his conversation with you Osman said the Chinese did not understand fair play, but he is wrong. I had done no deal with him, so I had no obligations towards him. But you are a colleague, and a Western friend. You had done a deal, so I did not like to stop him.'

Tony looked back at him, doubtful.

'I'm not sure what you're saying.'

'I am saying that I did not take a decision about Osman leaving China. But about getting him back, I have taken a decision. Because once he was out of the country I was no longer bound by your agreement.'

Bullshit, Tony thought. Absolute bullshit. The Captain had gone back on their understanding.

'Osman is a clever man, a cunning man,' Tang went on. 'And confident, Tony, too confident. He chose the wrong place to go, because with Mongolia we have just signed an extradition treaty, with security provisions. In a few hours he will be back in China. In Beijing this time, for greater security. That is what I have arranged in the phone call.'

Tony looked back at him, still taking it in.

'This man puzzles me, Tony. So arrogant, and yet he was an amateur, with a high estimation of his capacities. Forgive me, but I have heard of such British people before: the amateur in a high social position who believes he can turn his hand to anything. But terrorism is not for amateurs. And we Chinese, we are not amateurs.'

A hardness had come into the Captain's expression. This time it wasn't that he was putting on his official face: it was patriotism, pure and simple.

'His insolence I find amazing. The kind of person who can show contempt towards other people even without speaking. When I tried to interrogate him, it was as if he was the master! He told me about Chinese history, and what happened to the Tungans. How can a man so educated not understand that history is in the past, that we cannot take revenge for what happened centuries ago? What if we Chinese behaved like that too? I hope my country will not do that when we have more power.

'I see you are unhappy, Tony, but the reason your deal was broken was not your fault. It was – what is the word, that French word the English use –'

'– *force majeure?*'

'Yes, that is the expression. China was the *force majeure*. We needed two things, and now we have them. The attack in Lop Nor has been prevented, and we have Osman. Is that such a bad result?'

It depends on your angle of vision, Tony was thinking. When they read about a British citizen being lethally injected after a secret trial, even though he'd squealed on his fellow conspirators, the press may have other ideas. Not to speak of his own position. He could see the *New York Times* picture of him looking louche being re-played in the UK media, endlessly. *M15 Man Involved in China Execution.*

'The main thing', he said quietly, 'is that the Lop Nor attack was stopped. It was only because Osman promised to tell me about it that Benediktov informed you. You have to give the man credit for that.'

'Logically, what you say is true. But the fact is that I knew about the attack before you told me.'

There was something wrong with the reasoning here, it seemed to Tony, but there seemed little point in picking the Chinese up. Tang had Osman in his hands, he wanted him to die, and no amount of reasoning would persuade him to save him.

28

It was after midnight before he got away from Tang's apartment, too late to ring Collinson. Xinjiang was two hours behind Beijing and if he rang that night the poor man would be yanked from his bed at nearly 3 a.m. And after what he had to tell him he wouldn't get back to sleep.

A pointless scruple. Events had taken over, and at the hotel a message was waiting for him to him ring the Embassy, urgently. Collinson came on the line instantly. Before he could get in a word he told Tony that the *Guoanbu* had warned the Embassy minutes earlier that they intended to announce Osman's arrest the following day, on a charge of gun-running. When Tony replied that there was rather more to the story than the Chinese might let on, more than he could explain on an open line, and that he had reason to suspect he would be recalled to London smartly as a result, Collinson sounded panicky.

'Sounds like we need to talk', he said, 'quickly.'

'You can come out to the airport when I transit Beijing, like when I arrived, and I'll fill you in.'

'It'll be too late. The announcement's later today. There's an early flight to Urumqi. I'll come out first thing this morning and we'll travel back together. It'll save a few hours.'

Thames House would be breathing down the poor devil's neck to get the full story, pronto.

'If you can bear to, I think that would be wise.'

Collinson showed up at the hotel next morning in a tempestuous mess, hair flying, his jacket flapping from a finger on his shoulder, his forehead dripping sweat in the new surge of hot weather. He did what he could to soothe him with the offer of a drink before lunch but he refused both, anxious to get straight to work. They went to his room, sat down and began. At the mention of Lop Nor Collinson, appalled, began signaling frantically at the ceiling.

'Something wrong?' Tony glanced up, all innocence.

'It's just…what you're saying. I never imagined… Maybe we should talk somewhere else.'

'Here's fine. There's nothing I'm telling you the Chinese don't know. That's the point. They know everything.'

It was nearly an hour before he was through. After hearing about Tony's solo operations with Osman the Embassy man was in a worse state than before. As Tony recounted his story he made notes on his laptop, throwing him anguished glances. When it was done all he could find to say as he closed the lid was:

'It would have been nice to know.'

'Would it? If I'd told you, what would our bosses have said? That I should tell the Chinese about Osman, let them pick him up and to hell with the consequences? Or that I should help smuggle him out and keep the Chinese in the dark, in the knowledge that he'd scupper the attack once he'd gone? Not telling them – or you – was a service to you both.'

Collinson looked unconvinced.

'Don't worry, I'll vouch for you', Tony added, 'when I get home. Explain why you were out of the loop.'

Collinson threw him a glance that said, thanks a bunch, but Tony would have trouble enough vouching for himself.

'Now if you'll excuse me I'd better get ahead with my packing.'

On the assumption that Thames House would want him back instantly he planned to catch a four o'clock plane to Beijing, then an overnight flight to Heathrow late that evening.

Leaving Collinson to get off a coded report to Thames

House, he took out his suitcases and got to work.

'Help yourself to something from the fridge', he threw at him when he'd flashed out his message. 'You look terrible.'

This time Collinson didn't say no. Pouring himself a gin and tonic he sat there drinking forlornly and picking at a bowl of nuts. It was three quarters of an hour later, when Tony had pretty much cleared the room, that his laptop pinged. Collinson lurched at it, read the message and looked up from his screen:

'Tony, you're not going to like this.'

'From your face I'm sure I won't.'

'They've come straight back. It's three o'clock in the morning at home but the duty officer must have woken someone up.'

'And so?'

'You're not going home tonight. They want you to stay on in Beijing.'

'For what?'

'Osman. They want you to have another talk with him.'

For a long moment Tony stood at the side of the bed, immobile, a stack of cellophane-wrapped shirts in his arms. Interrogating Osman a second time was out of the question. In his fury over what had happened he would revert to his previous self – treat him like shit, or simply refuse to talk.

'I can't.'

'It's not a question.' Collinson searched his face, his attitude to Tony wary now, as if he was dealing with some headstrong child. 'It's an instruction.'

'The Chinese may not agree.'

'It says they'll clear it with them in London.'

'I don't see the point. I've nothing to ask him now.'

'*They* have. They'll be sending a list of questions.'

'Tell them I'm the last man to get answers, the way things

have turned out.' He looked down at Collinson. 'Why not have a crack at him yourself?'

Two bright young things together, he thought wryly. Should get along fine.

He laid the shirts in his suitcase, sighing.

'What is it they want me to ask?'

'The context,' Collinson said, 'will be home security.'

Ah. Six words that made it impossible for him to refuse. Which he saw, now that he'd calmed down, that he was in no position to do anyway.

*

At two o'clock a taxi took them to the airport. Urumqi wasn't the kind of place you got sentimental about, he reflected, staring from the window to dissuade Collinson from attempts at conversation, yet in a way he was. For him China had been both a discovery and a holiday from reality. The world talked about the country incessantly, yet for most it was a great abstraction: a vast productive machine operated by faceless people, a place with too much humanity to think of in human terms. And amongst Westerners who went there, how many had got to know a Chinese, let alone an intelligence official?

Though how far had he really got to know the Captain? Until yesterday he would have had no hesitation in describing Tang as a friend. Now he might hesitate. The gulf between them that had begun to close in their long talks together had edged open again over Osman. He didn't blame Tang for wanting Osman to face justice; he had no sympathy for the man. When it came down to it their perspectives on the world were different, always would be, reflecting their starkly different experience. Would they see each other again, in London perhaps? Difficult, after what had happened…

The idea that he could stay on in China, let go of his family duties and go off with Meili on a protracted tour of the country, that too had been an illusion. Now there could be no lingering on. A day or two in Beijing, and that would be it. Apart from the fact that they'd want him back in London, the idea of wandering the country with an exquisite twenty-year-old Chinese lover, how had he ever persuaded himself it was possible? When he'd phoned Meili to say goodbye she'd seemed genuinely sorry, though as she chattered on brightly it was clear who would miss whom the most.

All too late. For a man on the brink of retirement there could be no new freedoms, no release from his obligations, no going with the flow. Wild imaginings, all of them, an ageing man's escapist dreams. Instead he would go home and face the music, the enquiry Thames House would no doubt conduct into how it could all have happened. The outcome would cast a shadow over his retirement at best, at worst put his pension at risk. The pension he would need to go on helping his daughter.

Tang and Ling-Ling came to the airport to see him off. While Collinson chatted away to his daughter (he caught something about her coming to Britain to study – had Sanderson asked him to make contact?) the Captain drew Tony aside.

'My ministry tells me your people have asked for you to see Mr Osman in Beijing.'

'That's right. And I'm not looking forward to it'

'I understand why. He will think you betrayed him, and you can give him no hope.'

'Meaning?'

'I do not think he will escape the death penalty. You will say that if our government are not going to announce the Lop Nor plot, then how can they try him for it? But the gun-running is enough. About guns our government is adamant.'

'But China attaches importance to confessions and remorse, doesn't it? In that café he told me that in the end he couldn't do it. I think he was sincere.'

'Sincere in wanting to escape the country, certainly. Sincere about remaining unpunished. When he boasted about smuggling his guns he was no doubt sincere then too. The weapons he brought in killed over 90 people, policemen mainly. As well as the two young men in your jeep there were colleagues in the Bureau who died. They were brave people, they stayed to the end, disposing of papers. When they were forced to escape the flames, they were shot. One was young, 34, a deputy of mine, a thoughtful man with a modern outlook. He did not see enemies of China everywhere, and he didn't agree with locking up people simply because of what was in their minds. I had hopes for him...'

Tony had one more try. He told him about Osman's upbringing, his father's behaviour, his mother's sickness, but it was useless. Tang had assumed his stony expression.

The flight to Beijing was announced.

'Before you go, Tony, there is something I want to thank you for.'

'What's that?'

'Thank you for not agreeing to Mr Sanderson's request to try to recruit me.'

Tony gave a resigned smile. There seemed nothing the Captain didn't know.

'Imagine you had tried. I would have faced a dilemma. If I had told my bosses, they would think, why did they decide on Captain Tang? Does he have unpatriotic thoughts? A secret vice? They would become interested in my books, my friends, my views on everything. Even if I kept my job I would never be allowed to travel...

'And if I had said yes, and agreed to work for you? Then the problem would be the one you discussed with Mr Sanderson. Our countries are not at war, we no longer speak of spreading communism throughout the world, so what information could I have given you that is so important? I would have had to make it up, to keep my handler happy! And finally they would catch me and I would end up in a death cell, next to Mr Osman!'

By now he was laughing, but Tony wasn't. Officially the response was simple – deny all knowledge – but it was a bit late in the day for that.

'Just for interest, tell me how you found out?'

'We knew about Mr Sanderson, you see. He does some commercial work, but we checked with the firm he was visiting in Xinjiang and it was as we thought. The trip was cover, so we were interested in why he was coming.'

'When you say you knew about him…'

'He had come to our attention because he is – how shall I say? – a little hot in the head. No, hot-headed. I do not want to say anything critical about M16, your brother service, but –'

'– go ahead', Tony smiled.

'– Mr Sanderson knows the Chinese language, but he does not understand Chinese people. His views on China lack – there is a word, another French word …'

'Finesse?'

'That is it, finesse. Why do the English keep speaking French, I wonder? He made an approach to a businessman he had met at a trade fair, someone who supplies electronics to our army. The man's company was in difficulty. The business-man was a rogue but a patriot, a patriotic rogue. So he told us. We didn't throw Mr Sanderson out, because the British would have felt bound to reciprocate against our people in London. British face!

'The result of tit-for-tat would be that we would lose

someone in London and you would get somebody better here. Not a good trade! So we left him, and recruited the businessman as a double agent. Then it was the usual thing: he gave Mr Sanderson small things, for his appetite, your man became suspicious, and it ended. I should not tell you this but', he shrugged, 'it's an old case, it's over. And if people spend less time on these things perhaps it will save a lot of trouble on both sides?'

There was a debate to be had about that – the *Guoanbu* had front companies and intelligence agents scooping up technological secrets all over the West – but this was not the moment to have it. Tony had got the message: Sanderson was blown, and they'd be well advised to withdraw him, without fuss or retaliation.

'So you had someone there when we had dinner?'

'Yes, Kazaks, though they can pass for Uighurs. You remember the men playing chess? Well the queen' – Tang did his best to suppress a grin – 'the queen was –'

'– don't tell me.'

'Yes, a microphone, a new type. It's the first time we have tried it.'

'It seems to have worked.'

'Very well, though one of our men complained. It was his queen and he was forced to sacrifice it. The signal was too weak, we had to get it off the board into a closer position. Sacrificing his queen so quickly was a humiliation, he said. Very proud, these Kazaks!'

'But he came back, I noticed.'

'Yes, eventually he won, but he was indignant. You must miniaturise it further, he said, right down into a pawn! A pawn I do not mind losing.' He giggled. 'There, another trade secret I have given away! You may copy it, Tony, but promise never to use it against our people!'

'Against the Russians would be OK?'

Tang gave a rueful smile.

Tony thought back to Sanderson. '*I'm running ahead of myself*,' he'd said in the restaurant. He certainly was. He must have thought he'd been smart, switching to a downmarket joint at the last minute, so he could speak freely. But the concierge must have signalled that they were coming. He ought to have warned him, been more careful himself, but then he was on his way out, found it hard to care...

'I apologise for listening to your dinner table conversations,' Tang said, 'but I am obliged.'

Tony shrugged. His regret at the blowing of Sanderson's cover and the blight on his career was containable.

'It is in the nature of our work,' Tang went on, 'and sometimes our bosses have strange ideas. I even received an order that I must try to recruit *you*.'

'*Me?*'

Was this a joke? Should he laugh? Or was it to do with Meili? Ling-Ling said she hadn't told her father, but she wouldn't need to. Nothing would happen at the hotel that Tang didn't know.

'It was not my suggestion, it was someone at my ministry. A senior man, very old-world. He was never in favour of foreigners going to Xinjiang, but he insisted on knowing what you were thinking. So to keep him happy we showed him some things that had come to our notice. He saw a report of you saying admiring things about our country. That coming to China had given you the surprise of your life, and the Americans had better watch out! It was kind of you to say such things, but sometimes our superiors can be simple folk, so I was ordered to sound you out.'

Tony looked at him with wondering eyes:

'Is that why you invited me for sherry?'

'I was under orders. Obliged to – what is it you say? – go through the motions.'

'And what did you report?'

'I said that Mr Underwood was an experienced man, a thoughtful man, but he was about to retire, that he would have no secrets, and he was a patriot. Unfortunately, my boss persisted. Never mind secrets, he said, the Englishman can be an agent of influence! He had trained in Russia, you see, it was something he had learned in Moscow… The Russians like such people. For me,' he shrugged and smiled, 'agents of influence are not worth the trouble.'

'Maybe this is your disguised attempt' – Tony grinned – 'at recruitment?'

'Yes, my official approach! Now I can report back that I have cultivated him, that I have tried, but that while you were grateful for the offer, on consideration you decided to decline.'

Tang ruminated a moment, before saying:

'Maybe what Mr Sanderson said about you is true of me as well.'

'And what was that?'

'That perhaps you are in the wrong profession. I do not mean that you are not good at it, I have heard of your successes. But it is possible to be a success at something and still be in the wrong career. Me too, sometimes I feel that way.'

'Well I've enjoyed my stay, even if everything I've done has been a waste of time. The last few days especially. I should never have got involved. You knew everything.'

'That is not the case. Without your talk with Osman, things would have been different. You did your best to save many people, Uighur and Chinese people. I am personally grateful. I must thank you too for your advice to my daughter. She told me you had been very frank with her.'

'I told her modelling is a crowded profession. I wouldn't

want her to be disappointed. On the other hand, she seems very determined, very ambitious.'

'You don't think she will do some study? For a serious profession?'

'Can I tell you something? My daughter didn't want to go to university, she wanted to go into the music business. When she told me the first thing that occurred to me was: that means drugs. So I said no, she had to go. So she went to university – and got into drugs. We had a quarrel. She left home. And now she's…'

He threw up his hands.

'In the music business?'

'And the drugs business. Taking them, selling them sometimes I think. And I feel guilty. All those years I was working late, all those crises, so I was never at home with her.'

'With my daughter, it is the same, I too have guilty feelings. Spies, plots, state secrets – these are our lives, but in the end everything comes down to personal things. Like Osman and his father, the Colonel and his…'

A call for the flight. Tony had yet to check in. He felt in his pocket for his ticket.

'May I?'

Tang reached over, took the economy class ticket and replaced it with two, first class. One in his name, one for Collinson.

'How did you – ?'

'– it is nothing. I had a word with the airline. In Xinjiang it is me, the agent of influence.'

They went back to the others and Tony said his farewells. Ling-Ling pecked his cheek, her eyes even lovelier when they were sad. He looked forward to seeing her in London, he said, with her father perhaps, but she shook her head. After what had happened they would be going to Beijing, she told him.

And now that her father's boss, General Li Hesan, had finally been retired, he would be promoted. She didn't sound too happy about it.

As they went through departure he glanced round. They were still there, the Captain in his sober suit, his daughter in some abbreviated outfit, all legs, holding her father's arm with one hand, waving with the other. There would be trouble there, but for now at least they were together. He hadn't seen his own daughter in years.

29

'He's in the Beijing Number One Detention Centre', Collinson explained as they drove to the meeting with Osman after the *Guoanbu* had given clearance. 'It's the most select establishment, as the name suggests. Most people there are facing death sentences. Murder, drug dealing, big-time corruption – it's where they've built the new high-tech lethal injection centre. State of the art, they tell me.'

'And the accommodation, meanwhile?' Tony enquired.

'Usually they're in cells of a dozen, but foreigners tend to be held apart. Osman's in isolation. They won't want him talking to people about the Lop Nor business, even if they'll be meeting their Maker long before his trial. His cell's not as agreeable as the one in Urumqi, to judge by your account. The Consul tried to get him upgraded, but no joy. He's not allowed visitors, but then no one's asked.'

'So his prospects are zero.'

'They have seven categories of serious crime, and he's got himself into the lot. Between them they cover terrorism, murder, transporting guns and ammunition, intent to cause explosions, security of public property and endangering the People's Republic. That's a lot of death sentences. If they're going to cover up the Russian affair they can't cite them all, but they don't have to. It's like Tang told you: the guns alone will do for him. Anyway I doubt whether –'

Collinson's voice was drowned by a fury of klaxons as he tried to change lanes, tacking choppily across an ocean of cars. At the same moment Tony let down a window – something was wrong with the air-conditioning – but it didn't help. The car filled with the stink of the fume-infected air, and the racket from the road helped sever their conversation.

Which for Tony was a relief. Apprehensive about the meeting, he would have preferred to see Osman alone, but Thames House had specifically requested that they see him together. Irritating, but after his Mongolian escapade, unsurprising.

His stay at the Embassy had been useful in one respect. The military attaché, a great, bearish fellow and a veteran who knew his business, had helped clear up the mystery of Benediktov's likely target. Tony had been right about miniature nuclear warheads. Work on them had been in progress in Lop Nor, the attaché was convinced, and the Russian must have had the research installations in his sights. It was high level stuff, China's leading scientists would have been employed on the project, so there may also have been an assassination motive: to take out some of China's top people, like the Israelis had done with nuclear experts in Iran.

'Our Chinese friends have been upgrading their force ever since Bush deployed antimissile systems in Alaska and California. They had to make sure theirs would get through, which meant miniaturisation and Mirvs – multiple warheads. Stealing American techniques helped, which they did in the 1990s, but they've had their own research.

'Why would that worry their Russian buddies? Everyone focuses on the China versus American thing, and forgets how things look to Moscow. The Chinese are richer than them, with a bigger army and a growing navy, so how long are the Russians going to wait until their little yellow friends – that's the way they think about them over there – start catching up with them in nuclear technology too?

'All of which strengthens the possibility that Benediktov might have been something more than a wild card, though whether the Kremlin was involved is something we're unlikely to discover. If we still don't know about the chain of command leading to the poisoning of Litvinenko in London, how likely are we to find out about a Russian operation of this magnitude? The Russians are masters of deniability, which would be why they used Uzbek jihadis as cover.'

'Theoretically, of course', Tony observed, 'they're friends and allies.'

'For the moment allies, yes, but friends?' The attaché rocked his head. 'The Chinese don't have friends, they don't want friends, they don't *need* friends. I've worked with them on and off over thirty years. I like them, I admire them, and I don't believe they're out to start a war against us as soon as they're strong enough. But friends? That's the tricky part.' He shrugged. 'Maybe they'll never forget the way we booted them around in the nineteenth century, or maybe it's in the genes.

'Same thing between the Chinese and Russians. Never forget the vast tracts of Siberia the Czars stole from them. The Chinese won't. On the Russian side in the Far East they have 20 million people. On China's side there's 120 million. We're talking *Lebensraum*, potentially – and Siberia's warming up, so more people can live there. Reminds me of something I heard on a tour up there. Cross-border marriages are on the rise, apparently. How so, you might think, if the Russians are out-and-out racists? Because the Chinese abort female children, there's not enough wives, and Russian women are keen on marrying anyone who isn't a drunk and a layabout who's going to die at 50.

'But basically there's no love lost. It's a matter of time before they're at each other's throats again. How long did the great communist alliance last? 'Bout nine years, 1950 to 1959. Ten years later the Russians wanted to bomb Lop Nor and wipe out the nuclear installations Khrushchev had been daft enough to give them. What no one seems to have told

Benediktov is that the Chinese have begun thinking about closing Lop Nor down themselves. Or maybe they did, and the Colonel was looking to blow up the facilities before they were relocated underground.

'Thinking of turning the place into a tourism attraction, apparently. Come and see where it used to rain radioactive fallout! Sounds like a grisly joke, but they wouldn't be the first. As a civvie I once did a tour of Los Alamos, site of the Manhattan Project, the 'Atomic City' the Americans call it. So why not Lop Nor?'

At the Embassy there'd been a chance meeting with Sanderson, mercifully brief. He was being transferred, he told him, to Africa. 'Good for you,' Tony said with affected heartiness. 'The up-and-coming continent, I'm told. And plenty of Chinese there for you to work on.' Sanderson seemed less than ecstatic at his new appointment. Maybe he'd do a Le Carré, Tony smiled to himself: write a novel about his brief and uneventful experience in the game, then sod off out of M16.

*

Collinson was getting agitated. They were going to be late at the prison. Their car was getting nowhere. Hemmed in from all sides, it halted. Tony reached out an envelope from his pocket. The diplomatic bag had arrived just as they'd set out from the Embassy, and there was a letter from his wife:

Darling,

The communications are back on I saw from the news, but they told me you'll soon be on your way home, and I've just got time to get this in the diplomatic bag.

You must be pleased to be getting back, but it's awful about that Osman being locked up, the press is full of it. I hope you can help get him out, after all he's a British citizen, he has rights. And he was only trying to help those poor Uighurs. It's terrible the way they're treated, with those executions and things. I saw a TV programme about it, it's like the Tibetans, the Chinese walking all over them. There's questions in Parliament and they're getting up a petition about it, with film stars and people.

Anyway, some good news. The rehab place say Penny's getting a grip of herself at last and they think she's turned the corner, and the people at her work say they'll be taking her back. Such a relief. And the plumber's managed to get hold of the parts for the boiler, so that's one less thing to worry about.

Heather's fine, chattering away as ever, she wants to know all about China.

Love from us both,

Jean

There was also a message from Zach, sent via the US Embassy.

Tony, They just filled me in. Crazy stuff! You got him – congratulations! Great to think of the cocky little shit twitching when they stick in the syringe! And our Russian drinking partner! Unbelievable! But there you go, we're in new times. Lone wolves, gonna see a lot more like them. But don't let them spoil your retirement.

All the best,

Zach.

*

They arrived at the prison. Seeing the car with diplomatic plates draw up a smart young fellow stepped from the office: the *Guoanbu* foreign liaison man, Collinson explained. Greeting him with what seemed an exaggerated display of familiarity, he thanked him for arranging access.

'It is normal. It is natural that we cooperate.'

Collinson presented Tony.

'Ah yes, Mr Underwood. We have heard so much about you.'

Too much maybe, Tony thought, to judge by the curtness of his nod and the brevity of his handshake. When the paperwork was complete a peak-capped warder with clipped steps and an automated manner marched them along corridors punctuated by endless secure doors to what seemed a separate wing. Stale food, latrines – even in the modern building there were the usual punitive odours.

Chinese prisoners were allowed to buy things at a shop run by the guards, Collinson had told him. For Osman it was the sole concession the Consul had secured, and the first thing he noticed when the warder fed in the code and the door to his cell swung open was a scent of air-freshener, overlaid with a whiff of tobacco; he must be smoking again. Otherwise it was a dismal hole. The cell the two of them crowded into was smaller than in Urumqi, and this time there was no desk or genteel toilet.

Each time they met Osman seemed different, and now he'd undergone another transformation. He was sitting on the edge of his bunk, a book on his knees. Bare-chested in the heat, his physique had gone from lean to scrawny, his features no longer sharp and knowing but taut and drawn. A wreck of a man, it seemed at first sight, yet this was Osman, and the arrogance was undiminished.

As in their first encounter he took his time before raising his head and recognizing Tony's presence.

'Ah, it's you.'

Setting his book aside he looked up at him. Collinson he ignored.

'You shouldn't have troubled. I've seen the Consul and he's as much use to me as you were in Urumqi. I asked why I was in a condemned man's cell. I know because I heard the warders call it that. He said he'd asked them already, and they said it was' – he mimicked a po-faced official – *'fang bian*: more convenient. It's this side of the prison they've put the injection unit, I gather. Even more convenient to scrub the trial completely. They might just as well, the way they conduct them.'

As he spoke Tony frowned at the floor. Osman was more right than he knew. Given that most of the evidence was intelligence-based the trial would be *in camera,* Collinson had told him, and something of a formality.

'The British government is opposed to capital punishment, whatever the crime.'

Collinson spoke solemnly. Osman turned to him with a look that said, *and who are you, exactly?*

'My colleague, Mr Collinson', Tony explained. 'He's from the Embassy.'

*'The British Government is opposed...*Well thank you, Mr Collinson. That should do it, that'll swing the jury. Except there won't be one. And if they don't listen to the British government, what do we do? Send a gunboat? Bombard the Summer Palace?'

The M15 men were standing – there was nowhere to sit. Osman was looking up at them with the superior smirk Tony knew too well, though this time he felt no anger. Conscious of Collinson busily jotting notes, he did his best to focus on the task in hand.

'The Chinese have agreed we can ask you some questions. It's not to do with the trial.'

'Not to do with my trial? And there was I thinking you'd come to help.'

'It's about your activities in the U.K.', Tony pursued.

'How can I be of assistance?'

'I want to take your mind back to your student days. Of your Muslim friends at University, which one had the greatest influence on you?'

'Who got me into it, you mean? Nobody. I'm self-radicalised. And self-cured.'

'Have you been planning anything in Britain?'

'*Are you, or have you ever been…*' Osman mimicked. 'Come on Tony, you can do better than that. Anyway, it's a badly phrased question. *Planning operations in Britain.* For abroad, you mean – or the UK?'

'Operations inside the United Kingdom.'

'Still a dumb question', Osman shrugged.

'So a definite no.'

'It is. Only Central Asia.'

'And is there anyone you know who has anything planned against the UK?'

'No.'

'And is there to your knowledge anyone who might be contemplating some attack, even if it's not yet planned?'

He was reading from a notebook, paraphrasing the official questions, turning the page quickly, convinced the whole procedure was pointless and keen to distance himself from it.

'And what good would it do me if the answer was yes? Given there's no prospect of extradition?'

'It could do some good to whoever might be on the receiving end.'

Tony closed his notebook.

'If you're holding anything back', he went on in a softer voice, 'in what circumstances might you tell us of whatever you might know?'

Feeling a touch on his elbow he turned to meet Collinson's imploring eyes. *For God's sake no more unauthorised deals* was inscribed in his expression as clearly as if he'd spoken the words. Tony looked back at him, tight-mouthed. In a poor mood already, the man's pleading look riled him.

'You couldn't leave us, could you?'

'My instructions –'

'– I'm asking you to leave us for a moment, if you would.'

There could be no ignoring Tony's imperious gaze. His Adam's apple working as if he'd swallowed a stone, Collinson left the cell.

Tony sat on the end of the bunk.

'The way they got you back from Ulan Bator – I don't want you to think it was pre-arranged. It was because of me they let you on the plane at all. The airport security people picked me up. When they realised who I was, and there were doubts about your passport, it was me who cleared it. I assumed you'd transit Ulan Bator without problems. What I didn't know –'

'Never complain, never explain.' With a shake of his head Osman cut him off. 'I'm not complaining, so why are you explaining? Concerned about your honour? That's your problem. I have rather more pressing things to worry about. I'm not accusing you of anything. At this stage of the game there wouldn't be a lot of point. All I know is I did a deal, and I don't care whether it was you or the Chinese who ratted. From my viewpoint it doesn't make a lot of difference. I'm not going to argue the toss about who got me into this. All I know is that it's your duty to get me out.'

Always my duty, Tony thought, as if I'm his bloody servant. There were things he could have said about that, but it was hard to moralise at a man in a condemned cell.

'And how would I do that?'

'Use your media contacts. M15 has plenty. Let's see an article in the *Daily Telegraph* saying usually reliable sources suggest that the Chinese went back on an agreement set up by M15 to let me out. That they have a moral obligation –'

'– I'd go easy on the morality if I were you.'

'An obligation to release me.'

It was clear how Osman's mind was working. His last hope would be the press. The Consul must have told him he was front-page news, as pictures of the prisoner of Beijing had flashed around the globe. As a rich-kid student (it was the picture from his passport, the one with the longish hair and Continental scarf), then in jungle fatigues, sporting one of his guns (where the hell had they got that from?). How Osman would have loved it...

Tony had seen the editorials, and they were as he'd predicted. Gun-running for the Uighurs? For the Left he was a fighter for human rights and an intrepid revolutionary, pretty much the Che Guevara of Central Asia. The son of an oligarch yet a man of conscience, who'd renounced his playboy past to rescue an oppressed people. Rumours of Al Qaeda or ISIS contacts were downplayed: even the Chinese were not suggesting that, the editorials insisted. About Lop Nor the media, it was clear, knew nothing.

He looked down at him wonderingly. Even now, a man condemned, sitting there half-naked, and still that truculence...There could be no changing him. Born to privilege, a child of his caste and of his era, the child of entitlement, he had absorbed the worst of his adopted country. It was for him to indulge in his jihadi games and for others to rescue him when the games turned real.

But he'd chosen the wrong place to play them. This wasn't Africa, where public school men could dabble in coups and conspiracies and be pardoned by Gilbert and Sullivan dictators: it was China. It still hadn't hit him that this time there might be no way out.

'The British press are onto it', Tony replied, 'they didn't need encouragement from us. Though I'm not sure what good it will do with the Chinese.'

'Because of Lop Nor? But it was me who told them about

it. That was the deal.'

'I don't think that side of things will feature in the press', Tony said softly.

'Why not?'

'Because it won't be public.'

'I don't understand. You saw my message? At the airport?'

'Of course. But the Chinese have reasons to keep that side of things quiet.'

'Then why don't *you* brief the press, if they won't? Tell them it was me who tipped them off. Me who saved all those lives.'

It was a difficult moment, but Tony was prepared. He took a breath before saying:

'You didn't tell them anything. The Chinese knew already. Which rather undermines your bargaining position.'

He averted his eyes as he said it. At his words, Osman looked up sharply. For the first time he was shaken.

'Impossible. How could they?'

'Because Benediktov told them.'

'Who?'

'Colonel Benediktov.' Tony frowned. 'The man you were dealing with. You didn't know who it was?'

'The Turkman,' Osman said wonderingly, 'A *Russian?*'

'Turkman?'

'His code name. We never met, properly. He was the Urumqi link but he stayed out of sight, at the address I gave you. And the Chinese didn't tell me he was Russian.'

'Well he was. An FSB man, stationed in Urumqi. Whether he was working on orders God alone knows. With the Russians you can never be sure. When he got wind you were about to sell him out he told the Chinese he'd uncovered the operation and taken it over. That he was waiting till all the pieces were in place before telling the *Guoanbu.*'

'He's a lying bastard.'

'In the FSB', Tony sighed, 'it happens.'

Till then Osman had been tensed forward on his bunk, his hands on the edge, his arms rigid, a man held together by force of pride. As the implications of what Tony had said hit him his body seemed to collapse into itself: his arms buckled, his back folded, his shoulders sank.

For a minute nothing was said.

'Tell me something.' Tony spoke quietly. 'I know you were developing doubts, but – do you still pray?'

'Do you?'

'No.'

'Of course not. At least you're honest. I lied to myself.'

He closed his eyes and said in a chanting voice

Say he is Allah, the only one, Allah the Everlasting. He did not beget and is not begotten, and none is His equal.

I've said it a thousand times. Said what I had to. I was an intellectual believer. Told myself I felt things I didn't. And now that's a problem. How do you pray for forgiveness if you've ceased to believe?'

Reaching to a shelf behind him he took down a book. It was the translation of the Koran he'd sworn on in the café. He held it out:

'Here. Take it.'

Tony didn't move. Finally he reached down for it, frowning, but just as his fingers touched it, Osman snatched it back.

'No, don't.'

Tony let a moment pass before saying:

O son of Adam, if your sins were to reach the clouds of the sky and then you would seek My forgiveness, I would forgive you.

It was a passage from the Koran he'd memorised with a purpose: used with Muslim moderates he was courting in his agent-recruiting days, his quotes made a good impression. Though not with Osman. Sardonic again, he laughed.

'A quote for every occasion, even in the condemned cell! Who do you think you are, Tony? My confessor?'

His face was grey, abject, his eyes empty.

It would be the last time they would meet, Tony thought. Would it happen here, in the state-of-the-art-facility along the corridor? Or in one of the mobile execution vehicles the Chinese had devised, Collinson had told him, so that no one could say where and when a prisoner had died?

If so the end would be more terrible still. He'd be loaded into a van, like an animal to the slaughter, and transported God knew where. They'd strap him to a bed that glided automatically to the middle, for the convenience of the doctors waiting to inject him with a swift succession of drugs: the first to knock him out, the next to cut short his breath, the last to stop the heart.

All this to think about as he sat in his cell with nothing more to sustain him than the memory of a faith he had manufactured in his mind, to avenge himself on his father.

'Will you be coming again?'

'I'll try', Tony lied. 'You were on your way to see your mother. I'm sorry you didn't get there. Maybe you'd like to send a message?'

'Absolutely not. Why would I want her to know? She's a sick woman and it would make her worse.'

He ought to have felt pity, though something about Osman deadened feeling. Yet it seemed wrong to leave him with nothing. Turning to the door, he tried to think of a few consoling phrases, words Osman would be unable to throw back at him. For almost a minute he stood silently, but nothing came.